# The Cinderella Society

# The Cinderella Society

KAY CASSIDY

**EGMONT**
USA
NEW YORK

# EGMONT
*We bring stories to life*

First published by Egmont USA, 2010
443 Park Avenue South, Suite 806
New York, NY 10016

1 3 5 7 9 8 6 4 2

www.egmontusa.com
www.kaycassidy.com

Library of Congress Cataloging-in-Publication Data
Cassidy, Kay
The Cinderella Society / Kay Cassidy.
p. cm.
Summary: After winning a coveted spot on the high school cheerleading squad,
sixteen-year-old newcomer, Jess Parker, is still treated as an "outsider" by the
majority of the student body thanks to the harassment campaign led by
the popular cheerleader she displaced.
ISBN 978-1-60684-017-7 (hardcover)
[1. Cheerleading—Fiction. 2. Bullying—Fiction. 3. Cliques (Sociology)—Fiction.
4. Popularity—Fiction. 5. High schools—Fiction. 6. Schools—Fiction.
7. Georgia—Fiction.] I. Title.
PZ7.C268582Cn 2010
[Fic]—dc22
2009026157

Book design by Becky Terhune

Printed in the United States of America

CPSIA tracking label information:
Random House Production • 1745 Broadway • New York, NY 10019

For my mom

my role model, my friend, and
the world's first Honorary Cindy.

I love you, Mom.

# The Cinderella Society

# Chapter 1

**THERE ARE MOMENTS IN LIFE** when you know things will never be the same. When you're called to the edge of adventure and given the chance to break free, uninhibited by your past, and claim the life you were meant to live.

Relax. This was totally not that kind of day.

Everyone around me was either scribbling furiously to finish their advanced algebra final, talking quietly until Mr. Norman gave them dirty looks, or texting each other on cell phones discreetly tucked into pants pockets and Prada totes. Me? I was mostly trying to be invisible. Praying to end my heinous year without drawing more negative "new kid" attention from my cohorts at Mt. Sterling High.

The last bell finally rang, and the rest of the class rushed the door in hot pursuit of a summer of freedom. In two seconds flat, it was just Mr. Norman and me gathering up our stuff.

"Great job catching up, Jess," he said as he shoved our exams into his battered briefcase. "Transferring midsemester is tough, but your grades are top of the class. Your last math teacher would be proud."

*Super.*

Don't get me wrong. Usually, a teacher's compliment is not something I'd scoff at. I work my butt off to keep up my GPA. But right then, being a brainiac was about the only thing I had going. And when the one person who bothers to engage you in conversation is a fortysomething who reads *The Calculus News* cover to cover, you know you're inches away from rock bottom on the social barometer.

I waved my thanks—not wanting to alienate a teacher I'd have for trig next year—and headed for the door.

By the time I hit the hall, it looked more like a frat house than a high school. Or what I imagined a frat house would look like. High fives were being exchanged, and many a folder's contents had been unceremoniously dumped in the nearest trash. Kids raced outside, throwing confetti laced with M&M's and shouting reminders of upcoming parties to friends, while Janitor Joe bellowed about messes and respect and proper receptacle use. Even Rick, the hottie assistant janitor, was shaking his head, and he couldn't have been much older than we were.

And then there was me, silently making my way through the madness. I reached my side hall, but couldn't get to my locker because of the couple making out in front of it. Classy. Now I had to stand there looking like a gawker or find something to do, quick.

I leaned against a standard-issue gray door a few lockers down from mine and started doodling on my folder, keeping the writhing couple in my peripheral vision until I could make a play for my locker.

The bane of my existence walked by, flanked by her cronies, and slowed to look into my locker alcove. Lexy tossed her straight jet-black hair over one shoulder and whispered to her gang. They stared at me with undisguised contempt while Morgan, Lexy's chief suck-up, cackled with laughter.

Subtle, my enemies were not.

You'd think Lexy would've gotten bored of tormenting me after two months, even though I made an easy target. I'd only been there a couple of weeks when they'd had cheerleading tryouts for next year's team. Cheering was the one thing I looked forward to no matter how many times we moved. I loved it. The precision, the creativity, the high of nailing the perfect stunt. The problem was that by adding me—an outsider in the MSH cheer ranks—to the varsity team, there was one less spot for the insiders. Namely one Alexandra "Lexy" Steele. A defeat she did not accept gracefully. Or quietly.

So now, most people knew me by face, though I'd usually be referred to as "That New Girl." Spoken with disdain. That New Girl who stole super popular, nasty-as-a-Rottweiler Lexy Steele's spot.

Sometimes invisibility is bliss.

Knowing she had my full attention, Lexy turned into my alcove. She bumped past the heavy breathers and stopped inches away from me. "Rumor has it you've got big plans for the summer. Hanging with our Beaumont besties, are we?"

Lexy's sidekicks snickered at the infamous rumor that I'd wanted to cheer at rival Beaumont High because I thought the MSH team was "a bunch of stuck-up divas who wouldn't know a handspring from a hand-me-down."

I considered ignoring her, but it was kind of hard to do when she was close enough to smell the Tic Tac on my breath. I tried to sound bored. "Why would I do that when I've never met them? The rumor doesn't even make sense." Not that any of my teammates seemed to notice.

"Funny thing about rumors," Lexy said. "They don't

have to be true, now, do they? They only have to be believable enough to make an impact." A self-satisfied smile hinted at her lips. "Tell me, Thief . . . did it make an impact?"

*And there you go.*

I'd always suspected Lexy had to be the source of the rumor—given her personal vendetta against me—but I'd never expected her to own up to the lie so willingly. Or be so proud of it. Then again, what good was her power if she couldn't flaunt it when the mood struck?

And yes, of course it was a total lie. But it was also a lie I hadn't known about until the damage was done. With no one to back up my side of the story, the cheerleaders were keeping their distance.

I might've beaten Lexy for a spot, but she'd made sure they wouldn't accept me as one of their own.

"Why don't you just quit and save yourself the misery?" she asked, a mock sadness enveloping her. "Don't you ever get tired of being around people who think you're nothing?"

I bit the inside of my cheek to keep from saying one of the thousand rude things screaming through my mind. And to keep my emotions under wraps. I'd never yet let her get a rise out of me, but I suspected we both knew that day was coming. Cornered at my locker on the last day of school, however, wasn't the time or place.

Instead, I stared straight back at Lexy, giving her a carefully schooled expression of self-assured indifference. I'd perfected that look a long time ago to guard against bullies. You couldn't look angry or threatening (that only engaged them), and you couldn't look intimidated (a massive bully turn-on). It was a fine line to walk, but you couldn't afford to overstep it if you wanted any chance of being left alone.

"Not up to a challenge today, huh?" She gave a pouty

frown. "You disappoint me, Parker. I'd lower my expectations of you, but they're already six feet under."

Smug in the knowledge that she'd won another round, Lexy about-faced and headed for the main hall. She said something under her breath that prompted her whole crew to swivel their heads in my direction. They looked down their surgically sculpted noses, dismissed me as meaningless, and strolled out of sight.

Relief bubbled up, followed by a depressing sigh. After nine moves in sixteen years (thanks to my dad's environmental-consulting assignments) this was the worst case of new-kid-itis yet. Most people thought being a cheerleader made you an automatic insider, but no. I only skirted the edges of popularity by association. I'd spent most of my existence so close to the in crowd I could smell their designer perfume, but I had never once crossed the threshold of acceptance. It was like living with your face pressed against the window, your breath steaming up the glass, while the world twirled on without you. If I didn't love cheering so much, I'd walk away from that window and never look back.

I'd built houses for Habitat for Humanity, ladled out scoops of chili at soup kitchens, and taken countless pictures of abandoned animals to put on local adoption Web sites. I was the quintessential Volunteer Girl. Wasn't there supposed to be some kind of karmic payback for being a decent person?

My already sagging spirits were dangerously close to zeroing out when I heard the voice that made me swoon even on the worst day. I looked up, waiting for Ryan to turn the corner into the alcove across from mine.

"No way, man," Dale Boone was saying as he and my future husband came into view. "I heard Frau Gardner's given out the same German exam three years in a row. That's the only way Mike could've aced it. His sister had the Frau last year."

"The vocab killed me," Ryan said. He shook his head, spun the combo, and opened his locker. She didn't pick anything from the first eight chapters."

I watched Ryan's dark hair flick out from under his Braves hat. So silky, so dreamy, so perfect for running your fingers through. My yummy Ryan Steele. If only he knew my name.

Or at least knew me as something other than his sister's archenemy.

Ryan and Dale continued their German commiseration, and I let myself drink in the sight of him. Tall and muscular, with the chiseled jaw of Jake Gyllenhaal. Toss in major sweetness (even to the geeks and nerds) and good old-fashioned Southern charm, and he was 100 percent fantasy-worthy. The kind of guy who made me wish I were five-eight, blonde, and leggy, not five-three with a baby face, freckles, and a dull brown mop for hair.

The fantasies rolled free in my mind. If only Lexy weren't bent on destroying my best shot at belonging here. If only the cheerleaders had tried to get to know me before Lexy got her claws into them. If only Ryan knew I existed.

If only I could break out of my crushing social jail. Then my life would be perfect.

Ryan tossed his things into his Nike duffel, and as quickly as he'd arrived, he was on his way out. Out of school, out of my life, for an entire summer. I wondered if the world would swallow me whole from Ryan withdrawal.

And then, it happened. Just as Ryan turned toward the main hall and a clean getaway, he looked across into our alcove.

I froze. How could anyone's eyes be so mesmerizing? Even from twenty feet away, they made my breath hitch.

In one of the most shocking turns of events since I'd moved—and that was saying something—Ryan's face broke into a dazzling smile when he saw me. He lifted a hand in a half wave and called out a baritone "Have a good summer" that nearly melted me into a puddle.

O. M. G.

Long, excruciating months of new-kid-ness were wiped away in a glorious instant. Despite all of Lexy's slander, the eternal optimist in me still held out hope that someone—*anyone*—would recognize I wasn't a complete waste of oxygen. And for it to be Ryan? My heart morphed into a thousand butterflies, fluttering joyfully in my chest.

His grin was contagious, and my answering smile was so huge it made my cheeks ache. I waved back, butterflies soaring in formation. "You too, Ryan!"

Just as a male voice behind me shouted, "Back atcha, dude!"

The butterflies were flying in chaos as I choked down bile. Had he noticed? Had anyone else? Where was an invisibility cloak when you needed one?

But alas, Ryan looked at me. Actually *looked* at me, I mean, and now I could see the difference. He gave me a faintly apologetic smile before exchanging good-byes with another guy and heading off toward Jock Hall with his posse at his back and a crowd of admirers parting like the Red Sea.

At which point all the butterflies fainted.

The only saving grace was that someone shouted a party invite to the lip-attached couple, so I took advantage of their momentary pause for air and lunged for my locker. I nudged their intertwined bodies out of the way and quickly spun the combination, thanking everything holy that this was the last time I'd ever have to fight with the metal beast. I turned the knob, crossed my fingers and blew on them for good luck, and pulled up on the latch.

Nothing.

Now, I'm not someone who goes around damaging school property. I'm pretty much the poster child for good girls. But at that point, I had so many emotions clawing their way to the surface that I had no problem whatsoever taking it out on the piece-of-crap locker from hell. If Satan existed, surely he, Lexy, and my locker were in cahoots.

With the halls rapidly clearing out, I showed the contraption no mercy. I gave it a kick, a yank, and a kick-yank combination. Pulled while kicking three times in the bottom corner to jar it loose, which sometimes worked. Not loud enough to call attention to myself, I hoped. Just loud enough to shake it out of Sticksville. Not that it did.

I glanced around to make sure everyone wasn't staring at the dipcrap soon-to-be junior who couldn't open her own locker. Thankfully, everyone was otherwise occupied. My invisibility had belatedly returned, a single bright spot in my otherwise hideous day. On top of being tortured by She Who Must Not Be Named, the last thing I needed was to draw attention to myself while I clanged around with my locker like Neanderthal Jane.

I gave my locker one more swift thump with the side of my foot, which caused it to pop open and nearly bounce off my head. I cursed under my breath—words that would *not* make Coach Trent happy—and threw everything into my well-worn CHEERLEADING IS LIFE bag as fast as humanly possible. Folders, pens, the eye pencil I'd lost two weeks before—all went tumbling into the bag. With a firm slam and a barely restrained desire to flip off an inanimate object, I kissed my sophomore year good-bye.

* * *

The last day of school is always cause for celebration. That was true in my case too, though not for the usual reasons. Instead of looking forward to a summer of lying by the pool, hanging with friends, and ogling cute guys in board shorts, I was destined for a summer filled with work, work, and—did I mention?—more work. Working at Celestial Gifts with Nan, helping Mom get the nursery ready for the twins, volunteering. Cheerleading camp was a bonus, but this summer was all about keeping me busy while I maintained a low profile.

When you get off on the wrong foot at a new school, the best strategy is usually to go underground for a while until some new drama grabs everyone's attention. That was Master Plan à la Jess for the summer. Then I'd slide back into the mainstream come fall and hope I could fly under Lexy's radar for a while. Goal number one was to find somewhere—anywhere—I might fit in. Thanks to Lexy, that wouldn't be with the cheerleaders.

I pushed open the doors to the main drive and took a deep breath despite the oppressive late-May Georgia heat. My stomach loosened its knots as the end to my horrific year came into view. The relief lasted all of seven seconds, until the engine of the bus at the end of the line roared to life. I looked up in time to see the first in the long line of buses start to pull away.

My bus? Second in line.

I weighed my options in that split second and decided walking the mile and a half home was infinitely preferable to sprinting around the bend inhaling bus fumes and flailing my arms in hopes of getting the bus driver to stop. A few miles of exercise was way better than being known as the freak girl who steals cheerleading spots and can't tell time.

To put the kibosh on my afternoon thirst, I decided to grab a pop for the road. Or soda, I corrected myself, since that's what people called it here. One more entry on my "Things to Remember to Fit In" list. I spun around to head back into the building and walked right smack into a very broad chest.

Literally. *Smack*. Into a very broad *male* chest.

It wasn't even one of those cute "oopsie" kind of bumps, where you both sort of laugh and do a little shuffle to the side. It was the major "oomph" variety, where you smack really hard and your breath rushes out sounding like a defective tuba.

I looked up, dread crawling over me as I recognized the Cool Water scent of my beloved. My waking nightmare was confirmed when my eyes met the gorgeous silvery-blue ones of the Adonis otherwise known as Ryan. Strike two against the Ryan-Steele-plus-Jess-Parker-equals-happily-ever-after equation.

"Sorry," he said in that sexy Southern drawl. "I didn't know this part of the sidewalk was taken."

His voice was smelling salts for the butterfly brigade, and they started a new freak-out dance in honor of my latest disgrace.

"Sorry," I mumbled. "I was just, um . . ."

But Ryan had already sidestepped me at the urging of his bleached-blonde arm candy of the week. "Come on, Ryan," Fake Blondie nagged in her nasal, big-breasted way.

Yep, I know. Catty am I.

"We have to get to the lake before everyone else," she whined. "I need a shady spot or I'll freckle."

My nose twitched in defense. Good thing my freckles were limited to that region instead of all over like my neighbor Mrs. Cleavis, or I'd have been battling a full-body convulsion.

I watched them as they rounded the bend into the upper-classmen's parking lot. The irony that the first words Ryan spoke to me (actual words, not the imaginary, misdirected kind) were due to yet another social gaffe on my part was not lost on me. Why I couldn't have a crush on a guy my own age and in my own social stratum—that is to say, bottom-feeders—was beyond me. The older brother of the founder of the We Hate Jess the Spot Stealer Club was my least promising choice yet.

Besides, I was practically a walking, talking stereotype: the cheerleader drooling over the quarterback. Except I wasn't popular. At least it wasn't a total cliché.

Not that it mattered, anyway. The heart wants what it wants. I knew that from experience.

But the heart wants what it wants. I knew that from experience. And I couldn't seem to break my losing streak of crushing on unattainable guys. My heart currently wanted a certain hot quarterback with a movie-star face and delicious muscular chest to shower attention and kisses on me. If that wasn't possible, I'd settle for him knowing me as something other than his sister's nemesis. Or, dare to dream, that my name was not, in fact, That New Girl.

As standards go, those probably needed a little work.

I unzipped the bag over my shoulder and dug for my wallet, determined to get out of Dodge. I groped around but couldn't find it in the clutter, so I swung the bag forward and held it open to peer inside.

The push from behind—more like a blind-side whack—

sent me flying. My bag upended and hit the ground with a thud, scattering papers, personal junk, and the last few scraps of my pride across the sidewalk.

My first grab was for the envelope with my cheerleading camp itinerary. Thank God for quick reflexes, or I'd have lost two fingers by the heel of a very vampy sandal. Lexy's foot came down solidly on the envelope and did a quick but meaningful heel grind on my cherished paperwork.

Lexy and her gang walked on without so much as a backward glance but made sure to kick and shred as much of my stuff as possible as they walked through the mess. Things had begun to roll down the sidewalk toward the parking lot, and I double-timed it to grab them before they got run over. I snatched up a roll of mints and an assortment of gel pens, barely catching the lip gloss that was heading straight for the main drive.

I scooped up bits and pieces as I worked my way back to the scene of the crime. And there, shuffling papers into a neat pile, was the only person at MSH who'd ever been nice to me. (Aside from Mr. Norman, who I'm not counting for obvious reasons.) Heather Clark wasn't outwardly nicey-nice—I mean, we didn't bud or anything—but at least she didn't treat me like a social leper. Because she was one too.

As much as I appreciated the help, it really stinks when the only people who don't snub you are the ones who are snubbed themselves. Once you make nice, you align with them and become one of them. I've never understood why, but that's how high-school politics work.

I grabbed the last of my stuff and shoved it into my bag as Heather handed me her tidy little stack. "I didn't look at it," she said by way of greeting.

"You didn't miss anything." I looked at her and she

seemed more, I don't know, *open* than usual. Like she was waiting for me to say something else.

The few people still milling around were watching me with amusement, my stomach was in borderline vomit mode from the latest Ryan run-in, and there was Heather looking like it was a friends-forever bonding moment. Sixteen years of living in new-kid limbo, eight weeks of Lexy-induced suffering, and two embarrassing interludes with Ryan in less than five minutes all came crashing down on me at once.

I snapped.

Not on the outside, like a public meltdown that would fuel the grapevine for weeks, but on the inside, where it really counted. Everything I'd tried so hard to do to fit in one more time was reduced to a moment of pity help by a fellow outcast. Lexy was pure evil and yet surrounded by friends—or at least "friends"—and I was the loser *du jour*. Again.

Fate had a sick sense of humor.

I didn't want to connect with Heather. I didn't want her help or her pity or her bonding moment. I just wanted to go home and pretend tenth grade had never happened.

And I hated that I felt that way about someone who'd never been anything but nice to me.

I stared at the ground, feeling like a horrible excuse for a human. "Thanks." I nudged a stray stone with my shoe, exhaling slowly to tamp down the wave of guilt. "For helping and stuff. You didn't have to."

Heather shifted her weight from foot to foot, probably waiting for more. I finally glanced up and saw some of the light fading from her eyes.

"No problem. I don't have a bus to catch." She turned to go. "Have a good summer, Jess."

I squeezed the bridge of my nose to ward off the headache

13

coming on, watching my only friend prospect walk away. Lots of watching other kids leave, sad little progress being made toward my own departure.

I stood there debating my options: catch Heather and apologize for acting like a jerk, or cut my losses and get down to the business of becoming a recluse for the summer. I was almost ready to go the way of the hermit—Heather was a regular customer at Celestial Gifts, so I could always apologize to her while I was at work—but Lexy wasn't quite done stomping people into the ground.

"Where's your boyfriend, Clark Bar?"

My eyes narrowed as I watched Lexy and her girls move in. Heather stood her ground, but the quiver of her shoulders gave away her fear. She said nothing.

"What's the matter? Cat got your tongue? Oh wait, I know what's got your tongue." Lexy cocked her head. "Or should I say 'who'?"

I zipped my bag, eyeing the situation. Heather took a step back and stumbled off the sidewalk onto the asphalt.

Lexy's gang circled Heather in two beats, and Lexy stepped forward, the sidewalk height enhancing her position of power. "We can either do this my way, or I can take you down and *then* we'll do it my way. The second option is more fun, but I'm feeling generous, so I'll give you a choice."

Tears leaked out of Heather's eyes, helpless tears laced with anger. Only someone who'd cried them herself could recognize them at ten paces. My feet moved before my brain could even engage.

"Offer stands until Monday. After that, I get to choose. And I'll make sure my choice is one they'll be talking about long after we're out of this place." Lexy crossed her arms. "You're in this one alone, Clark Bar. And I come with backup," she added, nodding to the crony parade.

"Ready to go?" I asked, finding my voice as I brushed past Lexy and landed next to Heather. "Sorry that took so long. You know how cheer business is."

Out of the corner of my eye, I saw Lexy tense before she caught herself and resumed her haughty pose. "Well, this is interesting. I can't decide which one of you is slumming."

I glanced up at her. "Oh, hey, Lexy. I didn't notice you behind the mountain of makeup."

"*She's* your backup, Clark Bar?" Lexy looked from me to Heather. "News flash: two losers do not equal a posse."

I'd been without backup my entire life. All it took was one person to step forward and give you a fighting chance against a bully, but that was about as likely as winning the lottery when you were an outcast. I might not have been much on the social-power scale, but at least I could be a backup for Heather. Two was always better than one.

I squared my shoulders. "You're not the only one with backup power. We're sticking together, so you'd better get used to it."

"Is that right?"

"Count on it."

"You sure that's how you want it, Clark Bar?"

When Heather didn't respond, I stepped closer. She needed moral support, and I was more than willing to oblige. Anything to present a united front against the forces of evil.

Instead, Heather looked at me, tears dripping like apologies down her cheek. Her voice was barely audible. "I'm sorry, Jess."

She turned and walked away.

I was so stunned I couldn't move. I'd thrown myself on the social grenade, solidifying my status as Mt. Sterling's

Most Wanted to help a fellow outcast. Who'd snubbed me right in front of the people I was trying to save her from.

Worse, I wasn't even sure I could blame her. Heather had helped me pick up the pieces when Lexy blasted through my life, and I'd shunned her. Now she was the target, and I was pushing my way into her life like she didn't have a choice.

*Here, hypocrite, hypocrite, hypocrite . . .*

I could've ignored what was happening. Could've kept my distance like everyone else. But the breaking point Lexy had been pushing me toward for weeks had finally arrived. For my efforts, I saw the first genuine smile I'd ever seen on Lexy's face. I'd given her a front-row seat to my ultimate humiliation.

"It must be hard to be you, Parker. Lucking your way onto varsity only to discover they don't want you. Not a single friend to your name. Even the losers won't give you the time of day." Lexy turned to go, delivering her parting shot over her shoulder. "It must really make you wonder what's wrong with you."

By the time the humiliating fog cleared from my mind, Lexy was halfway across the parking lot. I stared after her, trying to erase the words ringing in my ears. But it was the car idling nearby that finally snapped me out of it. Fake Blondie's voice reached my ears as she gossiped with another soon-to-be senior. A string of Populars lined the car on both sides. When the crowd broke and Ryan's eyes met mine, I knew without a doubt that he'd witnessed my final downfall.

My misery was complete.

Drained by my lingering shame, I trudged back into school for my much-needed beverage of choice. I dropped my bag on a bench to dig one more time for cash. The sound of the bag's thump against the wood echoed through the nearly vacant halls. Funny how a place could be so alive and kicking one minute and completely devoid of energy the next.

I fished around for the money I hadn't thought to set aside while it was sprawled on the sidewalk. Since only a few people were hanging around, mostly outside, I dumped the contents of the bag in the corner near the vending machines. At the very bottom of the bag—big surprise—was my wallet. It came out almost dead last. Except for one small, lavender envelope that swept down to land on top of it.

In small, loopy letters it read: *For Jessica's eyes only*.

Almost no one calls me Jessica. It's always been Jess, except to Nan and receptionists in doctors' offices. Whoever had left this for me must not have known me very well. Which, given the givens, wasn't a shocking revelation. The fact that this person knew I even *had* a first name gave them bonus points.

I turned the envelope over in my hand. It was sealed with one of those old-fashioned wax thingies, where they drip wax on the paper and stamp it with a fancy seal.

I dropped it back on the pile, trying to process this latest development. Someone had given me a note that didn't look like hate mail. Because, really, anyone who puts fancy wax seals on hate mail has way too much time on their hands.

But a fancy wax seal on an elaborate joke? That would be right up Lexy's alley.

As tempted as I was to toss the stupid thing in the trash— *that* would show her—I couldn't. I've always been too curious for my own good. I also knew myself well enough to know I'd never make it home before I gave in to temptation, so I plowed ahead, determined to get the joke over with once and for all. I tossed some coins in the machine and grabbed my pop (soda, whatever), gathered up my stuff, and headed straight for the girls' bathroom.

I checked under the stalls to make sure they were free of

witnesses before locking myself in one so nobody would have a prime view of my private episode of *Punk'd*. Because, let's face it, that would've been on par with the rest of my day.

I peeled open the envelope, taking care not to break the seal in two. Somehow, the seal made the envelope's contents feel important. And wasn't it always the breaking of some seal that opened the portal to the seventh level of hell in movies? So yeah, case number two for keeping that baby intact.

My hand hesitated at the open flap. Part of me wanted to tear into it, but the bigger part of me—the one concerned with self-preservation—resisted. How had my life come to this? Where I feared opening random notes because they might be the latest in a long line of adolescent aggravations? Yes, there was a chance it could be a legit note, but the odds of that were minuscule. I might've been an optimist, but I wasn't an idiot.

Still . . .

I reached into the envelope and withdrew the matching lavender note card, which sported the same swirly design as the seal. I opened the card, my hands trembling in dread and the faint remnants of what I used to call hope, as a tiny silver high-heel pin bounced into my hand.

*What the . . . ?*

I juggled the pin for a second, barely managing to keep it from falling into the toilet, and flipped open the note with my other hand. The words inside were written in the same girly handwriting. Not a message but an invitation, one that sent shivers down my spine that had nothing to do with the blasting AC.

*Your presence is requested at The Grind.*
*Tonight, 7 p.m.*
*Wear the pin. Discretion MANDATORY.*

# *Chapter 2*

**I STOOD ON THE STONE SIDEWALK,** checking the silver pin I'd inconspicuously fastened to the ruffled hem of my shirt. Seven on the dot. I peered through the massive windows of The Grind, relieved to see it was wall-to-wall people. As intimidating as crowds were right now, this one offered a definite advantage. With that many people around, I could easily pass off the visit as a simple drink stop, and my pin wouldn't be noticeable until I wanted it to be.

*If* I wanted it to be.

I traced the outline of the pin with my fingertip. I'd spent most of the afternoon listing the zillion reasons why this was obviously a setup. Not to mention the fact that I had no clue when the note had even been put in my locker. (My locker wouldn't exactly win awards for tidiness.) *Tonight, 7 p.m.* could've been a week ago Tuesday.

On the flip side, the list of reasons why I *should* come was short and sweet: my curiosity was killing me, and my luck was bound to turn around sometime. Or at least that was the theory. Karma and all that.

But ultimately, it was the pathetic saga of my life that clinched the deal. I'd already withstood Lexy's campaign of torture, plus embarrassment (twice) at the hands of my dream guy. How much more could someone do to me in a public place like The Grind, where there'd be witnesses galore, including adults? Even Lexy wouldn't be that bold. I hoped.

I said a quick prayer for good luck and pushed through the glass doors, the chill of the coffee shop barely making its way to me through the throngs of people. Couples waited in line, kids chatted about summer events . . . everyone seemed to have a purpose for being there, and not one of them seemed to involve me.

I slipped into line and waited, keeping my eyes peeled for any unusual activity. I recognized some faces, but nothing made my inner danger signal ping. Mostly because there was no sign of Lexy or her band of merry gossip girls.

I was almost to the front of the line when Sarah Jane Peterson and Kyra Gonzalez, our cheer team cocaptains, stepped out from the hallway near the bathrooms. They looked like a teen cover shoot, Sarah Jane's glossy blonde hair and high cheekbones a striking contrast to Kyra's deep auburn hair and flawless complexion. They could've been straight out of any of the fashion mags I devoured every month. Even in glam-crazy Mt. Sterling, they still stood out as starlets. Except that Sarah Jane and Kyra were peacemakers, not divas.

Sarah Jane scanned the room, her eyes falling on me. She looked at me, expressionless, glanced from my eyes to my chest and back as if passing swift judgment, and continued on to scan the rest of the room. She and Kyra headed toward a table of girls in the corner, and I was quickly forgotten.

I would've brooded over the fact that Sarah Jane and Kyra were two of the nicest, most popular girls in school—not to mention my teammates—and they'd just passed me over as insignificant. Which I understood, given how the whole cheer rumor went down. Except why did Sarah Jane look at my shirt? Could it mean—?

"Showing your face in public so soon?" Lexy asked, loud enough to break through the din. "How brave. I would've thought you'd been snubbed enough for one day."

She'd snuck up next to me while I'd been lala-ing in fantasy land. It served me right for letting my guard down.

"It gets me right here"—Lexy tapped her chest where a normal person would have a heart—"to know you'll be flying solo this summer. But keep the faith. Maybe you'll find a friend by graduation."

I so wanted to remind her that I'd be spending part of that summer at the cheer camp she'd never go to, but I didn't. Partly because I didn't want to engage the enemy. I just wanted her to go away. But also partly because her words stung more than I wanted them to.

It was uncanny. Lexy had a knack for knowing exactly which buttons to push to hit you where it hurt. And how to push them in the most public way possible. It was like she had a giant cheat sheet listing everyone's biggest insecurities, and she got a gold star every time she nailed one.

I ignored her, studying the coffee menu like I didn't have a care in the world.

"Isn't that sad?" Lexy asked Morgan. "She's pretending she doesn't hear me so she doesn't have to face reality."

*Deep breath.* No way was I letting her get so much as a blink from me. Until a bump from behind her sent her coffee flying. Like my chest was a bull's-eye.

I gasped. The coffee seared through the thin material, scalding my skin like a hot iron. Lexy's fake apologies fooled everyone but me as Sarah Jane swooped in and grabbed my arm. Lexy looked irritated by Sarah Jane's interference but painted an innocent look on her face when the night manager came out looking peeved.

Sarah Jane hurried me to the bathroom, but not fast enough that I missed the behind-the-back low five Lexy and Morgan exchanged for a job well done. My face flushed redder than my throbbing chest at the injustice. How did girls like Lexy always manage to get away with it?

Sarah Jane pulled me toward the sinks as several girls exited the bathroom in a hurry. She quickly soaked a wad of paper towels with cold water and handed it to me. "Put this under your shirt," she instructed.

The cool relief felt like heaven on my scorched skin. Sarah Jane and I stood there for several minutes, resoaking the paper towels in cold water when they got warm, as an awkward silence engulfed us.

In all my years of wishing for backup, I'd never let myself imagine it could come in the form of someone like Sarah Jane Peterson. I beat back the needy hopes that I might be teetering on the brink of cheer acceptance.

After many rounds of cold paper towels, I pulled the neck of my T-shirt open and peered down. My bra was a total loss, and my chest was beet red, but no blisters.

Kyra poked her head in the doorway. "Everything okay in here?"

"It's just us." Sarah Jane motioned her inside. "She's got it on."

"Thank God. What was Lexy trying to prove?" Kyra turned to me. "Did she see the pin?"

"What?"

Sarah Jane flicked the hem of my shirt. "Did Lexy see this?"

"No clue. Does it matter?"

"Yes," they said in unison.

I tossed the paper towels in the trash as Kyra turned to Sarah Jane with wide eyes and dire news I didn't understand. "They left in *three* SUVs."

"What do they need with three? And what were they doing here, anyway? This isn't part of their tradition." Sarah Jane shook her head. "We need to get out of here."

"Already in progress." Kyra looked back at me. "Are you ready?"

*For what?* So far my little escapade was a mystery wrapped in disaster paper. With a skin-on-fire bow. I had no desire to play Nancy Drew.

"I think I'll head home," I said, easing toward the door. "Thanks for the towels, Sarah Jane."

"Not so fast, *chica*." Kyra wedged herself between me and the door. "Don't you want to know what that was all about?"

"It was about me 'stealing' her spot." I resisted the urge to make air quotes. For all I knew, Sarah Jane and Kyra agreed with her.

Or not. They looked surprised by that revelation, so I clarified. "I made the team—she's an alternate." Was any of this ringing a bell?

"That's just a cover, Jess." Sarah Jane dried her hands. "We'll explain it at Overnight."

"Overnight where?" All I wanted to do was crawl into my own bed and pull the covers over my head until I was twenty-five. "I've got plans tonight," I lied.

"I know you do," Sarah Jane said with a smile. "With us."

\* \* \*

They tucked me into the backseat of Sarah Jane's red convertible. On the way to my house, Kyra filled me in on the Overnight hostess, a former MSH cheerleader named Cassandra who'd just finished her freshman year cheering for Georgia. I acted like I was totally cool with being whisked away to sleepover heaven, but inside?

I was freaking.

A life spent being new on the block meant that by the time I got to be good enough friends with people to do group overnights, moving day was bound to be in the works. At sixteen, I was embarrassingly naïve about the whole deal.

What did you pack? What did you wear to sleep in? My comfort choice of cutoff sweats and ratty tees was so not making the trip. Did you bring munchies?

And then it hit me. These were not my biggest concerns. This wasn't Kyra and Sarah Jane's party—it was Cassandra's. Which meant—hello?—*Cassandra* should be issuing the invite to an outsider.

Would they turn me away if Sarah Jane and Kyra were vouching for me? How much of their social status would be ever-so-briefly extended to me? I'd never been this close to a party of their caliber to know for sure, but given the day's events so far, this was not the time to take another risk.

Not eager to add Sleepover Crasher to my long list of vile, Lexy-inspired nicknames, I tried to head off another fiasco. "So, will everyone be there?" I asked when the conversation up front hit a lull. Maybe I'd blend in okay if it was a cheer-team thing.

I thought of the rumor. *Or maybe not.*

Kyra turned down the music. "Everyone who?"

"The whole team?"

"The cheer team? A few people. Not everyone."

I took a deep breath. Better to get my concerns out in the open than descend on a surprised and potentially unthrilled

Cassandra. "Shouldn't I really be invited by Cassandra?"

Sarah Jane glanced up at me in the rearview mirror. "Have you met Cass?"

"No."

"Then how would she know to invite you?"

How could my distress be completely lost on both of them? "I don't want to crash the plans," I said, hoping for casual but delivering more on the side of lame and self-conscious.

"It's no big, Jess," Kyra said. "It's kind of a tradition, not a formal party or anything."

"More like a standing invitation," Sarah Jane added. "I'm not even sure who-all's gonna be there. We never know until we get there."

That's how it is with the in crowd. If they hear about a party, they just assume they can hang. Not so for the rest of the world. Most of us have to be outright invited or we run the risk of ridicule and banishment.

When Sarah Jane turned off the engine in front of my house and they started unbuckling their seat belts, I panicked.

"Be right back," I said, bolting out of the car. I didn't have a packing plan yet, didn't want them to see my room in hurricane mode, and definitely didn't want them to meet Mom in her current hormonal state. My life was ridiculous enough all on its own.

I nearly ran over Mom when I blew through the door. "Got invited to a sleepover," I called, taking the stairs two at a time. "I'm just grabbing my stuff."

I yanked my cheer duffel off the back of my closet door, tossed my ruined tee and bra in the trash, then remembered the pin and snagged it. I threw on my pink CHEER CHICK tank and surveyed the heap of clothing on my bed. In the time it took Mom to waddle up the stairs to grill me, I'd already thrown in shorts, yoga pants, and a couple of tees, and was pulling out whatever I had clean in my underwear drawer.

"Were you planning to ask?" Mom eased herself down onto my bed, huffing after hauling forty extra pounds of baby stomach up the stairs. "Whose house are you going to?" she asked between gasps for air. "Will her parents be home?"

"Sorry. Can I go? It's one of the girls who used to cheer here," I said, not liking the direction this was going. "Two of the other cheerleaders invited me to a sleepover they always have at her house."

I ran across the hall and stuffed my skin-care and makeup bin—what Dad calls my tackle box—into the bag and hoped I could make her see reason. For a woman who'd pretty much let me fend for myself since I was twelve, she'd turned into Super Mom of the Billion Questions since we'd moved to Georgia. Quitting her job as a big-shot auditor to stay home with the twins once they were born left her with a void she filled by grilling people for a living. Lucky me.

Mom sat perched on the edge of my bed, breathing hard and contemplating my story. Finally, she came to her senses. "It's a cheerleading sleepover?"

"I'm not sure who-all will be there, but Sarah Jane said some of them will. She's our cocaptain," I added for good measure. Captains were responsible, right? That had to help my case.

Mom nodded, somehow comforted by the idea of me spending the night with complete strangers whose parents may or may not be home as long as it was sports-related. Whatever.

"We need to get started on the nursery mural," she reminded me. "You'll be home in time to help in the morning?"

I stiffened a little. She'd never considered quitting her job for me, but for the twins? It was a whole new ball game. If the Parker household was the solar system, the twins were about to become our sun.

"Promise," I said. "I'll have my cell if you need me." I gave her a quick hug—extra gentle around the middle—and darted for the stairs before she could change her mind.

✳ ✳ ✳

Until a few years ago, Mt. Sterling was your average small town, tucked away between Atlanta's outer suburbs and the North Georgia Mountains. A quiet, friendly place filled with nice people like my grandma (that's Nan) and stores like her funky New Age gift shop. Then some fancy companies moved their big-kahuna offices to town, and it totally went upscale.

Cassandra's subdivision? Definitely Big Kahunaville.

I trailed Sarah Jane and Kyra up the front walk of Cassandra's McMansion and waited quietly, trying to look unobtrusive. Kyra pressed the doorbell, chattering comfortably the whole time. When the door opened and squeals of delight were exchanged, I changed my strategy from unobtrusive to blend-in-with-the-brickwork. But Sarah Jane was having none of that. She pulled me inside the gorgeous marble foyer and made formal intros.

"Cass, this is Jess Parker. She's new on the team this year. Her team in Seattle was top ten at nationals."

"The one who put Lexy out on her butt," Cassandra said, raising her eyebrows. "Your reputation precedes you."

After having spent time with Kyra and Sarah Jane, you'd think I'd have been used to being around beautiful people. But Cassandra made them look almost average. Thick, glossy hair the color of milk chocolate and a megawatt smile made her look like a walking advertisement for, well, anything you'd want to sell. Especially to the male population.

"I guess that's me," I said, unable to think of a snappy comeback to lighten the mood. "Sorry for crashing your party."

"Don't sweat it. SJ told me you were coming." Cassandra smiled. "And I think someone putting Lexy in her place is long overdue. Everyone needs a knock off their pedestal to keep them humble."

I was so relieved she wasn't mad about the Lexy thing— or the crashing thing—that I almost didn't register the voice behind me.

"Don't get your panties in a wad, Cass," said the hunky voice of my dreams. "I just forgot my iPod."

"Off-limits, Ry! You know the score. You forget something after seven, you go without until tomorrow," Cassandra yelled as Ryan jogged past us and up the curving staircase. Cassandra turned back to us, shaking her head. "Guys. They think rules only apply when it's convenient."

Three things went through my mind in rapid succession. One, Ryan Steele was here in this house, which meant . . . two, Cassandra was his sister, which also meant (please, *no*) . . . three, Cassandra was Lexy's sister too. If I'd been wondering about ulterior motives, a public face-off between Lexy and me on Lexy's home turf was about as juicy as any gossip I could think of. Apparently, I wasn't crashing the party after all.

I was the entertainment.

The doorbell rang again, and I stepped aside to witness another squeal-fest while my mind drummed up ways to make a quick escape without letting on that I'd figured out the game. Mental wheels spinning at hyper speed, I turned to pick up my bag, and rammed right into a now-familiar chest.

I rubbed my nose and snuck a glance at Ryan's face.

Just in time to see the corner of his mouth tugging up in a half grin.

"Is this going to be our thing?" He lost the battle to keep from smiling. "Running into each other everywhere?"

God, I hoped so. "I didn't hear you come back down the stairs."

"Not hard to believe with all the screaming."

He gave me a wink and moved toward the door before turning back. "Don't let Cass make you do anything you don't want to do. She's a devil underneath that squeaky-clean exterior."

"Ryan! Don't scare the guests." Cassandra swatted him out the door. "You're gonna make her run before we even get to check her out."

"Check me out?"

"Get to know you," Cassandra said smoothly, steering me away from the front door–slash–escape route. "Come on in, Jess. I promise we're harmless."

I must have hesitated a second too long, because Cassandra draped an arm around me. "Lexy's not here," she said in a low voice, while Kyra and Sarah Jane greeted two other girls I recognized from school. "She has her own plans, so it's just us tonight."

I wasn't buying it. Since when had I ever been an *us*?

"Look, I don't blame you for being suspicious," she said. "You're here for a reason, but I guarantee you it's not what you think. Do you have your pin?"

I patted my shorts pocket.

"That's your ticket for the evening, and Lexy definitely doesn't have one. Trust me, okay?"

I looked up at her in her all-American glory, and for some inexplicable reason, I trusted her. That had to mean something. The pin felt warm in my pocket, like it was trying to send me a message. *Believe,* it seemed to say.

To which I responded: *I am the person here; you are a piece of metal. Hush it.*

But I couldn't shake Cass's soothing mojo. She was drawing me in. Despite Ryan's warning and my suspicion that I might still be the evening's entertainment, I swallowed hard and let optimism reign supreme.

"Onward," I said. The time had come to meet my fate.

# *Chapter 3*

CASSANDRA LED ME BACK into the open, airy kitchen—
a modern wonder roughly the size of my whole house—where
girls were sipping delicious-looking shakes. That sounded
awesome, since I'd been too nervous to eat before I went to
The Grind. Except now I was a bundle of new nerves, and
harfing up a smoothie in front of the hostess was probably
frowned upon.

As we walked around the large island with its gleaming
countertop, I noticed the two girls on blender duty adding
dashes from all kinds of pretty bottles. I couldn't see the
labels, but hard liquor was an easy bet. Which stunk, since I
wasn't a big drinker. Or any kind of drinker, for that matter.
Yet here I was, finally on the fringe of social acceptance, and
*whammo*. The liquor dilemma.

I didn't get a chance to think of a graceful way to decline,
because Sarah Jane, Kyra, and a girl named Paige immediately
joined us with frosty glasses that smelled like a divine mix of
bananas and chocolate.

Cassandra lifted her glass in a toast to the four of us. "To
a successful summer."

"To a successful summer," we repeated, clinking glasses.

Everyone else took a long drink of the frozen wonder.

I hesitated.

Cassandra watched me over her glass. "You don't want it?"

"No, it smells great, Cassandra. I just . . ." Wanted to crawl under a rock. "I haven't eaten in a while."

"It's Cassie, or Cass, and don't sweat the shake, Jess," she said, grabbing several veggie-wrap slices from a nearby tray and handing them to me on a beach-print napkin. "There's no alcohol at Overnight."

A party with Populars and no alcohol? That was a jolt to my system. They'd have been laughed out of my old school. Most of my old schools, actually. Still, I couldn't help thinking someone hadn't gotten the message at the blender station.

Cassie followed my gaze. "Gwen," she called to one of the girls on duty, "what's on tap tonight?"

Gwen Fielding, an all-state volleyball champ who could've easily traded her sneakers for a modeling contract, held up the bottles in rapid succession. "Banana, mint chocolate chip, gingerbread, and peppermint."

"The Grind Exclusives," Cassie explained. "Best gourmet coffee syrups on the planet."

Clearly, these were *not* your everyday Populars.

By the time everyone had arrived, there were more than a dozen girls milling around the Steeles' state-of-the-art kitchen. For the next few hours, I sipped different shakes, nibbled on creamy, spicy wraps, and hung out with Sarah Jane, Kyra, and the other girls.

To my credit, I managed to contain my excitement about the fact that Ryan grabbed food out of that industrial-sized refrigerator every day (what was his favorite snack?) and ate breakfast at that table every morning (which lucky chair got to feel his cute butt on it?) and did a hundred other things in the space we were occupying. The giddy potential was staggering.

Just before midnight, Cassie announced it was time to "retire to the dungeon." I followed everyone downstairs to a massive rec room that was pure party paradise. The Steeles' basement came complete with a massive flat screen, a pool table, and a sleek bar area loaded with every drink and snack imaginable. A true shrine to teendom.

We set up makeshift beds around the room and got changed into our pajamas. I remembered the pin in my pocket and wondered what that had to do with tonight.

"It's for something special later," was all Cassie would say. "A little bit of mystery makes the evening more fun."

So far it was still Mystery 1, Jess 0. I hoped my record was about to improve.

The atmosphere was chummy and relaxed as we settled in for the night, with Sarah Jane, me, a beauty queen named Mel, and Kyra all in a neat little row by the sliding-glass doors leading out to the pool deck.

Sarah Jane stretched her long legs out in front of her. Her stars-and-moon pj's made a constellation against her deep blue blanket. My yoga pants and Gap tee looked impossibly generic by comparison. Why hadn't I thought to bring my cute lipstick-print boxer pj's? Couldn't I do anything right?

"You're lucky you have a job already, Jess," Sarah Jane was saying. "All the good ones were already taken by college students when I went looking last month."

"I heard Casey Sturgeon got a job at Harry and Marie's," Kyra said, referring to the retro diner in the heart of town that was notorious for great tips. "Debbie Maloney and Jay Carter did too."

"Wow, that's a step up for Jay," Kyra said. "Didn't he work at the car wash on Main last year? I know he's trying to save up for college. He doesn't think his parents will qualify for financial aid, but they can't swing tuition without it."

I nodded along with everyone else at Jay's good luck at landing the diner job, but I had no idea who Jay Carter was. Or Debbie Maloney, for that matter.

I knew more people than most new students would after only a couple of months, thanks to hours of studying last year's yearbook in the library. That was always the first thing I did at a new school, to help me get up to speed quickly on who's who. It's pretty easy to gauge who hangs in which groups from looking at the yearbook candids and group shots.

But I didn't know everyone. So I just nodded and smiled, taking my cue from everyone else's responses, as I pretended I knew what they were talking about. All the while feeling like a fake.

We chatted about finals, guys (not Ryan, thank goodness), and plans for the summer. After a while, I stopped having to pretend. I even contributed a few funny stories, including one that made Mel spit a raisin onto the carpet from laughing. Which made us all laugh even harder.

It was a little weird being there with no parents, though. Cassie's mom had died a year or two earlier, and Cassie's dad was out of town at a surgeon's conference. So it was just a dozen or so girls, yummy food, good music, and hours of chitchat.

"So where have you been volunteering since you moved here, Jess?" Paige wanted to know as she plopped down at the edge of Mel's sleeping bag.

I did a double take. I hadn't mentioned my volunteering

to anyone, certainly not here, where they might figure out I spent all my time volunteering to avoid having to sit home alone.

"At the Humane Society, mostly," I said. Helping abandoned animals sounded more glamorous than wielding a hammer on the porch of a Habitat house, even though I liked doing both.

"I wish I could do that," said Mel. "I'd love to volunteer there, but I'm allergic to cats."

"You could always do something outside or fund-raising or whatever. They're getting ready to do a big adoption day at the elementary school, and adoption days always need a ton of people helping with paperwork. You wouldn't even have to be in the cat area."

Mel didn't say anything for a second. I took the opportunity to mentally smack myself for sounding like Dillweed Do-Gooder. *Way to look cool, Jess. Suggest to the beauty queen that she spend a Saturday being a paper pusher. What's next? Friday night at the old folks' home?*

"That could work," Mel said. "They usually separate the dogs and cats anyway, right?"

"I'm planning to be there," Paige told Mel. "I can pick you up, if you need a ride. You too, Jess."

I sat there, stunned. Paige was definitely a power player among these girls. Not in a bad, Lexy kind of way either. She was totally nice and down-to-earth, and I'd already noticed how the other girls looked up to her. Looked up to Cassie too. Plus, Paige had just graduated, and yet here she was offering up rides to piddly high schoolers she'd just met. Could she *be* any cooler? When I grew up, I wanted to be like Paige Ellis.

Or Cassie Steele. Or Sarah Jane Peterson. Or really, anyone but me.

Kyra leaned her head back against her lavender pillow embroidered with a fancy *K*. "It's so nice being here, just us," she said. "This is the first time I've been able to relax all week."

This time, when I nodded, it wasn't just because I could relate to sleepless nights of finals anxiety. It was because I agreed with her sentiment about us.

For once, I actually felt like an *us*. Or part of an *us*, anyway. Which really brought the bizarreness home for me. I mean, come on. A bunch of good-girl Populars who mingled outside their assigned groups—cheerleaders, jocks, brains, an actress who'd already earned her SAG card—*and* managed to make an outsider like me feel welcome? Despite my lack of a social life and my do-gooder ways? It was enough to give a girl hope that she might finally, by some strange twist of fate, fit in. Most of the girls were socially out of my league, but if I could hang with them for one evening, maybe I could do it again sometime.

*And yet . . .*

How on earth had I gone from being Lexy's emotional punching bag and Heather's big snub to having a group of awesome girls treat me like a normal human being all in one day? Especially when we were camped out in the very place where Lexy hung her tall, pointy hat?

Too many years spent as an outsider made me suspicious. There had to be a catch. In my experience, there always was. Nothing was ever this easy.

I'd already scanned the rec room looking for hidden cameras or microphones that Lexy might have planted. Not being obvious about it, but Lexy had to know everyone was there, right? Decking it out seemed like her style. So I paid attention to our surroundings, even getting other people snacks as an excuse to check out the bar area up close.

But everything looked kosher. Felt kosher too, with nothing sending off a danger signal. And I had a pretty well-tuned danger meter when I was paying attention to it. Tonight? I had it tuned to extra-high frequency. Maybe gadgets were too high-tech for a hands-on girl like Lexy. Either way, I vowed not to let my guard down like I had at The Grind. No way would she catch me off guard twice.

Despite the Lexy connection, Cassie and the girls had done nothing to make me doubt Cassie's words of welcome. If my paranoia was front and center, I couldn't blame *them* for it. Lexy, maybe. But not them.

Paige's yawn spread like wildfire, and we began to form lines outside the various Steele bathrooms, laughing like old friends as we endured the nightly rituals that made us girls.

I ended up in the upstairs hallway waiting my turn, half listening to people rattle off their favorite spring-break hot spots.

"I don't think you can beat Daytona for action," Gwen said. "I found a pickup volleyball game on the beach every day while we were there."

"I'll take Manhattan over Daytona any day." Cherie, the resident actress, shifted her Clinique bag to her other hip as we waited. "Broadway, baby."

I leaned against the faux painted wall, my eyes settling on the room across from us. Light from the hallway spilled into a neat and tidy space with a color-blocked comforter and a soft painting of a single dandelion gone to seed. The guest room, I assumed.

The line moved, and I started to turn away but caught a glimpse of the opposite wall, which housed a bookcase full of trophies. An image of a curvaceous, scantily clad female was taped to the closet door. Unless the Steeles' guest room was frequented by teenage boys, I had to assume the room was Ryan's.

The room slid out of view as I moved on, but it didn't stop me from basking in his pseudo-nearness. While maintaining an air of normalcy, of course. No need to alert the others about my obsession. Ryan's room was so close I could've reached out and touched it. Good thing I was surrounded, or I might've succumbed to temptation and stepped inside the private world of my fantasy guy to explore. Just for a minute.

Later, as I lay wrapped in my fuzzy blanket in the rec room, I replayed the image of Ryan's room. In an instant, my mind had memorized the details. I tried to picture him in it, wondering what he thought about when he turned off the light. But eventually, days of cramming for finals did me in, and I drifted off to sleep, hoping to dream about Ryan and a pair of tasty lips locking with mine.

Sweet bliss.

\* \* \*

Long before it was light out, I woke up after having one of those dreams where I had to go to the bathroom really badly, but everywhere I went, the bathroom stalls only had little half walls around them and no doors. Plus, the stalls were outside on a patio in the middle of a party, and I was completely mortified that I couldn't find anything to shield myself with while I, you know, did the business.

I think that's supposed to mean I felt vulnerable in my real life (that's what my dream encyclopedia says, anyway), but as I lay there wondering why I was dreaming about toilets instead of about Ryan, my bladder suggested it might just be because I had to pee.

I tiptoed through the sleeping masses, careful not to step on anyone in the dark. I crept up the stairs into the kitchen and made a beeline for the hall bathroom. I was washing my hands and admiring one of the worst cases of bed head ever when I heard voices outside the door.

"Chill, you guys. Cass, where are the candles?"

"I think—"

"I've got 'em. Ouch!"

"Shhh!"

"That was my foot, Cherie. Are you trying to cripple me before camp?"

"Give me a break. We're working like it's the Dark Ages in here."

I opened the door, wondering what the heck was going on. "What are you guys—?"

"*Geez.*" Sarah Jane slapped a hand to her chest. "You almost gave me a heart attack, Jess!"

I stepped out, keenly aware of my crazy-haired look in contrast to the girls in the hallway. They looked radiant, decked out in long white dresses that definitely weren't nightgowns.

I looked at them.

They looked at me.

Some of them looked to Cassie for guidance, but she was frozen in place. Finally, she shook her head. "I don't know what protocol is. No one's ever caught us mid-setup before." Her eyebrows knit together, which I hoped meant she was thinking hard and not trying to decide if a family of canaries had built a nest in my hair. "You guys take Jess downstairs and wake the others. Just give us a few extra minutes to finish up."

Sarah Jane herded me down the stairs, while a few

other girls in white followed. Quietly, they woke the sleeping beauties.

My eyes snapped to the high heel I'd pinned to the corner of my pillowcase so I wouldn't lose it. If this was the "special" part of the night, why couldn't they have given us some warning? I gave my hair a quick brush while Sarah Jane helped someone find her contacts case, but I still felt way underdressed and undercoiffed for whatever they had planned.

Once everyone was fully awake, we single-filed it up the stairs, through the kitchen, and out the back doors onto the Steeles' massive deck. I don't know what I was expecting, but a full-on ceremonial setting wasn't it.

The moon cast its rays through the overhang of trees, giving a bluish dappled effect to everything. In the middle of the deck, Paige stood in her flowing white gown, the gauzy fabric billowing in the night breeze. She looked like an ancient Greek goddess. Almost ethereal. She stood behind a large round table with a white tablecloth draped over it and welcomed us silently with a gentle wave of her hand.

We moved closer, and the older girls led us behind a half-moon of chairs covered in more white fabric and tied with bows that shimmered under the stars. I glanced around and noticed we were arranged in two neat rows behind the seven chairs. Everyone except for Gaby (another brainiac like me) and Cassie, who both stood off to the side observing the procession.

The girls forming the back row—Sarah Jane, Kyra, and the others—each had a hand on the shoulder of the girl in front of her. The girls in my row seemed lulled by the quiet chirp of crickets and wore peaceful, if curious, expressions of acceptance. I, on the other hand, was holding up the skeptical end of the bargain. My latent fears of being punked had officially kicked into gear.

On the table in front of Paige sat an elaborate white pillar candle burning on a brass tray, two sets of long taper candles, and a small crystal bowl that twinkled as though it held secrets just beyond our grasp. Paige raised her hands, palms up, and addressed us in a low, melodic voice. "Who enters the Sacred Circle?"

"We, the Sisters of the Society," said Sarah Jane and the back row.

"What brings you to the Circle?"

"We seek to refill the well of Sisterhood."

"The Sisterhood accepts your quest."

The "Sisters" made sure everyone in the front row was seated before they approached Paige. Cassie moved in to assist and handed Paige a long white taper candle. Paige lit it from the elegant pillar as each Sister took a darker taper candle from the table. One by one, Paige lit the tapers—purple, I could see from the glow—and the Sisters quietly returned to their positions behind us.

I tried to scan the yard for Lexy, but everything was obscured by white fabric woven through the lattice around the deck. Pots of tall, bushy plants huddled together where the lattice ended to close us off from the open deck space. It gave our whole area a private, almost secretive feel. I focused on Paige and tried to get my bearings for the upcoming event. Whatever they had planned was not a drive-by affair. They'd spent a lot of time orchestrating our party game.

Paige lifted her white candle, the Sisters raising their purple ones in answer. "We come forth tonight," she began, "in the name of Sisterhood, to bring new Sisters into our fold. We present to you an opportunity, young Sisters. We are the new face of women. Our leadership will bring the dawn of a new era."

A chorus of voices responded behind me. "We celebrate our true strength."

"Each of you," Paige continued, nodding at our seated group, "has been selected for your potential to continue our mission in a tradition befitting the beloved Sisterhood. But first, we celebrate the glory of you in the present."

The standing Sisters moved as one to Paige's table and took the second group of taper candles. Sarah Jane motioned for me to stand as she approached and handed me a pale candle.

"We celebrate you as you are, young Sisters," Paige said. "Accept our light as a reflection of your own. Your candle acknowledges the triumphs and challenges that have made you who you are today."

"I celebrate the glory of you, Jess," Sarah Jane whispered, lighting my candle with hers.

She stood next to me now, her purple candle and my lavender one casting a warm glow on our faces. Sarah Jane looked so tranquil, completely at odds with my thumping heartbeat. Could anything this serene be evil? My suspicions about Lexy wavered.

Sarah Jane must've been reading my thoughts. "Don't be afraid," she said softly. "You're meant to be one of us."

Again with the *us*. My heart beat a little faster. How many times had I dreamed of being one of the chosen few? To be truly accepted by the in crowd instead of sitting on the sidelines of my own life?

"We come together tonight," Paige continued, "to honor our Sisterhood, celebrate the glory of you, and embrace you on your mission. Each of you comes to the Sisterhood with a special purpose and unique gift to share with the world. We seek to help you bring forth those treasures and contribute them to the greater good."

The chorus of voices sounded. "We embrace our future."

The Sisters moved to the table again, each reaching into the crystal bowl. Sarah Jane returned to my side, her hand in a loose fist over her heart.

"With loving hearts, we pay tribute to your potential," Paige said. "We believe in the power of our shared destinies."

The voices chimed once more. "We shall be extraordinary."

Paige turned toward the opposite end of the half-moon. "Melanie Davis. You possess an amazing gift of serenity and calm. You bring peace to those around you and settle disputes with a pure heart. We embrace your pursuit of the greater truth." Kyra placed something in Mel's palm and whispered in her ear.

Paige called each girl by name as she moved around the arc—Katrina Walker, Chandi Prasad, Hannah Campbell, Nalani Akina, Alicia Gallagher. I was last, my breath coming short and quick. *Please don't let me be the punch line.*

"Jessica Parker. You possess an exceptional gift of leadership. We honor your unwavering determination and your steadfast loyalty. You are a champion of justice and a visionary guardian of the world."

My mouth dropped as Sarah Jane placed a beautiful silver butterfly charm in my free hand. "Sister Jess," she whispered, "we celebrate your potential and welcome your gifts to the Sisterhood."

I was so shocked I could barely keep up with the rest of the ceremony. Me, a champion of justice? A visionary guardian of the world? Had these people even *met* me? I couldn't even guard myself against Lexy!

I felt ambushed, the fantasy and reality shocking me in equal measure. This was real. I understood that now. It wasn't some elaborate hoax. They intended for me to be here, wanted me in their secret Sisterhood. And they had no *clue* who I really was. Why had I explained about the volunteering? I was only helping a few puppies, not saving an entire galaxy of them.

Disappointment washed over me. They were gifting me everything I'd ever wanted, everything I'd ever glimpsed on the other side of the glass. Yet no matter how much I ached to belong—to be part of something real and true and special—this was never what I'd imagined.

I might've been the queen of worthy causes, but these were the most extraordinary girls at MSH. The best of the best in every facet of high-school life. I wasn't even in the same league. The Sisters were shining stars, so intent on welcoming others like them that they never realized one exception had slipped through undetected. An exception who was the epitome of ordinary. I was the only one who knew my invitation was nothing more than a case of mistaken identity.

An unwanted tear slipped down my cheek, and Sarah Jane wiped it away with the sleeve of her dress. "I cried too," she whispered, and I glanced around, surprised to see a tear glistening on Mel's cheek at the far end. But Mel's and Sarah Jane's joyful tears and my miserable ones had nothing in common.

*Just like us.*

"Are you sure"—my throat seized up for a second—"you meant to choose me?"

I hated to ask it, dreaded it more than all the Lexy confrontations in the world. But I knew I couldn't live with it if they were the ones who realized the mistake later. I couldn't handle their pity.

Sarah Jane held up a finger to Paige, who paused mid-sentence. Sarah Jane turned to face me square on, her eyes full of compassion and wisdom and a strength I could never match. "You are the guardian, Jess. The truth is inside you if you look for it. Trust that you're here because you're destined to be."

She didn't know how crazy her request was. Someone like Sarah Jane could never understand. She was asking me to tear down my defenses, walls that kept me protected in my lonely but safe little bubble. A bubble that let me believe I *was* good enough, that people just hadn't gotten the chance to really know me.

I closed my eyes and took a deep breath, praying for some kind of sign. No lightning bolts appeared in the sky, but a momentary shower of peace rained over me. It came and went so quickly I wondered if I'd imagined it, but in the end, I knew. If ever there was a time to trust, this was it. "Trust the universe and go with God," as Nan would say. It scared the living heck out of me. *What happens when they realize I'm just me?*

"Young Sisters," Paige continued, "we honor you now and celebrate who you will become. With this charm as a reminder of your greatest potential, the time has come for you to choose." Paige beckoned us forward to her table. "In every life there is a moment of truth. Will you stand as you are now, or will you accept the call to fulfill your greatest potential?"

Cassie stepped up to place a wide, flat candle in the center of the table. One glance at the shape of the wicks—one at the top and seven more in a half-moon around the bottom—and I knew it represented us. Paige lit the wick at the top and raised her candle to the Sisters standing tall behind our abandoned chairs. "Long live the Sisterhood," they said, blowing out their candles as one.

"Each of you must choose your future," Paige said, turning to Mel. "Sister Melanie, do you accept the call of the Sisterhood?"

Without hesitation, Mel lit the wick on her end of the half-moon. "I accept the call."

Each girl accepted without showing any flickers of doubt that this was exactly where she belonged. The wicks came to life until every one was lit except mine.

"Sister Jessica, do you accept the call of the Sisterhood?"

Trust warred with fear. Only one thing was worse than being forever on the outside: to feel the magic of belonging only to be banished back behind the glass when the dream came crashing down. Was it ever worth the risk?

Peace swept over me again, stronger this time but just as fleeting, and I steadied myself to quiet the fears. I listened to the small, still voice inside me and lowered my trembling candle to the wick, my voice barely a whisper. "I accept the call."

"One last thing remains. The candle that burns bright on our table represents each of you as cherished Sisters of the Society. Where one journey begins, another must end. When you are ready to begin your new journey, extinguish your flame and release the fears that bind you to your past."

One by one, the girls blew out their lavender candles. I looked back at Sarah Jane, who was silently encouraging me as she clutched Gwen's hand atop my chair. Years of being alone flooded my memory, dragging me toward the safety of my bubble. Palms sweating, I resisted the temptation to cower from the unknown and did the thing that scared me most. I took a leap of faith.

Wisps of smoke curled from my darkened candle as I gazed up at Paige.

"*Namaste*, Sisters," she said. "Welcome to The Cinderella Society."

# Chapter 4

NINE HOURS LATER, I was back at The Grind for lunch. Jittery from excitement and lack of sleep and achy from two hours of mural painting with Mom, I trailed Sarah Jane up the same front walk I'd traveled the night before. Same stone pathway, same etched-glass doors with their stylized coffee cups. Everything was the same . . . and everything was different.

Last night, I'd stood outside those double doors, pondering my fate as a perpetual outcast. In a matter of hours, I'd crossed that elusive threshold of acceptance. Back at the scene of the crime, I was facing the door to my future. I was no longer Jess Parker, persona non grata. I was Jess Parker, newly initiated Sister of the Society. The world was my oyster.

I slowed, feeling the tiniest bit overwhelmed and uncertain. And yes, a little melodramatic.

Sarah Jane glanced over at me. "Are you ready for this?"

"Only one way to find out." I took a deep breath, pushed through the doors, and boldly stepped into my fabulous new life.

As rites of passage go, it was pretty anticlimactic. No one showered me with confetti or asked for my autograph. No one knew there was anything different about me at all, save the fact that I'd shown up with Sarah Jane Peterson, resident it girl. The rest was status quo.

Which, on the one hand, was kind of a letdown. Would a little celebration have killed anyone?

"When do we get started?" I asked Sarah Jane as we waited in line. The nerves and anticipation combined to make me sound more like a six-year-old at Christmas than a sixteen-year-old Cinderella, but I couldn't help it. Ever since Sarah Jane had given me the scoop on our Society and its ultimate life makeovers, visions of fairy godmothers had filled my head.

As far as I was concerned, we could skip lunch and hit the mall on empty stomachs. A new wardrobe was first on my makeover agenda, with shimmery amber highlights a close second.

"Let's get our drinks first," Sarah Jane murmured, turning toward the counter. "Hi, Audrey. I'll have a tall mocha latte."

"Hey, SJ. Coming right up."

Audrey London moved with the kind of grace you'd imagine from a top model, though you'd expect to see it on a catwalk instead of behind the counter of an upscale café that was giving Starbucks a run for its money.

I started to ask, "Do you guys hang out here a lot?" but closed my mouth. Because, hello? Audrey London had called Sarah Jane by *name*.

I know! A two-time *Sports Illustrated* cover model who reportedly dated Matthew McConaughey (Sarah Jane says that's just a rumor) and now owns a chain of super trendy coffee shops chatted with Sarah Jane like they were old friends.

The Grind in Mt. Sterling was Audrey's first café and,

since she'd become a franchising phenom, her headquarters. I'd read an article where she'd talked about her best friend being some big professor at Montgomery University. That was less than twenty minutes from The Grind. But still, settling in a small town like Mt. Sterling instead of kicking it in New York or Milan or her native Sydney?

Naturally, I thought that was mental. But then, I'd never had a best friend, so what did I know?

Audrey liked to stay visible, so it wasn't unusual to see her behind the counter talking to customers. Which was part of what made The Grind *the* see-and-be-seen place for the entire MSH student body.

But when she asked about Sarah Jane's boyfriend by name *and* how she did on her French final, my celeb-o-meter went on overload. I suffer from one of the worst cases of celebrity fright. I'm as much of a watcher as the next girl, but to actually be in the presence of one? Totally different story.

I got tongue-tied when it was my turn. After stuttering out my order, I played mute and listened to Sarah Jane finish her story as a counter guy handed Sarah Jane's latte to Audrey. Aside from making the best pumpkin muffin tops in the world—according to *Seventeen* magazine—one of The Grind's claims to fame was the picture they sprinkled on the tops of their to-die-for drinks. They held a cool shaker thing over the cup, gave it a quick tap, and you had a perfect image on the top of your designer coffee. I'd gotten everything from a butterfly to a megaphone to a heart on mine.

Audrey picked up a purple shaker I hadn't noticed before and gave Sarah Jane's coffee a topper. My extra-tall caramel latte came up next, and Audrey picked up the bright pink shaker I recognized as the dragonfly. She paused with the shaker in her hand and looked at Sarah Jane. "She's with you?"

"This is Jess Parker," Sarah Jane said. "We're hanging out today."

Audrey extended her free hand across the counter to shake mine. "Nice to meet you, Jess. I've seen you in here with Rosemary."

*Whoa.* She even knew Nan's name. "Hi, Miss London. It's nice to meet you." And I only stuttered once. *M-meet you.*

"Call me Audrey. We're among friends, right?"

I nodded uncertainly, struck mute by my celeb fright, while Audrey switched shakers and popped a quick picture from the purple one. She snapped on a clear lid and handed me the cup as I pulled out my money.

Audrey shook her head. "It's on the house. Welcome to town, Jess Parker."

I thanked her profusely, still amazed that she'd said my name not once, but twice. As I looked down at my free latte, I saw a picture I hadn't gotten before. It was starting to disintegrate into the steamy mixture, but it looked distinctly like a shoe. A high heel, to be exact. Like a . . .

"No way," I whispered.

"Way," Sarah Jane whispered back, as Audrey gave me a wink before turning to help the next person in line.

A lump formed in my throat. One moonlight initiation and I was already rubbing elbows with the rich and famous. I watched as the picture dissolved away into nothing. But my first glimpse at how the other half lived was imprinted on my brain. Fame, fortune, and a latte topper in the shape of a glass slipper.

I hoped the clock would never strike midnight.

We grabbed a booth along the front as some girls I

recognized from gym were leaving. Audrey came over with a cute red bistro towel and did a quick wipe of the table. She slowed her last swipe and lowered her voice. "Rumor has it there were fourteen at The Range last night."

Sarah Jane's eyes widened. "Fourteen?"

"Fourteen what?" I asked, forgetting I was the tagalong.

"People." Sarah Jane glanced at Audrey. "They doubled?"

Audrey nodded, finishing the wipe-down with a flourish. "Strength in numbers, honey," she said before moving back to the counter.

Sarah Jane sat motionless, still in shock over the number fourteen. Kyra and Mel came in, and Sarah Jane waved them over. Kyra motioned toward the counter first, and she and Mel went to grab drinks of their own.

By the time they got to our table, Kyra's expression matched Sarah Jane's.

"Fourteen?" she asked Sarah Jane quietly. "How did we miss that?"

Sarah Jane shook her head. "I don't know, but we'll have to pass it along."

I was about to ask, "Fourteen what?" again, figuring Sarah Jane would realize it was rude to keep talking in cryptics, when two hunky seniors arrived on the scene. Mark Evans and Ben Harper came strolling in, looking divine in polos and cargo shorts. Just like that, the mood went from dark to sparkling.

They pulled up chairs next to their respective girlfriends, Mark by Sarah Jane and Ben by Kyra. Sarah Jane made introductions for Mel and me, and the conversation shifted to finals-week war stories. I listened quietly and tried to pretend I belonged there. Until Ben looked over at the door and yelled, "Steele!"

We all turned, and there in the flesh—very *fine* flesh—was fantasy boy himself. Ryan lifted his chin in greeting and headed our way. The guys exchanged a fancy testosterone handshake before turning to the girls. My heart stopped as I saw recognition dawn on his face.

"So you made it?" A smile lit his eyes. "I thought that might be the last we saw of Jess Parker."

"Yeah," I said, trying to think of a witty comeback. Instead, all I could think was how he actually knew my full name and how white his teeth were up close, so nothing else came out. Just "yeah."

He turned his attention back to the rest of the group and joined in the conversation about the party at Nick Case's last night. I refrained from kicking myself under the table.

I tried to look casual and cool, but there was no escaping reality. For someone who was totally at ease with adults—thanks to years of working with them on volunteer stuff—I was pretty awkward with people my own age. Especially guys. I might be a Sister, but I had miles to go before I'd ever blend with Sarah Jane's crowd.

When the guys finally stood to go, Mark gave Sarah Jane a quick peck on the cheek. "What's your plan today?"

"Hanging out with the girls," she said. "Maybe working on some cheers."

What?! *Noooo!* Sarah Jane had promised we'd spend the afternoon working on makeover stuff, not test-drive new material for . . .

*Oh.*

So *discretion* meant no boyfriends either. Interesting.

Ben gave Kyra a peck—earning both couples brownie points for low-key PDA—and the guys headed toward the door. It wasn't until Sarah Jane stifled a laugh that I realized

I was wearing the most blatant puppy-dog expression.

"Ryan?" she asked.

My face went from pasty to scarlet in two seconds flat. "I didn't know he'd be here."

"They travel in herds, but that's a story for another day." She looked around the table, a glint in her eye. "Right now, we've got work to do."

*　*　*

When you're about to enter the mysterious world of a secret society, back toward the café bathrooms and through the employee-entrance door probably isn't the first place you'd expect to go.

Sarah Jane paused to make a call from the pay phone in the employee hall, but she didn't actually talk to anyone, as far as I could tell. She swiped a credit card–looking thing and punched in some numbers before we heard a buzz and click from the door marked MANAGEMENT ONLY. We followed her through that door into another hallway . . . and another . . . burrowing deeper into the heart of the building. The Grind must've been built around a maze.

I wondered if I should leave a trail of bread crumbs. Which made me hungry, since between Audrey's presence, the number fourteen, and three very distracting hotties, we'd forgotten to order lunch.

We finally stopped in front of a door with a keypad and waited while Sarah Jane punched in more numbers. The butterflies were busy in my chest, tapping out Morse code for *Are you sure you're ready for this?*

Sarah Jane pushed the door open and held it wide as Kyra and Mel stepped inside. I followed suit, stepping into the secret hideaway of The Cinderella Society.

The ritzy setup looked like a huge, posh boardroom. But

instead of catering to corporate-y types in suits, it was just the four of us and Gaby, who was busy laying binders around the giant table.

Warm, shiny wood and big, comfy rolling chairs in gorgeous deep purple suede gave the room a high-class feel while still making the huge space feel homey. Homey or not, the fears from the night before crept in, reminding me I was out of my league. I laid my hand on top of a chair, nervously stroking the soft leather.

"Faux, of course," Sarah Jane said. "Soft and animal-friendly."

Vanilla candles burned on a crystal platter down the center of the table, and ornately framed pictures lined the walls. The walls themselves were a soft shade of lavender and, upon closer inspection, were covered with photographs of celebrities: classy actresses and pro athletes and Grammy winners. Exactly the kind of women you'd expect The Cinderella Society to consider role models. All positive, all powerful, all dazzling.

Yep. Light-years out of my league. A different galaxy, even.

I stepped closer to peer at a collection of silver-framed group photos near the door, some of which included Sarah Jane or Kyra or Paige surrounded by other girls. Everyone looked luminous and happy. With some framed Asian graphics for joy, wisdom, prosperity, and harmony, the room was a tribute to girl power.

Gaby waved us around the table, where thick binders awaited us. Sarah Jane led me over to one by her, and Kyra led Mel to another. I reached for the binder.

Sarah Jane stilled my wrist. "Gab?"

"Hang on," she said, still bustling around the room, lighting candles, pulling supplies from shelves, and grabbing bowls for snacks. "We have to wait for everyone else."

"No worries." Sarah Jane leaned toward me. "This is Gaby's first time as Alpha Chair. She's gonna be great."

"Alpha Chair?" I asked.

"Sit tight, J." She looked up at Gaby, who was pouring trail mix into jewel-toned glass bowls. "Did Audrey tell you about the number spike?"

Gaby glanced up, losing her concentration and pouring trail mix on the table. "She has news already?"

"Fourteen," Kyra said.

Gaby set the bag down with a thump. "That's double."

Sarah Jane, Kyra, and Gaby looked at each other, each mulling over the magic number fourteen, while Mel and I exchanged looks of cluelessness.

I cleared my throat. "What does fourteen mean?"

Gaby shook her head to clear it, bending to scoop up the trail-mix mess. "I guess I'll have to include that." She steadied her hands on the table. "As Gwen would say, *Game on.*"

"Game on," Sarah Jane agreed.

．＊　＊　＊

The other girls from the initiation ceremony began to arrive, and Sarah Jane and Kyra retreated to a row of chairs against the wall behind us. When everyone was seated, Gaby moved to the head of the table and opened a large leather book with a lock on the side like a diary.

"As you all know, my name is Gaby Winston. I'll be your Alpha Chair for the next year. My job is to lead your Alpha-level meetings and get you ready to take the next step in the Sisterhood.

"Since this is your first time back to the Club, here's the lowdown. This is our meeting place for Cindys only. No one else knows it exists. There are security locks on the outer management entrance and on the door to the Club. You'll each be given your own code, and the security system will log every time you enter the facility. You're free to come back here whenever you want during business hours to study and work on your projects."

She stretched out her arms to encompass the room. "This is what we call Study Hall. Through that door"—she pointed to her left—"is the Alpha office. That's where I'll be when I'm on duty this summer. If I'm not on duty, you can leave me a note in my mailbox."

Gaby gestured to the other doors farther down on her left. "The next door is the leader's office, Paige Ellis. She's a camp counselor this summer, so she'll be MIA for the next week or so during counselor training. The last door is the Gamma office. It has its own keyed access and is off-limits unless you've got Gamma security clearance."

She pointed a thumb over her shoulder. "Behind me is the Cindy lounge. We've got a great setup in there: a kitchenette with a couple of tables, two laptops, a TV, and a bathroom. Audrey keeps us well stocked, so have at it if you get the munchies. If you want a sandwich or something from the front while Audrey's here, instructions for ordering are next to the laptops. Audrey will bring it back."

Security clearance and a supermodel waiting on us? Who *were* we?

"From now on, you only hang in the front if you're here to socialize. If you're here for the Society, you enter through the outside door near the bathrooms and come straight back through the employee entrance. You leave the same way you came in. No one should see you enter or exit if you can help it. If anyone questions you, just tell them you're doing some work for Audrey."

"Audrey hires students for a lot of things around the store," Kyra explained. "That helps us with the cover."

They weren't kidding about secrecy. I wondered if fingerprinting was far behind.

"The binders in front of you," Gaby continued, "are your Sisterhood training manuals. The *CMM* on the cover stands for *Cinderella Makeover Manual*. The *CMM* is one of the most top secret documents in the Society and does *not* leave the Club. There are lockers in the lounge for you to lock them up when you leave."

Since when did makeovers require training? My fantasies about simple before-and-after photos were looking more and more like a pipe dream.

Gaby consulted the book in front of her, leaving her finger on the page to mark her spot. "It goes without saying that nothing you see, hear, or do in the Club goes beyond the Club. You're not to mention the *CMM* or anything about The Cinderella Society to non-Cindys."

"What about Audrey?" I asked. "Doesn't she know?"

Gaby smiled. "You're quick. A group like ours can't function without help, so we have a dedicated support system for what we do. Audrey has a lucrative contract with us for the space, so that works for both of us."

I couldn't imagine what *lucrative* meant to a millionaire supermodel, but the Cindys had to be seriously well funded. I made a mental note to get the scoop from Sarah Jane on who was financing our little group. She'd sworn it was strictly a "no dues" thing. Which was good, because my allowance couldn't support a hamster, much less a supermodel.

"She's also our eyes and ears," Sarah Jane added. "That's part of why she's so chummy out front. She's like that anyway, but she picks up a lot from people who come into the store.

If it's detrimental to us or to"—she paused—"other people, Audrey lets us know."

"And those other people are exactly why you're here," Gaby said. "The Cinderella Society's creed is simple but powerful: Celebrate your strength, embrace your future, and be extraordinary. Every Cindy, no matter what level, has the same creed. It's what drives everything the Sisterhood is about."

It seemed Sarah Jane had left a few things out in her explanation about the Cindys. Or maybe I'd glossed over them the minute I'd heard the words *you* and *makeover* in the same breath.

Gaby had us flip open our *Cinderella Makeover Manual*s to a slick chart that shed light on the whole ranks thing. "The Society has four levels," she explained. "Alpha, Beta, Gamma, and Delta. As soon as you accept the call during initiation, you're officially an Alpha. As Alphas, your priority is to learn about the Society's mission and complete the first part of your Cindy training to prepare you for the battle ahead."

Training, training, and more training. When did we get to the—

*Wait. Did she say "battle"?*

"We work hard to be the best we can be and to contribute to the greater good. But for every one of us, there's someone on the opposite end of the spectrum. Kind of like in physics, where—"

"Gab," Sarah Jane cut in. "Ix-nay on the science lecture."

"Spoilsport. What I mean is that for every Cindy there's an opposite."

"A Wicked?" I joked, but stopped chuckling when I realized none of my Alpha sisters got the reference. "You know, like Cinderella's wicked stepsisters?"

Gaby lost any hint of a smile. "We never joke about the Wickeds. But yes, they're our opposites. For the most part, Wickeds live a surface existence. Very superficial, very interested in the now. Casual sex, drinking, sometimes drugs, even small-time illegal. They push the envelope without worrying about the repercussions. Or if they worry, they don't let it cramp their style."

An Alpha named Kat nodded. "Taking the Me Generation to the extreme."

"You got it," Gaby agreed. "Cindys, on the other hand, understand the need to sometimes sacrifice the now—*sometimes*, not always—to get the bigger win later. There's a grander plan in motion, and we're only one piece of the puzzle."

"So," Mel said, trying the idea on for size, "the Cindys are good and the Wickeds are bad. Like a high-school battle of good and evil?"

"The Wickeds aren't one hundred percent bad, just like the Cindys aren't one hundred percent good," Gaby cautioned. "But otherwise, yeah. The Wickeds gain power by manipulating and dominating other kids. Mostly the Reggies—that's what we call kids who aren't Cindys or Wickeds. It's short for regular kids, but don't let the name fool you. Every one of them has the strength and the ability to make a major impact. You don't have to be a Cindy or a Wicked for that."

I'd been a regular kid all my life, so I had to agree with her on that one.

"The Wickeds' mission is to rule the Reggies and make them do the Wickeds' dirty work. Our mission is to protect the Reggies and ultimately take the Wickeds down."

The Cindys versus the Wickeds. Battling for the souls of the Reggies?

Gaby slid aside the bulletin board on the wall behind her to reveal a whiteboard beneath. "To defeat the Wickeds, we follow the two Sisterhood commandments."

She picked up a blue marker from the tray and wrote commandment number one on the board.

## PROTECT YOURSELF

"The Sisterhood can help by offering backup when you need it," Gaby said, "but you have to be able to go head-to-head with a Wicked and win. That means preparing yourself so you don't let their mental games get inside your head."

She turned back to the board and wrote the second Cindy commandment.

## PROTECT THE REGGIES

"Power is key. Give a Reggie the tools to save herself, and step in as backup to give her confidence. The best way to protect a Reggie is to help her protect herself. When she asserts her own power, the Wickeds start to lose theirs."

Gaby capped the marker and put it back on the tray. "It's not an easy mission, but by the time you're done with your Alpha and Beta training, you'll be ready to do battle with the Wickeds and come out on top. Any questions so far?"

Her question met seven glassy-eyed stares around the table.

"That's normal. It's a lot to take in at first." Gaby took a deep breath and launched into her last topic. "Okay, about the fourteen . . ."

My system got a dose of verbal caffeine.

"To continue building the Sisterhood, we offer bids to seven girls every year. Until now, so have the Wickeds. But if Audrey's intel is right—and she's rarely wrong—the Wickeds have stepped it up a notch and recruited fourteen girls this year."

Hence the "double."

"So they'll have more than we do," Mel said slowly, trying to grasp the significance. "The scales tip in their favor. But how does that affect us as Alphas?"

Gaby held up a hand. "In more ways than we can get into on day one. I'm sure there are already people hot on the trail of that particular problem. For now, just focus on your *CMM*. That's the best way to prepare for whatever they've got planned."

We opened our binders and started reading about the history of TCS while Gaby retreated to her office and our mentors (or "Big Sisters," according to Gaby) headed into the lounge. Who would've guessed a secret society dedicated to defeating the mean girls of the world had thrived in Mt. Sterling for more than a century?

I couldn't help sneaking a peek at the other sections Gaby had mentioned, though. Behind history, there were several more tabs, including the much-anticipated appearance section. Sadly, they were all empty except for an overview.

Gaby peeked her head out of her office, and I let the pages drop. "If you guys need anything, I'll be in here for the rest of the day," she said. "Since tomorrow's your first Alpha class, try to get through the history section and the other overviews before then so you're ready to dive into phase one of your makeover."

Visions of gorgeousness and Sarah Jane–caliber popularity toyed with my focus. We might have to learn about our history first, but that didn't mean I couldn't dream about what came next. I was surrounded by the in crowd, I held a top secret guide to coolness in my hands, and I had the junior prom queen playing fairy godmother for my very own ultimate life makeover. It had all the makings of a full-blown fairy tale.

Except that everything about our mission prickled the hairs on my neck.

The Cindys might veer onto the path of Makeoverland, but the Sisterhood was a force to be reckoned with. And unlike the movies, they weren't battling evil villains in a far-off land. Our villains were right here at home.

I would've bet my cherished Kate Spade purse that Lexy was as Wicked as they came. And if she was, this was way more than I'd signed on for.

How could I ever do battle with Lexy and win?

# Chapter 5

BEING IN THE CLUB for the second time didn't take away any of the awe factor. Mel and I showed up late morning the next day to get through the rest of our *Cinderella Makeover Manual* overviews before the first Alpha class that afternoon. Gaby, of course, had been there since the first pot of coffee went on out front. She greeted us in the lounge, sporting a BlackBerry on a lanyard and an apple crumb muffin in one hand.

Gaby nabbed us each a soda as we stowed our gear in the cute pink lockers. She had David Cook playing on the iPod speakers in the kitchenette, which she promptly turned off. "Sorry," she said. "I needed a little pick-me-up."

I could totally relate. David Cook could pick me up anytime.

Mel and I grabbed our binders and settled into the yum Study Hall chairs as Sarah Jane and Kyra were coming in the door. They stowed their stuff and joined us at the table. Sarah Jane set down her enormous binder next to mine. Even laying it gently on the table still resulted in a loud thud.

I eyed the monstrosity, suddenly glad mine only had a few dozen sheets of paper in it, and wondered what hers could possibly be filled with. She was a third-level Cindy, I'd found out—a Gamma—so who knew what-all was in there?

From what I'd learned so far, Alpha stage was mostly about the *celebrating your strength* part of the creed, and Beta stage got deeper into *embracing your future.* Clever girl that I am, I reasoned that Gammas were all about *being extraordinary.* As for Deltas . . . sheesh, what came after being extraordinary? World domination?

We all dug into our *CMM* work—Mel and I on the last few overviews and Sarah Jane and Kyra on their special projects. The air hummed with productivity vibes.

The door to the Club opened again, and Paige entered, with Audrey trailing her. They both looked serious as they headed for Paige's office. Our Big Sisters eyed them solemnly and quietly closed up their *CMMs.* By the time they'd finished putting their binders away, Paige had opened her door. She gave Sarah Jane a silent nod and slipped back inside, while Audrey headed out of the Club without a word.

Sarah Jane and Kyra keyed into the Gamma office and closed the door behind them.

Mel and I looked at each other.

"What was that about?" I asked.

Mel tapped a staccato rhythm with her pen. "Did you see the news this morning?"

Mom had The Weather Channel on every morning like clockwork, but something told me that wasn't what Mel meant. "What about it?"

"Miss Teen Blue Ridge was stripped of her title last night." She leaned in closer, lowering her voice. "A video of her smoking a joint in the woods behind her school was mailed to a local TV station. Once they identified her, they called the pageant office for an official comment. The pageant called her family, confirmed it was her, and took away her crown."

Brutal. But who in their right mind would be out behind their school smoking a joint? First of all, I like all my brain cells, thanks. And second, a local teen celebrity doing *anything* wrong in public is a dumb move. Add illegal to dumb and what did she expect?

"What does that have to do with us?" Before "with us" was even out of my mouth, I knew the answer. The question wasn't why she'd been so dumb—it was why the TV station had ended up with a prime-time video of the event.

The Wickeds strike again. "Who has it in for her?"

"Lexy and Morgan used to do pageants," Mel said. "Lexy was runner-up for Miss Teen Blue Ridge and 'retired' right after she lost to Alyssa."

"Looks like she's coming out of retirement."

"Looks like."

I thought about the way Lexy had launched a steaming drink on me when I dared to ignore her. How far would she go to get revenge when she felt wronged? Had I been a Cindy long enough that they'd always have my back if she stepped up her attack on me?

"I hope she doesn't come after us that way." I shuddered. "My reputation's already taken a beating. One more blow and I'll be back to loser status."

"No Wicked chatter out here," Gaby said, striding toward us. "Do you two want to order up a late breakfast? I've been going on muffins all morning, and I'm craving a pesto egg sandwich. Snacks and drinks are on the house, but we usually pay Audrey for meals. Any takers?"

My stomach rumbled. I couldn't get within a hundred feet of The Grind without hunger setting in. This was not going to bode well for my cheer uniform future.

"Sure," I said. "What's Wicked chatter?"

Mel and I followed Gaby into the lounge to grab our wallets as she elaborated. "Any kind of general negativity. Swearing, gossiping, putting people down. Including ourselves." She gave me a pointed look at the last part. "Even Wicked chatter that goes on in your head."

Mel looked amused as she handed Gaby a five. "You monitor our thoughts?"

"Haven't gotten the patent on it yet, but give us time."

Sarah Jane had said that the higher up you went in the Cindys, the more independent study you did. The way Gaby joked about the patent gave me the sneaking suspicion she'd love to have a crack at that project. There seemed to be very little a Cindy couldn't do if she set her mind to it. Myself excluded, of course.

Ah. *That* kind of Wicked chatter in your head.

Good thing the patent was just a joke. (Probably.)

* * *

After all the Alphas had arrived and were eagerly seated around the table, Gaby got us rolling.

"Welcome to your first Alpha class," Gaby said. "We'll be covering a lot of ground today, but here's the main thing you need to know: Alpha training is all about making you stronger. Remember, our goal is to prepare you to go head-to-head with a Wicked and win."

She passed out an outline of the Alpha program. "The Wickeds prey on weakness. If they can hone in on your insecurities, they'll knock you off your game nine times out of ten. Your Alpha work is designed to help you get over your insecurities and focus on your strengths. If the Wickeds don't have anything on you that'll hit a sore spot, that puts you in the power position. To win against the Wickeds, you have to keep the power on your side."

I craved the win. Especially if it meant Lexy was the loser. Lexy and all her Wicked minions.

Gaby slid aside the bulletin board to expose the whiteboard again. Yesterday's commandments were still printed in bold capital letters.

She pointed to *PROTECT THE REGGIES*. "We'll cover more about this part of the mission later. For right now, our focus is on this," she said, drawing a giant red circle around *PROTECT YOURSELF*.

"If you want to beat the Wickeds, you've got to keep them from getting inside your head. You already know the Wickeds prey on weakness, but the tricky thing is that they know exactly where to look for it. They go straight for the three areas most likely to let them take advantage."

Gaby picked up a purple marker from the tray and wrote an equation on the board.

$$Power = Personality + Appearance + Strengths$$

"To become truly powerful, you have to be completely comfortable with what makes you *you*. You have to be confident about who you are as a person." She put a check mark above *Personality*. "You need to be comfortable in your own skin." She made a check above *Appearance*. "And you have to understand your strengths *and* know how to use them to your advantage."

Gaby put a final check mark above *Strengths* and recapped her pen. "It sounds simple, but those are the three things most girls are insecure about: how they act, how they look, and whether they have anything to offer. The Wickeds know that and go after it with a vengeance."

She made eye contact with each of us to make sure we got the message. "If you've got insecurities in any of those areas, consider yourself a target. It's just a matter of time before they use your insecurities against you."

I thought about how easy it had been for Lexy to hit my sore spots. If she was able to tune into that for everyone, that was a pretty powerful bag of tricks.

Gaby eased up a bit at our grim faces. "You don't need to stress," she said. "The upside is that once you nail all three pieces, you've taken away most of the Wickeds' power over you. And you *will* nail all three pieces. It's our job to make sure you do."

Our Big Sisters had begun to gather just beyond the doorway to the lounge. *Please let that be a sign our makeovers aren't far off.* I was ready to take back my power in a big way.

"Let me ask you a question," Gaby said. "How many of you have something you wish you could change about how you look?"

Every Alpha's hand went up. Even Mel, the beauty queen.

"Look around," she told us. "Ninety-two percent of girls want to change something about the way they look. The Wickeds know that too. That's why the first thing we're going to focus on in your Power Plan is your appearance."

A cheer went up around the room. *Makeovers and shopping sprees, here we come!*

"Just don't confuse a great appearance with being a fashion diva," she cautioned, "or feel like you need to spend a ton of money on a new look. It's about getting comfortable in your own skin."

My baby face and I nodded like we believed her.

"The core of your appearance is what we call your signature style. Your Big Sisters will walk you through what signature style is in more detail, but before I turn you over to them, I want you to remember two things."

The room was still abuzz with the news of our impending makeovers, so Gaby waited until she had our full attention.

"Two things," she repeated. "First, beauty is not cookie-cutter."

I looked around the table at my Alpha sisters. *Cookie-cutter* was definitely not the first word that came to mind. We weren't even all from the same part of the world. Chandi had moved here from India a few years earlier, and Nalani was born in Hawaii but lived in Japan until she was nine.

"Second, there's no such thing as perfect," Gaby continued. "Focus on making the most of what you have and making peace with what you can't change. It's easier said than done—trust me, I *know*—but it's essential to mastering this part of your Power Plan. Confidence equals power."

To drive her point home, each of the Big Sisters stepped forward and told the Alphas one thing about herself she would change if she could. Even Gaby shared one. Gaby's nose was too wide (her glasses balanced it nicely), Cherie wished she could gain weight (she did have a Calista Flockhart thing going on beneath her breezy clothes), Kyra carried too much weight around her hips (her babydoll tops hid it well). The list went on and on.

The funny thing was, I'd always just thought of them as pretty. But when you stopped and looked hard at the flaws they pointed out, I guess you could kind of see what they meant. That was the thing, though. You didn't see the flaws. You saw the whole package: positive, polished, confident.

Still, I couldn't imagine a time I'd ever stand up in a room full of people and willingly point out my physical flaws. If my makeover gave me a smidgeon of their confidence, it would be a win of mythical proportions.

Gaby passed around a packet of Power Plan prep work for each of us while the Big Sisters came around the table. "These assignments will help you lay the groundwork for your entire Power Plan," she said. "Take your time with them, be true to who you are, and you'll do great. They're actually pretty fun once you get into them, so remember to enjoy it too. You're only an Alpha once."

With promises from us not to go crazy with our makeovers, Gaby turned us loose to our fairy godmothers, aka Big Sisters. While the other Big Sisters cozied up to the table next to their Alphas, Sarah Jane strolled up to me with keys in her hand. "Are you ready?"

I looked from her keys to my binder to the other Alphas around the table. Mel was standing up to go somewhere with Kyra, but everyone else looked to be here for the duration.

"I don't have to do the prep stuff?" I asked. Did I pull a rockin' big Sister card or what?

"Oh, no, you definitely do. You can't launch the new you until you know who she is."

*Thanks, Dr. Phil.*

"But first, I'm going to introduce you to signature style the same way my Big Sister introduced me."

"Which means . . . ?"

"Reconnaissance mission."

* * *

Blue Ridge Park is a jumbo-sized sports complex with baseball diamonds, soccer fields, basketball courts, a skateboard park, and several playgrounds for the preschool set. In the summer months, every Mt. Sterling resident under twenty inevitably finds his or her way there.

"First things first," Sarah Jane said as she turned off the engine. She pulled a small glittery box out of her purse. "A gift for my little Sister."

*Presents!* I unraveled the ribbon and lifted the top. A shiny silver charm bracelet twinkled at me from inside. Even with no charms on it, it was totally glam.

I slipped it on and slowly turned my wrist, watching the beveled links catch the sunlight, and noticed it actually did have a charm on it. The butterfly from initiation that I'd returned to Sarah Jane after the ceremony for "a special something." I got choked up seeing it again and had to blink hard against a sappy show of emotion.

"Every Cindy gets a charm bracelet when she goes Alpha," Sarah Jane said. "The first charm is a butterfly to symbolize the change you're about to make in your life."

"A metamorphosis." I *so* wanted to be the butterfly.

"You'll get new charms as you pass other milestones, but this one's a constant reminder that real beauty is there all along. You're just making sure the real you shines through in the end."

As cornball as her spiel sounded, I bought it like a large buttered popcorn on movie night. "It's awesome, Sarah Jane. Thanks."

"Remember what it means, and you'll never go astray. That's the secret to surviving the Alphas."

I knew she was kidding. Then I thought about her enormo binder and decided there was probably a hint of truth in there too. After surviving hundreds of pages of training and projects, I'd deserve every charm and then some.

"Okay, let's talk basics." Sarah Jane unbuckled and turned

toward me. "The goal of the appearance part of your Power Plan is to refine your image to make you feel completely comfortable and confident."

I barely resisted pumping my fists in the air in triumph. Finally, the good stuff!

"Signature style is the ultimate example of you being comfortable in your own skin. Gaby was right about that being the key to confidence with your new look. It's where you pull all the pieces together—hair, makeup, wardrobe, accessories—to show who you really are. Are you casual or glam or girly or sporty or a combination of two or three? Once you're clear on that, you've got your signature style."

To help me understand, we wandered through the park and checked out the hodgepodge of people. Skater boys with down-to-there waistbands and basketball players in cut-off muscle shirts and high-tops. Not exactly the fashion mecca you'd expect for a signature style intro.

SJ slowed in front of a baseball diamond, where I recognized some kids from school. Some teachers too.

"This is the annual Student-Teacher Summer Slam," she explained. "The teachers and students always play each other for bragging rights the next year. Yesterday was the basketball game—we crushed 'em—and today's the baseball game."

SJ steered us toward some empty bleachers near the outfield to give us a good view of the grandstand, the real reason we were there. With so much of the in crowd in attendance, it was practically a fashion event waiting to happen. We climbed up a couple of rows, made ourselves as comfy as the metal benches would allow, and shifted our attention to our fellow classmates.

Inadequacy hit me like a wave. I'd rarely fit the bill for trendy anywhere I'd lived. Oh, I'd tried. But after breaking the bank trying to overhaul my wardrobe every time we moved—only to find out I was unforgivably last year or, worse, the poster child for generic—I'd learned to become a savvy observer of fashion and style.

SJ leaned back, propping her elbows on the bleacher behind her. I followed suit, and we let our sunglasses hide our gazes from the world.

"Let's start with one close to home," SJ said. "How would you describe my signature style?"

*Um, perfect?* I glanced over at the ever-fabulous Sarah Jane Peterson. Sarah Jane had classy prep down to a science. If Ralph Lauren or Tommy Hilfiger made it, it inevitably found its way into SJ's closet. With her classic blonde good looks and natural makeup, it was a freak of nature she wasn't the latest face of Cover Girl.

"All-American classy prep?" I ventured.

I saw SJ's eyes widen. "I call it all-American dockside prep, but you nailed it. What about Kyra? She's sitting second row from the bottom."

I squinted at the crowd and found her sitting next to Mel, cheering for Ben at bat. Kyra had a totally fun and flirty style—she was decked out in a super cute Nicole Miller sundress that was one of my favorites on her. Plus, she had that amazing auburn hair and perfect skin that needed almost zero makeup to look fabulous.

"Fun and flirty girl-next-door."

"You've got the gift, J. Kee calls it 'flirty and fresh romance,' but again, bull's-eye. Your makeover's going to be a breeze." She scanned the grandstand again before giving me my final test. Top row, dead center. Black shirt.

My eyes skimmed the row until they landed on the last person I wanted to see. I stifled a groan and dutifully studied her signature style. I hated to admit it, but Lexy had a way tight style. She favored form-fitting Hugo Boss for getting noticed (always high on Lexy's agenda) and Diesel jeans with Urban Chic tanks for slumming. With her custom-dyed, blacker-than-black hair and pale skin, she definitely made a statement: Welcome to *Sex and the City, The Early Years.*

"Pure slutty rich girl?"

Sarah Jane gave me a gentle but disapproving look. Definitely a no-Wicked-chatter kind of girl, our Sarah Jane.

"Lexy has a powerful style, I'll give you that much," she said. "Try to take your emotions out of it and give it another shot."

I watched Lexy slouching with the Wickeds, doing her best to draw attention to herself while pretending to be oblivious to everything around her. I narrowed my eyes at the ruse. "Calculated sexy chic."

"I would've said 'carefully planned,' but I think you're coming around to the same kind of thing. The effect is thrown together and sexy, but it takes a lot of effort to pull off. You have to be fully committed to that kind of style."

Bottom line? These were no mere mortals. Master fashionistas roamed the halls of Mt. Sterling High. How could I possibly compete with them? Ryan knowing my name was one thing. Putting it in a sentence that included "wanna go out?" was another.

SJ sat up, giving me a huge grin. "You're a natural at style, Jess. Way more savvy than I was when I first started my Power Plan."

I didn't believe that for a second, but it still made me glow. Until she said, "What would you call *your* signature style?"

Truth was, I had no idea. I'd always been a chameleon

about clothes, so I'd never bothered to put my own stamp on fashion choices. Scrambling to catch up was as much as I could handle.

"I don't have one," I admitted.

"Really? What do you want it to be?"

That was a tough one. Stylish, for sure. Fun and carefree, but not girly. Sporty, but not boxy or boyish or too body-conscious. Memorable, definitely. And hot enough to get Ryan's attention away from someone like Fake Blondie without being blatantly sexy.

I glanced at Lexy again and shuddered. Sexy was definitely not my game.

How did you condense all that down into one signature style? I mean, I read *Vogue* just like the next girl. But looking at clothes and putting together a style of my own were totally different. While other girls had been perfecting their trendy looks, I'd been racking up volunteer hours by the dozen. Which wasn't super helpful at solving the dilemma at hand. "What do you recommend?"

"You need to figure it out for yourself. Try some different styles on for size and see how they feel. When you find one that makes you feel comfortable and confident, that's the signature style for you. And when we hit the mall"—I nearly fainted with excitement—"give yourself permission to try new things and see what you think. You don't always know if something's *you* until you give it a shot."

That seemed fair. Plus, hello? The mall was in my future, with Sarah Jane at my side!

With recon complete, we wandered over to the Snack Shack to grab a slush freeze and some seats in the grandstand. I managed to stumble only a little when I saw Ryan get up from the bench to warm up for his at bat. I carefully focused my eyes straight ahead so he wouldn't think I was stalking him. But when his head turned to watch us go, it was all I could do to keep my cool. As soon as our backs were to him, the thrill overpowered me. Ryan Steele had just watched me walk by.

Me. *Walk by.*

Now, before you go assuming I think I'm all that, yes, I was walking with Sarah Jane, who could probably turn the heads of half the MSH faculty. But since she was dating one of Ryan's best friends, I didn't think he'd be bold enough to show it even if he did have the hots for her.

I could barely contain my glee as we stood in line. I was in such a tiz that I almost missed seeing Heather pay for her drink and head around the side of the shack.

"Cherry Jubilee or Grapetastic?" SJ asked.

"Grape, thanks." I handed her my money. "I'll be right back."

I stepped around the side of the building to catch Heather before she hit the stands again. I hadn't seen her since the last day of school and didn't want her to get away before we had a chance to talk.

I was almost around the back when I heard her voice. Not her, Heather, but *her*, Lexy.

I peeked around the back and saw Lexy, Morgan, and Tina—the Three Musketeers of the Wickeds—crowding around Heather like the menaces they were. Their backs were to me, so I could only see one pink-sleeved arm of Heather. Lexy's voice was low, but a lifetime of drawing attention to herself made it impossible to muffle entirely.

"Quit acting like a baby, Clark Bar. A few more favors and you'll be free and clear."

Heather's voice was drowned out by a massive roar from

the stands. I started to move toward them but hesitated. She'd already snubbed me once when I'd tried to help.

"Don't forget what got you here to begin with. I can make it your worst nightmare or"—Lexy snapped her fingers over her right shoulder—"make it all go away." They moved past Heather, knocking her arm so her soda landed with a splat on her Keds. "Don't call us, Reggie. We'll call you."

Heather stood there shaking, looking pale and terrified. The orange soda soaked into her dirty shoes, turning the canvas to a mucky brownish swirl. She swiped at a tear, suddenly and with a ferocity I wouldn't have imagined her capable of, and bent to grab the remnants of her battered cup.

I hurried over, beating myself up for playing the bystander. Since when did I hesitate to do the right thing? I'd let Lexy win. Again.

"Hey," I said quietly, trying not to spook her. "You okay?"

She chucked the cup into a nearby trash can, not meeting my eyes. Her body was so tense I thought she might shatter.

I tried again. "If there's anything I can do—"

"You *can't*," she cried, the tension fizzling into heartbreak. "No one can."

I opened my mouth to tell her I could if she'd let me, but she was already darting around the building in the opposite direction Lexy and her cronies had gone.

Lexy had done her job. Heather looked as victimized as any target I'd ever seen.

"What was that about?"

SJ's voice made me jump. How long had she been there? "Lexy and the crew," I said, opting for brevity. "Ganging up on Heather Clark."

"Any idea why?"

"She wouldn't tell me jack."

SJ chewed her lower lip and watched the puddle of orange carbonation sink into the grass. "They never do."

"Why did Lexy call her Reggie?"

Lexy was known for nicknames. Clark Bar, I got. Thief—her favorite name for me—I understood too. But I'd thought Reggie was a Cindy term.

SJ's eyes focused on me for a second, but several more ticked by before her brain seemed to follow. She glanced around to check our privacy status and leaned in close. "Reggies was originally their word, a derogatory name for ordinary people who could be manipulated because the Wickeds considered them weak. We adopted the same term in a positive sense. Ordinary can be extraordinary with the right motivation."

That seemed like a pretty tall order. "The meek shall inherit the earth?"

"They're not meek, but yeah. There are way more Reggies than there will ever be Cindys or Wickeds. The real power is in their hands, but they have to embrace it for it to do them any good."

"Why not just let all of the Reggies become Cindys?" If every Reggie had access to our training and backup, the Wickeds would have no one to rule. *Bye bye, Lexy.*

"There's no way we could train them all," she said. "Besides, you don't *need* to be a Cindy to have power. That's what Gaby was trying to explain. Being a Cindy doesn't make you superior."

"But it gives you tools to fight them with, right? And a built-in support system?"

Sarah Jane looked uneasy now, so I wisely shut my mouth. I was the new kid here, not the boss of Sarah Jane. Instead, I asked, "Does Reggies cover everyone? I mean, everyone who's not a Cindy or a Wicked?"

"As far as girls go, yeah. Most guys are Reggies too, except for the ones who are all into the Wickeds and their mental games. Those are the Villains."

"What about the good guys?"

"Like Ryan?" SJ teased. "Those are the Charmings."

I blushed, despite knowing Sarah Jane would never blab about my crushing ways. Ryan *definitely* did the name justice.

Sarah Jane turned to go, handing me my grape freeze. I took it from her, humbled by how lucky I was to know the Cindys had my back. It seemed impossible that I'd gone from total loner to full-fledged Sister in a matter of days. I wished Heather could too. Or at least that I could offer real protection from whatever Lexy was grinding into her.

We headed over to squeeze in near Kyra and Mel and watch a very close baseball game. I tried not to ogle Ryan's fine form as the teachers pulled off a victory with a home run by Mr. Darden, the football coach. The crowd began to disperse with plenty of good-natured—or mostly good-natured—ribbing, and Kyra and Mel waved off as they headed over to tease Ben.

Fake Blondie had plastered herself to Ryan's side, so I turned around to search the stands for Heather. Not surprisingly, she was nowhere to be found. I would've bailed too.

We found Mark in the crowd and followed the masses out to the main parking lot. I felt like a genuine part of the gang, hanging out with Sarah Jane and Mark as people stopped to gab about tomorrow's Summer Slam obstacle race. I might be a tagalong, but at least I *was* along. That was a step up already.

When everyone had scattered to the winds and Mark had deposited us back at the convertible, Sarah Jane turned to me and said the words I'd been dying to hear.

"Are you ready to play Cinderella?"

# Chapter 6

SAFELY ENTRENCHED BACK in the nearly empty Club—most everyone else was probably off hashing out makeover plans at the mall—I pulled out my *CMM* and dug in. If I needed to try out some signature style ideas before we could launch my makeover, I was all over it. I'd promised Mom I'd be home for dinner and to help her in the nursery, so I didn't have all night.

I settled in next to Kat and reviewed the appearance section. The overview was like a style bible itself, supported by articles written by everyone from top designers to Hollywood makeup artists. It didn't take me long to devour words of makeup wisdom from Bobbi and figure-flattering advice from Stacy. But the coolest part of all? Some of the big names had gotten together and created a *CMM* style quiz just for the Cindys.

But I had to tackle my first project before I could hit the computer and pay a visit to Quiz City.

I knocked on the door of Gaby's office, and she lifted her nose from a binder to rival SJ's. "Back from the front lines?" she asked.

"I got here half an hour ago. You were on your cell, so I didn't want to disturb."

"Sorry." Gaby rubbed her eyes. "I'm trying to finish my

final Beta project. I'm also going for the Girl Scout Gold Award®, so it's more juggling than I'm used to."

"You're in TCS *and* in Girl Scouts?" Talk about a girl-power one-two punch.

Gaby nodded. "I'm usually fine with balancing them, but I've got a bunch of things hitting at the same time right now. I'll get it done, though. Somehow."

Overachiever, thy name is Gaby. "I heard you're shooting to be the youngest Gamma in the history of TCS," I said, not bothering to mask my awe.

"That's the goal. Some girls have done it the summer between sophomore and junior year, but I skipped second grade, so I'm a year younger."

*Dang.* Brilliant after skipping a grade? Einstein had nothing on Gabrielle Winston. "Your parents must be really proud of you being the youngest soon-to-be Gamma."

Oh. Except they probably didn't know.

Gaby chuckled at the look on my face. "Yeah, I wish I could tell them. I'm kind of overshadowed by my sister, Angie. She was born eleven minutes before me, and she's been the one to watch ever since. She's on the fast track to Juilliard as a dancer." She rolled her pencil between her fingers. "A little advice? Don't treat your sibs like two halves of one person. Every twin is a whole person all by themselves, even if parents forget that."

I felt bad that I let my resentment toward Mom and Dad spill over onto the babies. It wasn't the twins' fault they'd have things I never had—parents who were actually there for them, a place to really call home. Plus, they weren't even born yet, so how petty was I? At least I'd never had to fight with anyone for my parents' attention. When they were *paying* attention, I mean.

I told Gaby I'd keep her advice in mind, then shifted back into *CMM* mode. "The binder says I need to get materials for my Signature Style Portfolio from you?"

Gaby pulled out a large, chunky envelope and handed it to me. "Instructions for the Signature Style Portfolio are inside, and magazines are in the storage cabinet in the lounge. But I have three words for you: *Zen is queen.* If a style gives you even the tiniest twinge of nerves, it's not for you. Make Zen your mantra and you'll do great."

"Whatever it takes, captain," I said. I'd make *Lexy is queen* my mantra if it meant getting to my makeover faster.

The butterflies revolted at the mere thought.

Okay, maybe not that. But I'd do just about anything else to rock this project. My social status depended on it.

\* \* \*

The Signature Style Portfolio was broken down into sections: Styles I Admire, Styles That Make Me Nervous, and Styles for the Real Me. For each one, you had to find examples in magazines that fit that particular statement for you. Then you cut them out and created a collage, along with words to represent each section, like *carefree* for things I admired or *dramatic* for things (and people) that made me nervous.

My chameleon ways were having a fit.

Instead of gluing my heart out and writing words and slogans in curly script, I mostly just shuffled my pictures around among the three poster-board cards. Just when I thought I'd finally figured out the difference between styles I admired and styles that were really me, Gaby's mantra would pop into my head: *Zen is queen.*

And I'd realize that the "real me" page was actually the "really *think* this should be me" page. Which is not at all the same.

Good thing I hadn't been gluing, changing my mind, and peeling things off the whole time. My boards would've looked like a three-year-old had been learning to use a glue stick. Instead, my trusty glue stick sat next to me, still capped, waiting for me to commit.

Kat's chair squeaked as she sat back, rolling her shoulders in slow circles to loosen up her neck. Without even thinking, I started doing the same thing to ease the crick in mine. Sitting hunched over for long stretches did not make muscles happy.

"Pretty amazing stuff, don't you think?" she asked.

"Amazing and then some," I said, leaving out the *and also insane-making* part. "I don't know what I'll look like when I'm done, but I can't wait to see the new me."

"Do you think they can make me look like Halle Berry?" Kat joked. "Only shorter and heavier and without the knockout cheekbones?"

"If they can, maybe I can get a Leighton Meester makeover." I glanced over at her. "Have you done a full-out makeover before?"

"Nah. My dad doesn't believe in that stuff. He says everyone should just be happy with what God gave them."

Easy for him to say. Kat's dad was former Hollywood stuntman Roscoe Walker. He was a dead ringer for Dwayne Johnson (aka The Rock), so what God gave him was pretty darn nifty. Even if Kat got embarrassed every time someone told her that her dad was a hottie.

"He's my *dad*," she'd groaned when someone joked about it at Overnight. "It's just . . . ack, you know?"

Kat flipped her *CMM* shut and stood to go. "But I figure God wants us to make the most of what He's given us, right? I can be the best me, inside *and* out. Nothing wrong with getting a little help from our friends," she added, with a wink.

Especially when those "friends" were people like Bobbi and Stacy.

I looked at my watch as she left, shocked to see that more than two hours had gone by. I'd never make it home in time for dinner. A quick negotiating call to Mom that involved me promising extra nursery painting plus a dreaded outing to Babies "R" Us as a bribe, and I was off the hook for the night.

I fished around in my locker to check my cash situation and settled on a ham and cheese panini. I popped my head in to see if Gaby wanted anything. Her bleary eyes were ready for a break, so I ordered for both of us.

I'd almost decided to just cut out every photo of Reese Witherspoon to make my "admire" page complete when Audrey came to the door with savory food and lively company. Gaby came out of her office, her nose leading the way toward our most excellent yummage, and Audrey asked if we minded if she took her dinner break with us.

Cut. It. OUT.

What alternate universe had I fallen into where a former supermodel chummed with two sixteen-year-olds over a panini and a Cobb salad? I glanced down to see if my clothing had suddenly transformed into ubercool threads. Sadly, no. Apparently this dimension also had red-tag clearance sales at Target.

We got to talking about most embarrassing moments for some reason—or Audrey and Gaby did—and I sat there stunned at what they were tossing around like they didn't have a care in the world. Audrey mistaking a hot new fashion designer for the coffee runner at Fashion Week and getting screamed at by the prima donna live on the Style Network. Gaby strutting around the entire cafeteria with a tampon wrapper clinging to her pant leg. I would've crawled under a very heavy rock to avoid giving the details on something like that.

Which must have showed on my face, because Audrey let out a gusty laugh. "Come on, Jess. Time to fess up."

I shook my head and chomped a monster bite of panini to buy time.

She handed me another napkin. "Being embarrassed is part of being human. No one's as perfect as you think they are."

"Can't," I said around the mouthful. I took my time chewing, my cheeks puffing out like a chipmunk. I swallowed the bite in a series of large gulps, even took my time wiping the mustard from my mouth. But did my stalling tactics let me off the hook? That would be a no.

"Seriously, you guys, I can't. I'm still sweating stupid stuff that happened in first grade. If it all came out, I might implode."

Audrey sipped her green-tea smoothie through a bendy straw. "That's far too long to be harboring embarrassments. They can't all have passed the Rule of Fives."

I shared a look of bewilderment with Gaby.

"The Rule of Fives," Audrey said. "Every time something embarrassing or horrible or stressful happens, stop and take five slow, deep breaths. Then ask yourself the 'five' questions: Will this matter in five hours? Will this matter in five weeks? Will this matter in five years? You'd be surprised how things that seem earth-shattering at the time don't even pass the five-week test. It puts things in perspective."

Not spending half my life dwelling on my never-ending stream of faux pas? Now there was a novel idea.

"It's only good if you use it, though. Pick an embarrassing moment and put it to the test."

Embarrassing moment? Gee, maybe cheerfully greeting my total crush *who wasn't talking to me?*

Okay, deep breaths. One . . . two . . . three . . . four . . . five.

I did a quick body check-in. Still felt squeamish about it, but not like I was going to throw up, so that was an improvement. Did it matter in five hours? Um, *yes.* Since I managed to run into him (literally!) twice in those five hours.

Deep breath.

Would it matter in five weeks? I drank my water and pondered. That was harder. He might remember me as the groupie from the hall. But since he'd seen me with SJ and the other Cindys after that, maybe he'd associate me with them, instead. Five weeks was looking pretty iffy.

Would it matter in five years? That almost made me laugh. No way would he still remember that five years from now. He'd be off doing some fabulous thing, graduating from college. He wouldn't remember me at all.

Okay, not a fun line of thought.

"So, what's the verdict?" Audrey asked, popping the lid onto her empty salad bowl. "Can you spill?"

"Time limit is an iffy five weeks."

"Excellent."

"But it just happened on Friday, so we're not in the clear yet."

Gaby laughed. "I'll hit you up for it later."

Perspective could come in mighty handy. I had a feeling I'd be seeing a lot more embarrassing moments at the hands of Lexy. Might as well have a defensive strategy ready to go.

We headed back through Study Hall, and Audrey glanced over at my project. Clippings lay scattered around the far end of the table like a tornado had struck.

"How's the Signature Style Portfolio coming?" she asked.

When I looked aghast that she knew the name of my *CMM* assignment, Audrey laughed. "I've been coming in and out of here for several years, Jess. I've seen more than you can imagine. Don't worry—what happens in the Club stays in the Club. It's kind of like Vegas that way." She nodded toward the piles of magazines. "You want to know a secret about those?"

Even Gaby snapped to attention. Who wouldn't want to hear a supermodel's secret?

"No one's as polished as you think they are," she said. "The me you see on a cover or a billboard? That's the airbrushed, meticulously styled me. Usually attended to by a whole team of well-paid, extremely talented professionals. It's not the me I wake up to in the mirror every morning. Professional photos create a snapshot in time that sends a specific visual message: *We're having the time of our lives* or *Don't you wish you were part of* our *crowd?* Whatever message they need to convey."

The scattered images in my portfolio seemed to say, *Don't you wish you could make up your mind? 'Cause we sure wish you could.*

Audrey gave my shoulder a squeeze. "Stay true to the real Jess, and you'll do fine."

Great advice. If I knew what the real Jess looked like.

It took me a ridiculous amount of time to finish my boards. I handed Gaby my Signature Style Portfolio to review and went to grab a juice from the kitchenette. I plunked down at one of the tables in the lounge and stared longingly across the room at the laptops with the style quiz, wishing for the password that would finally kick-start the makeover phase.

As if in answer to my prayers, Gaby walked into the

kitchenette clutching a small card and my portfolio. "Chic, sleek, and memorable?"

I cringed, hearing some of the words I'd listed on my Styles I Admire board. Definitely a difference between admiring and being me. "There were more words than that," I defended.

"It's not a criticism. I think you've got great images and words on there to get you thinking. You did me proud." She stepped forward to lay a card and my style boards on the table. "Log-in instructions are on the card. It should only take you about twenty minutes."

*Bingo.*

A few quick keystrokes, and I was on my way to style heaven.

QUESTION #1: *It's a lazy Saturday morning, and you're going to be hanging out at home all day. You:*

*A) Wear your pajamas until your parents force you to get dressed. Come on, it's Saturday!*

*B) Get all dolled up, including full makeup and hair. You never know who might swing by for a visit.*

*C) Wash your face, throw on a headband, and put on your favorite comfy outfit. Clean is good, but comfort is the main attraction.*

*D) Hop out of bed, get cleaned up, and put on whatever is handy. Who has time for a lazy Saturday?*

*B* was definitely out. Someone swinging by to visit me was not exactly a concern. *A* was a little too on the lazy side, and *D* was too high-strung. I clicked on *C* and hit Enter.

I couldn't keep the smile from creeping across my face. One question closer to my makeover fantasy. Tomorrow couldn't come fast enough.

Jess Parker was about to make Cinderella look gooooood.

# Chapter 7

**IN A LOT OF WAYS,** playing Cinderella is like watching a train wreck in slow motion. You're terrified of what you might see as it unfolds, but you can't *not* look.

Especially when you suspect that *you* might be the train.

A day I thought would be filled with magical pampering and glass-slipper fantasies started bright and early with a posh salon, a gold coin, and an elitist hairdresser named Leopold.

We'd arrived at Avalon Salon and Spa in plenty of time for my nine thirty appointment, only to be told by the rail-thin Amazon passing for a receptionist that we couldn't possibly have made an appointment on such short notice. They were "simply booked months in advance." My glass slippers had barely been donned, and it looked like we were out on our butts. Which was fine with me, actually, because one look at the granite counters and silicone clients told me there was no way my allowance could sustain a hit of this magnitude without resorting to Old Navy clearance for the wardrobe part of our adventure.

In true Sarah Jane style, however, she gave the twenty-something a patient smile and stepped to the side, where they spoke in muffled voices, the girl continuing to shake her head.

It wasn't until SJ passed her a two-inch gold coin thing that the girl suddenly went from "Nuh-uh" to "Whatever you say, Miss Peterson." Amazon scurried away to the back room, while SJ came to sit next to me, looking pleased with herself.

I pretended to be engrossed in the latest issue of *Celebrity Hair* and gave her a fake-cheerful smile. "Are you sure everything's okay?" *Please say it's not.*

"All taken care of."

I put Jessica Biel's new do faceup in my lap. "I don't mean to be tacky, but how much is this gonna cost?" I whispered, casting furtive glances at the upper-echelon clientele. "I figured we'd be at a regular salon for a quick haircut and some highlights. I didn't budget for a hair extravaganza."

SJ smiled serenely in her Sarah Jane way. "Don't sweat it, J. This part is on the house. It's one of our traditions."

At that, a tall man dressed head to toe in flowing black came out, clapping his hands in delight. "Welcome, Sarah Jane!"

He and SJ exchanged air kisses, and he held her at arm's length to take in her Tommy Girl gloriosity. "Always magnificent to see you, darling. The gold chili rinse was pure genius. You look radiant!"

SJ accepted the compliments graciously and took his hand to face me. "Leopold, this is my good friend Jessica. We're here to have you work your magic."

Leopold pursed his lips and sized me up in 2.3 seconds. "Flat and forgettable. You brought her just in time."

"Don't worry, Jess. Leopold is the best there is."

Good thing, because he was already steering me toward the blood-red curtains in the rear of the salon, saying, "Much work ahead. Not a moment to waste."

"Look, Leo," I said, starting to panic. I didn't want a

drastic makeover—I just wanted a little primping! "I'm only here to—"

"Leo*pold.*"

Stupid nerves! "Leopold, right. I'm *so* sorry." *Note to self: Never insult the person who holds your follicular future in his hands!* "I didn't mean to drop in on you like this. If it's not a good time, I can totally make an appointment." Or say I'm going to and then not.

"Tink, tink," he scolded, firmly guiding me by the forearm. "I do not take appointments like a common stylist. I am the owner of Avalon. I am only available for celebrity emergencies."

"But I'm not a celebrity."

He stopped short of the curtains and gave me another appraising look. "You are emergency enough to make up for it."

✳ ✳ ✳

A haircut is usually just a haircut. But a hair consultation by Leopold is like a religious experience for *Glamour* groupies. After drilling me with questions for ten minutes—describe my morning ritual, what's my signature style (he definitely knew his Cindy lingo, even though I couldn't fully answer that one yet)—he and Sarah Jane discussed my best features, my coloring, high maintenance versus low maintenance, and other essentials as though I were nothing more than a chimp in a chair.

For two hours, I was served more sparkling water than I could possibly consume (with the bladder pain to prove it), suffered more veiled insults at the hands of a sadistic stylist than Lexy could hurl in a week, and had every inch of my head pulled, twisted, clipped, capped, gooed, and even plucked.

In short, I'd never been happier in my life.

To say that Leopold is a complete flippin' genius is to say that Ryan Steele gives 505s a good name. Understatement of the century. My hair was magically transformed from mouse-turd brown to a shimmery mix of chocolate, copper, and gold that looked almost iridescent under the lights. My once-boring longish bob was shaped and shagged and nipped and tucked until it was full and free and looked like an ad for a top styling school. Flirty to the tenth degree.

*Imagine . . . me, flirty.* I suppressed a jolt of laughter.

With my hair in dazzling shape, I was ready for round two: makeup.

A cosmetologist named Chiniqua took over and redid my face so I could see the result she was after. Totally babelike, if I do say so myself. Clean and fresh with a hint of shimmer to match my hair.

*Rock on, Chiniqua.*

Then Chiniqua did me one better. She washed it all off and had *me* redo the whole thing, with her coaching every step. It wasn't as good as her version—not by any stretch—but my confidence went through the roof knowing I could attempt a decent copy of the look.

Leopold came in to judge the final result and fluttered his hands so much I thought he'd pass out from exhaustion. Or take flight. In the end, I was deemed exquisite enough to be in the presence of his exalted Sarah Jane.

Leopold plied me full of conditioners and styling products while Chiniqua filled a shiny black bag with cosmetics and skin-care products. New look, new goods, new me . . . major windfall. I'd hit the makeover lottery in a *big* way.

With a boisterous farewell (and plenty of patting himself on the back, I noticed), Leopold bid us good-bye, and Sarah

Jane took me to The Grind to celebrate. And to show me off to Audrey, of course.

"Jess! You're a bombshell!"

Okay, a supermodel mini-screamed and told me I looked hot. I could officially die a happy girl.

Audrey had one of her counter kids watch the front while she took me back to her office. She forced me to tell her everything, from the moment we'd arrived to walking out the door. I was feeling so light and breezy that I even told her about the "emergency enough" comment. Which didn't surprise her at all, since she knew Leopold personally.

"Why, Jess Parker, is that an embarrassing moment you just shared?"

I laughed and tipped my imaginary hat. "It didn't even pass the five-hour test. Mostly because he was right."

Audrey pulled me into a bear hug (don't ever think supermodels are wimpy; that woman hugs like a grizzly), then stepped back to look me over one more time. She shook her head, grinning from ear to platinum-studded ear. "Once you get your new wardrobe, you're going to be a stunner. Ryan Steele, look out."

Okay, did *everyone* in the universe know I was crushing?

We rounded the corner on our way back from Audrey's office, and I managed to sidestep just in time to avoid running into Ryan himself for the third time in a week. One out of three wasn't bad, right? Maybe my new hair was bringing me good luck.

Except that I tripped on a chair leg (push them *in*, people!) and ended up being launched straight at Ryan's body. He caught me and set me upright, holding me a second longer than was technically necessary. Or so I fantasized.

"You okay?" he asked, his voice rolling over me like a warm wave.

"Fine. At least it wasn't a full-on crash this time."

He looked at me for a second, a dazzler of a smile lighting his face. Then his eyes widened and he looked closer. "Jess?"

"Yeah?"

"Wow." He dropped his hands. So sad was I.

"Wow . . . ?" I prompted.

He stared at me for a few more seconds, then tucked his hands in his pockets. "Just, wow. You look really great."

I couldn't help it. My knees turned to mush, and I grinned like a big goober. "Thanks."

Makeover, phase one? Success! Finally, I was in a league to catch Ryan's eye.

"Really great," he said. "So . . . I guess I'll catch you later."

Or maybe not quite there.

"Yeah," I started, but he was already turning away. My shoulders slumped in defeat. *Great.* My side of the conversation consisted of gems like *Wow? Thanks. Yeah.* A spoonful of smooth for your tea? No, thanks, I've got plenty.

Sarah Jane was giving me a half-hidden thumbs-up sign. I started to correct the direction of her thumbs when Ryan turned back.

"Are you going to Kyra's party on Friday?" he asked.

I saw SJ in my peripheral vision, giving me subtle visual cues that still managed to scream, *Tell him yes!*

"I think so."

"Cool. I'll see you there." He gave a gentle tug on my newly cropped mane. "Don't get any more gorgeous before I see you again."

I managed to let him get all the way out the door to the

patio before I pulled SJ into the ladies' for a totally girly squee moment. "No way, no way, no way . . ." I started to hyperventilate.

"You know what this means, J?"

That Ryan remembered my name again? That he thought I was gorgeous? That he thought it was cool he'd see me at the party???

My smile wattage could've lit Mt. Sterling for a month. "Game on, baby."

# Chapter 8

**AFTER A LONG DAY OF WORK** at the store—during which five different customers complimented my new look!—I thought I'd drop into bed exhausted. But who could sleep the night before a day of power shopping with the Sisters Fabulous?

Or Sist*er* Fabulous. Turned out Kyra and Mel were catching up with us later, because Sarah Jane had more than a simple mall excursion on the agenda.

Mrs. Peterson dropped us off at the curb in the ritzy Buckhead part of Atlanta and made plans to pick us up at noon. Just like that, we were on our own. In Atlanta. On the sidewalk in front of the famed Fashion Academy of the South.

And we were going *in*.

My first appointment was with a modeling coach named Lorraine. Her goal was to help me "carry myself" better. Which basically meant walking.

"I need training to walk?" I whispered to SJ while Lorraine turned on the spotlights above the runway.

Thankfully, she didn't respond. I probably didn't want to know the answer.

"The first thing every model needs to learn," Lorraine

said after guiding me up onto the catwalk, "is to carry herself with grace and confidence. She must wear her clothes, not let the clothes wear her."

She turned me to the side so I could see my profile. "Do you see how your shoulders are rounded forward? That draws your eyes to the ground and creates a gap in your cleavage area."

*I'm sorry, what cleavage area would that be?*

She pulled my shoulders back, lifted my chin slightly, and curved my hips forward so my stomach tucked in. All of which left me feeling like I was falling over backward. "Tummy, tummy, tummy," she said. "If you remember to hold in the tummy, all the rest naturally falls into line." Then she stepped away to give me a clear view of my disastrous new profile.

My posture was model perfect. So this was what it felt like to walk upright.

From there, we transitioned into walking. "You have a naturally wide stride," Lorraine said, watching me critically but not unkindly. "An athlete's walk. Am I right?"

"Yes, ma'am."

"Call me Lorraine, dear. That type of stride is appropriate for the field, but not for every day."

Lorraine showed me how to adjust my stride to a glide, walking on a single line without dislocating my hips. I made several laps on the catwalk that way before she had me go back to walking normally. Magically, my new stride was a little shorter and a little narrower and looked much more feminine without being prissy. *Très* cool.

I worked on my turns, trying to spot things on the wall to keep my head up and shoulders back. "I never knew I looked down so much," I said, doing my spotting-best pivot. "I feel like Gisele Bündchen."

I gradually relaxed into my new posture, realizing it wasn't that different from my posture on the field. I'd just never realized that looking up into the stands while cheering was the only thing keeping my chin up. Off the field? I was a tried and true ground-looker.

"Many girls look at the ground when they walk, particularly when they turn. Unless you're walking down stairs you're unaccustomed to, a simple glance down with your eyes—head up, of course—is all that's required." She moved to a desk along the wall. "You wear a size six shoe, Jessica?"

"Yes, ma'am. Lorraine." I sensed the imminent danger as soon as she reached for the box. "Do I really need those?"

Lorraine removed a pair of stiletto heels. "Wearing heels changes your center of gravity. If you want to look confident in any fashion, you need to learn to walk as gracefully in heels as you do in your sandals or sneakers."

SJ stored my sandals under her seat next to the runway. I sat down to slip on the heels and wobbled my way to standing. I felt like a baby giraffe on new legs. I'd rarely worn towering high heels before—though I had to admit they made my calves look awesome—so I was public klutz number one. It took me seven laps to make it down the runway and back without tripping. *Seven.* I gave myself extra credit for not doing a complete face-plant, but I wasn't exactly setting the world on fire with my walking prowess.

Lorraine worked with me to center my hips and change my stride to accommodate the heel height. By the end, my feet ached, and my right ankle throbbed where I'd twisted it, but I looked like a model ready for her first assignment. At least posture-wise.

Still, whenever I started analyzing my inadequacies

instead of being in the moment (always a battle), I felt like a big-time fraud. Even Lorraine could tell when those fraud thoughts crept in, because my shoulders started to roll forward and my posture drooped. Like my body was sending out *I'm not really all that* signals.

"Don't be self-conscious, Jessica. You are a smart, beautiful girl who deserves to be noticed. Walk like you know that."

Did I mention self-conscious habits are hard to break?

But with more needling from Lorraine, catcalls from Sarah Jane to lighten the mood, and some background music with a great beat, I started to feel the power of being noticed. It sank into me, and before I knew it, I owned the runway. I belonged there. *This must be what it feels like to be Sarah Jane,* I thought. *What Fake Blondie must feel like around Ryan when she knows all eyes are on her.*

It was a heady, potent, scary-as-heck mix.

Lorraine gifted me the shoes (love that woman!) and sent us on our way to my next appointment.

Despite my rocky beginning, I'd passed my first test. Bring on number two!

＊　＊　＊

Stephan the designer had an airy studio on the top floor of the academy. Large windows overlooked the city and flooded the space with natural light. The clothes and fabrics were tucked behind screens—to protect them from sun damage, he explained—and mannequins lined another wall. Stephan greeted us like long-lost friends and immediately put me at ease.

"The key to fashion is confidence and individuality," he said, helping me up onto the round platform in front of a tall trifold mirror. "Trends are worthless if the clothes don't flatter *your* figure. If it doesn't make you feel confident and gorgeous, don't waste your money."

Stephan did a quick color analysis, deciding I looked best in clear, crisp colors with warm undertones. "Not bold colors," he clarified, "but not subtle or muted. You need the bright, fresh tones to bring out the warmth of your eyes and hair."

He draped me with different fabrics to show how they perked up or dulled my coloring and then helped me combine colors to create a palette that didn't clash. Stephan swore I didn't need to take notes, but I wasn't an honor student because I relied on my memory. Sarah Jane hunted down a notebook and pen, and I jotted down all of his recommendations.

"I'll never keep all this straight," I moaned, writing like crazy while Stephan disappeared behind a room-dividing curtain. Fashion mags were great, but you'd have to read ten years' worth to get this kind of detailed information. Even then, it wouldn't be customized for you.

"Once you figure out what works for you, shopping's a no-brainer," Sarah Jane said. "You'll know right away which new styles will work and which styles are a fashion disaster waiting to happen. Like, I know I can't wear anything with single spaghetti straps, because my shoulders are so wide. It saves me a lot of time sifting through the racks."

I looked at her cami with its triple set of thin straps fanning out on top of her shoulders. I'd never noticed that detail before, but I guess that was the point.

"Excellent example, Sarah Jane," Stephan said as he wheeled out a rolling rack of clothes. "Camis are in this year, so you found camis that worked for you instead of wearing something that worked against your figure." He tapped her affectionately on the nose like a prized fashion pupil.

He turned his attention back to me. "Time to dress the princess. Tell me your signature style, Jess."

I dutifully handed over my style description from the style quiz:

> *Sporty and classic are words to live by. Whether it's an athletic cut or simple pieces with clean lines, you'll always look your best in tried and true fashions. Aim for outfits that flatter your figure but leave plenty to the imagination and fabrics that move with you to give you the freedom to be yourself. Comfort and confidence are key.*

Stephan looked over my sheet, and I smiled patiently, waiting for a tap on my nose to let me know I'd earned brownie points for being prepared.

"That's nice," Stephan said, looking up from the paper. "But it's just what a computer says about your style. What do *you* have to say about it?"

*Phooey.*

I thought about my Signature Style Portfolio, the words and images I'd played with for so many hours. Yes to feminine and sporty; no to dramatic and bold. Definite no to body-conscious (I felt ill just thinking about Lexy's sex-kitten look). Clean-cut style, a little bit flirty without being girly. And I liked the "fabrics that move with you" part of my style description.

So that left me with . . . "Fun, feminine, and sporty?"

Stephan chuckled. "Are you asking my permission, or are you undecided?"

"Fun, feminine, and sporty," I repeated with conviction. It was as close as I got to feeling Zen when I thought about my new look. That had to be a starting point.

Stephan pulled clothes off hangers, and I tried them on behind the curtain.

"Wow," SJ breathed when I came out with the first outfit. "That fitted blouse looks amazing on you!"

"And the hemline just above your knees makes your legs look long and slender. It's the perfect combination for your figure. You came out with your head held high—that's a dead giveaway that you've found the right outfit." Stephan tweaked the collar a bit. "Confidence is sexy, Jess. That may not matter to you now, but someday it'll make all the difference in the world."

I tried on the rest of the collection Stephan had put together, totally loving how the clothes looked. Basking in the glow of how they made me feel. I didn't know about the sexy part, but they definitely made me feel stronger and ready to take on the world. Never underestimate the power of the right skirt and a couple of tucks.

No gifting this time—so sad—but Stephan did treat me to a CD of digital pictures with me in the various outfits. "Remember how you felt in these when you go shopping, and don't give in to temptation just because something's 'in.' It's only in for you if it fits your signature style."

"Any final words of advice from the fashion king?" I asked as we helped Stephan put away the clothes.

"Find what works for you and work it for all it's worth. Confidence breeds confidence."

✳ ✳ ✳

We met Kyra and Mel for a late lunch at Kyra's house and discussed shopping strategy.

"I only need a few things," Kyra said as she double-checked her list. "A new outfit for my party, a teal shirt to go with my tropical sarong skirt, and a new pair of light-brown sandals."

Mel needed a few pieces too, and Sarah Jane only wanted a silver ankle bracelet to wear with her metallic flip-flops at the lake.

"What about you, J?" Sarah Jane asked, scooping salsa with a tortilla chip.

I glanced down at the list I'd created on the way back from the academy. "I want a few outfits like what Stephan had at the studio." Sarah Jane had downloaded my photos to her phone so we'd have them for shopping. "And some accessories to finish the outfits I already have."

"You should definitely wear one of the new outfits to my party," Kyra said. "You can launch the new Jess Parker. Especially since *somebody will be looking for you . . .*," she added in a singsong voice.

I felt the heat wave coming on, my cheeks prickling as the blush arrived full swing. "Word travels fast."

"Ryan's a catch. If he went out of his way to make sure you were coming to my birthday, he's definitely into you."

My butterflies perked up their little heads. I distracted them with a swallow of water.

"Kee's right," SJ said. "You should unveil Jess 2.0 at the party. It'll be like your debut."

*Parties and launches and Ryan, oh my.*

With shopping strategies set, we hit the mall like Cindys on a mission. Not only had everyone come prepared with lists, but Mel had come armed with fabric swatches. The pageant circuit had taught her well.

In less than an hour, they'd managed to cross off nearly everything on their lists. I found a few accessories but mostly stood in awe of their shopping expertise.

With everyone else in good shape, they turned their attention to helping me find something for the party.

I never saw it coming.

SJ marched us down to the biggest department store at the mall and had me describe my fun-feminine-sporty signature style. Even a few hours later, I was still a little geeked at how natural that style felt for me.

"Who's up for a little contest?" Sarah Jane asked as we wandered to the Juniors section.

"I know that look," Kyra said, grinning. "You want a PSC." She turned to Mel and me. "A Power Shop Challenge. It's great for keeping your fashion skills sharp. We each have to pick out three outfits on a certain budget in twenty minutes."

Mel looked game, but no way could I hold my own with this crowd. "I'll sit this one out and watch the pros at work."

Sarah Jane tucked her arm in mine. "That works out great, since you're our model. You tell us what kind of outfits you're looking for, your size, and the colors you're after, and we do the rest. Think of us as your personal shoppers."

The only catch was that I had to try on everything—even if I looked hideous in it—so they could give it the thumbs-up or thumbs-down. Which, of course, made SJ remind everyone in her most serious, don't-mess-with-the-Big-Sister voice that my personal thumbs were the only ones that mattered.

Like I'd really trust my judgment over theirs.

I gave them my sizes, what I was looking for (two casual outfits and one dressy thing), Stephan's color advice, and a very limited budget to keep my debit card from conking out on me. Sarah Jane tossed in her two cents about what she'd liked on me that morning, we synched our watches (you think I'm kidding, but no), and they scrammed to different sections.

I met them at the dressing room twenty minutes later. With only seconds to spare, the shopping queens handed over their outfits and stood guard outside the door. Nine outfits of varying cut and color were draped around the small room. Most of them would've made Stephan proud, but a few were flashy enough to make my palms sweat. And that was inside a locked dressing room.

True to my word, I donned each one and headed out to the mirror at the far end of the dressing rooms, bracing myself for their comments. But instead of giving me simple yea or nay reactions, I got my second master class of fashion that day.

Sarah Jane showed me how certain fabrics draped better on me, Mel was all about how tiny tweaks in tailoring could make the clothes perfect for my figure, and Kyra gave me a crash course in how to combine patterns without looking like Krusty the Clown. We studied the colors against my new highlights and makeup palette, deciding that Stephan was right on the money with his "clear, crisp colors" analysis.

They smoothed out wrinkles, had me turn this way and that. I felt like a fairy princess with a whole team of fairy stylists at her disposal.

The last outfit was a not-too-girly-but-still-flirty dress that I never in a billion years would've picked but that made me feel totally knockout. I put it on, did a little spin in the dressing room to watch the fabric swirl, and I knew it was the one. Kyra was the queen of dress shopping.

I walked down the dressing-room hall, only to hear a commanding "Stop!" from Sarah Jane as I approached the mirror. "How do you feel in that dress?"

"Awesome," I admitted, unsure why it warranted a major halt in the action.

"Look at your profile."

I turned to the side and saw that I looked every bit as confident and powerful as I had during my walk of fame in Lorraine's studio. I hadn't even thought about posture or walking or anything. I'd just let the dress's happy vibes get the best of me.

I ended up choosing four outfits, because the Cindys had been such awesome bargain shoppers: the killer coral dress (Kyra), a cute shorts outfit for knocking around in (SJ), embroidered capris and a gauzy shirt and cami set (SJ again), and a dynamite mini-and-tank combo (Mel). The funniest part was that even though I looked completely Mt. Sterling–worthy, nothing I bought was major name. Not even one. Proof that you could definitely dress hot on a budget, with a little help from the Cindys.

We took the four outfits to the accessories department and played with different combinations that fit my fun-feminine-sporty style. I'd never been a big necklace fan, but the tiny silver chain with the swirl-enameled butterfly begged to be taken home. Combine that with a pair of small silver hoops (I'd never be a dangly earring kind of girl) and a thin pearly watch (for time-obsessed me), and I was a happy shopping camper.

A trip to lingerie for a low-back bra and some no-show panties and we were on our way out. Even with the extras, I had a few dollars to spare on my debit card until next payday. Enough to celebrate with a triple-decker sundae and four spoons, a token of my gratitude for my savvy Sisters' help.

We sat at a big umbrella table on the patio outside the food court, surrounded by a dozen bags of clothes we adored, and quickly scooped the ice cream before it melted in the heat. All in all, a definite check in the win column of my *CMM* progress. Nothing could've ruined my day at that point, not even Gaby with a fistful of projects.

Nothing, that is, except seeing my archenemy watching me from the parking lot.

Lexy stood outside her sleek black Lexus, her ultra-expensive sunglasses reflecting the afternoon sun.

Some girls from school were blocking the rest of our table as Lexy headed in my direction. She was almost to the sidewalk surrounding the patio when the girls in front of us moved on and the rest of the table came into Lexy's view.

She pulled up short.

It was the first time I'd seen her since my adventure with Leopold, and I could see the wheels turning in her head. Me with my new babe hair and bags of clothing at my feet, chumming with my super popular friends. I'd gone from being public enemy number one to being a living nightmare. Her favorite target was surrounded by people every bit as strong as her.

*Life's tough when your targets are protected, isn't it, Lexy?*

She watched me a few seconds longer, then let her attention drift away when two newly minted grads stopped to congratulate her on being crowned Miss Teen Blue Ridge.

*By default,* I wanted to yell.

Lexy headed out to the parking lot, but not before throwing me a look over her shoulder. Despite the sunglasses, her message came through loud and clear. I might've built a safety net, but she wasn't done with me yet. And given her success with the Alyssa video, bullying Heather, and the coffee spill at The Grind? I didn't doubt she could still take me down.

# Chapter 9

**THE GONZALEZES' DOWNSTAIRS REC ROOM** (was I the only person without one?) had been transformed into a tropical paradise. Kyra's mom waved at me from her virgin piña colada station at the bar, and I looked around for somewhere to set my gift.

Kyra came rushing over with Mel and Kat hot on her heels. "You're here!" she yelled, hugging me tight and whispering in my ear. "You look *hot*. Ryan's out back throwing the football around."

I figured I'd play it cool and wait until everybody came in from outside so I didn't look obsessed with him. We headed over to see Gwen and Sarah Jane on the couch. Everyone oohed and aahed over my new look and gave my capri outfit— which Sarah Jane had picked out—the coveted double snap of approval. With my charm bracelet on my wrist for good luck, the launch of Jess 2.0 was officially underway.

Awkward Jess Parker had been put to bed for good.

From what SJ had told me, Kyra's birthday parties were major events. Her mom is Irish and her dad is Cuban, so she'd had a big bash for her *quinces* (the Cuban equivalent of a Sweet Sixteen, except you get it when you're fifteen) and then another blowout for her Sweet Sixteen the following year. She was turning seventeen this year, but the festivities still looked way more elaborate than anything I was used to. Especially my piddly ones with a few neighbor friends and my parents.

Dale came in from outside, mildly sweaty and bent on giving Gwen a hug. Pretty soon, the rest of the guys came streaming in. A few of them hunkered down on the sofa with us, and it didn't even faze me. For once I felt like I fit. Until Cherie came down the stairs, and Kat and Mel got up to find out how her audition had gone.

I looked around at our little group. Gwen and Dale, Sarah Jane and Mark, Kyra and Ben. And me.

*One of these things is not like the other . . .*

I caught Cherie's wave out of the corner of my eye and turned to wave back, getting up to make my escape from Couples Central. What I didn't see was a certain someone approaching from behind who took an elbow to the arm on account of my wave. The arm carrying a large virgin piña colada.

White frothy slush smelling strongly of coconut dripped down his shirt to the tile floor, while he hugged the glass in question against his chest to safeguard against a second attack.

A beat passed. Ryan looked at the glass and extended his hand. "You looked thirsty."

I took the nearly empty drink, suddenly aware that my back was feeling mighty chilly. "At least my shirt's thirst is quenched," I said, unable to think of anything less lame to say to disguise my mortification.

"Nice job, Parker!" a familiar voice cackled. What was *Lexy* doing here? Did evil roameth everywhere?

Mrs. Gonzalez was there in a flash. "Don't worry, honey," she said. "That's why we put tile down here."

I bent to help her clean up the latest mess of my life, but she shooed me away with a smile. "Towels are in the bathroom around the corner. Why don't you two go get cleaned up?"

I thanked her again, apologizing like crazy and feeling like a grade-A dweeb. I headed for the bathroom, trying not to look at the gawkers. I didn't look at Ryan either, but I could hear the squeak of his Nikes behind me. Perfect. Now I had to face him alone in the bathroom while we tried to rid ourselves of our Frosty the Snowcolada costumes.

A major gaffe, and I'd only been there twenty minutes. That might've been a new record, even for me. Dorky Jess Parker wasn't going down without a fight.

"Don't do anything we wouldn't do!" Lexy called.

My eyes sent hate darts in her direction.

Alone with Ryan in the spa-like bathroom, I handed him a fluffy white towel and took one for myself. All while avoiding eye contact. I wasn't normally a clumsy person. I wasn't! So why did I catch the freak bug every time Ryan came near me?

I ran a washcloth under warm water and wiped away the remnants of slush on my arm and calf. I glanced up in the mirror to see Ryan watching me and quickly looked back down at the sink, fumbling with the terry cloth. "Sorry for ruining your shirt," I mumbled.

"Oh, this old thing," he said in a girly voice that made me laugh in spite of my nerves. Or maybe because of them. "It was the first thing I put on."

My face heated up as I thought about how many clothes I'd tried on in that changing room looking for the perfect outfit to impress him. Only to have it covered in coconut yum.

I swiped at my back a few times before a warm hand closed around my wrist. "Let me get it."

He took the washcloth out of my hand and gently wiped the back of my shirt in long, slow strokes, catching the icy mix with each pass and dumping it into the sink. The sensation of his warm breath on my neck, the cold wetness of my shirt and cami, and the burning insult of my latest public humiliation made a powerful combination. Complete sensory overload.

"All set," he said quietly, handing me the washcloth over my shoulder.

I tried to look cool and composed, but all of my Jess 2.0 confidence had gone to Tahiti the minute I'd demolished his drink. So I tidied up the mess we'd made of the sink at super speed and turned to leave. But Ryan was right there.

*Right* there, like he'd never moved. Which meant he was about eight inches away from me.

I looked up into his face and saw a glimmer of ice clinging to a lock of his hair. Before I even registered the motion, I reached up to wipe it away with my finger. I was touching Ryan Steele. And he wasn't moving away.

He flicked a glance to my lips. "You look really good, Jess."

I could barely get air into my lungs. "I'll bet you say that to all the wet T-shirt girls." I was aiming for a joke, but it came out all breathy and Marilyn Monroe.

I tried again. "Sorry for being a klutz. I'll get out of your way so you can finish cleaning up."

I moved around him to escape, but he stilled my progress. "Wait."

He leaned in, and I knew—*knew*—that my life would never be the same after this. I was about to be kissed by the only guy I'd ever truly fantasized about, and nothing could possibly, in my whole entire life, top this moment.

He hesitated mere inches from my lips, and then I felt it. One amazingly gentle whisper of a kiss.

On my cheek.

"Mmm . . . ," he said, licking his lips. "Coconut."

My dream state disintegrated in a heartbeat. My first fantasy-worthy kiss was a minor-league cheek brush to capture the dripping mess caused by my geeky, spork-like tendencies.

But the saddest part? It still rocked my world.

In the end, I did what any self-respecting teenage girl would do when faced with her own ridiculousness. I fled like the coward I was.

I wouldn't bail on Kyra until we'd done cake and presents, so I tried to find a way to blend into the wallpaper. I also got a private pep talk from Sarah Jane about the importance of keeping up appearances of calm even when I was dying inside. Which was easy to say, it seemed to me, when you were as close to perfect as Sarah Jane.

So I did the next best thing to leaving: I manned the iPod station.

Manning the iPod station wasn't actually as lame as it sounds. Because pretty much everyone at the party, at one point or another, came over to request something. And suddenly, I was the Girl in the Know. The only people who didn't come over were Lexy and Morgan (which was fine) and Ryan (which was also fine, *obviously*). My shirt was drying and not nearly as cold anymore, the flames of my mortification having long since warmed up the fabric.

SJ asked me to hang out after the party with the other Sisters for a Sisterhood birthday tradition, and I gladly obliged. Man the iPod to keep a low profile, do the Sisterhood birthday thing for Kyra, and then I'd be out of there. *I can do this.*

Of course, that was also the moment my luck took a bathroom break. Avril Lavigne faded out, and I heard a tempting voice behind me. "Got any John Mayer?"

I played it chill, no pun intended. "The classics or his new album?"

"The classics. What's your favorite Mayer album?" he asked, copping a squat on the floor next to me.

"*Any Given Thursday.* I love hearing him play live."

Ryan nodded, the lock of hair I'd touched drawing my attention. I curled my fingernails into my palms to restrain myself from further inappropriate urges. "I like acoustic versions the best," he said. "Acoustic always gets to the soul of the song."

We ended up talking music for so long I lost track of time. People still stopped by to request songs, and we all did the cake thing for Kyra (with much laughter over Ben's serenade of "You Say It's Your Birthday"). But other than that and a quick trip for nonfrosty drinks, Ryan hung by the iPod for the rest of the party, until Mark came by to ask if he needed a ride home.

I looked up and realized the whole rec room had emptied out, save the band of Sisters cleaning up the bar area. And Lexy, tapping her foot impatiently by the stairs while Ryan talked to Mark. She glared at me and, after checking for Mrs. Gonzalez, snapped an *L* against her forehead.

*Loser.*

I looked at Ryan, then back at her, and realized her real beef was that the big brother she idolized was paying attention to her sworn enemy. The thought made me smile. I discreetly touched the tips of my thumbs together and flicked up my forefingers in response.

*Whatever.*

Ryan turned back to me, his keys dangling from his thumb. "I need to give my sister a ride home. See you around?"

"Probably."

"Keep rockin' John Mayer."

I smiled to hide my disappointment, thanks to Sarah Jane's half lecture, half pep talk. "Always."

He nodded and turned to go, but only made it a few steps before he turned back. "Jess?"

"Yeah?" I said, a little too quickly and a lot too eagerly.

"My dad's out of town this weekend, so we're having a pool party on Sunday. Are you coming?"

Was that an invitation? "Um, I don't know."

I wasn't toying with him. I seriously didn't know if it was kosher for me to go, since I was pretty sure Lexy would be there. But if Ryan wanted me there . . .

Ryan shrugged, and my excitement snuffed out like a candle in a tornado. "That's cool," he said.

He headed over to Lexy before I could clarify the situation. Lexy gave me a smirk, then plastered on a cheeky smile for her big brother. He let her go up the stairs first as I watched, my heart crushed by my stupid lack of response. Why was it that people like Kyra and Sarah Jane could simply say, "Yep, I'll be there!" anytime a party was hosted, but I had to worry about being booted out on my butt?

Ryan started up the stairs after Lexy, but at the last second popped his head back around the corner and winked. At me. With a grin, he disappeared to follow his heinous excuse for a sibling.

A new bathing suit was definitely in my future.

Working at Nan's store was a little like being the ringmaster at a circus. Not that her clients were a bunch of sideshow freaks. Most of the customers at Celestial Gifts were totally normal. Even the few who gave new meaning to "quirky and eccentric" were really nice. But when events like summer solstice came around, people tended to get a little carried away with their preparations.

The morning had started off fine until one of Nan's regulars knocked over a pyramid of gems I'd painstakingly arranged, just because the one he *had* to have for his talisman was right smack in the middle. I was trying to clean up the scattered amethysts so no one stepped on them when a woman with a chunky amulet on a long chain got herself tangled up in the pendulum display. Then, right as Mary Alice Higgenbotham launched into a deep, booming chant in front of the incense holders, the dragon phone rang. That's Nan's cue for scurrying away and closing her office door to answer it in private.

If Mary Alice doesn't make Nan bat an eyelash, I don't want to know what kind of clients make Nan feel the need to hide them from the world.

To say Nan embraced the New Age movement would be a massive understatement. The only thing keeping her from a completely bohemian lifestyle was her mysterious draw toward science professors and an uptight daughter—that would be Mom—who got creeped out by braless women in broomstick skirts. Mom's clearly a good match for the bean counter profession. Or was. How they could possibly be mother and daughter, I had no idea.

The good thing about days like this was that I was usually too busy trying to keep track of our customers' bazillion requests ("Where did you find a jade pillar in such a brilliant shade of blue? Can I custom-order one with nine sides?") that I didn't have time to dwell. Today was definitely not a dwelling day. Not when I was battling a serious case of nerves about the Steeles' pool party.

"Jessica, can you refill the fountains while I package the garden gnome for Mrs. Bertrice?" Nan asked, back from her office to help me with the last of the gems.

"Sure." I nabbed the water jug from the back room and starting making the daily fountain run. Water was constantly evaporating out of them, so you had to refill them every day or they'd run dry and the motors would burn out.

I didn't really mind, though. I love fountains. Maybe it's because I'm a Pisces, or maybe it's because my favorite places we ever lived were Seattle and Cleveland (both by the shore), but gently moving water has always been really soothing for me.

At the moment, soothing was good, because in only twenty-six hours and seventeen minutes, I'd see Ryan again. At his pool party. In my new bathing suit.

*Breathe in. Breathe out.*

A guy seeing you in next to nothing is a big step. Sarah Jane had wanted me to get this super cute bikini, but I almost had a cow trying it on, so that was a definite no-go. Better to err on the safe side with a turquoise tankini that left a little to the imagination. The style quiz would be proud.

I finished with the last of the fountains, rubbing my shoulder from the nerve pinch I'd gotten reaching up onto the top shelf. Nan and I swapped spots while she went to weigh the package in the back room. The door chimed with another customer. She stepped in, saw me behind the counter, and turned to make a quick exit.

"Hi, Heather!"

New Kid Rule #37: If you wave at someone and use her name, only a truly mean person will completely ignore you.

True fact. Most people at least grunt a greeting in return. Nan says using someone's name engages them. I wanted the scoop on the Lexy torment and was happy to dip into my bag of newbie tricks to get it.

Heather, being the nice person she is, froze after hearing her name.

*Gotcha.*

She paused for a second, then turned and came in with a half smile on her face. "Hey, Jess."

"What can I getcha?"

"Oh, a bunch of little stuff. Just stocking up, you know?"

"Gotta keep the good stuff on hand." I gave her my warmest *you can trust me* smile. "Want a basket?"

Heather took the small woven basket from my hand and started shopping. As skittish as she was, I wasn't pressing my luck. Better to give her some room and see if she loosened up. I'd never seen her be distant—at least not with me—so the Lexy thing must've really shaken her up. Or she was mad at me about the last day of school, even though she'd definitely gotten me back in front of Lexy. Whether she'd meant to or not.

I cleaned the mirrored display counter and waited patiently while Heather filled her basket with goodies. She kept stealing glances toward the back, and I realized she was waiting for Nan so she could check out. Fortunately, Nan was lugging a shipping box and her purse when she came back up front. "I'm running this to the post office and picking up something to eat. Would you like soup and salad or a sandwich?"

"Salad, no soup. Thanks, Nan." No sense getting anything heavy in my stomach that would turn to lead from the stress. Me in a bathing suit with Ryan. And Lexy.

*Help.*

Nan gave Heather a little shoulder hug as she passed, stopping for a second to say hi. Nan is like that . . . she makes all her regulars feel like the store is their second home. Heather's shoulders sagged when the door closed behind Nan, and I knew I had her. Not that I let on. I pulled out a small box of rings and took my time choosing rose quartz, tourmaline, and citrine ones to refill the empty slots in the jewelry display.

Heather looked like she was waffling about whether to pay or leave her basket and come back later, so I made the decision for her. "All ready to check out?"

Heather reluctantly set her basket on the counter, and I made small talk about the amber ring I really wanted and the cool new Willow Tree statue I'd been eyeing. This seemed to put Heather at ease, and she mentioned the angel pendant she loved to look at when she came in.

I scanned each of her items: patchouli incense, sage for smudging. Small bottles of geranium, vanilla, and clove essential oils, with a larger bottle of rice-bran oil. I glanced up at her and saw the blush forming. We both knew a love potion was in the making—adding a drop or two to a relaxing bath was always a nice touch if you planned to be mulling over a romance—but I gave her a relaxed smile to show her that I wasn't about to call her out on it.

Even with my patented *your secrets are my secrets* Celestial Gifts smile, I saw Heather tense up as I reached my hand into the basket again. Looking down, I knew why. Frankincense, juniper berries, dried fennel, and rosemary oil.

All the fixings for protection incense.

I looked up at her again, but this time she wouldn't meet my eyes. I finished up the sale and put everything in a bag while Heather shakily rummaged through her purse. She handed over the cash, and I took my time putting it away as I waved to another customer on her way out.

When we were the only ones near the register, I made my move. "She bullies me too, you know."

I said it quietly, nonjudgmentally, but the point was clear. *You don't have to go through it alone.*

"I know," she said, averting her eyes. "I picked up your papers."

"I'm sorry about that day. None of it went the way I planned." I handed her the bag. "I offered before, but seriously, if there's anything I can do—"

"It would only make things worse. If I do what they want, they'll move on."

That didn't sound like the Lexy I knew. "You really think so?"

She nodded optimistically, still not meeting my eyes, then slowed the nod and shook her head. "Not really."

"You can get out of it. I'll help you."

She didn't respond, and I could almost hear the cries for help in her head. I knew that feeling of being trapped well. All it took was one person who wanted to help. But you had to open up and let them.

"You can't," she finally said. When she looked up, I saw tears glistening. "It's not like with you, Jess. It's more"—she searched for the word—"involved. She's not just being a bully. She needs me."

The way she said it made me want to shake her. "Lexy doesn't need anyone, Heather. She just uses people."

"As long as . . ."

"As . . . ?"

"As long as she keeps her end of the bargain, she can use me."

My eyes popped in surprise. "No one deserves to be used, Heather. That's not how the world works. You need someone to—"

"I don't need someone to do anything except butt out."

It was the most blunt I'd ever heard Heather be. It didn't come out rude, just . . . final. And it made my heart hurt, because I'd so been there. But this wasn't my fight, and I couldn't tread where she didn't want me to.

"Thanks for the stuff, Jess. And for caring," she added softly. She walked out of the store, and there wasn't a single thing I could do to stop her. Or help her.

# Chapter 10

"**REPEAT AFTER ME:** I will not stoop to her level."

"I won't, Sarah Jane. Trust me." Sarah Jane had been calming my fears on the drive over to the pool party, but now that we were rounding the bend to the Steeles', I was starting to have a bad feeling. It might have been a bright, sunny day, but a cloud of doom could be right over the horizon.

SJ pulled in behind the long line of cars. "You can't let her see she's gotten to you either. She can sense fear like a cougar."

"Comforting, thanks." I pushed open the door, adjusted the wrap skirt around my tankini, and grabbed my beach bag. "I'm going to ignore her and stick with people I can trust. And be myself."

SJ met me on the expanse of lush green grass standing between me and my future. "Spoken like a true Cindy," she beamed.

We trudged across the grass, catching up to Gwen and Dale on their way to the wrought-iron fence. Mark was en route to his great-grandma's for her eightieth-birthday bash, so I had Sarah Jane all to myself for the day. Given the upcoming event on Lexy's home turf—with Lexy there this time—I was grateful for the full-time support.

"Looking good, Jess. Trying to impress anyone we know?" Dale teased.

Gwen punched his offensive-tackle shoulder.

"Hey! I'm just saying someone might be impressed is all." He turned to me. "Remind me never to date anyone stronger than me again."

I'd never spent much time around couples before—hello? Not so fun—but the Cindys and their boyfriends were pretty entertaining to hang with. They didn't overdo the PDA, they all joked around like the old friends they were, and they teased each other in a playful but nice way. Best of all, the guys treated the girls like equals instead of acting like possessive jerks. No wonder the Cindys called them Charmings.

I quickly discovered, however, that this kind of good, wholesome fun did not extend to every male at MSH. The Villains were nowhere near as stable and had a tendency to snarl and get into arguments at the drop of a hat. Or sarong skirt. They thrived on the same kind of drama as the Wickeds. I shuddered to think what kind of offspring they'd produce if given the chance to procreate.

Satan Jr. came to mind.

Dale nabbed us chairs in the corner by the outdoor kitchen, where Ben was guzzling a Coke and Kyra was sipping a peach freeze.

Ben and Kyra scooted their chairs so we all had a piece of sun, and Dale helped Gwen tuck her towel over the chaise. We settled in and watched the drama unfold in the middle of the pool deck, where, naturally, the Wickeds and Villains had positioned themselves. The perfect place to command attention.

I'd begun to realize something about the in crowd. The Cindys/Charmings and the Wickeds/Villains had to coexist in the social fabric of high school. Case in point: Lexy and a few other Wickeds being invited to Kyra's party. Exclude them all and it could turn into a big nasty deal. But invite a few and you kept things kosher. A definite irritation, but I had to admit it was smart politics.

The groups weren't chummy by any stretch, but they were civil. Even friendly, if only on the surface. A few people, like Ryan, seemed equally at ease with both groups. But for the most part, people stuck with their own. It made me glad I was firmly on the side of the Cindys, because the Reggies didn't have the benefit of an unspoken truce. Reggies were fair game, as Heather and I knew too well.

Ben and Dale got up to take orders. A peach freeze for Gwen, another for SJ, and a—

"I thought a Coke would be safer to start," Ryan said, sneaking up behind me. He handed me a tall blue cup, still foaming from the pour. "I'm glad you came."

"Me too."

We stayed like that, grinning at each other longer than we should have, before Ryan looked away. "Pool volleyball starts in fifteen minutes. Coed teams. Dale and I are captains."

"It's a summer tradition," SJ explained. "Ryan and Dale have been playing against each other since the summer before sixth grade. It's the only time they're ever on different sides."

Gwen stripped down to her athletic Speedo in record time and huddled close to Dale, whispering about strategy. Strategy for pool volleyball? Were they serious?

The series was tied at three and three, so this was a critical year. I couldn't wait to watch. Seeing Ryan dive and pound the ball, muscles a-ripplin'? I should've brought popcorn.

The rules were that they had to alternate girl and guy picks. I made Ryan promise not to pick me before he hopped into the pool to join Dale. Ryan won the coin toss, gave Dale an evil grin, and took the all-state Gwen to get back at Dale for winning last year's battle. Dale sized him up and called out his own first pick. "I get Jess!"

I froze. I was *not* a volleyball player. Dale gave Ryan an evil grin right back, and I saw that Ryan's own smile had disappeared. But there was no way I was jumping into the fray and making a fool of myself, so I resisted the pressure of thirty or so pairs of eyes.

"Sorry," I begged off. "I hurt my shoulder at work yesterday." A slight exaggeration, but a small price to pay for my self-esteem.

Dale narrowed his eyes at me in mock suspicion and looked at Ryan, who had a triumphant gleam in his eye. Dale nodded knowingly, then went on with the picking. With everyone's attention on Dale, Ryan gave me that killer smile again. With a wink like we had an inside joke. My heart skipped a beat.

They finished picking sides, and the game started. My refusal to play had given Sarah Jane an easy out to keep the teams even. She collapsed next to me after a quick conference with Dale and Ryan. "Thank you," she said. "I'm always the worst player on the team."

A few minutes later, I understood why. This was no ordinary pool volleyball game. These kids were pros.

They bumped and set and spiked the ball, diving over each other, calling shots. I would've been a total nuisance to Dale's team. Or Ryan's team. Which reminded me . . .

"Why did Dale—?"

"Exactly why you think." She turned to me, her eyes

lit with mischief. "Ryan's definitely got you in his sights."

I couldn't help it. I panicked. "But he's way out of my league. What could he possibly see in me other than I'm a new challenge?"

"No Wicked chatter. You should know exactly what he sees in you. You're smart, funny, and a total cutie. And you've got a good heart. Charmings always go for the girls with good hearts."

I thought about Fake Blondie. "Always?"

"Well, mostly," she hedged. "Sometimes big boobs override their common sense."

I took a sip of the drink poured for me by the object of my affection. I couldn't deliver much in the boobs department—me and my just-barely-Bs—but I might be okay if he went for good-girl types. Somehow I couldn't see Fake Blondie fitting that bill, though.

I took another sip, wondering how much of Sarah Jane's view was based on reality, when the volleyball came blasting onto my chaise, splattering Coke down the front of my new suit.

"Oops!" came the snarky voice. "My bad."

I looked blandly at Lexy, and she gave me her best Wicked Witch of the West smile until Ryan turned around and yelled at her. She scowled at him and splashed away to her position in the back row. She flipped me off, then proceeded to ignore me.

I went over to the hot tub and splashed water on my suit. SJ wiped down my chair and came over to join me.

"What is it with me and drink spills?" I complained. "I'm like a human magnet for stains." With aim like that, Lexy should've been playing varsity volleyball instead of cheerleading. Though I'd never sic her on Gwen.

"The Wickeds love public fights. You handled that perfectly."

"The Wickeds love public everything," I grouched.

"They crave attention like other people crave air. It's how they measure their power. Being ignored is like having their power stripped away." She bent to scoop bubbles from the jet into her cupped hands. "They don't respond well to that."

"Do they respond well to anything?"

"Not that I've seen. That's why the Reggies are so afraid of them." She let the water stream through her fingers. "They never know what'll set the Wickeds off."

We dangled our feet in the jetted water as we watched the game. I'd never seen that kind of volleyball ferocity off an actual court. Even with Gwen being first-team all-state, I was shocked at how many other kids held their own against her power spikes.

The game wore on, and it was down to the wire, with Dale's team serving. The volley lasted forever, with a brilliant save by Dale that I thought for sure was going out-of-bounds. Kyra set up the shot to use the surprise save to their advantage, and Dale spiked it for the win.

You'd have thought it was the Olympics. Dale's team erupted in cheers and screams and several loud renditions of "We Are the Champions" as Ryan's team faked heart attacks and moved to slap hands with the winners. Ryan and Dale tried to dunk each other for the next few minutes, but neither one showed signs of superiority or grief.

Life without drama was bliss.

"Too bad Parker bailed with her fake injury," Lexy said too loudly from her prime location mid-pool. "We'd have crushed 'em for sure."

Morgan and Tina giggled loudly. Not that I cared. In fact,

it was hard to be upset about anything. We were having fun, Ryan might really be into me, and it was a perfect sunny day among the Populars.

Ryan came out of the pool. "Got any hugs for the losers?" he asked, dripping all over the concrete.

*Always.* "Sure," I said, forcing myself not to stare as water dripped off pecs worthy of a Calvin Klein ad. *Football does a lady mmm-mmm good.* "Go dry off," I teased, "and I'll see if I can find a girl to soothe your ego."

"What?" He faked another heart attack. "You'd forsake a dying man his final wish? After being humiliated on the battlefield—"

"Pool."

"In the pool. I guess I'll have to play the part of conqueror, then," he said, wiggling his eyebrows at me.

I shrieked as he made a grab for me—totally girly, I know—and he chased me down the length of the pool. I dodged people, laughing like a fool, and even put Dale in his path as I came around the far end, but Ryan still gained on me. I'd almost sprinted away when Lexy gave me a huge bump with her shoulder. I was going so fast that the change in direction sent me sailing out over the pool, where I promptly took out the volleyball net.

It toppled down on me as I went under, my feet getting caught up in the netting. I tried to right myself but couldn't shake loose and couldn't push off the bottom with my feet to stand up. I groped for the pool floor to push off with my hands, but my fear made me disoriented. Were the net poles floating on the surface above me or hovering below me?

Water bubbles burped out of my mouth as panic set in. I tried to free my feet, but I couldn't get a good grip on the nylon. I thrashed around, trying to clear my limbs from the tangle—

And then Ryan was there, pulling me up to safety. We broke the surface and I gulped fresh air. He untangled me from the net and hauled me against his side as I caught my breath. He smoothed my hair off my forehead and cupped my face in his hands. "You okay?"

I put a shaking hand on his and nodded, a lump in my throat that tasted like adrenaline and fear.

He put my hand on the side of the pool for support, even though it was shallow enough to stand, and hoisted himself out of the pool in one fluid motion. He stalked over to Lexy and got right in her face. "What were you thinking? She could've gotten hurt!"

Lexy's eyes were twice their normal size. They filled with tears before her normal defense—pure hate—surfaced to cover it. "What do you care about the freak?" she spat. "Why did you even invite her when you know what she did to me?"

Excuse me? What I did to *her*?

"Pool party's over!" she blurted out. "We have to have the pool sanitized. For STDs," she added with a glare in my direction.

Another rumor had just been unleashed.

"Shut up, Lexy," Ryan growled. "Go make yourself useful and get the net out of the pool." He turned to me and leaned down to pull me out. "Let's get you cleaned up."

By now, Lexy's tears were full force, and she was making a dramatic exit up the stairs to the deck. As Ryan handed me a towel and helped me dry off, Lexy stopped short. "For God's sake, Ryan, don't let her infect you. Use gloves!"

"How would you know about it unless you'd given it to her?" Dale asked loudly.

Lexy stormed away as several people snickered. Ryan

gave Dale a *watch your step* look but didn't say anything. Apparently, it was okay for siblings to fight, but big brother's protective instincts didn't permit outsiders to trash-talk his little sister. Even though she was the queen of trash talk herself.

SJ handed me my beach bag and towel, and I realized the party really was breaking up. Nothing like a little Wicked drama to ruin a great afternoon.

People were already heading out through the gate, waving thanks to Ryan and gossiping quietly about me and Ryan and Lexy and, probably, the odds of me actually having herpes or something even nastier.

Despite Lexy's attempts to embarrass me, I experienced a fleeting moment of superiority. From someone who always managed to hit the sorest spot in your psyche, this was a pretty generic rumor. Especially to use against someone who didn't have a slutty reputation (unless she'd given me one I hadn't discovered yet). Lexy must've been majorly flustered about Ryan choosing me over her for it to knock her off her game.

The thought pleased me to no end.

Ego and emotion were Lexy's weak spots. Sarah Jane was right on the money about Lexy's need for attention, and being ignored by the brother she adored trumped all. I tucked the information away.

"Let me walk you out front," Ryan said, easing the beach bag from my scraped-up shoulder. Ryan's offer pleased me even more. Maybe this wasn't such a disaster after all.

People continued to offer their thanks to Ryan for the party and high fives to Dale for winning. A few even stopped to see if I was okay, though I suspected some of that attention was more to get fodder for the grapevine than out of concern for my well-being. But at least they acknowledged me by name.

SJ and I exchanged hugs with Kyra and Gwen and headed to the convertible. Being the super-cool Big Sis she is, Sarah Jane skirted the car and busied herself with something in the trunk to give Ryan and me privacy.

Ryan leaned a hip against the passenger door. "I'm sorry about my sister. She's not really as bad as she seems." When I didn't meet his eyes, he retracted that. "Okay, maybe she is. My mom died a couple years ago. She's had a rough time."

"I know. I'm sorry." From what Nan had told me, Mrs. Steele's death in a car accident had been a blow to the whole community. "But hasn't it been rough on all of you?"

Now Ryan wouldn't meet my eyes. "It's been worse for her."

I remembered that part too. *Because she was in the car.*

"Let me make it up to you," Ryan said, perking up. "The new Adam Sandler movie came out last weekend. Why don't we grab dinner and go check it out? How about tomorrow?"

"I can't."

"Oh." He straightened and slid my beach bag into the backseat, looking disappointed but casual. "No problem."

What? *Oh.* "No!" *No no no no NO!!!* "No, I mean . . . it's not that. . . ." I stopped and tried again. "I have to work tomorrow, that's all."

"Tuesday?"

I could breathe normally. "Tuesday would be great."

"Awesome." He opened my door for me like a gentleman, and I laid out my towel so I wouldn't wreck SJ's leather seats. "I'll pick you up around six?"

I nodded, and he knocked me out with another For Jess Only wink. I feared an addiction to them was not far off.

"See you then, gorgeous."

He patted the car and sent us on our way with a double-finger swing toward the road before heading back across the lawn. I watched him go, but movement in an upstairs window caught my eye. Lexy stood there looking like her head might spin around in fury.

I stood my ground—sat it, whatever—and stared right back. She held my eyes and pointed at me, then pointed to the ground. I might be protected with SJ at my side, but Lexy had no intention of backing down anytime soon.

The wickedest of the Wickeds was plotting to take me down.

* * *

Our latest Alpha class included a recap of the appearance work we'd done so far and a progress powwow for each of us with Gaby and our assigned big Sister. I was keeping up with my assignments and had gotten an enthusiastic thumbs-up for creating a signature style that was genuine and made me feel confident. Definitely a day for the win column.

Best of all, I'd finally found my comfort zone in the world of belonging. That alone was worth the price of admission. Despite the abrupt ending to the pool party and Lexy's not-so-veiled threat, things had been going surprisingly well on all fronts.

We started clearing our stuff out of Study Hall when Sarah Jane and the other Gammas came out of the Gamma office. Paige led the pack.

"Hang on," Paige said. "We've got a tradition to take care of before you leave."

More Cindys piled into Study Hall from the lounge, until we were packed around the huge table. Gaby had everyone take a step back, and she hit a button next to her office door.

A buzzing sound followed as the legs under the table folded and the whole thing lowered itself until the top was flush with the rest of the floor. Very James Bond.

Kyra and Gwen unrolled a gorgeous geometric-patterned rug over the tabletop now embedded in the floor, and girls moved chairs into the lounge to give us more room. We spread out in a giant oval. It was the first time all of the Cindys had been in one place at the same time. Girl power pulsed off the walls.

Paige stepped inside the circle. "I'd like to formally welcome our new Alpha members and welcome back all of our returning Sisters. Apologies for my absence since initiation. I just graduated"—a chorus of snaps went up around the room—"and I'm staffing at Worthington Estates this summer."

More snaps followed. Part of the secrecy thing, I decided. If almost thirty girls started whooping and cheering, there'd be no way for us to stay a secret in The Grind.

"As part of our tradition, we elect a new leader every two years. The incoming leader is always identified during freshman year and trains for her new position during sophomore year. She officially takes office when school starts her junior year."

I looked around at our Alpha class, all soon-to-be sophomores except for me, the sole junior. Kat had a total go-getter vibe. Mel was thoughtful and sweet, the kind of person you knew you could trust. Chandi was our voice of reason. Not that the other Alphas weren't awesome, but I was putting my money on one of those three.

"The Cinderella Society is deeply rooted in tradition," Paige was saying. "But sometimes doing what's best for the Sisterhood means taking a bold step in a new direction.

We have new challenges to face and more battles to fight than we've ever seen in our history. I trust you'll join me in welcoming and supporting our new leader as we witness a historic event in our Sisterhood."

Paige nodded at Gaby, who turned out the lights, but I didn't miss the tiny flicker of a smile Paige shared with Sarah Jane in the split second before the room went dark.

The Wickeds increasing their ranks. A secret smile between Paige and my Big Sister. A historic event . . . meaning it wasn't an Alpha being tapped?

*Sarah Jane's going to be our new leader.*

Paige lit a candle, illuminating her face. I felt a rush of pride having Sarah Jane at my side. She was everything a Big Sister should be and more. It was comforting to know the rest of the Cindys recognized how amazing she was too. With Lexy firmly on the side of the Wickeds, it was a huge relief to know our side would have Sarah Jane leading the charge.

Paige stepped back to become part of the circle. The candle started to move, passing from Sister to Sister, as the Cindys quietly began to sing:

*Oh, Sister dear, we join thee here,*
*To cheer your grand occasion.*
*When time has come, our battles won,*
*We'll join you in celebration.*

The candle made its way around the circle. Past Kat, past Mel—

*Oh, Sister dear, we join thee here,*
*To cheer your grand occasion.*

It came toward us. Pride filled me, knowing I'd be the one to hand it to her. Two away, one away—

*When time has come, our battles won,*

Finally, it was in my hand. I turned toward Sarah Jane, my face aglow with happiness as I reached out to present her with the candle.

*We'll join you in celebration.*

SJ beamed at me, her look of pride a mirror of mine, as she leaned forward and blew out the candle.
While it was still between my fingers.

# Chapter 11

"HOW CAN I POSSIBLY BE the new leader?"

I was pacing in Paige's office. *Our* office. Or at least mine for the sharing until Paige handed over the reins for good. "I thought you were talking about Sarah Jane."

Sarah Jane looked confused. "Why would you . . . Oh, you saw that? No, the new leader never knows until the candle's blown out. It's usually done by her Big Sister, but not always."

I flopped down on the chair opposite Sarah Jane. "This can't be right."

As soon as Sarah Jane had blown out the candle and the lights had come up, I'd been surrounded. Girls rushed forward to hug me; other girls snapped like crazy. The entire time, my mind heard only two words.

"Why me?"

Paige leaned back in her chair. "Why not you?"

It wasn't like I was a complete waste. I'd taken the lead on tons of volunteer things before. But this was a totally different deal. If they were going to break tradition and only give the new leader a couple of months to prepare—instead of a whole year like normal—it should be for someone who was already a Cindy rock star. Someone like, just to be crazy, *Sarah Jane.*

"Look, Jess, I know we've caught you off guard. It threw us for a loop too." Paige held up a hand to flag off my obvious question. "Not because we don't think you'll be great, but because we've never been in this situation before. Our incoming leader's mom got an ambassadorship in Europe, so she had to move mid-year. The Powers That Be told us to hold off naming a new incoming until the new Alphas were selected. And then you arrived on the scene, the Wickeds' recruitment surge came into play . . . and everything sort of happened at once."

Questions swirled in my mind. What did a leader do? How much time before I had to officially take over? My senses went on alert, and I knew I had to voice the question I dreaded most. "Who's the leader of the Wickeds?"

Sarah Jane shifted in her seat. She looked at Paige. Paige looked at me. They confirmed my suspicions before Paige's lips ever moved.

"We think Lexy's the incoming."

Sarah Jane started talking before I could object. "Don't worry about Lexy. Focus on *your* job not hers." She gave my hand a squeeze. Like that helped. "You're a natural leader. You wouldn't have been chosen if you weren't the right person for the job."

"There's no way I can be the right person. No one here even knows me yet. I'm a year late in my training in the first place—"

"Because you didn't move here until a few months ago," SJ clarified. "We brought you on as soon as we could."

"What difference does it make? I'm still a year behind where a leader should be." But that wasn't the worst of it.

"How can I lead the Cindys when I can't even protect myself against Lexy? You have to know she targets me too."

"That's what makes you so valuable as the leader," Sarah Jane explained. "It's not just theory for you. You know what it feels like to be a target. We suspect they knew we had our eye on you from the minute you got here; that's why Lexy didn't waste any time in targeting you."

"How could you know you wanted me when you didn't even *know* me?"

Paige gave me her *Cindys know all* smile. "It'll all make sense in the end, Jess. Once you adjust—and I know it's a lot to adjust to—you'll understand why you need to be the one. I'll help you as much as I can. I'm staffing at camp this summer, but I'll be available by cell or e-mail if I'm not here, and we'll meet as often as we can. I won't let you fail, okay? I promise."

Paige handed me a folder as Sarah Jane excused herself. She keyed open the adjoining door to the Gamma office and slipped through, closing it gently behind her.

Paige motioned toward the door. "You have your own entrance to the Gamma office. As leader you have full access to all parts of the Club. You won't have access to all the Gamma systems, but you'll be able to use most of them."

She opened the folder and pulled out a chart showing all the Cindys. Not just our Cindys, but *the* Cindys. The whole shebang. Above our group was Paige's name (with a dotted line to mine as the new leader), with Cassie above Paige as our regional liaison. No wonder Cassie was around so much.

Above Cassie was a whole level of other groups, like the Financial Advisory Board (which I assumed was responsible for Audrey's "lucrative deal"). At the very top of the chart was a single box: ISIS.

"What's ISIS?"

Paige tucked her ankles underneath her. "You know the Cindys have been in Mt. Sterling for over a hundred years."

A statement, not a question. I nodded, remembering the history section of my CMM.

"Well, the Cindys have been around a lot longer than that. The Cinderella Society is the recruiting arm of ISIS, an even more secret society of the most powerful women in the world. ISIS was founded in Boston in 1790 after women discovered that all the hard work they'd done during the war to keep homes and families and businesses running was being ignored by the Constitution. So they took their cause underground and created ISIS to forward the agenda of those who had no voice."

"What does ISIS stand for?"

"It's not an acronym. Isis was one of the most powerful ancient goddesses, honored for being ultrafeminine *and* super strong."

Definitely Cindy material.

"Name just about any positive, powerful woman you can think of—athletes, actresses, senators, talk show hosts, teachers, doctors, scientists—and odds are she's probably a Cindy. There are hundreds of thousands of Cindys making an impact on the world."

I thought about the framed pictures on the Study Hall walls. Those weren't just celebrity role models; those were high-powered Cindys one and all. My head started to spin.

"Come with me," Paige said, leading me into the Gamma's office through our private entrance. "Welcome to Gamma Central," she said. "Better known as the War Room."

Compared to the feel-good Study Hall and lounge areas, the War Room was high-tech and all business. Monitors and keyboards lined one wall, with a plasma screen and video console in one corner. Sarah Jane sat at one of the keyboards, typing with her earbuds in, and Gwen was leaning back in a chair, reading some kind of report filled with graphs.

Gwen looked up from her reading. "Welcome to the next level, Jess." She handed Paige the report. "The weekly just came in, and it shows another spike."

Paige shook her head, flipping through the first few pages while she spoke. "The weekly is the communication summary from ISIS that monitors the activity level between high-school Wickeds and their mother organization, ATHENA."

Athena. "The Greek goddess of war?" *Nice.*

"The Wickeds aren't big on subtlety."

"They don't call themselves Wickeds, though, right?" I asked. "That's just our shorthand for them?"

"Right. Inside the ranks they call themselves the *Delectae*. It's Latin for the Chosen Ones." Paige handed the report back to Gwen. "We've been tracking a trend showing an increase in communication between the Wickeds and ATHENA. There was a spike in early spring, which we assume was when the Wickeds got their recruitment-surge instructions, and again the week leading up to initiation. If it's spiking again, odds are something new is in the works."

Sarah Jane pulled out an earbud. "The system upgrade's been delayed two weeks. I'll update the master calendar. And it sounds like Albuquerque may have a breakthrough on the codes."

"Sarah Jane is our intelligence liaison," Paige explained. "She listens in on the twice-weekly conference call from ISIS and passes along any information we might need. They're upgrading our computer systems to give us digital access to the entire ISIS archives, so SJ's taking care of anything they need from our end. The Albuquerque Wickeds have been using some sort of code to communicate to the Reggies they're targeting. Sounds like their Cindys have a shot at cracking it."

Fire lit Gwen's eyes. "That would be huge, especially if they can crack it without the Wickeds knowing. Breaking the secrecy barrier is a huge step in winning the war against the Wickeds."

Back in the leader office, Paige grabbed a Yoo-hoo for each of us from her mini-fridge.

"So you've got the basics," she said. "ISIS leads our efforts, and ATHENA leads the Wickeds. ATHENA's goal is to dominate in every way they can. That means sliding into influential positions in government, the media, anything that gives them power over other people so they can push their own agenda."

She cracked open the cap to her Yoo-hoo, then did the same for mine when I showed no signs of doing it myself. My limbs felt heavy.

"That same fight plays out every day on the high-school battlefield. We're fighting to create a level playing field for the Reggies, while the Wickeds are fighting to dominate them. What our Wickeds are doing to our Reggies? That's happening from Maine to California. In different ways, but always with the same intent. To control through fear and manipulation. Why do you think the Wickeds bully the Reggies?"

My head hurt to think, and my comfort zone had jettisoned to somewhere in the vicinity of Mars, but I tried to sound coherent. "To get them to do their dirty work?"

"In a general sense, sure. But their primary goal is to teach the Reggies to be subservient to people stronger than them. The more ingrained it is in them when they're young, the easier they are to manipulate when they're older."

"So find them young, train them early, and take advantage of them when they're older." It was a sick plan, but I could see the logic behind it. If you wanted to grow your power, you needed to keep feeding the pipeline with people who would let you. "But how does ATHENA know which people they'll need to target when they're older?"

"That's just it. They don't. The Wickeds' goal is to cast a wide net and catch whoever they can. The more the merrier."

Paige ran her finger around the condensation ring on the table. "The worst part is that their information system follows their targets beyond school. Have a Reggie who does your dirty work in high school and is heading off to college? She doesn't get away simply by leaving town. Everything is filtered back through ATHENA. The Wickeds at the college will be there to greet her the minute she arrives, taking over where the high-school Wickeds left off. No chance for the Reggie to build a support system that could help her."

My stomach churned. How could a Reggie ever win? Once you were targeted, it was a lifetime sentence. No one deserved a life like that.

"Wickeds are everywhere, and their intelligence about Reggies at every stage of the game far surpasses anything we have. That's why our battle matters." Paige grimaced at the look of horror on my face. "It's ugly, I know. But you have to understand what's at stake to do your job effectively. The more Reggies who stay out of their web now, the more Reggies who'll stay free beyond graduation. That's your primary focus as leader."

I picked up my bottle to take a drink but set it back down. I wasn't sure my stomach was up to it, even for chocolaty goodness.

"What matters most to you as leader is the here and now," Paige said. "Priority number one is to figure out how our Cindys can head off whatever Lexy and the Wickeds have up their sleeves. Keeping the Wickeds contained is hard enough, but throw in the recruitment surge and it's a whole new ball game. Your first job is to figure out how you plan to deal with the surge."

"You'll help me with that, right?" I'd barely gotten my feet under me as an Alpha. Without the help of an insider like Paige, the Cindys were doomed from the word go.

"I'll try. Here's what we know so far. The second communication spike between ATHENA and the Wickeds happened right before the recruitment surge launched. They've doubled their recruitment class, so we're assuming it's part of a phased-in surge. Double their incoming class every year, and pretty soon they've got fifty-six Wickeds to our twenty-eight Cindys."

Twenty-eight Wickeds targeting the Reggies was bad enough. But thirty-five today . . . forty-two a year from now . . . fifty-six when they hit full capacity?

"Now, here's what we don't know. First, the communication is spiking again, but we don't know what it's leading up to. Second, we don't know why the surge is going on in the first place. Why now? How does it factor into their bigger agenda? Third, we know there's got to be a specific use for those new members. We just don't know what. And fourth— here's the biggie—we don't know how to fend off twice as many Wickeds without increasing our own ranks."

It didn't take a math wiz to figure out there were way more things we *didn't* know than things we did.

"If things had stayed on the track they'd been on," she said, "you'd be in good shape. But with the recruitment surge . . ."

"My job just got a lot harder."

"Unfortunately, yeah. By sheer volume, they're going to have the advantage. Your plan has to blow that out of the water before they get a stronghold." She gave me a bittersweet smile. "I don't blame you if you're feeling overwhelmed. I'd have freaked if I was being sworn in, without a year of preparation, just as the Wickeds were launching their surge."

*Not exactly words of comfort.*

"One last thing." Paige handed me a long, slim box. "This is yours. You'll get your leader charm during the induction ceremony."

I lifted the top and stared. JESS PARKER, indelibly etched in brass. A nameplate of my own to put outside the door when I was manning the leader office.

This wasn't a dream. For better or worse, this was my new reality. I hoped the better part would show up soon.

I put the lid back on the box and stood to go. "When will you be in the office again?"

"I tucked a copy of my schedule in your folder. Take a couple days to let this sink in. You need to come to terms with all this on your own before you can dive in and make sense of it as leader. When you're ready to talk plan, let me know."

I nodded and turned to leave, my head throbbing.

"Jess?"

I looked back at Paige.

"Being new works to your advantage. You're not bogged down by seeing things the way they've always been. A lot of the next two years is going to be running on instinct. You're absolutely strong enough to take on the Wickeds and win. You just have to trust yourself."

I could only pray she was right.

* * *

Our second unofficial cheer practice of the summer was grueling. It was only nine a.m., and the heat from the asphalt track was scorching. I finally felt like I was on the verge of proving to my teammates that I did, in fact, belong on the team and wasn't some lucky duck who got in because Lexy supposedly hurt her ankle the day of tryouts. That's the excuse she'd given everyone about why she'd gotten beat, even though it was clear as day to *me* that her "injury" was questionable at best.

But she'd planted that seed, and the question had lingered among my teammates. *If Lexy had been up to full potential, would Jess still have gotten the spot?* they wondered.

To which I wanted to yell, *Yes! Because she wasn't really hurt!* Which I did not yell, of course, because yelling rarely helps your case.

Sarah Jane and I had talked about Lexy's rumor in the lead-up to our first unofficial practice a few days earlier and decided the best way to deal with it was to face it head-on. As cocaptain, SJ had been up-front with the team at that first practice about the fact that everyone had heard the rumor and we needed to get it out in the open so it didn't divide us. For my part, I'd given my little spiel about how I didn't even know anything about Beaumont's cheerleaders—they competed in a different division at nationals than my old team—and I'd never thought anyone here was a diva anyway. And I'd said it all without laying the blame firmly where it belonged. On Lexy's waiflike shoulders.

I didn't expect to win everyone over with a two-minute speech, no matter how heartfelt, so I was more than a little surprised when everything seemed hunky-dory after that. They'd been so quick to assume the worst without knowing anything about me. But all it took was one person they trusted to vouch for me, and all was forgiven.

*Ridiculous, but I'll take it.*

Just to prove my worth, I'd been trying to fit in extra practice time on the cheer SJ and Kyra had taught us at our first practice. Today was my day to shine. To show them I was all about being a team player and prove I had the skills to justify my spot. No more sharing the spotlight with Miss Nasty in people's minds.

Except that Miss Nasty was *there.*

Sarah Jane had been as surprised as I was, because neither she nor Kyra had gotten Coach Trent's e-mail before practice about wanting Nichele and Lexy to come. Coach had invited them to make sure they learned the routine early in case we needed them to fill in later on.

Which I understood. Truly. Competitive cheerleading can be pretty grueling on your body, and you never knew when an injury could sideline you. I had the separated shoulder–dislocated kneecap–concussion battle wounds to prove it.

But still, a little notice would've been nice. Rule #1 when it came to dealing with Lexy: *Be prepared.*

"Okay, Lexy and Nichele are here to learn the routine so they're ready in case we need them. We're so glad you're here!" SJ could make anyone feel appreciated. Even when they didn't deserve it.

"We're glad to help," Lexy said in an irritatingly sweet voice. "We'll do whatever we can to help you be awesome this year. Right, Nichele?"

As alternates went, Nichele was way preferable to Lexy. Not only was she super nice, but she was an amazing flyer. Tiny and totally fearless in the air. I wasn't huge, but because I was really strong for my size, I'd always been a base. Flyers astounded me, especially when they were as good as Nichele. But she didn't have a consistent back handspring–back tuck, so she'd been relegated to second alternate.

Apparently, I was the only one on the track who saw through Lexy's fakeitude, because everyone else was nodding cheerfully. Too cheerfully for my taste. But since I had to assume none of them had death wishes—nor did I—being agreeable was probably the wise choice, all things considered.

League rules stated that teams couldn't officially practice until August, so Coach Trent wasn't allowed to be present at our unofficial summer practices. SJ was the girl in charge, taking her job seriously as she led us in stretches. Cassie had stopped by to give us a pep talk at our first practice and teach us some college-level drills we could use in our warm-up. Sarah Jane led us through the drills this time, followed by two laps around the track. After that, it was nonstop cheering until eleven. We did digs, lunges, and jumps until my quads were burning and my hamstrings were screaming for a break. Not that I'd admit it. Not for all the Golden Oreos in the world.

We stopped several times to work out the kinks of the new routine. Despite the fact that Lexy was only an alternate, I was surprised by how often my teammates deferred to her judgment. It was almost eerie the way people handed over their power to her even when she was clearly not in the power position. Sarah Jane and Kyra didn't, of course, nor did I. Thanks to our Cindy support system. But most of our teammates did. All the while acting as though it were perfectly natural.

I definitely had my work cut out for me if I expected to defeat her in two short years.

I shook off my leader role and focused on the task at

hand. At eleven, we stopped counting through the stunts and focused on nailing them. Lexy and Nichele were extra spotters—which totally helped, especially since Lexy didn't spot *my* group—and we finally called it a day after wrapping the triple-based heel stretches. SJ adopted the same three-five rule we'd had on my competition team in Seattle: Stick it three times in a row for five seconds each and you're done. It only took *my* stunt group six attempts to get a triple whammy.

*Take that, Miss Nasty.*

\* \* \*

We were throwing our cheer gear back into our bags and making plans for lunch when the construction trucks rolled in. Kids from the other sports fields gathered around the main entrance to school but were pushed back as workers roped off the area. The news filtered back from the front lines: water-main break.

Why don't these things ever happen during school when they'd be useful?

The water-company trucks were joined by a flatbed truck with an excavator thingie. It looked like a massive undertaking—and not very interesting unless you were a construction-truck fanatic—so we headed toward SJ's car. We were halfway across the parking lot when a bunch of dark-windowed sedans came streaming in. A woman who looked like Jennifer Aniston in thirty years stepped out of a Mercedes with a crisp white folder in her hand and went straight for the guy in charge.

After a heated exchange, the guy threw his hard hat on the ground and snatched the two-way from his belt. While he yelled into it, Grandma Aniston gave a slight nod to the other cars in the procession, and immediately, seven other women exited the vehicles and went straight into the school. The only ones I recognized were Principal Zimmer, Vice Principal Starr, and Coach Trent. Not that I'd have stopped to say hi or anything.

Between the trucks and the sedans, we were blocked in. SJ and I gave up and went over to hang out on the bleachers, guzzling water like we lived in the Sahara.

Half a bottle later, we saw Paige heading across the field. We waved her down, and she joined us next to the announcer's hut, which offered a tiny bit of shade and the perfect view to keep an eye on the parking lot.

"What do you know about Heather Clark?" Paige asked me after we'd caught up on Sisterhood stuff.

Where had that come from? "She's nice."

"Did you figure out what the deal is with Lexy targeting her?"

"How did you . . . ?" I looked at SJ, remembering she'd been at the ball game too. "Sarah Jane saw the same thing I did. That's all I know."

"Doesn't she come into Celestial Gifts?" SJ asked.

"Sometimes."

SJ looked at Paige, and Paige gave her a *go ahead, then* gesture.

"We need you to do a little digging," SJ said. "On the down low."

That piqued my interest. "What kind of digging?"

"We need to find out what's up between Lexy and Heather."

"Why?"

"Heather's one of the people we've identified as being a key target of the Wickeds," Paige said. "We haven't been able to crack the others, so we need you to try to get through to Heather."

Cracking people? What were we, the Mafia? "Did you put them under a lightbulb and toothpick their eyelids open?"

Paige did not look amused.

"This is serious, Jess. The Wickeds doubling their bid class *and* stepping up pressure on the Reggies? Something's up, and we need to know what. *You* need to know what, so you can figure out how to stop it."

I didn't like where this was going. "What exactly does this mission entail?"

"It's not impossible, if that's what you're thinking. I'm not going to self-destruct in three seconds." That was as much of a joke as Paige would allow. Times were grim. "We need someone to get Heather to open up. Find out what Lexy's targeting is about. Anything to give us something to go on."

I squirmed on the bleachers, and not just because the perspiration on my legs was suctioning them to the super-heated metal. I didn't mind going out of my way to help Heather, but constantly getting in Lexy's business to do it? Did I *look* insane?

"Let's face facts here," I said in my most reasonable voice. I ticked off the strikes against me on my fingers. "One, I've already tried talking to Heather, and she was about as helpful as a mute guppy. Two, if Lexy finds out I'm trying to help the Reggie she's targeting, she'll end me before I can even take over as leader." I couldn't even fathom how low she'd stoop beyond what she'd already done. Especially after she found out I was going to be the new leader of the Cindys to boot. "Three, I'm the new kid here. Why do you think I can help Heather if you haven't been able to help the others? You guys wield the kind of social power that would make Madonna jealous. I'm a nobody."

"No Wicked chatter."

*Thanks, Sarah Jane. Not helpful.*

"First, Heather needs to be guided, not chatted with," Paige said. "You need to show her she can trust you. Second, Lexy won't *end* you. That's your drama talking. And the Cindys have your back if you step on her toes."

Step on her toes? *Thanks for the understatement, Paige.*

"Third, being the new kid is exactly why you have a connection with her. Heather's always been guarded, but she reached out to you. That has power."

I thought about how Heather had stopped to help me pick up the Lexy mess just a few hundred feet from where we sat. Something I realized the Cindys must have witnessed too. But if Heather had really been reaching out that day, why had she pushed me away when I'd gone to bat for her against Lexy? I'd offered her backup when no one else had, but she'd chosen to go it alone.

"Promise you'll think about it, okay?" SJ asked. "I know we're asking a lot with everything you've been through since you moved here, but you don't have to throw it in Lexy's face. Just, you know, be sly about it. See what you can find out."

*Love potion, protection incense, one more favor for the Wickeds.* The pieces of the puzzle were already forming, but my intuition was still on alert. "No promises, but I'll think about it."

"I knew we could count on you, J."

Trouble was, I didn't know if I could count on myself not to chicken out. "Is this part of my leader training?"

"Not officially, no. But it goes along with everything you'll be up against come fall, so think of it as a chance for you to show your stuff."

*Fabulous.* The candle was barely cold and they were already asking me to prove my worth.

We watched the guy in charge have more heated words with Grandma Aniston before saying what were, we guessed, some pretty choice ones and leading his crew off campus. They'd already moved the sedans so people could leave, and everyone had pretty much disbanded. Except for Lexy, who was hanging around under the overhang of the concession stand on the outskirts of the sports complex. By herself.

The muscle near my eye twitched.

Lexy Steele is always surrounded. *Always.* If she's out and about, her cronies are there to support her, cater to her every whim, and make sure she looks powerful. The fact that she was alone was suspicious. The fact that she looked excited while alone made me worried.

"Jess? You still with us?"

I snapped back to the conversation. "What?"

"Let's head out. Do you want to get wraps at The Grind or pizza at Cuomo's?"

"You know, I think I'm gonna hang out for a while and practice more." Good thing I wasn't standing, or my legs would've given out in protest. Even though they knew it was a lie.

SJ looked out past me and saw the same thing I did. "Don't even think about confronting her. Discreet, remember?"

"Do I strike you as unstable? Of course I'm not gonna confront her. I just want to see what's up."

Paige didn't look thrilled. "Focus on Heather. If Lexy knows you're getting close, she may change tactics."

"Then I'll make sure she doesn't know." When they didn't look convinced, I pulled out the big guns. "You gave me the mission. Trust me to do it right."

The tap of Paige's fingernail on the bleacher sent tinny echoes around our feet. "Sounds like you're done thinking it over."

"Sounds like."

*　＊　＊

Lexy stayed off to the side while the sedans filed out of the parking lot, then made a quick call on her cell that involved lots of animated gestures. She shoved it back in her purse, did a quick perusal of the area where the workers had started to dig, and headed back to her Lexus for destinations unknown.

I considered the clues and had to admit they intrigued me. Despite my hesitation to play amateur sleuth that first night at The Grind, I was a sucker for puzzles. And if helping Heather meant bringing Lexy and the Wickeds down in the process, I was all over that. As long as it was Lexy who went down and not me.

But before I got sucked into the mystery, I had a mission of a different kind competing for my attention. One that would take everything I had to complete successfully with minimal damage to my well-being.

I had a date to get ready for.

# Chapter 12

"THE JAMBALAYA CHICKEN is really good here," Ryan told me as we slid into the booth for dinner. "I get it every time we come."

"Yum," I said, even though I was thinking the heartburn and gas special wasn't my first choice for date food. I picked up my menu. "I love their chicken Caesar salad."

"That's what Lexy always gets," he said. Our eyes met for a split second over the tops of our menus, and we both looked away. Dating your enemy's brother was a messy business.

A too-chipper waitress girl came to take our orders, fawning a bit too much over Ryan for my taste. I slowly turned my charm bracelet around my wrist to calm my nerves. I'd stressed out in a major way deciding what to wear, but a quick call to SJ had reeled me back in. I wasn't Fake Blondie's caliber, but my fun-feminine-sporty look had been holding Ryan's attention so far. I could do this.

She took away our menus, and the moment arrived. With no entrée options to impede our views, there was nothing to shield us from looking at each other. To keep us from engaging in more than idle chitchat. The time had come to act like two people on a real date.

Why don't they make coloring menus for kids our age?

The silence stretched on for hours—okay, more like a few seconds, but it seemed like three lifetimes—before Ryan broke the ice. "Sorry about the Lexy comment."

Not my first choice of topic. "She's your sister," I said, folding my napkin neatly onto my lap.

"Yeah, but she's been tough on you."

True, but I wasn't letting her rain on my date. "What's your plan for the summer?"

"I work at the car wash and the Tri-Eight. So mostly that and working out before football starts."

"You work at the movie theater? Do you really get to see all the movies for free?"

"Mostly." He grabbed some sugar packets and started building a mini house of sugar with them. "I didn't see the Sandler flick, since I knew we were going."

How sweet was that? "I've only seen one movie since we moved here."

Ryan smiled. "Orlando Bloom."

*Typical.* "You know, just because most girls are in love with him doesn't mean that's the one movie I would've seen."

"You came with your mom and got there after the previews started. You were wearing a red shirt that said EAT-SLEEP-CHEER."

Oh.

No. *Way.*

"She doesn't like to sit through the previews." My face felt like fire. "I didn't see you that day. How did you see me?"

"I always notice cute new girls. But back to Orlando. What were you saying about the movie you saw?" He laughed at my deepening blush. "That's okay. As long as you know we can't all be Orlando Bloom."

He thought my embarrassment was about being caught as a bona fide Orly groupie. I couldn't have cared less about that. I was just trying to hold it together after the bomb he'd dropped. Ryan Steele had noticed me all the way back then.

And he'd remembered.

"Why didn't you . . . ?" I stopped, embarrassed that my brain-to-mouth filter didn't seem to be working. Did I really want to ask the question swirling in my mind?

"Why didn't I what?"

I folded my napkin, gliding my finger along the crease to give my nervous hands something to do. "I don't know. Talk to me back then or something."

Ryan looked surprised. "I did. You got bumped in the hallway one day, and I tried to help you pick up your books."

And by *got bumped* he meant got tripped by his sister's BFF while Lexy looked on and beamed.

*Lovely of you to remember that shining moment.*

"I tried to introduce myself," he said, "but you couldn't get away from me fast enough. I figured I'd blown it somehow."

I thought back to the day I'd much rather have erased from my memory banks. The cheer-team list had just been posted, and Lexy had already gathered her friends for the Jess hunt. I hadn't known much about Ryan then—I'd only been at MSH a few weeks—so I'd assumed he'd been in on the torturefest, being Lexy's brother and all. I'd gotten away from him as fast as I could. It wasn't until later that I realized Lexy was the Steele family devil, and Ryan was prime crush material.

Fate has such ironic timing.

"Anyway," he said, letting me off the hook. Just like a

Charming. "I'm a total movie buff. Sandler might not be Orlando Bloom, but I think the movie will be a blast."

I latched on to the change of topic, despite the Orly teasing, and we were off and running just like when we'd talked music at Kyra's. Ryan continued his construction of the sugar building—a castle, we decided—and I passed him sugar packets while we talked. White ones for the first floor, pink ones for the second floor.

By the time our food arrived, we'd already contemplated girls' obsession with romantic comedies, guys' fascination with shoot-'em-up, crash-'em-up movies, and why musicals were so popular. We couldn't think of anyone who would burst into song in the middle of the caf. Not even the drama club.

Ryan snatched a handful of packets from the empty table next to us when we ran out. Our castle was now a monstrosity with a blue-packet tower I was afraid to breathe near for fear of it taking a nosedive into our spinach artichoke dip. His hands were amazingly steady. I couldn't imagine my hands ever being that steady, much less on a first date. The guy had some seriously talented hands.

I wouldn't let myself think about how talented. Or how experienced.

I cut my salad into small pieces with a knife, a little trick Nan had taught me so I could avoid making a spectacle of myself. The chicken salad was awesome, and Ryan raved about his jambalaya. We managed to debate chicken versus turkey, whether buttermilk ranch was better than regular ranch, and even whether spinach artichoke dip was better hot or cold.

"You're so easy to talk to," Ryan said as he pushed his

plate aside. "I can't remember ever having this much fun talking on a date."

I couldn't remember ever *having* a date. At least not a real one in public. I swallowed another bite of chicken and lettuce. "What do you usually have fun doing on dates?"

I wasn't trying to be coy (if that means what I think it means). It was actually an innocent question. Being the dateless wonder, I had no clue what people usually did during dates where dinner was involved. Was the conversation usually stilted? Did girls blather on about pedicures or gossip or other froufrou stuff? These were the questions on my mind.

But that's just where *my* mind was.

Ryan, being the experienced dater I knew him to be, leaned back against the faux leather seat and studied me. His eyebrows raised a millimeter. "Looking for details?"

All the blood drained from my face, then rushed back with the heat of a dozen jambalaya dinners. *Do-over!* "I wasn't asking . . . I mean, I know you've . . ." I hung my head. "Can we talk about movies again?"

Ryan laughed and reached out, careful not to knock over the castle, and put his hand on mine. "I'm kidding, Jess."

I knew he was, but it didn't make it any easier. Neither did having his nice cozy hand covering my clammy one. With one innocent slipup, I'd managed to derail my carefully formulated plan to convince Ryan I was a completely normal, dating-is-no-big-deal kind of girl.

Ryan polished off the last of his soda and patted his stomach. "You're gonna have to roll me out of here."

Ryan drawing attention to his rock-hard abs was not helping my cause. I was so out of my league. I mean, what *did* usually happen on his dates? We talked like old friends, so it felt more like hanging with a buddy. A really hot, drool-worthy buddy you'd rather make out with than talk to. Except I had the distinct impression the make-out part was sadly a one-sided fantasy.

Thankfully, we had to motor if we wanted to catch the movie, so Ryan paid and I bailed to the ladies' to get my act together. As I suspected, my face still had the faint telltale blotchiness known as post-blush syndrome. At least we were headed for an Adam Sandler movie. Some laughs would be the perfect thing to ease the tension and put us back into relax-o mode.

Ryan grabbed a large popcorn to share (how could he be hungry again?), a bottled water for me, and a soda for him, and nabbed us some middle-of-the-theater seats. The previews were ready to start, so there was little time for small talk. That worked out perfectly, since I was looking to chill my nerves anyway.

Now, if you've seen an Adam Sandler movie like *Mr. Deeds* or *50 First Dates* or whatever, you know it's mostly a guys' comedy with a pinch of romance thrown in, so Adam always gets the girl. What I didn't think about was what happens when Adam *gets* the girl.

I know. I'm slow, right? They *kiss*.

So I'm sitting there next to Ryan, knowing this is coming and not knowing how to react. Do I sit there and watch the on-screen kiss like it's no big deal (which—hello?—it *is*. Their heads are two stories high!) or do I reach for a drink to distract myself without looking like I'm trying *not* to look? Since my water was gone, option number two was a no-go, and option number one wasn't even a possibility, since I could already feel the embarrassed flush superheating my skin. I'd be shocked if I didn't set off the emergency sprinklers. So I did the next best thing and reached into the bucket of popcorn to distract myself.

Twining my fingers with Ryan's in the process.

Just as Adam went in for the lip-lock, Ryan gave me a questioning look and squeezed my fingers. Was that code for *Wanna make out now?* or *Nice try, honey, but it's not that kind of date* or *Nice of your fingers to join mine; now please vamoose them so I can eat?*

Why was dating so complicated?!

Fortunately, it was a quick kissing scene, so I was off the hook, even though it took me a full ten minutes before my heart slowed to a normal pace. When the credits rolled, Ryan steered us out of the theater, and I went straight to the ladies' again. A large bottled water had a way of doing that to a girl, but I also needed a chance to fully recover before the final leg of my dating adventure: the good-night moment.

I didn't want to look in the mirror this time, knowing full well my blotches would've sprouted blotches of their own, but I couldn't resist. I covered up what I could with powder, ran a fresh coat of gloss over my lips, and popped a tiny mint. I rummaged around for a breath strip with no luck, so a second tiny mint joined the first. At least I hadn't eaten the jambalaya.

By the time I reached the hallway, Ryan was surrounded by people from school. Some guys, but mostly girls. Including Fake Blondie.

"I've missed you, Ry," she purred, rubbing her chest against his arm in front of everyone.

*Self-control . . . ever heard of it?* Clearly, Fake Blondie hadn't.

Ryan looked perfectly comfortable being the center of attention, but his eyes perked up when he saw me, and he waved me over. A few quick introductions later, including one to Gennifer (with a *G*, she informed me—yep, that's Fake Blondie), and he was leading me by the hand out into the evening air.

"Thanks for the save back there."

"You didn't look like you needed saving," I grumbled, feeling catty and insecure. But really, how could I compete with Fake Blondie and her blatant chestiness on my very first date? A girl could only hurdle so many obstacles in a single bound.

"Sometimes I like being alone." Ryan squeezed my hand. "And sometimes I just want to be with you."

My cattiness melted into a little kitty puddle.

We'd parked off to the side, and Ryan held my hand the whole way across the parking lot.

A point of distinction: Ryan has the most amazing hands. I'd admired them in the restaurant, but that didn't hold a candle to feeling them up close and personal. They're big and strong, with really nice fingers (not stubby at all) and clean fingernails. Holding his hand was the most amazing, solid, wonderful thing in the world. Our hands fit perfectly together, obviously a sign they were meant to be linked for all eternity. You can't argue with hand destiny.

My hand felt small and dainty in his, and when he wove our fingers together, I could've sworn I heard my heart sigh. Even if I'd had a lifetime of other hand-holding experiences to rate this one against, I was positive it still would've topped the scale.

Ryan opened my door. "So, where to?"

I still had an hour till curfew (a curfew being the latest, and least well-received, addition to the Parker family rulebook), so I danced a mental jig that he wanted to stay out longer.

"Where do you usually go?" *Don't answer that!* "I mean, what's your favorite place . . . you know, like a hangout?"

"You're cute when you blush."

I grimaced. *Cute.* Not gorgeous or hot or fantasy material, but cute. Like a little sister or a baby. Or a puppy.

*Arf.*

"That was supposed to be a compliment."

I stared at my sandals. "Thanks."

"But?"

"It's just, you know, *cute.* Cute is your best friend's little sister." *Or Chihuahua.*

"Ah, not the girl I'm having a blast with. The girl I can't stop thinking about kissing."

"Uh, yeah."

"Then let me rephrase that." He lifted my chin so I had to look up, then slid his warm hand up to cradle my jaw. "You're amazing."

Errant thoughts ambushed my already rattled brain. *Is this our first kiss? Our first real one, I mean? Do I have bad breath? What if I—?*

Oh. My.

*Heaven.*

The kiss was so gentle and perfect I thought I might be dreaming it. Small kisses, firm and full, followed by deeper kisses that left me flushed and breathless. His lips eased mine apart, and the tip of his tongue brushed my lower lip. Once. Twice. He slipped his other hand into my hair as my arms slid around his waist, tucking my body in close to his.

I let my tongue gently touch his and felt his intake of breath. He angled my head and deepened the kiss, my toes tingling from the magic of his mouth on mine. I wished it would never end.

"Get a room!"

Except that we were in a parking lot.

The magic evaporated in an instant. Ryan backed away from me as the car of teenagers drove by. "Come on," he said hoarsely, tucking a stray hair behind my ear. "Let's go."

My lips felt puffy and full, and I hesitated long enough to convey my uncertainty. He put both hands behind his back and motioned with his shoulder toward the open door. "There's no pressure, Jess. We don't have to rush this."

I slid into my seat, and he closed the door behind me. He climbed in the driver's side, gave me a quick glance I couldn't read, and started the engine.

I took an extra long time clicking my seat belt into place to keep my hands busy. "Where?" I asked, after my voice revived itself.

"Somewhere public, so I have to keep my hands off you." He shifted the car into drive. "Even though that's the last thing on my mind."

\* \* \*

We ended up at The Grind for mocha shakes. Audrey gave a smile of approval at the sight of Ryan and me together. I could only hope my lips weren't as swollen as they felt. So busted.

Ryan was leading me toward a cozy table in the corner when we were interrupted again. "Steele! How you doin', man?"

I saw a flash of frustration cross Ryan's face before he turned around to smile at the voice behind us. "Hey, Nick," he said, dropping my hand. "What's up?"

Nick Case looked me up and down, sizing me up with his dreamboat eyes. "Who's the sizzlin' new girl?"

"Jess Parker, meet Nick Case—Mt. Sterling's answer to

Hugh Hefner," Ryan said. "Don't worry, I'll protect you."

I liked the sound of that. "Nice to meet you, Nick."

"The pleasure's all mine," he said, lifting my hand for a showy kiss before Ryan smacked him. Nick laughed. "We've got the round booths by the windows. Come on over."

Ryan tensed. "We're not staying long."

"All the more reason to grace us with your presence." Nick glanced at me. "We're going into hero withdrawal now that we don't get our daily Ryan fix at school."

I could've sworn I saw Ryan's jaw twitch, but his smile never wavered. "I don't mind," I offered just as Ryan said, "Maybe some other time."

*Oh.*

We looked at each other. "Another time is fine too," I hedged.

Ryan looked over at the table filled with—I was sorry to see—several Wickeds, a couple of Villains, and some other kids I didn't know. Ryan glanced at me, then back at them, before shaking his head. "Some other time."

Nick studied him for a minute. Shrugged. "You're probably right." He gave me a lady-killer smile that had zero impact on me. "Nice to meet you, Jess. Let me know if you need a private tour of our fine town. I know all the best spots."

*I'll bet you do.*

Nick sauntered away like the player he was, and when I turned back to Ryan, he was already headed toward the opposite corner. Without my hand.

After a few minutes of painfully stilted small talk—Adam Sandler was funny in the restaurant scene, the theater always puts too much salt in the popcorn—I noticed we were out of napkins. I mentioned it offhand, but Ryan immediately hopped up to grab some, even though neither of us had an urgent need for cleanup supplies.

I watched him at the counter, wondering how we'd gotten off track so quickly. Ryan got waylaid by a girl whose breasts put Fake Blondie's to shame, and I suffered my second insecurity of the night.

To avoid my reality, I focused on the Wickeds and Villains holding court in the opposite corner. In contrast to the pool party, the power positions at The Grind were the two large round booths anchoring the side wall. Since they were booths instead of tables, no one sat with their back to the audience. I mean, the action. Everyone had a full view, which meant every seat at the booth had power.

I watched as kids from school came in and out, trying to pretend that Ryan abandoning me was but a momentary thing that we'd mutually agreed upon. As if.

It was easy to tell who the Reggies were. Their eyes immediately went to the power tables to see who was staked out there. They gave the tables a wide berth, even faking a trip to the restrooms so they could approach the counter from the side opposite the Wickeds when they came out. One even turned on her heel and fled the moment she laid eyes on the booths.

Some seemed just fine, chatting away with friends, until they noticed that one of the Wickeds was watching them with interest. Which led to an immediate departure, usually out the side doors by the restrooms. The Wickeds didn't even have to advance on them. The mere prospect of being a target was enough to put most Reggies on edge.

How on earth was I going to defeat that? Their power was relentless.

I shifted my attention back to Ryan and Boob Girl, which didn't inspire a boost in my happy quotient. A surprise visitor on her way back from the ladies' didn't help matters either.

"Nice shirt, Parker." Tina sneered. "I used to have one just like it before I gave it away to the Salvation Army. Glad it found a needy home." Even though it was a brand-new purchase *thankyouverymuch*. "No wonder Ryan's hiding you in a corner."

"Aren't you sitting in a corner too?"

"You wish." Tina looked over at their table, which was—thank you—*in a corner*. She scowled. "At least where I sit is by choice, not because someone's too embarrassed to be seen with me. Have a nice date."

She flipped her glossy mane over her shoulder, swatting me with the strands, and rejoined her Wicked and Villain buds.

I kept a neutral expression on my face as I watched Ryan smile and talk to Boob Girl, but my nerves were shot. Just like Lexy, Tina had managed to find a weak spot and poke at it. Ryan finally glanced over at me, as did Boob Girl (who, I'm pretty sure, thrust her chest out a little extra on my behalf), and he gave her a final smile before heading back my way with a noticeably less enthusiastic smile in my direction.

"Napkin trouble?" I joked, wading in self-pity.

He stuffed the napkins in the holder. "Sorry about that. I got sidetracked."

"That happens to you a lot."

Ryan paused. "Yeah. I guess it does." He looked at his watch, and I took that as my cue to wrap it up. Jess Parker as date material was about to get the boot.

I tossed the rest of my shake in the trash, giving a subtle

shake of my head in response to Audrey's questioning look, and kept pace with Ryan to the car.

The car ride was over before either of us could think of something to fill the dead air, and within seconds, we were on my porch. I would've gladly walked myself to the door to avoid the humiliation of being let down easy.

"Sorry about The Grind." Ryan stuffed his hands in his pockets. "I didn't really want to sit with them."

Because he was embarrassed by me. "No problem." I put on my cheerleader face. "Thanks for dinner and the movie. It was fun."

"I had a good time too," he said. I wondered if his pants would catch fire from the lie. "Maybe I'll call you?"

Was he asking permission or deciding if that was really going to happen? "Sure. I'll see you around."

Ryan looked like he was going to be sick. He nodded. "Yeah, around." He looked into my eyes—the first time we'd made eye contact since The Grind—then flicked a glance to my lips. The promise of another kiss hung in the air, and I thought maybe, just maybe, everything might be okay. Then he looked at his shoes, and the flicker went out. He gave me a quick peck on the cheek and stepped back to watch me walk into the house.

I gave him a cheery wave and closed the door. I turned the lock, the resounding click of the dead bolt shattering my reserve. The tears let loose and I ran upstairs, ignoring Mom's voice from the kitchen. A glutton for punishment, I hid in the shadows of my dark room and watched out the window.

Ryan walked slowly around his car and got in. The engine roared to life. He gave one last look at my front door, shook his head, and drove away.

I grabbed a box of tissues and burrowed under the

covers as a torrent of tears streamed down my face.

It was official. I was the girl you could only like in private.

✳ ✳ ✳

GlitterGirl: how did it go tonight???

WillCheer4Food: dinner, great. movie, fun. first kiss, yum.

GlitterGirl: FIRST KISS?!?!?!!!!

WillCheer4Food: running into Wickeds at The Grind, disaster. no goodnight kiss.

Which wasn't technically true, because he had kissed my cheek. But compared to the soul-searing lip-lock after the movie, it wasn't even on the same scoreboard. Sarah Jane would understand the difference.

GlitterGirl: {{{Jess}}}

WillCheer4Food: are you embarrassed to be seen with me?

GlitterGirl: i'm sure it's — —

GlitterGirl: what? of course not!!

I gave SJ the Tina rundown. She made all the right comforting noises (emoticons, whatever), but it didn't make me feel any better. Neither had spilling the whole thing to Mom over a bowl of Chunky Monkey.

Boy, that had been nice, though. It was the first time Mom and I had really talked in what seemed like forever. It made me remember how cool she could be when she wasn't obsessing about the twins.

But our talk hadn't changed my mind about Ryan. No matter how many people told me it wasn't me, I knew better.

It was Dan Carter all over again. I'd let myself get sucked into the fairy tale with him too. But in my defense, what was

I supposed to think when Dan hung out with me all summer, flirting and sneaking kisses? It's not like he ever said, "Oh, and by the way? If you can't hang with the Chosen Few come September, I'm ditching you like last year's soccer cleats."

I mean, when the big brush-off happens once, you can chalk it up to the guy being a loser. Which I did. In red Sharpie across his yearbook picture.

But here I was—new town, new guy—and it was like Dan: The Sequel. Ryan's mind-blowing kiss in the parking lot snuffed out by the cold shoulder I'd gotten when we'd crossed paths with the evil ones. When would I ever learn? I might as well have *gullible* tattooed on my forehead.

*No Wicked chatter.*

I braced myself, determined not to give in to the pity party I could feel brewing. I'd been to that party enough to know that no one cool ever crashes it.

I wrapped up with SJ, not wanting to prolong my misery, and was about to shut down when another IM knocked the wind out of me.

First&Goal: jess?

I stared at the screen. I'd taken my Internet safety class like a good little doobie and knew better than to respond to an unknown IM. But could it be . . . ?

First&Goal: it's ryan

How did he get my screen name? More to the point, why in the heck was he IMing me at almost midnight? Like he hadn't already done enough damage to my fragile ego? Or was this Lexy and Morgan having a little fun at my expense?

WillCheer4Food: what did you eat tonight?
First&Goal: spinach dip (hot IS better), chicken jambalaya, and too much popcorn

Yep. Definitely Ryan.

First&Goal: i hope it's okay to IM u... cass gave me your screen name... do u mind?
WillCheer4Food: that depends. are you IMing to break my heart a second time?

I know. I deleted that before I hit Send. As if I'd let on I was fool enough to think the spark was real.

WillCheer4Food: no problem. what's up?
First&Goal: i wanted to say i'm sorry
WillCheer4Food: for?
First&Goal: how things ended
First&Goal: nick and i... there's a lot of friction there
First&Goal: it has nothing to do with u
WillCheer4Food: np
First&Goal: can i make it up to u?

I stared at the screen again, afraid to let myself go there. *Fool me once, shame on me. Fool me twice, and I'll put your butt in a sling.*

Whoa. That didn't even sound like *my* Wicked chatter. Maybe my heart was finally rebelling against the male species.

WillCheer4Food: no need, but thanks. have a good night!
First&Goal: WAIT

First&Goal: okay, you're mad... i don't blame u... i acted like an idiot

First&Goal: let me show u i'm not a jerk

First&Goal: at least not all the time

WillCheer4Food: you're not a jerk. and you don't have to prove anything. i'm used to not fitting in

First&Goal: who don't u fit in with?

WillCheer4Food: everyone at the round table? most of the kids in Mt. Sterling? your sister? take your pick

First&Goal: u fit with me

It caught me right square in the heart.

First&Goal: jess?

I couldn't give in. The Cindys had my head in fairy-tale mode already. I couldn't afford to let it spill over into my real life. I'd been burned enough to know better. I wasn't one of the fortunate few destined to have it all.

First&Goal: i have to work early but i don't want this to be over before it even gets started

First&Goal: i want another chance

First&Goal: i'm working a double shift tomorrow, but how about mini golf and really bad hot dogs Thu night? around 7?

First&Goal: i felt something with u, Jess

First&Goal: something I want to feel again

Was I delusional to give it another shot? To open myself up again, only to be picked off by a Wicked sniper or sleazy competitor ready to step in at the first sign of weakness?

First&Goal: are u going to make me beg?
WillCheer4Food: no

I hadn't planned to do it. Didn't even realize I had until I'd typed the word. But deep down I knew I couldn't live with the what-ifs.

First&Goal: no u won't go out with me or no u won't make me beg?
First&Goal: because i'm not above begging
First&Goal: groveling is good for the soul
WillCheer4Food: no, you don't have to beg. but you don't have to prove anything either. if it works, it works. if it doesn't, no big.
First&Goal: deal... but jess?
WillCheer4Food: yeah?
First&Goal: i can't stop thinking about u... or that kiss in the parking lot
First&Goal: see u thursday, beautiful
<First&Goal has signed off>

# Chapter 13

**PAIGE WAS TALKING TO SARAH JANE** about the system upgrade when I got to the War Room for our first official leader meeting. I'd been racking my brain over the surge stuff, but so far I'd come up with zip. No idea what the surge was for; no idea how to battle it.

If I'd been a baseball player, I'd have been one step away from striking out. Not an impressive start for the new leader.

Once she'd turned Sarah Jane loose on the latest intelligence briefing from ISIS, Paige led me over to a magnetic whiteboard filling a large section of wall space. "Our intel isn't anywhere near complete, but here's what we can confirm: fourteen primary targets and about two dozen secondary targets." She pointed to a group of photos gathered in the upper right corner. "Those are the primary targets: favorites of the Wickeds for a year or more. The rest are ones we've identified in the last twelve months."

The targets were small photographs, each attached to card stock that listed the name, year in school, address, and any other notes the Cindys thought might be important.

"That's it?" In a school of more than fifteen hundred students, forty or so targets didn't seem like a very wide net. Although I'm sure it seemed plenty wide to those forty girls.

"Those are just the top two tiers. Reggies we've been able to document being bullied on a regular basis. That's targeting. The Wickeds gain power by dominating people who are strong. They might occasionally bully someone weak just for kicks, but it's pretty rare, because it doesn't increase their power. In their eyes, anyone can bully a weakling. But dominate someone strong, and the Wickeds' power—and egos—get a boost. Plus, it makes that person less of a threat to the Wickeds' empire."

She settled us into chairs along the bank of computers on the side wall. "The hard part is that there's been an upswing in new targets over the last couple of months. We're still trying to get a handle on the new group. There could be dozens more, even hundreds. It's like the rules changed overnight, and the Wickeds have taken their game to a new level. We don't know how they've been able to manage it so quickly. And now we've got the surge on top of it."

"Is this my pep talk?"

Paige laughed and relaxed a little. "Sorry. It's just frustrating to be turning all this over to you. I feel like I should be able to give you more. Instead, I'm handing off a bunch of problems and no solutions."

Paige showed me how to log in to the intelligence system and get background information on the Reggies. It felt intrusive, like I was spying on them. Yes, the Wickeds had far more information—and more embarrassing information, to be sure—but it didn't seem right to be reading about Heather's dad, the town drunk. Or that her mom had died when she was born, leaving her with no female role model and a father who could barely care for himself, much less a daughter. At least she'd had her grandparents until she was ten. Since then . . . there hadn't been much of anything in the way of support.

Paige excused herself to deal with a system issue, and I stole a minute to search the Cindy database for Mom. Given that she'd never mentioned a word about the Cindys since I'd joined their ranks, it wasn't very likely she was a Cindy herself. But if people like Sarah Jane's mom could be lifelong Cindys, making Sarah Jane a legacy, part of me still clung to the hope that Mom might be. Just to give us something in common, something the babies couldn't take away from us.

The search came up empty. My insides felt a little like that too.

My gaze fell on the board again. Looking at it from across the room gave me a different perspective. Up close, they were people I knew. Maybe not personally, but I'd passed them in the hall or seen them in a yearbook. From farther away, the pictures were a pattern. Groups of rectangles sorted around the board in various ways.

My math-geek tendencies came out of hibernation. Success leaves clues. If the Wickeds had been successful at growing the ranks of the targeted, it wasn't by accident. Not if all the communication evidence from ISIS was any indication. There was a pattern to what they were doing; they were systematically targeting people who fit into the bigger plan.

If we could uncover the pattern, we could unravel the plan. Just like the Albuquerque Cindys were doing with the code.

I moved toward the board and studied it, looking for patterns. Paige had said I could move the targets around as long as they all stayed up, so I shuffled them around in different ways. By grade level, by last name. Even tacked up a map of Mt. Sterling and grouped them according to where they lived.

I stepped back again. There was something about how they grouped on the map that called to me, but I couldn't put my finger on it. What would location have to do with it?

In less than a minute, I'd printed off a roster of the Wickeds, complete with addresses. Maybe that was the connection. Start near home and move out, so you'd have easy access? I used little red magnets to mark where the Wickeds lived compared to the Reggies.

There were a few clusters in the nicer parts of town, but nothing that seemed organized. With income came status, though, so maybe that was the key. The Wickeds were all about status, even when it meant stealing someone else's to give them more power.

Shuffling them by social status was harder, because I didn't know people the way the Cindys did, so I peeked into our office and asked for Paige's help. I pulled off the red magnets—bye-bye, Wickeds—and Paige helped me break the targets into groups by popularity.

"We looked at that too," she explained, "but there wasn't anything obvious that sent up a red flag."

There were three groups: those at the top of the social pecking order, those at the bottom, and those in the middle. Not exactly earth-shattering.

Rather than group them by where they seemed to be in the social hierarchy, we started looking at them individually. What did the Wickeds have to gain by targeting them?

"We looked at that too," Paige said. "Some are pretty easy to figure out. Like the student-council president and the editor of the school newspaper. They're in power positions the Wickeds would want to control." She pulled out those two, plus a few other Reggies in key positions, and lined them up along the left edge of the board. "But the strategy falls apart there. Not every target is a power player at school."

Maybe that was our problem. We were looking for an explanation that would justify every target.

"If it's true targeting instead of random bullying, there's got to be a reason for it. But it doesn't have to be the same reason for everyone, right?" I asked. "What does each of them have that the Wickeds want?"

Paige and I shuffled things around and looked for more groupings that seemed logical, but nothing gave us that "Aha!" moment we were looking for.

What made the girls desirable targets if they didn't hold a position of power? "What about connections to high levels that *aren't* targets?" If you couldn't get to the person you wanted, getting to a person close to them would be the next best thing, right?

Paige pulled a clipboard off the wall that contained more detailed profiles of each target. She flipped some pages, nodded, flipped some more. A slow smile spread across her face. "You might be on to something."

"Yeah?" My face broke into a grin. There was nothing a good math puzzle couldn't fix.

Paige wrote KEY PLAYERS above the first column of people she'd lined up on the left. Next to that she wrote KEY FRIENDS and moved nearly a dozen targets to the new column.

"If you're right, that means they're definitely targeting the power positions first. Either directly targeting those people or targeting people close to them as a way of getting to them indirectly." Paige beamed at me. "First day on the job and already putting the pieces together. Throw in a confirmation of what they're targeting Heather about, and you've got a game changer on your hands."

* * *

By the time Thursday night rolled around, I was pretty far gone. I'd already done the new-Jess look twice—using two of my best outfits from the mall—and it hadn't been enough to keep me out of the corner in Ryan's life. If this was my last chance to cross the barrier of acceptance, I wasn't going down without a fight. Instead of fun-feminine-sporty, I'd shake it up a little and go for fun-*flirty*-sporty. *Flirty* was just *feminine* kicked up a few notches.

The doorbell rang, and I heard Dad answer, the male voices drifting upstairs as I swept one last brush of powder over my cheeks and kissed my charm bracelet for good luck. I headed downstairs, and we made a quick escape when I saw Mom waddling forward for the Great Date Intercept. After the less-than-stellar first date and my Chunky Monkey woes, Mom wasn't exactly thrilled about the idea of round two.

"You look amazing," Ryan said, letting go of my hand to open the car door. "I didn't plan anything fancy, though. Is miniature golf still okay?"

"Oh, this old thing," I joked, trying to climb into his white Escape as gracefully as possible without showing off my new undies. Fine, Kyra's flirty dress choice and two-inch wedge heels may have been a tad much for the occasion. "You don't like it?"

"It's great." Ryan's smile made it clear just how great. "But you don't have to dress up on my account. I think you look great no matter what you wear."

A nice sentiment, but I knew better. Even if he didn't know it himself.

The Fun Zone Family Fun Park is crammed with

everything from go-karts to batting cages, arcade games to a miniature golf course complete with a two-story waterfall. It's a couple towns over from Mt. Sterling, so I'd never been there before. The night wasn't too buggy, which meant that every rug rat in the tri-county area had begged to come out for a night of fun. Not exactly romantic.

It turned out Ryan was every bit as competitive as me. Not in an out-for-blood way, but in a fun, teasing kind of way. By the sixth hole, the competition was fierce, and I had my game face on. "If you hit it up the left side, it'll bounce off the clown's nose and shoot through the tunnel in his arm," I offered, as Ryan lined up his shot like Tiger Woods.

"And risk having it ricochet off the squirting flower on his suspenders?" He never took his eye off the ball. "Not a chance."

He hit a graceful shot up the right side. The ball rebounded off the back wall, hit the bounce peg in the middle, and made a clean shot into the tunnel. We leaned over the edge of the clown's bed and watched it shoot out the tunnel and straight for the—

"Hole in one!" Ryan shouted, thrusting his putter to the sky.

"Lucky shot."

Ryan grinned. "Luck got me here with you tonight, so I'll take it." He helped me line up my shot, then stepped back. "I'd go a little more to the right if it were me. You may need to bend more so you can see straight up the clown's nose."

"I can see it fine." But I leaned over a little more, because he was kinda right. The heels were a definite disadvantage. "Better?"

He paused long enough that I glanced up to find him totally checking me out. *Clown's nose, my butt.*

Literally. That's what he was checking out. (My butt, not the clown's nose.) Fun-flirty-sporty? Score!

I opted for a banked shot that bounced around in the clown's leg and wobbled out onto the green below. I putted it in for two.

"Thirteen to thirteen," I said, picking my ball out of the cup. "Looks like we're evenly matched."

Ryan kissed the top of my head. "I wouldn't have it any other way."

I was lining up my shot at the pirate-ship hole when I heard someone call Ryan's name. I sighed and looked up, wondering who the intruder would be this time. For once, Ryan seemed genuinely pleased with the interruption.

The boy couldn't have been more than twelve, but he already had the makings of a heartbreaker. Adorable dimples, a charmer of a grin, and the kind of lanky walk where you knew he'd just hit a growth spurt.

He and Ryan fake-boxed a few moves before Ryan scruffed up the kid's hair. The boy looked back and forth between us. "Sorry. I didn't know you were on a date."

"Matt Taylor, meet Jess Parker."

Matt ambled over and shook my hand, a firm handshake and good eye contact that would make him aces with a girl's dad someday. "Nice to meet you, Jess. Is he treating you okay?" he asked, with a nod in Ryan's direction. He rubbed his hands together. "I can rough him up for you if you need me to."

"Save it for someone your own age, Romeo," Ryan mocked. He gave Matt a joking punch on the arm. "This one's taken."

*Faint. I feel faint.*

Matt pretended to be insulted, then grinned like the kid

he was. Oh, boy, the girls were going to love him in a few years. Although if they were half as boy crazy as I'd been they probably already did.

Ryan and Matt exchanged a few more playful barbs as the people behind us came up to wait their turn at our hole. We stepped aside to let them play through. Ryan and Matt leaned their heads together for a minute, did some kind of guy bump-bump-pop handshake thing, and Matt waved a friendly good-bye.

Ryan helped me off the tee area to give the other players more room. I leaned close to Ryan's ear, his warm hunky scent filling my lungs. "He's adorable. Is he your neighbor?"

Ryan kept his eye on the players, obviously trying to get tips on how to beat me on the hole. I wasn't sure he'd even heard me until he bent down toward my ear. "I'm his mentor."

"You're a mentor?" Could he *be* any more Charming? "That's awesome. Especially with school and football and working two jobs."

Ryan shrugged off the compliment. "He's a good kid—just has a rough home life. He's an only child, so I'm more like a big brother."

"Well, I think it's really cool." How many times had I wished for a big sister to talk to? Yet another reason I was grateful for Sarah Jane.

Ryan still wasn't looking at me, so I turned his head. "You're my hero, Ryan Steele."

Big mistake. We'd been whispering, so our heads were close together. Now our faces were inches apart. His lips were so close I lost my breath, prayed he'd lean in. But one look in his eyes, at the pain there, and I knew something was wrong. His blue eyes pierced mine, and he closed them before kissing me on the forehead. "You're up, Equal Girl."

It took a few more holes for the tension to ease. I'd never been more grateful for the easy banter and playful rivalry. The last thing I wanted to do was smack down the magic.

We ended up tying after twelve holes—25 to 25—which seemed a fitting end to the game. Ryan handed our clubs and balls to the attendant, then treated us to the massive Winner's Circle sundae, a mountain of ice cream large enough to hide small children. Only on a date could you eat dessert before dinner and not feel the slightest bit guilty. Would the perks never end?

We opted for one sundae and two spoons and took it outside to the bench by the go-kart track. I had the bowl balanced on my lap, Ryan had his arm around my shoulder, and every few bites our spoons would click together. He had to lean in to me so he didn't drip ice cream on my dress or his pants. It made my insides zing every time he did. Every time, like clockwork.

Tick, tock, *zing*. Tick, tock, *zing*.

If I were that kind of girl (and by *that kind of girl* I mean Fake Blondie), I would've ditched the sundae and pulled him into the bushes next to the parking lot. But of course, I'm the polar opposite of that kind of girl, so I kept the ice-cream bowl on my legs and suppressed shivers each time he leaned in.

When we reached the bottom of the huge bowl, we headed for the car to get to the lake before the hot-dog vendor closed up for the night. Not that I was hungry anymore, but an evening stroll by the lake with Ryan? Sign me up.

We'd parked near the road, and I stood unusually close to Ryan, hoping for a kiss before he deposited me in the car. Unfortunately, Ryan had better control than I had—or didn't feel the same urges I did—so I sat down feeling like I'd somehow failed a test. Should I have made the first move? Was the new Jess a first-move kind of girl?

He stepped back and swung the door closed as a dark blur shot past us, heading straight for the main road. I thought it was a dog, but before I'd even registered that it was a tiny rug rat, Ryan was sprinting after it.

Everything froze for a second, then seemed to go in slow motion. The little boy running through the grass next to the gravel road, the semi coming over the hill at the other end of the complex, the mother's screams from the parking lot. Ryan trying to close the gap in time. I watched the disaster unfold like a movie. Fear paralyzed me, rooting my butt to the seat as the truck came barreling toward them.

The boy stumbled as he reached the gravel, the movement enough to catch the driver's eye. The horn blared and the brakes squealed as the truck's back end shuddered with the abrupt change in momentum. Ryan lunged to scoop his arms under the boy and yanked, pulling the boy to his chest as they tumbled sideways onto the grass. The truck swerved, spitting gravel up over them, and finally came to rest on the shoulder farther down.

Ryan lay on his back, his chest rising and falling in rapid succession. The boy looked into Ryan's eyes, cheeks quivering, and promptly burst into hysterics. Ryan tucked him into his chest as he regained his breath, then pushed off the ground with one hand.

With that simple move, everything broke loose.

The driver jumped out of the truck and rushed over, two terrified parents descended on the grass, and a dozen bystanders mobbed Ryan and the boy. The boy's mother clutched her son for dear life, crying as loudly as her kid, while the father pumped Ryan's hand until I thought it would fall off from sheer force. The mother grabbed Ryan's arm and drew him into a crushing hug, nearly smothering the poor child·in the process.

Mayhem ensued as people comforted the parents, scolded the driver (who hadn't done anything wrong), and drew even more onlookers to the road. The scene amassed such a giant crowd I couldn't even see Ryan anymore. Once again, he was surrounded by the adoring masses.

Tears streaked down my cheeks as I thought about what could've been. What would've been if I'd made the first move. Thank God for my uncertainty. All things for a reason, even if we couldn't see it at the time.

I had just started wondering if I should go over or wait until things settled down when the driver's-side door opened. Ryan ducked into the car and quietly closed the door, shaking his head firmly when I opened my mouth to speak. Not that any words would've come out anyway.

He backed out carefully and took the far exit. I didn't fully realize what had happened until I saw the parents emerge from the throngs of people, looking everywhere.

Life was so tenuous, so fragile. Fifteen seconds could change a life forever. Ryan knew that better than anyone. The lives of those three people—a nameless mother, father, and little boy—were forever indebted to one person. A seventeen-year-old guy who'd slipped away like a shadow.

Ryan stared straight ahead and took back roads to the lake, never looking back and never saying a word.

# Chapter 14

AFTER FINDING ONE LONE HOT-DOG CART still open for business and loading up with ketchup and mustard, we wandered down the boardwalk skirting the lake. The sun dipped low on the horizon as we settled under a tree. I picked at my food, not because I was full from the ice cream—even though I was—but because neither of us had broached the topic hanging in the air.

I watched him polish off his second hot dog. Saving lives must make a person hungry. "That was pretty incredible," I said. The ultimate understatement.

Ryan gazed out over the lake, seeming a million miles away. "It was . . . I don't know what."

I couldn't imagine what it felt like to save the life of another human being. The rush of adrenaline, the relief. The what-ifs plagued my mind. What if the boy had run by an empty car instead of ours? What if we hadn't seen him run by? What if Ryan hadn't gotten there in time?

What if he'd leaned in for the kiss?

"You saved his life, Ryan."

He stayed silent, eyes focused on the lake.

"You're a—"

"Don't," he said sharply. He looked at me and softened, brushing my hair off my forehead in a way that was so intimate, and so sweet. "Right place, right time. I got lucky."

Every time I thought I understood him, he mystified me. "Why do you downplay it? It's not like you can hide from being a hero."

"I'm not hiding from anything." His anger snapped at me again. "And I don't play the hero game."

I thought about the agony in those parents' faces, the joy when they had their son safely back in their arms. "Why can't you just admit you did a good thing?"

He pulled me up to stand close to him. "I'm sorry. It's a sore subject, okay? Let's go for a walk."

I gathered up our trash to pitch. Ryan slipped his hand in mine, linking our fingers together in the fit I'd so quickly grown accustomed to. I wondered if there was a guys' equivalent to ISIS. If there was, it would be a sin if Ryan wasn't destined for it.

The boardwalk went all the way around the back of the lake except for the sandy beach area, which had already started to clear out. We walked in synch, our feet moving in an even, unhurried rhythm. Ryan planted a kiss on the top of my head, and I felt him relax for the first time since we'd left the Fun Zone.

He pointed out where he and Dale used to fish when they were kids. Where they'd spied on Cassie getting her first kiss (then followed her around for a week calling her Goose Lips).

We stopped at a secluded section of the boardwalk and watched the sun as it touched the horizon. Ryan snuggled in behind me and put his arms on either side to grasp the railing. The sky glowed with honeyed hues of pink and red, and I leaned back into his warmth, tuning into the quiet evening sounds and the solid feeling of being with Ryan. Just being.

The sun slipped from view, and Ryan nuzzled my temple with his jaw, a tiny bit of stubble abrading my skin. "This feels right," he whispered.

A sigh escaped my lips as he turned me toward him. His eyes were deep and intense, and I lost myself in them, in the moment, in Ryan.

"You make me feel alive, Jess." He slid his fingers along my neck and wove them through my hair. "I can't get enough of you."

His lips were gentle as they found mine, but when he angled my head, the kisses went deeper, pulling every sensation out of me. Our tongues found each other, wove together in a slow dance. He slid a hand behind me to cushion where I leaned against the railing. His other hand caressed my neck, his thumb grazing tiny circles that turned my skin to flame.

It was well after dark when the kisses became shorter and lighter, and Ryan finally set me away from him. His eyelids were heavy and hooded, matching the rush of emotions I felt in my chest, and I knew it had cost him. The realization made me feel vulnerable and thrilled. And cherished. Very, very cherished.

We took our time walking back toward the car, my head resting on his shoulder and our fingers laced together in perfect harmony.

We drove home in companionable silence, my hand missing the intimate contact with his but my mind relieved that he was a careful driver. Which made me think of his mom. "I know I already said this, but I'm sorry about your mom," I said into the dark.

The oncoming headlights cast his face in shifting shadows.

I saw him swallow. He reached for my hand and planted a soft kiss on my palm. "Thanks."

When we got to my house, the walk to the door was so different from last time. Standing on the porch, awash in bright parental-induced light, he touched his forehead to mine. "See me again."

"Will you be at the banner party?" I'd been crossing my fingers since Sarah Jane had mentioned that the football team usually made an appearance at the cheerleaders' annual banner-making shindig on Sunday.

"I have to work the whole weekend." He nuzzled my ear. "I definitely want to see you again, though. In private."

"I'm working Monday and Tuesday. Tuesday night?"

He groaned and placed my palm on his chest. I felt his heartbeat beneath my fingertips, the quick rhythm almost matching my own.

"That's so long. But I'll take what I can get." He lifted my hand to his lips. "Don't forget about me before then, okay?"

I smiled, feeling the distinct sensation of getting pulled under by something that felt a lot like love. "Ditto."

He smiled and dropped my hand as he stepped back onto the path, waiting for me to go inside. I turned inside the doorway and blew him a kiss before closing the door.

Mom stood in the archway separating the kitchen from the hall, a mug of hot cocoa warming her hands. She took one look at me and gave a fleeting smile. "Is he The One?"

"I hope so."

She nodded her head and blew on the steaming mug. "God help us."

* * *

I took the most luxurious bath imaginable, indulging in two of Mom's fizzy apricot tabs and a full cap of my almond oil bubble bath. I rested my head on the spa pillow and replayed every minute of our date (okay, I replayed the kissing part several times) until the water was lukewarm and Mom was knocking to ask if I was a prune yet.

By the time I'd dried off, I was completely exhausted, exhilarated, and on emotional overdrive. It would be Tuesday before I managed to get any sleep, at the rate I was going. I turned on my computer to see if Sarah Jane had e-mailed the schedule for our next few practices. Ever on the ball, she had. I just hoped Lexy wouldn't be at all of them.

I scanned the junk that had snuck through my spam filter, deleting it before closing down. My cursor hovered over Shut Down when an IM popped up.

> First&Goal: tuesday's too long i... i'll find a way to be there on sunday

My butterflies fluttered their approval. Definitely The One.

> WillCheer4Food: that would be awesome ☺
> First&Goal: i don't think i can sleep tonight
> First&Goal: will u be up for a while?

Mom knocked, and I closed my laptop.

"We're going to bed, honey. I'm glad you had fun on your date." She shuffled over and brushed the bangs off my forehead in her Mom-ish way, so different than when Ryan had done it. "How did you manage to grow up so fast?"

*I didn't. You just weren't paying attention.*

I gave her a break, thinking about Mrs. Steele. "Get some sleep for the little guys."

Mom's hand supported her back as she made her way

to the door. "I would if they'd stop playing soccer with my bladder."

"Yuck, Mom. TMI."

"I'll try to keep the *I* to myself. Oh, can you help me pick out a rocking chair for the twins' room tomorrow? I thought you'd want a say, since you'll be helping out with feedings."

The feeding thing was news to me, and I felt the lingering resentment simmering in my stomach. *I'm not the hired help,* I wanted to say. "I already have plans. You can pick out whatever you want."

"I wanted you to be comfortable in it too." She leaned against the doorframe. "You're gone so much lately. I feel like I never get to see you."

Except when she needed me to do something for the babies. "That's because I finally have a life." It came out like a dig, even though I tried to keep my tone in check. "I'm happy. Can't you just be happy for me too?"

"I'm always happy if you're happy, Jess. How could you ever think I'm not? I know we haven't always . . ."

Her voice drifted away, cutting off this line of questioning, and I breathed a tiny sigh of relief. This wasn't the time.

Mom turned and waddled out the door, looking sad. "Not too late," she reminded me, and clicked the door closed.

I listened to her feet retreat down the hall.

WillCheer4Food: sorry. parents are off to bed.
First&Goal: can i call u?
First&Goal: i want to hear your voice
WillCheer4Food: sure

I grabbed my cell and flicked it to stealth mode right before it started to vibrate. I went into my closet and camped out on the floor so I wouldn't disturb the parental sleeping beauties. "Hey."

"Hey, beautiful." I could hear the smile in his voice. "Am I crazy to be calling?"

Calling this late? Calling this soon? Calling at all? Why were guys so cryptic???

"I'm glad you did," I said. "I had fun tonight."

"Me too. Our dates are so different."

"Well, yeah, unless you save people's lives every time." I said it without thinking and smacked my forehead for being such an idiot. "Sorry. I know you don't want to talk about it."

"I do." He sounded sad. "I just can't. Not right now."

"No problem." I changed the subject, and we started talking about football and school and summer jobs.

"Why do you work so much?" I wondered aloud. "I mean, it's great, but . . . you know."

"Know what?"

How could I say it without sounding snobby? "Well, I mean, I've been to your house. I figured kids who live in houses like that, and whose dads are orthopedic surgeons, wouldn't have to work two jobs."

Ryan considered that. "I don't have to, I guess. But I want to. I need to. For me, I mean. I'm saving up for something."

"A car?" Now, that I could understand.

"Sort of, yeah."

"Me too. Though at the rate I'm going, I'll be out of college by the time I scrape together enough for something that's not a complete embarrassment." I settled back against the wall, propping my feet on the shoe boxes I'd lined up neatly along the floor. "What kind of car do you want? Isn't the Escape yours?"

"They're more like community cars in my family, but I usually get dibs on it. The one I'm saving for is a vintage Mustang. My mom's favorite."

I couldn't fathom what it would be like to lose my mom. All the attention she was heaping on the twins' arrival might've been getting under my skin, but I couldn't imagine life without her. "Do you miss her a lot?"

"All the time." I heard him shift and figured he was on his bed. "She painted a picture right before she died. I have it in my room, so it's the last thing I see every night."

"The dandelion," I said, as much to myself as to him.

Long pause. "How did you know?"

*Oh, crap!* I almost did another forehead smack but heard a grin in his voice. "Have you been in my room, Jess?" he teased.

"It was maybe a teeny-weeny little peek at the overnight," I said, feeling my face flush. "I didn't go in or anything, but your door was open, and—"

"It's okay." Ryan chuckled. "It's kinda cool, actually. Now I can lie here on my bed and imagine you standing in my doorway." I heard the mattress squeak and visualized him stretched out with his arms behind his head. "Oh, yeah. I can see me getting a lot of mileage out of that image."

My heart pitter-pattered at warp speed.

"What does your room look like?" he asked. "I want to picture it."

I leaned around the closet door and took in the apple-green walls, obnoxious flowered comforter from fifth grade, and ancient white wicker furniture. Even *I* didn't want to picture it. "It's very girly." *And babyish.* "It doesn't really fit me anymore, but I haven't gotten around to updating it. With all the moves, redoing my room was never a big priority."

"Yeah, I can see that. My mom was big into decorating. She'd make our room a project with us every few years to make sure it reflected our personality. She was big on 'the space makes the person' and all that."

*I bet I would've liked her.* "What does your room say about you?"

I pictured him looking around his room, taking it in with fresh eyes, as I'd done with mine. "It's calming. Just like she was. I can be sort of intense, so it works. I shut down when I get overwhelmed."

"You're hard to get to know."

"Am I?"

I nodded as though he could see me. "I feel like I catch these glimpses of you, but most of what I come away with is surface."

"Maybe it's better that way."

"Safer, maybe, but not better." *Wasn't it?*

"You really get to the heart of it, don't you?"

I cradled the phone on my shoulder and picked lint off my pink chenille robe. "I'm not big on games, I guess. Probably why I haven't dated."

"You haven't dated?"

I could *not* believe I'd said that out loud! The exhaustion and easy conversation had lulled me into a false sense of security, wreaking havoc on my brain. "Well, plus, I move a lot, so it's hard to get to know people." Plaster that neon LOSER sign to my chest, thanks.

"Wow." This news clearly blew him away. Nothing like clueing in a potential boyfriend that no one else wants you. At least I hadn't mentioned that I'd pseudo-dated once. That debacle was the last thing Ryan needed to know about.

"Wow," he said again. "That's—"

*Loserish.*

"—pretty cool," he finished. "We're going through this together."

*In what universe?* "You've had a million girlfriends. And that's just since I moved here."

"That was harsh. I'm not a player, Jess."

"I didn't mean it like that. But you're a lot more experienced than I am."

"Not when there's a connection like this. That's a first for me. It's like . . ."

I thought of that scene in *Sleepless in Seattle* that always made Mom cry. "Magic."

"What?"

Had I said *that* out loud too?! "Huh? Nothing. Just a yawn." *Must shut mouth!*

"Magic," he said, trying it on for size. "Yeah."

My skin tingled all the way to my toes.

I heard Ryan yawn, which made me yawn for real this time. "I'm glad you were still awake," he said. "I never get tired of talking to you."

"Same here." I could talk to Ryan for hours. "I'm glad you called."

"Me too. I have to get up early for work, so I'd better get going," he said, his reluctance obvious enough to make me smile through my disappointment. "But Jess?"

"Yeah?"

"I hope you dream about the lake."

# Chapter 15

**AFTER A LONG NIGHT** spent beating myself up for admitting I was the Dateless Wonder to the first guy to take an interest in me since Dan had shown up in our old backyard for a game of Frisbee, I was pretty much the walking wounded by the time Mom and I waddled into the yuppie-mom heaven known as Babies "R" Us. Things had been going so great until I'd spilled about my lack of dating savvy. Why couldn't I be smooth with guys? Just one time?

To top it off, now I was stuck in my personal version of Hades. The land of babies and pregnant women with impossible-to-predict mood swings. Yes, I'd been the one to suggest the outing as a bribe for not making it home for dinner in the early days of my *CMM* work. But now . . . now I could see the error of my ways. I'd thought it would just appease her. Instead, she saw it as me taking an active interest in preparing for the babies.

The fatal flaw in my plan had been revealed.

First, we hit the ever-important rocking chairs. Two full rows of them lined up like an assembly line for moms-to-be, putting mine over the edge. A woman who was once famous for her brilliant snap decisions was reduced to an indecisive mess.

"I like the blue and the beige," she said, running her hand over the twill cushions. "But should we get two of the same or one of each?"

*This is my penance.* "Whatever you want," I said, forcing a smile. I propped my feet up on a footrest and discovered it moved just like the glider. Cool, not that I'd point it out to Mom.

She walked halfway down the aisle in the other direction. "I like the natural wood finish, but I don't know if it's too light. They don't make a rocking chair that coordinates with the other furniture I chose, so I'm not sure if I should coordinate or go with something that's different."

"They're babies, Mom. Do you really think they'll care?"

"Of course they won't. But other people will see it when they come to see the babies."

"Like who?"

As soon as it was out there, I regretted it. Nan had been trying to convince Mom to move back to Mt. Sterling for years, but Mom's high-school days were something she'd rather forget. Her friends had been kids like her, the ones totally rebelling against their hippie parents. Just like Mom, they scattered to the winds after graduation. Unlike Mom, they hadn't returned twenty years later to raise a family in their hometown when—surprise, surprise!—they ended up pregnant with twins at age thirty-nine.

Talk about a major life shake-up. Mom and Nan might not always get along, but when you're closing in on forty with two babies on the way, I guess you need all the help you can get.

So here we were, in the house Mom grew up in so Nan could downsize into something that required less upkeep. And here Mom was . . . pregnant, not working, and trying to put down roots for the first time in her adult life. She'd been trying so hard to make the house feel like home (a real and true *home*, which was a novelty for us, with our transient ways) that she hadn't gotten out to meet people. I could count on one hand the number of visitors other than Nan that we'd had since we'd moved here.

"I mean, how many people are going to go into the nursery?" I said, trying to cover. "Don't you usually bring the babies down to show people?"

"Not if they're sleeping."

"If they're sleeping, the lights will be low. Who's going to notice if the rocking chairs coordinate?"

Logic was still the best way to get Mom back on track when hormones got in her way. She thought that over. "So you think one of each in the darker wood?"

"Sounds groovy." Mostly, it sounded like a decision that put us one step closer to getting out of there.

We wandered over to the changing tables. She'd already chosen one, so that saved us time. But now she was considering the options for covering the changing pad. Knit fabric or terry cloth? Or maybe a cute yellow gingham? One gingham and one stripe?

All for something the babies would end up rubbing their bare butts all over.

I was counting the minutes until I could get back to the Club and figure out how in the heck to defeat Lexy and the Wickeds while saving Heather. But yeah, let's debate the pros and cons of poly-cotton knit over cotton terry.

Mom seemed to sense my waning enthusiasm and shifted

her attention to me. She brushed my hair out of my eyes. "I like how you've been keeping your hair down," she said. "These lights really pick up the highlights in it. Where did you say you got it done?"

*At a place you can't get into without a gold coin you definitely don't have.*

I knew it wasn't her fault she wasn't a Cindy. But it didn't make it okay. Innocent questions and no way to answer them without lying were turning me into a very stressed girl. I needed to figure out which Cindys didn't have Cindy moms and see what they told their parents. Gaby's mom wasn't a Cindy—her sister wasn't, either—so I'd start with her. I hated lying to Mom, but I felt stuck in the middle between family and Sisterhood.

"It's this place where Sarah Jane goes. Do you have everything you need here?" I rolled the shopping cart out into the main aisle as a hint. "I think the lights are giving me a headache."

She put her hand on my forehead. "Do you think you're coming down with something? Maybe you shouldn't go in to work today."

"It's just a headache. Fluorescent lights do that to me sometimes."

Mom went back to the rocking chairs and pulled tags for the ones she wanted. I used the lights as an excuse to wait outside in the sunshine. My head did hurt, but the lights weren't to blame.

I found a wooden bench in a courtyard and planted myself there to wait. They'd probably installed it for all the soon-to-be-dads who had to escape their pregnant, hormonally insane wives while they discussed the merits of the Diaper Monster versus the Diaper Annihilator.

Ten long minutes later, the stock guy was helping us load up the minivan with this week's haul. I'd survived, and I even managed to finagle a lunch out of it at my favorite chain restaurant across the parking lot.

We walked over, much slower than normal because of Mom's sore back, and out of the corner of my eye, I caught movement behind the bushes. I circled around to Mom's other side and saw Leah Michaels crouched down behind the row of hedges lining the restaurant sidewalk. She was staring at Corrine Duncan, one of the nicest Reggies I knew, as Corrine got into the car of someone who was definitely not her boyfriend.

I told Mom I'd just seen a friend and would meet her inside the restaurant. She nodded, still muttering to herself about swollen ankles and being on her feet all day. I waited until she rounded the front of the building before slipping around the other side.

I watched Corrine's date open her car door and help her into his Camaro. He went around to his side, and as they drove away, I saw Corrine lean her head on his shoulder. Just as Leah held her phone out and snapped a picture.

With the car safely out of sight, Leah got up from hiding and dialed a number. She paced along the sidewalk in the rear of the restaurant as she talked quietly on her cell. She made a couple of nervous gestures with her hands, then settled a bit as she listened to whoever was on the other end. Visibly relieved, she said a few more words and disconnected.

The wheels in my head turned as she got into her car and drove away. Corrine was nice, but she wasn't a power player that I knew of. And Leah definitely wasn't a Wicked. She was more of a loner like Heather.

If the Wickeds were using Reggies to get dirt on other

Reggies, they could expand their reach exponentially. No wonder they'd been able to take their game to the next level so quickly.

Double the Wickeds plus an entire network of spies at their disposal? It might just be a hunch, but my hunch was telling me things were about to get ugly in a hurry.

* * *

"Can you mind the counter while I take these boxes to the back?"

"No problem, Nan." I slid the duster into the basket under the cash register and plopped down on the stool as the bell above the door jingled.

An older guy came in, holding a small black notebook in his hand. "Is Rosemary around?"

"She's in the stockroom. Do you need me to—?"

"In here, Stan." Nan stuck her arm out the door and waved him back, her thin metal bracelets jangling.

With Nan in the back and no sign of Heather, my mind wandered to its usual place. *Welcome to the land of Ryan.* I knew I shouldn't get my hopes up, but I wanted Ryan to be at the banner party. It would be the first time we'd be together with our friends since we'd started dating. And I could say that now. I was dating Ryan Steele. In fact, I could say it over and over and never get bored.

I was dating Ryan Steele.

I was dating *Ryan Steele.*

As much as it gave me a case of the golden giddies just thinking about that fact, I wasn't sure if it qualified me as his girlfriend. We hadn't talked exclusivity or anything. But our late-night chat left me feeling like he wasn't interested in dating anyone else, so that had to be a good sign.

My butterflies gave a cheer.

"I haven't heard anything," Nan said as she and Stan came out of the stockroom a few minutes later, "but I'd rather you leave that business to the police and write something positive for a change."

"Reporting the news is my job, Rosemary. Not all news is rosy." Stan rolled his eyes at me as if to say, *Women.* Like I wasn't one of them.

"More of it is than you print. Look at the boy Jessica is dating."

"Nan!" *Please don't print that I'm Ryan's girlfriend!*

Nan gave me a startled look. "It's a prime example of what I'm talking about. Jessica's date last night saved a little boy from being run over in the street. But did that make the front page?"

"At the amusement park?" He shrugged. "We ran that one, but the rescuer wasn't identified. You know him?"

"Ryan Steele," Nan said. "His mother, Elizabeth, was killed at the corner of Green and Main a few years back."

"Sure. I know the Steeles. Ryan's the quarterback over at the high school." Stan turned to me, suddenly interested. "You're his girlfriend?"

"We're just friends," I clarified, nailing Nan with a glare. "But Nan's right about last night. It was at the Fun Zone."

I relayed the story as I remembered it. It still stung that I hadn't been able to get Ryan to feel good about what he'd done. Shouldn't he trust my opinion more? If enough other people supported him, maybe he'd finally accept that it was okay to be a hero. The world needed more guys like Ryan Steele.

"Sounds like a good kid," Stan said, his pen scribbling on the pad. "Anything else I should know?"

I scrunched up my nose at him, even though I knew it was

rude (and not very flattering). "Isn't that enough?"

He looked at Nan and laughed. "Like grandmother, like granddaughter." He flapped his pad at us. "Thanks for the tip, ladies. You let me know if you hear anything about the shoplifting ring."

Nan patted my shoulder as he left. "Some people need to be trained to see the good that's around them. You remember that, Jessica. All it takes is a little redirecting of their energy and"—she snapped her fingers—"magic."

I thought of Ryan. *Magic.*

✳ ✳ ✳

With Nan back out on the floor, I excused myself to finish dusting and take out the trash. I'd just tied the bag and dragged it to the back door along with the broken-down boxes for recycling when I heard a scuffle outside.

I looked through the peephole Nan had installed for safety and saw Lexy, Tina, and Morgan. I so did not want to deal with them today. I looked to the side to see what they were focused on—

*Oh, no.*

I reached for the handle to put a stop to it once and for all.

"What do you mean you won't tell us?" Lexy barked at Heather. "Who put *you* in charge?"

Heather was standing up to Lexy? *You go, girl!*

I plastered my ear against the door, not wanting to save a girl who was ready to save herself. I could hear Heather sobbing. "He'll hate me."

"You should've thought about that before you went slumming with a freakin' *janitor*, Clark Bar."

I gave Lexy the evil eye through the peephole, my hand on the doorknob in case Heather needed me.

Heather straightened as the tears continued to fall. "I won't let you do this anymore. What you saw was a private thing between two people. A *private* thing," Heather argued, and I pumped my fist in the air at her nerve. "It was an innocent kiss and a mistake. You have no right to use it as blackmail!"

"Is that right?" Lexy smirked. She reached into her shocking pink bag. "Doesn't look so innocent to me."

Heather took the large envelope Lexy shoved in her face and pulled out some sheets of paper. Heather's face crumpled, and her body followed, sliding down the side of the steel dumpster until she was sobbing and hugging her knees to her chest.

"You didn't think he actually liked you, did you?" Tina jeered. "He only liked the hundred bucks." Morgan laughed along with her.

Lexy plucked the papers from Heather's hand and slid them back into her bag. "Do we have a deal?"

Heather rocked back and forth. She nodded in response and wiped her nose on her sleeve.

"That's what I thought. Keep your cell on."

I waited until Lexy, Tina, and Morgan had disappeared before yanking open the door and dragging Heather inside. Makeup ran down her face, and she was crying so hard I was afraid she'd start dry-heaving. I pulled her straight into the tiny break room, giving Nan a quick *I'll explain later* look. I closed the door behind us, pulled out a chair for Heather, and set a box of tissues on the table. I grabbed a chair for myself and hunkered down to wait.

If you think there's a limit to the amount of liquid a human tear duct can produce, let me clear that up for you. Heather cried so long and so hard, going through eleven tissues (not that I was counting), that she could have filled a two-liter bottle.

Her tears finally ebbed to a trickle, her sobs more like hiccups. She blew her nose, a couple of hard toots that would've made me laugh if she hadn't been such a mess. She took one deep breath, then another. The firestorm had subsided. It was time.

"Do you want to talk about it?"

She sniffed and hiccuped, and her voice caught when she tried to speak. I thought we were in for a fresh parade of tears, but Heather pulled it together enough to shake her head.

I reached across the small table to squeeze her hand, making sure it was the one without the tissue. "I can't help if you don't tell me what's going on."

She exhaled on a long breath that sounded eerily like her soul deflating. "You can't help me anyway."

"You don't know that."

She looked up at me, smeared mascara circling her eyes like a raccoon mask, and my heart gave a little tug on her behalf. She looked lost.

I waited.

She shredded the tissue in her hand, then a second. Another long-suffering sigh. She balled up the tissue confetti and threw it back on the table. "I didn't mean for it to happen."

Finally, an opening. "But it did?"

"Cameron and I were fighting. I thought we were breaking up."

"Cameron?"

"My boyfriend."

I remembered reading about him in Heather's file in the War Room. Cameron was one of the few people listed in the Support Network box on Heather's profile, but I hadn't realized they were an official couple. "Cameron Cole is your boyfriend?"

"You sound surprised."

"Not at all. I just didn't know you guys were exclusive. Cameron seems pretty cool."

"He and his dad don't get along. That's how we started talking. We bonded over alcoholic dads and moms out of the picture. Romantic, huh?"

"Not the greatest way to build a relationship?"

"It is what it is. Things with Cameron were going great until he and his dad started fighting about the money Cam was making playing gigs with the band. Cam wants to save it to get his own place, and his dad wants it for 'the house.' That's alkie speak for *booze*." She shifted in her seat, her hands gathering the tissues into a neat pile. "Cam's been getting more and more distant. He won't talk to me about what's wrong, and we had a big blow-up about some stupid concert tickets." She shook her head. "And then he was there."

"Cameron? Or his dad?"

"Rick." She looked like she was going to be ill. "Janitor Joe's assistant?"

Oh. *Ohhhhhh.*

"He's not that much older than us, you know. And he was so nice, and he listened and said all the right things. I didn't mean for it to happen."

*Janitor, mistake, blackmail evidence. Oh, crud.*

"You and Rick got together?"

Heather nodded.

"And Lexy saw."

Her head bobbed like a marionette.

*Double crud.*

"At first she was going to tell Cameron unless I did what she wanted. But it turns out she has pictures too." Heather fisted away a fresh batch of tears. "It makes it look a lot worse than it was. We only kissed under the bleachers, but the angle of the pictures makes it look like he was lying on top of me. There's no way Cam's gonna listen to my side when he sees those."

I gritted my teeth, wanting a piece of Lexy more than ever.

"I thought Rick would support me in standing up to them," Heather went on. "And to tell Cameron the truth."

"But he didn't."

Heather shook her head and the tears started anew. "It was all a lie." She hiccuped. "They paid him to do it."

A setup, heinous and premeditated, to get a Reggie under their thumb. It was one thing catching other people's mistakes in action. But to purposely set someone up to try to get dirt on her? The Wickeds were pure evil.

"Did you see her take the picture?"

"I didn't see anyone. Nichele Stanton was hanging around for a while, but I didn't see her afterward."

Nichele definitely wasn't in with the Wickeds. It was possible she could be a target, but I figured it was more likely that a Wicked had been lurking nearby. The Wickeds were master lurkers when they wanted to be.

I squeezed Heather's wrist for reassurance, trying to figure out how to help. "What are you gonna do about Cameron?"

This was clearly the wrong question since it prompted more tears.

"Sorry, you don't have to tell me. But Heather?" I waited

until her bloodshot eyes met mine. "What does Lexy want from you?"

I watched as her mind slowly reengaged. "She wants me to give her opinions."

Lexy asking other people's advice? That didn't compute. "What kind of opinions?"

"Weird stuff. Like she wants me to picture things and tell her what I see. Or hold a piece of something and tell her what I think about it."

I'd been around enough of Nan's clients to know a gift when I saw it. "Are you a clairvoyant?"

"More of an intuitive. I don't see ghosts or the future or anything. I just get a sense of things sometimes." She paused thoughtfully. "My mom had a real gift. She used to help the police with cases and stuff. Before she died."

Guilt about my constant annoyance with Mom ate away at me. I needed to give her a five-alarm hug when I got home. "I'm sorry about your mom, Heather."

"She died when I was born, so I never knew her. People tell me I look like her, though." She smiled, a tiny crack in her misery. Then her face fell. "I don't know how they even knew about the intuitive thing. It's not like I go around advertising it. Besides, I can't even control it. Sometimes I get little glimpses, and other times, nothing."

"Did it work for Lexy?"

A light glinted in Heather's eyes. "Not usually. And even when it did, I didn't tell her. I just made it up as I went along."

I couldn't help it. I burst out laughing. Ten points to the Reggies.

Heather laughed too, and it felt good to let loose for a minute. We laughed harder than we really needed to, but it was more of an emotional release mixed with a mini-celebration of finally getting one over on the Wickeds.

When the laughter subsided, we sobered up again. "So," I said, drumming my fingers on the Formica tabletop, "what happens next?"

"I think Lexy's on to me. She thinks I've been sending her on a wild goose chase, so she said she's gonna test me." She shuddered. "There's something they want at school. I've figured out that much. Something under the school, I think, but that doesn't make sense." Heather focused on a point near the microwave like she was trying to picture something in her mind. "I can't quite get it. But whatever they want, they want it bad. The look she gets in her eye when she thinks I've given her a lead gives me the heebies."

I thought about the day after cheer practice. The excitement on Lexy's face had given me the heebies too.

"Even if I could help her, I couldn't live with myself if I used my . . ."

"Gift?"

"It sounds weird to say that. Like I'm a circus act or something. I'm always afraid people will run away screaming."

"Have you forgotten where I work?" I deadpanned.

That earned an honest chuckle from Heather. "I couldn't live with myself if I used it to help someone like Lexy. That would be like spitting on my mom's grave."

"What if you don't help her?"

"She'll give the pictures to Cameron."

I sighed. "You need to tell him, Heather."

"I know. I just don't know how."

I couldn't imagine how I'd feel if Ryan ever cheated on me, and I wasn't even sure we were boyfriend and girlfriend. I didn't envy Heather the job ahead of her. "If you tell him, the pictures have no meaning."

"If I tell him, our relationship has no meaning."

*Touché*. "I'm here if you need me, okay?" I jotted down my cell number on a napkin. "Call me anytime."

"I wish I was more like you. The way you stand up to Lexy . . . you're a role model. And not just to me." She shook her head. "But you don't want a piece of this, Jess. You're already on her list."

I already had a piece of it. This was exactly what I needed to know to put the full weight of the Cindys behind me. As glad as I was that I'd achieved my mission and confirmed their blackmail scheme, knowing I could help Heather mattered more.

"Don't worry about me. Just watch your back where she's concerned, and call me if you need backup." I got up to go, since I was technically still on the clock. "There's a bathroom through there if you want to clean up. Take as much time as you need. My grandma won't care."

"Okay," Heather said, picking up her stack of tissues. "Jess?"

I paused at the door. "Yeah?"

"Thanks for listening. And for helping."

"That's what friends do."

# Chapter 16

**GRATEFUL FOR MY OFFICE,** I slid into the seat and exhaled a long breath. I was feeling guilty about having to cut my volunteer hours way back right when the Humane Society was gearing up for their big summer adoption event. I'd recruited Mel to come, and now I wasn't even going myself. Some example I set.

But I was already an assignment behind in my *CMM* because of work and my leader stuff plus the Heather mission on top of it. Most days, it felt like my head was spinning.

And that little tiny bit of brain space I had left over? That part was devoted to Ryan.

Or to Tina, more specifically, and the nagging suspicion that she might be right. That Ryan *didn't* want to be seen with me in public.

After moving past the disastrous meet-up at The Grind on our first date, things seemed to be going so well. Yet all of our bonding had happened off the beaten path. On IM or on the phone, we were golden. But that was private. He'd taken me to the Fun Zone, but that wasn't in Mt. Sterling. The only person we'd seen there was Matt. And at the lake, Ryan carefully kept us on the far side, away from the beach where everyone usually hung out.

I'd been trying to tell myself it was because Ryan wanted to be alone with me. But I couldn't shake the feeling that I wasn't measuring up. I might look better than I had, but I was no Fake Blondie.

*Not the time to dwell.* I shook my head to clear the woe-is-mes and pulled out the recruitment-surge file Paige had given me. I started jotting notes about what we knew for sure and what we suspected was true.

1. Doubling their new recruit class (strength in numbers)
2. Targeting people in key positions (either directly or by getting to someone close to them)
3. Getting the Reggies to do their dirty work (building spy network to boost intel?)

We were looking at the pieces—a lot of them, anyway—but something was still missing. The bigger plan of what they were trying to accomplish. Where did the recruitment surge fit in? Why the sudden need for extra Wickeds if they had spies doing their work for them?

Paige walked in, stopping short when she saw me at the desk. "I keep forgetting you might be in here."

"Sorry. I thought it was okay that we shared the office."

She opened a drawer and tossed in her purse. "No, it's fine. I'm just so used to coming in here when I need to regroup. It's nice to be able to close out the world when you need it."

I'd been an almost-leader for less than a week, and I could

already see where that would come in handy. "Want me to scat for a while?"

"Not on your life. You need to be here more than I do." She inclined her head toward my folder. "How's it coming along?"

"Slowly. It's hard, because I know some of the players but not all. I don't really understand how the Reggies operate."

She pulled up a chair next to me. "You've been to a lot of schools, so it's probably similar to what you're used to. The Reggies aren't one group—they're a community of little groups. *Community* isn't really the right word, though, because they rarely connect, thanks to the Wickeds. The Wickeds get antsy if any groups show signs of merging. Size matters to the Wickeds, in their own ranks and with the Reggies."

She flipped to a new page of my notebook and drew a diagram of the cafeteria. Just like at any school, mapping out the cafeteria was the easiest way to show how the groups split out. The drama club, student government, class leaders, athletes, brains, goths . . . the list went on and on. Her map looked slightly different from my lunch period, but the groups were mostly the same. Whether you were sophomores or seniors, groups were groups and cliques were cliques.

I tucked her map into the surge folder for future reference. Being an outsider might help in some ways, but it was hard to keep all the major players straight with a student body of a thousand and a half. All I wanted was to wrap up my mission and find my new comfort zone.

"Oh!" I dropped my pen—I'd nearly forgotten my good news. "Mission accomplished with Heather, *and* I've got intel about the Reggies."

"Really?" Paige opened the door to the War Room and pulled Sarah Jane away from her earbuds. I filled them in on what I'd seen at the restaurant.

Sarah Jane looked at Paige. "Any chance that's a one-time thing?"

"I'd be shocked it if were," Paige said. "It's a brilliant strategy for them. They can't be everywhere at once, but the Reggies can. We need to get a research team together for that."

"Why Corrine?" I asked.

We wandered around the War Room, talking about possible connections. The two columns Paige had separated out—*KEY PLAYERS* and *KEY FRIENDS*—were still there. No matter how hard we tried, we couldn't figure out where Corrine would fit in.

"Is she a threat to them?"

Sarah Jane gave a half laugh. "Corrine isn't a threat to anyone except for the Class Nicest award. She's friends with everyone."

Paige and I looked at each other. Could it be—?

"She's a floater," I said at the same time Paige said, "She's a connector."

"So it's not what she has—it's what she's capable of?" Sarah Jane asked.

Paige nodded. "Her strength is that she's easy to talk to and people respect her. She's one of the few people who could go back and forth between Reggie groups to connect them."

"So they're not just targeting people who have something they want," I said. "They're getting rid of anything that poses a threat."

I grabbed my notebook from the office. Two more pieces of the puzzle went on my list.

4. Keep the Reggies isolated
5. Eliminate any strength that poses a threat

Paige made another column on the board called *THREATS* as Sarah Jane passed her the cards for people with strengths that could threaten the Wickeds' power. People who were connectors (like Corrine), people known for voicing their opinions no matter what the opposition, go-getters who craved success the way the Wickeds craved power. If a target could change the status quo, she was a threat to the Wickeds. The status quo was their friend.

But Heather didn't fit in that category. Her strength wasn't a threat to the Wickeds; it was something they wanted to exploit. I added a sixth puzzle piece to my list.

6. Exploit any strengths that can be used to their advantage.

When they'd separated out everyone they could, Paige turned back to me. "That's huge stuff right there," she said. "All this and you got through to Heather too?"

I gave them the scoop about Heather's meltdown, leaving out the more personal details about her and Cameron bonding over their dads.

"I was worried it might be something like that," Paige said. "A few years ago, the Wickeds got a picture of someone in a compromising position with a substitute teacher."

Sarah Jane's eyes nearly popped out of her head. "A *teacher*? Geez, I'm naïve about people."

"Better naïve than photographed," I said. "Heather's pretty sure they're looking for something at school. Maybe under it? What would the Wickeds want underneath a school?"

Paige tapped her lower lip. "Nothing I'd give any merit to."

"Meaning?"

"There are rumors about a vault under the school, but no one's ever confirmed it."

I thought back to the day of the water-main break. Grandma Aniston showing up with Principal Zimmer and the other power women in tow. Lexy looking way too excited about the hole the workers dug before being turned away. Now it made sense. "Who fixed the water-main break?"

Paige sighed. "You don't have the clearance, Jess."

"Then what's in the vault?"

"No one knows," Sarah Jane chimed in. "But if the Wickeds are trying to find it . . ." She looked at Paige.

Paige shook her head. "I don't have that kind of clearance either. Let it go, Jess. You did good getting through to Heather. Now we know for sure that blackmail is part of their arsenal. That gives us more to go on."

I didn't agree it was enough *or* that I should drop it. "How can I not have clearance? I'm the new leader. You're the ones who gave me the mission in the first place." Did they choose me as the new leader because they thought they could use me as their puppet? That I'd do whatever they said, no questions asked, just because I was grateful to be selected in their big "break with tradition"?

"Yes, we did and, like you said, mission accomplished," Paige said. "There's more going on here than just your mission, Jess. If we're going to stop the Wickeds, we need to do it across the board. One person at a time won't get us there fast enough."

"But they still want Heather. Lexy said she's going to test her."

"That's Heather's cross to bear. You can't always fight other people's battles for them."

"But I can help. Isn't that the point?" I looked from one Sister to the other. "Or are we just doing spy work here?"

"Of course we want to help Heather," SJ soothed. "Paige just means we need to look at the big picture and figure out how best to do that."

*By sticking up for her, obviously.* Was I really the only one who saw that? "If we let them use Heather, they'll keep blackmailing other girls because they know they can. How many Reggies do they have to hurt before you step up?"

Sarah Jane tried to calm me down in her peace-and-light way, but Paige simply studied me like I was an experiment gone awry. When she spoke again, there was a hint of admiration in her voice laced with caution. "Don't get in deeper than you can get out of, Jess. There's only so much we can do to protect you."

Given Lexy's fascination with torturing me, that wasn't a news flash. "I'm not turning my back on Heather. If she needs me, I'm there."

"As long as you understand the consequences."

"Crystal clear."

Paige gave me a stiff nod and picked up her stuff to go to the lounge. Space was a good thing for both of us right then. If they gave me a mission, they needed to trust me to see it through and not run away at the first sign of trouble. And if they wanted me as their leader, they needed to know I wasn't going to back down from doing the right thing just because Paige wanted me to keep my nose clean.

Yes, I worried a little that I'd made her mad. I liked Paige.

But I had to think she'd have been disappointed if I'd let an innocent Reggie get hung out to dry. She would've taken the same stand, wouldn't she? Because if she wouldn't have . . .

I didn't even want to go down that road.

* * *

Sarah Jane set down the last of the paint buckets on a tarp covering the gym floor. We'd set up shop for the banner party there, and the other cheerleaders were starting to stream in. I dropped the box of paintbrushes with an echoing thud. "How exactly does this work?"

She had me unroll the giant paper, stopping every fifteen feet or so to let her cut the banners. Nichele, the awesome alternate, put the rocks we'd collected on the corners to keep them from rolling back up, and Kyra started outlining the slogans with a thick black marker.

"We can start painting as soon as Kee's done sketching the letters," SJ said. "We try to knock out as many banners as we can before the guys get here. Things usually get a little crazy after that."

The door burst open as Lexy dragged in a heavy tarp and positioned it along the far wall. It was the most work I'd seen her do since I'd moved to Georgia.

"We'll do a massive banner on that tarp." SJ gestured toward Lexy. "The football players put their handprints and signatures on it, and we fill in around it with markers."

A shiver ran down my spine in anticipation of seeing Ryan again. I *had* dreamed about the lake, the jerk. Not once, but twice. Talk about not wanting to wake up.

Kyra made quick work of the slogans, and we started working in groups of three or four on different banners. SJ, Kyra, and I huddled together to paint *Mt. Sterling ROCKS!* in a glossy rainbow of colors.

"So," Kyra said, way too casually. "Ben and I saw you and Ryan at the lake."

"Why didn't you say hi?" My voice gave nothing away. "I didn't see you."

Her auburn curls hung down, half hiding her grin, as she painted the exclamation point. "I'm not surprised."

My face flushed, and I shushed SJ and Kyra's laughter before they drew attention to us. Fortunately, everyone else was involved in their own chat fests and didn't notice my flaming glow.

I gave them the abbreviated version of our date. Very abbreviated.

"As long as he gave you a good-night kiss this time," SJ teased.

"Ryan's a great guy." Kyra dipped a brush into a container of vivid purple. "It's been a tough couple of years for him. I'm glad to see him happy."

"What was he like? After it happened?"

SJ's brush slicked a red ribbon of paint inside the M. "He never talked about the accident. Not to us, anyway. Mark said he never talked about it with him either."

"It's against the guys' code of silence." Kyra made a face as she swirled purple paint in the dot over the i. "It's like they think talking about something other than football will suck the testosterone out of them."

I painted the R in bright blue strokes and wondered if Ryan would talk to me about what happened. If I was his girlfriend—a yet unknown status—it seemed like he probably would. What kind of relationship would it be if we only shared the surface stuff?

All I knew about that day was that Lexy and her mom were driving in town the fall before last when a drunk driver ran a stop sign and hit the driver's side. Already drunk at five o'clock, and the driver walks away with barely a scratch. Lexy suffered a concussion and a broken arm, and Ryan's mom was killed instantly.

A life extinguished all because of someone's stupid buzz fix. I didn't know how Ryan could stand it.

I wanted to ask them more about the accident, but I didn't want to risk Lexy overhearing. Although when I looked around, Lexy had conveniently disappeared. Probably to take a spa day after doing five minutes of actual work. Nichele and Penny were left to paint the *Go–Fight–Win* sign by themselves.

Nichele looked much more relaxed with Lexy gone. I couldn't get Heather's comment out of my head: *I saw Nichele Stanton hanging around for a while.* Nichele would no more take a photo of Heather in a compromising position than I would. Then again, I would've said the same about Leah Michaels. With Nichele acting so nervous around Lexy, I couldn't rule out blackmail as a possibility.

I needed to catch her alone and pump her for information. As subtly as possible, of course.

We moved to a *Panther Pride—Catch the Fever* sign, and Sarah Jane eyed Kyra's giant bubble letters. "This would go faster with the wider brushes. Do we have any in Coach Trent's office?"

"I can check." I was starting to get antsy knowing the guys would be showing up soon. It would do me good to work off my nervous energy. Not nerves about seeing Ryan—those butterflies were in good shape—but nerves at how everyone would react to Ryan and me together. I'd never been on the social scene as part of a couple before. It was the ultimate moment of acceptance: when the whole world could see that someone chose *you* over everyone else.

I'd even dressed in a sparkly tank for the occasion. It was a little clingier than I was used to—more *sleek* than *sporty*, but they were in the same ballpark, I figured. I'd decided the occasion called for a little extra spice. I didn't want any of the Wickeds or Villains to think Ryan was settling for a frump.

I headed down the back hall and took the shortcut across the science wing to get to Coach Trent's office. I rounded the corner by the chem labs but pulled up short at a loud clattering in the janitor's closet.

"I swear to God, Lexy, if a mouse runs over my foot, I'm out of here."

*Lexy.* In the *janitor's closet*? I stepped back to look at the door plaque. Not janitor's closet, but electrical room.

"Keep your voice down, you idiot. Where's the light?"

A tiny strip of light peeked out from underneath the door.

"Lock the door and put the blueprints up here."

Their voices got quieter, and I strained my ears to pick up what I could. Science wing . . . bomb shelter . . . equipment room . . .

Blueprints of the school? This had to be about Heather's blackmail.

"That little witch sent us to an electrical closet!" Definitely Morgan's voice. I'd recognize that hiss anywhere.

The little witch had to be Heather. They were definitely on to her.

"She thinks she screwed us over," Lexy said, "but this might be exactly what we're looking for."

I pressed my ear against the door, hoping no one would come wandering down the hall. Or worse, that Lexy would swing the door open without warning. I figured I'd at least hear the door unlock before it crashed into me.

"There!" Lexy sounded way too excited. "Look at that switch panel. Science wing, shelter, storage, equipment room. It follows the layout of the school, so it should match the blueprints, right?"

"Do I look like I know anything about electricity?"

"It's a standard circuit panel. Anything with power running to it is hooked into here. It follows a straight path across the school, so it should match the blueprints."

Morgan sounded bored. "I guess."

"The blueprints go from the science wing to the bomb-shelter stairs straight to the equipment room. Nothing about a storage area. If the vault is underground and supposed to be secret, where do you think it would be?"

Long pause. *Loooong* pause. I could feel Lexy's impatience radiating through the door. What a drag it must be to have friends who were mentally vacant. Of Lexy's favorite Wicked pals, Morgan was definitely the lap-dog sidekick, along for the ride as Lexy's number one groupie, but not contributing much beyond that. Tina was the one who could match Lexy play-by-play in their manipulative games.

"*Here,*" Lexy growled, giving up on her sidekick entirely. "It would be right next to the bomb shelter, and not on the blueprints where anyone in the county clerk's office could see it."

I heard feet shuffling and bolted to safety a few classrooms down, ducking behind the edge of the locker row. The electrical-closet door opened a few inches as Lexy made sure there was no one around. I watched Morgan finish zipping a long duffel bag around the blueprints as Lexy locked the door with . . . a set of keys?

Assistant Janitor Rick. It looked like money could buy all sorts of interesting resources if you knew where to lay it down. I wondered who else was on their payroll. I just hoped they weren't as well funded as we were.

"Take the bag out to the car and put it in the trunk," Lexy instructed. "We'll need the prints when we put the screws to Clark Bar."

"What are you going to do?"

Lexy linked her elbow through Morgan's. "I'm going to figure out how to make the little schemer pay."

* * *

By the time I got back to the gym, the first carload of guys was arriving. Just like that, the gym went from assembly line to flirting session.

The girls poured the trays for the guys' hands, and the football players got to work. Mike Braille chased Lexy around the gym, trying to put two red handprints on her butt (which I actually thought was pretty funny), and the other guys filed into the locker room to wash their hands. I handed them markers on their way back out so they could sign under their handprints, all the while keeping one eye on the open gym doors and trying to figure out how to keep Lexy from making Heather's life a living hell.

"He's not here yet." Nick Case pulled a green marker from my grasp. "He's probably out signing autographs and kissing babies."

Nick clearly didn't like Ryan being in the spotlight. Even though—hello?—who did he think threw him all those passes?

I gave him my polite cheerleader smile and tuned him out. Guys were streaming in, but half an hour went by with no Ryan to be found. There were only a few guys left in the gym when I finally got my wish.

Ryan and Dale gave each other a quick punch on the arm and traded insults (why is that a bonding experience for guys?) before Ryan made his way over to the banner. He smiled at me but made no move to kiss me. Nor did he give my clingy ensemble a second glance.

I laid my best double-wide cheerleader smile on him and got him set up with the paint. So he wasn't a PDA kind of guy in crowds. No big deal. I was kinda squeamish about it too.

But, really . . . nothing more than a smile?

Ryan planted his palms on the paper, joking around with another player, then went to wash up. He hung right inside the door of the locker room, BSing with the offensive line and drying his hands, while I waited patiently like the Good Marker Fairy and wrestled with Tina's comment from our first date. I hated the feeling that she'd been right.

"I can take it from here if you want a few minutes alone," SJ offered.

"I'm good, thanks," I chirped. *Happy, happy outside equals happy, happy inside.*

The other guys came out, and Ryan waited for them to pass before checking that the coast was clear and tugging me around the corner. His lips were on mine like white on rice, only way tastier.

"I had to see you." His kisses were soft and quick, like little love bites punctuating his words. "I missed you."

"I dreamed about the lake," I whispered, hating that all it took was one kiss and I'd forgive him for anything. He gave a groan that made me feel all girly and satisfied in spite of myself.

We broke way too soon, and he rested his forehead against mine. "At least my day finally stopped sucking."

I relaxed a little. He was just preoccupied, that was all. "Do you want to talk about it?"

He shook his head. He left a trail of kisses from my cheekbone to the corner of my mouth before planting his lips on mine for one last mind-blowing kiss that left both of us breathless. "This is better therapy."

"Mmm." It was so natural being with Ryan. Why did I always have to overanalyze?

He held my hand as we walked back out into the gym and right into Nick Case. Nick gave us both a quick once-over and smirked, then turned back to the twenty or so people still left in the gym. "Ladies and gentlemen," he said in a mock announcer's voice. "May I present Mt. Sterling's own Superman. Faster than a speeding semi, able to leap small children in a single bound . . ."

Nick made a show of clapping and bowing to Ryan, and this time I knew I didn't imagine it when Ryan's jaw clenched. "Shut up, Case."

Nick looked him square in the eye. "What's the matter, Steele? You got a problem being the local hero?"

The muscle in Ryan's jaw jumped, and I thought he was going to take a swing at Nick.

Satisfied that he'd gotten under Ryan's skin, Nick strolled away to flirt with Nichele (who needed a bonk on the head from the Good Sense Fairy if she thought he was worth fawning over). I reached over to link my fingers with Ryan's, since he'd let go of my hand when we ran into Nick. Ryan shook it off.

"He's jealous," I said. "He doesn't like sharing the spotlight."

"He can have the spotlight for all I care. They all can."

I stepped in front of him so he'd have to look at me instead of staring at the far wall. "Why do you hate being appreciated?"

"Anyone who knows me knows I'm not a hero."

"And yet," I countered, "everyone who knows you thinks you are one. Doesn't that strike you as odd?" I reached for him again, determined to break through the wall. "There's nothing wrong with being a hero, Ryan."

Our eyes met, and I saw a flicker of pain behind the anger. But the wall stayed up, and he dropped my hand after only a few seconds. "Don't make me into something I'm not. I'm not Superman."

"Don't confuse me with Nick Case," I snapped. "And don't shut me out if there's something wrong. Lay it on me. I can take it."

He looked at me for the longest time, completely unreadable. "And if you can't?"

"Give me some credit."

His frustration was palpable, and I watched in awe as he reined it all back in before it could break the surface. At the rate he was going, he'd be ulcer city by the time he hit college.

"Drop it, Jess." Ryan's voice was dead serious and so low it came out like a rumble.

He stepped around me to leave, but I blocked his path. "Don't dismiss me like I'm second class." I didn't care if it pissed him off. *I* was pissed. Why was I so easy for guys to kiss and so hard for guys to be honest with? "And don't pretend you're some villain. Because I know villains, and you're not even close."

"Stop putting me on a damn pedestal. I'm no saint."

"Neither am I."

He worked the muscle in his jaw as he ground his teeth in irritation. Make that ulcers *and* dentures by college. "It's been a rough day," he said after a minute. "They reran the story with my name in the paper, and people have been giving me hell about it all day. Front-page news, my ass."

Front page? *Go, Stan!* "Why are people giving you grief about it? That's ridiculous."

"They're not giving me grief. But it's all anyone's talked about all day. Why can't they give it a rest?"

"Why can't you take the praise?"

His eyes darted to my face, then back to the wall. He shook his head. "I don't want to fight with you. Let it go and I'll see you Tuesday, okay?"

"Okay. But I'm glad Stan put it on the front page. That's where it deserves to be."

He didn't move for a second. Didn't even breathe. When he did, I could almost see smoke coming from his nostrils. "*You* did this?"

He sounded stunned. And beyond pissed off. But I hadn't done anything wrong, and I stood my ground. "Nan did, actually. But I was there and filled in the blanks for Stan when he asked." Ryan opened his mouth, but I cut him off. "Nothing I told him was untrue, Ryan. You need to get over whatever your hang-up is."

"It's a lot more than some stupid hang-up."

"How would I know that? You never let me in."

"Be careful what you wish for." His eyes were cold. "See you Tuesday."

I watched him go, barely registering the footsteps behind me. "Leave it alone, Thief."

I turned toward Lexy and saw the same intensity I saw in Ryan. I glared back, sick of her trying to destroy everything good in my world. "Stay out of my way and it'll be fine."

"He deserves better than you. Don't ever forget that." She leaned in close to me—personal space, what's that?—and I resisted the urge to lean away. "You'll never be enough for him."

The knife in my heart twisted. If I were the girl for him, he'd let me in. If I could measure up, I'd be a part of his life off the phone as much as on. If I could only be enough, I just might be his One.

If only.

I looked back at Ryan stepping out into the sunlight, surrounded by people who'd been in his life forever, and watched his easy smile return. He looked like the Ryan I'd always admired from afar. And here I was again, admiring from afar, even though he'd kissed me senseless not five minutes before. In secret, of course. It didn't take a genius to figure out things were no longer what I'd thought they were between Ryan and me.

The sad fact was, they probably never had been.

# *Chapter 17*

"LAST TIME," CASSIE CALLED as we got back into formation. She'd led us through our paces all morning so she could give us pointers while Sarah Jane did the full routine with us.

We'd started cheer practice extra early to beat the heat, but Mother Nature still had the last laugh. Sweat soaked our shirts; empty water bottles overflowed the recycling bin at the edge of our practice area. It was like cheering on the sun.

We lunged and rippled and stunted our way through the aggressive routine, botching the dance sequence but nailing the stunts. Except the swan-dive basket toss that turned into a pike. Still, not bad for only a few practices. The team totally had competition potential.

Sarah Jane had errands to run and wanted company, but she needed to talk to Cassie about job-shadowing her as regional liaison for her Gamma training. I headed to the bleachers where Nichele had been cheering us on. Time to dig for information.

"The stunts are really sharp," she said as I met her coming off the last step. "You're going to be great at camp."

"Thanks. I wish you were coming too. You're an unbe-lievable flier."

Nichele blushed. "I keep working on my back handspring–back tuck. It just makes me nervous."

"That goes away after a while. When it does, you'll be a shoo-in for the team."

We found shade under the bleachers—an ironic choice of location, for sure—and I popped open a water. "Man, it feels good out of the sun. I'll never get used to the heat here."

I gazed out over the practice fields, watching Nichele's furtive glances toward the other end of the bleachers out of the corner of my eye. She even positioned herself so she wouldn't have to face it head on.

I glanced over that way and shook my head. "So that's where it happened? You'd think they could've chosen somewhere a little more private."

Nichele nibbled her thumbnail.

"I mean, who'd have thought it?" I took another swig. "But if it's meant to be, it's meant to be. I just don't think someone should be holding the photos over their heads."

"I don't think it's meant to be," she said quietly. "Cameron's the one who'll be hurt."

She looked away, and I waited. Seconds ticked by as I watched the lightbulb go on. She turned back toward me, her eyes growing wider as it hit her full force.

The Wickeds had been careful to keep a lid on the pictures—can't use them as blackmail if the story gets leaked—but Nichele had just acknowledged their existence. Since Nichele wasn't a Wicked, the only way she could've known about them was if she'd taken them herself.

"I'm not going to out you," I said softly, when I thought she might burst into tears. "And you don't have to tell me why. I know you wouldn't have done it if you'd had a choice."

Nichele blinked hard, but stayed silent.

"I know you're scared. I've been targeted by her too. But I want to help, and I'm trying. Trust me that I'm going to fix this, okay?"

She nodded, mute and fighting back tears. She gathered up her purse and water, but I stopped her before she ran. Until I had a plan to take down the Wickeds, the least I could do was tell her the one strategy I was sure of. "Just promise me one thing?"

Nichele looked like promises were the last thing on her mind, but she gave a tiny nod.

"Promise me you'll find yourself some backup. Don't ever let her get you alone."

* * *

Sarah Jane and I grabbed some drive-through food and parked under a tree near the library. After feeling the wind in my hair for a while, I was able to stop dwelling on Heather and Lexy, and on Nichele getting sucked into a fight that wasn't hers. But the momentary reprieve from that mental anguish was quickly replaced with the Ryan drama. How was it possible I could feel so much for him so fast, even when it looked more and more like it was a one-way street? Was it love or lust or just being caught up in the romance and bigness of it all?

"Can I ask you something?" I swallowed a bite of cheese-burger. "Something personal, I mean."

Sarah Jane munched a fry. "Shoot."

"How did you know you were in love with Mark? Like, when it first happened?"

"Wow. I don't know, J. That was a long time ago."

"Can you think about it? It's kind of important."

Sarah Jane sat back, sipping her drink.

"I'd been crazy about guys before I met Mark," she said

after a while. "Always wondering what they were doing—were they thinking about me, were they going to call? But that was more like infatuation."

Which sounded exactly like what I was doing with Ryan. "How'd you know when it changed?"

"I think it was when I got to know him. Really *know* him. And I stopped wondering what he was doing and started wondering how he was feeling. If he had football practice, I'd wonder how he did and if his knee was aching from wind sprints and down-ups. If he had an argument with his parents, I'd want to know if he was okay and if he needed to talk." She lifted a shoulder in a half shrug. "To me, that's love. It's knowing someone well and connecting with them deep down. Caring about the person inside, not just the person they let the rest of the world see."

"What if they don't let you see the person inside?"

She sighed. "It's hard to know Ryan. It was horrible when Mrs. Steele died. Cassie, Ryan, Lexy . . . none of them knew how to cope, I don't think. Cassie's come a long way, mostly because of the Sisters. But Ryan and Lexy changed in really fundamental ways."

My heart went out to Ryan, and I wished again that he'd open up to me. Though I wasn't holding my breath after the incident at the banner party. Lexy, on the other hand, didn't get nearly as much sympathy from me. I felt bad about that, but it's hard to sympathize with someone who treats the world like her ashtray. "How did Lexy used to be?"

"Like us."

That took a minute to sink in. "'Like us,' as in like the Cindys?" No way was I buying that. Lexy was Wicked to the core.

"Cassie was already a Cindy, and her mom was a high-level Delta. Lexy would've been in the freshman recruit class that spring. She was already pegged for the invitation."

"Lexy *knew* about the Sisterhood?"

"She'd been groomed for it, but never in a way that compromised Society secrets."

"And then she went over to the dark side?"

"Lexy and I had been friends since we were in gymnastics together in middle school. She couldn't face me after she confessed what happened in the car that day. Once the painkillers wore off, and she realized what she'd said . . ." Sarah Jane's voice trailed off, and she busied herself putting our wrappers and boxes into the bag. "She pushed us away after the funeral. And the Wickeds embraced her because she's incredibly strong. Our loss was their gain. She would've been a good Cindy."

"If you say so."

"I do." Sarah Jane pushed open her door, ready to toss our trash and get rolling. "Don't underestimate her, J. There's more to Lexy than you think."

I'd never seen the Range before—the Wickeds' home base—so Sarah Jane took the long way back into town and gave me the grand tour. We passed a palatial estate surrounded by a regal wrought-iron fence. "That's Worthington Estates, the camp where Paige is working this summer."

My eyes bugged out. It wasn't like any camp *I'd* ever seen. "Are you serious?"

"It's a training ground for daughters of the most famous Cindys on the planet. They also invite high-potential legacies whose moms aren't famous, but it's a huge deal to get an invitation. It's where they go to get their first taste of Cindy ways. All done without compromising our secrecy, of course."

How cool was that? "But why the daughters of famous

Cindys? Don't they already have all the opportunities?"

"They're also under the microscope more than other girls. Everything they do is news, so there's no incentive for them to stretch. No one wants to see their personal failures, even the small ones, on a cover in the checkout lane. But like I said," she added, "it's not just for famous legacies. Other legacies can be nominated too. They want it to be a mix of backgrounds: the famous daughters need time to be around regular girls who don't want anything from them, and the regular girls need to get comfortable around the rich and famous. It puts everyone on the same level."

I wish I'd had that. Maybe I wouldn't have been so starstruck around Audrey in the beginning.

"Not that the girls know any of that." SJ chuckled. She glanced in the rearview mirror as we left the fence behind. "They just think it's a posh resort camp their moms send them to every summer."

The estate faded out of view as we drove on toward the Range. "The selection process for camp counselors is super competitive. Paige had the Cindy leader job, Girls Inc. Discovery Leadership credentials, and tons of volunteer work swaying the odds in her favor, but she still had to go through three sets of interviews, plus get recommendations from five Deltas, before she landed the job. It's a major win for her." She turned onto a gravel road a few miles down. "You should try to meet her there at least once while she's on staff. It would be good for you to see that piece of the Society. And here we are."

I'd been so caught up in tales of the estate that I'd stopped paying attention to our immediate surroundings. If she hadn't looked serious, I'd have thought she was playing a joke on me.

The Range was an abandoned driving range owned by

one of the Wickeds' families. It had closed years ago when the side road it was on hadn't been paved with the rest of the county. Over the years, the paved roads grew with homes and businesses until few people even ventured down the old private road. We pulled off onto the shoulder, shielded by an outcropping of overgrown bushes, and SJ cut the engine.

As obsessed as the Wickeds were with the appearance of power, the Range was anything but a commanding presence. Inside, I had no doubt it had been upgraded to the Wickeds' usual over-the-top standards. But outside, it was forgettable. The clubhouse sat back from the road, looking old and battered and lifeless. Paint peeled from the siding, shutters hung haphazardly around blacked-out windows. Weeds grew up in tufts through the parking-lot gravel. Most people wouldn't give it a second look. But the second look would've given them a clue that everything was not what it seemed.

Underneath the leaf-filled gutters on the overhang hid high-tech security lights. Surveillance cameras were tucked into crevices on the old floodlight towers that would've lit up the Range for night practice in its heyday. Chains draped across both entrances, but an unobtrusive electronic fence at the far end provided access to the grounds. A large storage barn had been built next to the clubhouse, probably offering space for parking away from prying eyes. Even the door to the clubhouse, though weathered and worn in appearance, was solid and reinforced with double locks.

It gave new meaning to the phrase "hiding in plain sight."

SJ started the car and drove the rest of the way toward the dead end. A beat-up El Camino was parked crookedly near the steel fence that marked the dead end. Sarah Jane made a slow three-point turn and drove back past the clubhouse again. But instead of heading straight for the main drag that would take us back into town, she slowed by a stand of trees on the far edge of the parking lot. She rolled to a stop, squinting her eyes into the woods.

I couldn't see anything at first, but movement near the base of a tree caught my eye. One of the Wickeds seemed to be standing there talking to someone, waving her hands in anger or frustration, I couldn't tell.

Sarah Jane started to roll forward.

"Wait," I said, squinting more closely. That couldn't be right. Not a Wicked but—"Is that *Heather*?"

We watched as Heather disappeared into the woods, only to reappear guiding a man by the elbow. The man stumbled over the exposed roots, clutching the remains of a six-pack under his opposite arm. Heather looked around the Range, deemed it safe to cross, and stepped out onto the gravel, heading for the far side of the property near the dead end.

That's when Heather saw us. And Lexy saw Heather.

A figure had emerged from the barn area while we were focused on the woods. A string of Wickeds followed her, all striding purposefully toward Heather and her dad.

I'd unbuckled my seat belt and opened my door before Sarah Jane could get out a word of warning. "This isn't your fight, Jess."

"How can it not be?" Leaving Heather to fend for herself was bad enough. Leaving her to fend off a crew of Wickeds on their home turf while keeping her dad upright was inconceivable. "I'm going whether you help or not."

My backup reluctantly opened her door.

The Wickeds snapped pictures on their cells as they closed in, Tina using hers for video. I hoped it wasn't a live feed.

"Just when I thought the day couldn't get any better," Lexy told Heather as we approached from behind. "You couldn't make this more fun if you planned it."

Heather turned to her dad. "Go wait in the car. I'll be there in a minute."

Lexy took in his dirty shirt and frayed jeans, disgust curling her lip. "And while you're at it, try to remember the last time you showered."

Mr. Clark puffed out his chest as if indignant, causing the remains of the six-pack to slip out from under his arm. He made a grab for it before it hit the ground. The remaining can burst and sent a stream of beer sailing toward Morgan's capris.

"Freak!" she screamed.

Mr. Clark's anger—probably at losing his last beer—centered on Heather. "Don't give me orders," he growled, slurring his words just enough to be noticeable. He lifted his chin and made his way unsteadily across the parking lot toward the waiting El Camino.

Lexy looked like she'd been given the gift of the century. "What to do with these new pictures." She clucked. "What to do, what to do . . ."

"How about nothing?" I said as we came up behind them.

Lexy whipped around, as did the other Wickeds. A flurry of camera clicks followed.

"Pretty bold, aren't you?" Lexy said. "This is the first time any of you have been brave enough to set foot here."

"That you know of."

She narrowed her eyes. "This is private, Thief, and you're trespassing. You have no business here."

"Heather against the six of you? That hardly seems fair. At least Heather's strong enough to stand on her own. She doesn't need a posse of hangers-on to shadow her every move."

"But she needs you."

"I'm here because I want to be. Because we"—I made eye contact with Sarah Jane—"want to be."

Sarah Jane gave a curt nod but said nothing.

Lexy turned back to Heather. "Don't think this is over, Clark Bar. I have special things planned for you."

"I already told Cameron the truth. He's not speaking to me, so I really don't give a crap what you do with the pictures." Heather jutted out her chin. "Go vent on someone else."

The Reggie had finally found her voice. Maybe it was a backup she could count on. Or maybe this was just her time.

Lexy looked taken aback but quickly recovered. "I'll use those pictures to wrap my Christmas presents this year. Don't you have any pride?"

Heather looked past us to the El Camino, where her father was unsuccessfully trying to open the door. Her eyes met Lexy's. "What do you think?"

She pushed past us before Lexy could respond. We watched her go: Lexy calculating her next move, the Wickeds snapping pictures, Sarah Jane in silence.

"She may not have any pride left, but I know someone who does *and* who likes his privacy." Lexy and Tina shared a look of anticipation that made me uneasy.

Mr. Clark might have his pride, but I doubted even he could believe he had any kind of privacy. His drunken escapades were legendary all over town. With only one person left in Heather's Support Network box, it wasn't hard to figure out what Lexy had in mind.

Cameron might not be speaking to Heather, but he was about to get called on by the leader of the Wickeds.

The chairs in the leader's office aren't nearly as comfortable as they look. Sure, they have a soft microfiber finish and nice high backs, but when all you want to do is flop down and chill out, they kind of miss the mark. I really needed a chill chair.

I'd been hiding out at the table in the office, working on different scenarios that could explain the Wickeds' big plan. Meanwhile, the hot ball of anger in my stomach grew. The butterflies were getting scorched. Having to share the office with Paige at the moment wasn't helping matters either.

Sarah Jane had lectured me all the way back from the Range on choosing my battles. If I stepped in to save every one of the Reggies, they'd never learn to fight for themselves. As far as I could see, *never* stepping in wasn't the answer either.

Here I was, busting my butt for a Sisterhood who a) would only back me up when I played by their rules, b) kept me in the dark about the whole secret vault thing, and c) wanted me to leave Heather for the wolves after she'd confided in me.

I felt like a pawn. A mouse in a maze trying to find my way to the finish line while giant, hovering people closed off this turn and that, all the while telling me it was for my own good.

"Just be proud that you accomplished your mission *and* gave ISIS a critical heads-up about the vault at the same time," Paige was saying. "ISIS is impressed."

Right then, I didn't give two snaps about ISIS. Who cares about the big picture when the Reggie you're trying to save is sinking?

But Paige couldn't see that either. "I know you want to save everyone, but you have to keep your emotions in check. You're leading the fight, but you're not doing it alone. You can't win if you don't have the Cindys behind you."

*Keep my emotions in check. Sure.* "You don't know what it's like to be a Reggie with no support system, Paige. For you, this is all strategy. For me, it's personal."

"Do you think you're the only Cindy who was ever a target?" she asked incredulously. "When I was a freshman, there was a senior Wicked who had it in for me. I'd just about given up on ever getting away from her the day she tripped me in the cafeteria and my lunch and I went flying." She paused, her eyes getting that distant look of recall. "I still remember the sound the tray made when it hit. The noise was deafening. I don't think there was a single person who wasn't looking at me sprawled out on the floor with milk pooling around my knees and tuna surprise in my hair."

I shuddered. Lunch was the most vulnerable time for anyone's social status. Getting hammered by a Wicked in the middle of Social Central was a fate worse than tuna surprise itself.

"I wanted to cry," Paige said, "but I wouldn't give her the satisfaction. And then Cassie got up from the cheerleaders' table. She walked over like it was the most normal thing in the world, helping me pile things back on my tray and dump it."

Paige's shoulders relaxed, nightmare over. "If Cassie hadn't stepped up when she did, I probably would've let the Wickeds win. I would've just given up. But I didn't because Cassie, that one time, showed me I was worth helping. The next time the Wicked came after me, I decided to help myself.

I stood my ground, and that's when things finally started to shift. Bit by bit I climbed out of the grave I'd let the Wickeds dig for me."

She looked back to me. "You don't have to save everyone, Jess. Sometimes a random act of kindness that seems like no big deal to you can mean the world to someone else."

We worked in silence after that. There was comfort in knowing Paige had gone from Reggie target to well-respected Cindy leader. And I understood what she meant about the random-acts-of-kindness thing. SJ stepping in at The Grind that first night had given me hope for the first time since Lexy had set her sights on me.

But instead of those facts having a soothing effect, I was still swigging raspberry iced tea to cool the fire in my stomach. How could we beat the growing ranks of Wickeds with a strategy of one-hit wonders? The Wickeds were miles ahead and here we were, constantly gathering more intel and offering random bits of help instead of real protection.

An idea started to gel in my mind. It was time to stop playing catch-up and go on offense.

* * *

A few hours later, Paige swiveled around in her chair. "I need to run a quick errand," she said. She logged off the computer and locked the lap drawer. "I'll be back for our meeting at three. Don't work too hard, okay?"

I sat back to rub my eyes after she left. I felt betrayed. By the Cindys, who wanted me to lead but only if I did it their way, and by Ryan, who acted like I was his world but barely acknowledged me in the real one. I was trying so hard to be what everyone wanted me to be, and yet every time I looked around, I was failing.

If I followed my heart where Heather was concerned, I

ran the risk of losing the Cindys' acceptance. If I gave in to Cindy pressure, I hung Heather out to dry. Maybe life had been easier when I didn't fit in. At least then the only person I let down was myself.

I wasn't an expert on leadership, but here's the thing I did know: no good leader ever bowed to peer pressure instead of doing the right thing. I might not have been making a splash with my makeover (if I had, wouldn't Ryan be proud to have me at his side?) or keeping up with my *CMM* assignments or figuring out how to defeat the Wickeds' recruitment surge. But I was still me: Do-Gooder Volunteer Girl, champion of worthy causes and people who needed help.

I poked my head out to make sure everyone was otherwise occupied in Study Hall, then closed the office door.

The leader office wasn't glamorous, but it was well equipped. The computer desk, a round table and chairs for spreading out, bookshelves filled with reference materials, and a locked file cabinet.

If we wanted to beat the Wickeds, we needed to stop reacting and take control. Let's see how the Wickeds liked being in scramble mode.

How do you create a plan of attack when your enemy is everywhere?

Rule #1: Start at the top.

The question was, how did we handle Lexy? If it was up to me, I'd go at her with everything we had and take her out the way she deserved: with as much humiliation as possible. If we could take away Lexy's power, the Wickeds would battle each other for her place. That would create chaos in their ranks and give us a chance to strike again when they weren't so well protected.

But even I knew that wasn't the Cindy way. The Cindy way would be to try to get through to her. If Sarah Jane was right about her having been groomed for Sisterhood, some of that had to exist in her somewhere, right? At least in theory. Like Gaby had said, no Wicked was 100 percent bad. Although I personally thought Lexy was about as close as you could get.

Getting to Lexy meant I needed to understand Lexy the way she understood the Reggies. Or me, for that matter. The only thing I really knew about her personally, other than that she was a Cindy legacy, was that she adored Ryan. If Ryan paying attention to me could throw her off her game enough that she'd start a generic rumor like her lame STD attempt, family definitely played into her psyche. Maybe it was the key to getting through to her.

I only had access to personnel files for our group of Cindys and profiles for the Wickeds and targeted Reggies. What I needed was detailed background intel on the other Cindys in Lexy's family, and on her as a legacy. What had they seen in her back then, before the accident? Paige and Sarah Jane were both playing mum, so if I wanted answers, I was going to have to find them myself.

I poked around in the desk drawers, looking for anything that caught my attention. The drawer Paige had locked wouldn't budge, and the others held nothing useful. I trailed a finger over the locked file cabinet.

The legacy files for recent Cindys were in the leader cabinet. The new system upgrade would make those files obsolete, but we still had a few weeks before Sarah Jane got us up and running with the digital archives.

The Steele women had been Cindys for generations, and

now one of their own was a leader of the Wickeds. That had to be significant.

I went back to the desk and scrounged around in the drawers for a key. Lip balm, loose change, a couple of barrettes, a box of paper clips . . .

Paper clips?

I picked one up and examined it. I knew you could use paper clips to pick locks—I'd seen it on an episode of *Crime Watch, Vegas*—but how did it work? I put it in the file cabinet lock and turned. The paper clip twisted, but nothing happened. I pulled it out and tried to think about the episode. A bend here, straighten that part out, slide it in, and give it a little jiggle. Stop, bend again, more jiggling.

Nothing. I clearly wasn't a lock picker, and I was running out of time.

Except . . . wasn't the little lock part supposed to be pushed in when it was locked? That's how the file cabinets worked in Mom's old office. So if it wasn't pushed in . . .

I pulled the handle of the top drawer, and it opened like a breeze. *Bingo*. I made a mental note to always push in the lock once the office was mine.

I quickly scanned the contents of the file drawers to get my bearings. Meeting minutes, curriculums for Alpha, Beta, and Gamma levels, files on the current Cindys . . .

The legacy files.

There weren't many, so I quickly jumped to the *S*s, hoping to hit the jackpot. *Steele*.

I pulled out the Steele family file. A different color file lay on top, with *Elizabeth (Harrington) Steele* on it. It wasn't a full file like ours were, but a smaller folder, with only a couple of documents in it. Her full file was probably housed wherever they archived high-level records.

I hesitated, but only for a second. If Mrs. Steele had been half the Cindy I'd heard she was, she would've understood that desperate times called for desperate measures.

I opened the cover. Her photo smiled up at me. She was an older version of Cassie, every bit as beautiful, with the same warmth in her eyes. I could see Ryan in her too, and even Lexy, though she lacked Lexy's harder edges.

I gently set the picture aside and looked beneath. There was a brief list of family connections in the Society: Mrs. Steele, her mom and grandmother, Cassie, and a note about Lexy with a reference to chart 4.7. I flipped through the pages. What was chart 4.7? Was it about Lexy being a legacy? Something that had to do with the Wickeds?

A knock sounded from my private door to the War Room a split second before it opened. I closed the cover and plastered both hands over the top of the file.

Sarah Jane noticed the leader-office door was closed and stopped. "Sorry. I thought you were studying." She took in the open cabinet drawer, the folder on the table. Her eyes flicked to Mrs. Steele's picture, a few inches from my hands. "I didn't know Paige had given you the keys already. You must be making great progress."

I stared back, understanding in that split second what the term *a deer in the headlights* meant. I'd never been caught doing something bad before. How did people react when they got caught?

Suspicion crept into Sarah Jane's eyes. She looked more closely at the cabinet this time, and I heard her sharp intake of breath. The paper clip stuck out of the lock like a beacon of shame. "You *broke into* the files?"

"No! Paige left it open."

She didn't look convinced.

"I didn't know that until after I stuck the paper clip in," I admitted.

Sarah Jane looked appalled. Rightfully so, even I had to admit, but it still put me on the defensive. "I wouldn't *have* to break in if someone would tell me what I need to know for once."

"Oh my gosh, J." Sarah Jane looked as flustered as I'd ever seen her. "You can't . . . if Paige finds out . . . Cassie's going to flip—"

"Nobody is flipping out, because nobody is going to tell anybody." I spoke with a defiance I didn't expect, but enough was enough. "Am I the new leader? Did you specifically choose me as the new leader in a break with tradition?"

"That doesn't give you the right to *break into the files.*"

"If you wanted a figurehead, you should've picked someone else. What you got was me, someone who's willing to do the *right* thing. If that means digging into Lexy's past to save Heather, so be it."

"Things are the way they are for a reason. You can't just do whatever you want without getting approval. That's not how the Sisterhood works."

"It's easy to take the high road when you don't have anything at stake, isn't it, Sarah Jane? I don't see you taking on any missions against Lexy. I don't see you being told to let somebody get squashed by the Wickeds because 'we have people working on it.' All I see is you being silent the only time I've ever asked you for backup and then lecturing me about being too impulsive. At least I'm doing *something.*"

Sarah Jane blanched. "Just because you don't see doesn't mean no one's doing anything. There's a lot more at stake than you know."

"Exactly. My. Point."

Kyra and Gwen entered the Gamma office at the far end, and I pushed the door between us closed, locking Sarah Jane in with me. I was teetering between freaking out and blowing up, so I pointed to the chair opposite my desk.

Sarah Jane sat down; I stayed standing. Power was all about positioning. I knew that from the Wickeds.

"Here's how this is going to play out," I said calmly. "You're not going to say a word about this to anyone. I'll explain it to Paige after I'm done, leader to leader. In the meantime, I need to figure out how to get Heather away from Lexy. You're always telling me to trust you? Well, it's your turn to trust me now. I know what I'm doing."

She looked skeptical, so I aimed for the bull's-eye. "If you stop me and Heather gets hurt, you'll never forgive yourself. Don't add that to your conscience, Sarah Jane."

SJ's face paled as the arrow hit home. But the hands on the wall clock above her made me uneasy. Paige would be back any minute for our meeting, and I needed to get this cleaned up in a hurry. I nodded toward the private door to the Gamma office. "If you don't want to get yourself in any deeper, walk back through that door and forget this ever happened."

Sarah Jane's face started to heat. Her usual Zen-like nature was waging war with her emotions. Fear, anger, sadness, desperation. So much passed across her face. Silently, she turned away from me.

The door closed behind her with a barely audible click.

I slipped Mrs. Steele's picture back into the file, rubber-banded everything together, and slipped it back in the cabinet before grabbing the incriminating paper clip and stuffing it in my pocket. Thanks to Sarah Jane's interruption, I hadn't found anything I could use with Lexy. I'd either need to find another time to scout out the office when no one was around or come up with a plan B. Either way, I was on my own. Flying solo on a cloud of righteousness.

A new sheriff had come to town, and she wasn't taking any prisoners.

# Chapter 18

I SAT IN MY ROOM studying my closet for date-worthy clothes, tapping an aggravated rhythm on my bedspread. Sarah Jane had been hinting for a while that I needed to stop worrying about what I thought I should look like and focus on what made me feel best about myself. She'd even taken me aside after the banner party to let me know that some of the guys had been making comments about me. Nothing horrible, but enough for her to remind me that I didn't have to dress to get attention.

"You don't have to push the envelope," she'd said. "More isn't always better."

"Easy for you to say," I'd snapped. I wouldn't have had to push the envelope if I looked like Sarah Jane. She could wear a Hefty bag and tutu and still look like a million bucks. But let her walk a mile in my flip-flops and see what she thought then.

The kicker was that the guys had noticed me, but Ryan had barely even looked my way. He noticed Fake Blondie and Boob Girl, so why not me? What good was a signature style if the guys you liked didn't think you were attractive enough to date in public?

But no, the Cindys had to remind me that I'd chosen my fun-feminine-sporty signature style for a reason. I needed to honor that and stick with what was really me. I'll admit I'd been gradually amping things up image-wise, but I'd only been trying to blend with Ryan's crowd. I was tired of feeling like an afterthought. Or worse, an embarrassment. Besides, who were the Cindys to say I'd gotten it right the first time? Who were they to assume they knew the real me?

I wanted to feel like I belonged by Ryan's side no matter where we were. So I kept tweaking the image to make it a little more hip, a little more sassy, a little more sexy. The last part made me uncomfortable—like the banner-party tank he hadn't even noticed—but I'd never admit that to SJ. All I wanted was for Ryan to put me in the same class as his other girlfriends. Maybe it was time to be bold instead of clinging to my fresh-faced girl-next-door ways.

So I sat on my bed, stewing about Sarah Jane's criticism and Tina's nagging comment about Ryan hiding me in the corner. Not to mention Lexy's reminder that Ryan deserved better.

I couldn't make it work no matter what I did. My new look was too much (but not enough—how's that for irony?), and Ryan saved his laid-back smiles for everyone but me.

I was fed up.

I'd spent my entire life trying to fit in with people who didn't want me. Parents who cared more about their careers than their own daughter. Cheer teams who hung with me at games but went their merry way after, never realizing I didn't have anyone to hang with off the field. A next-door neighbor who flirted with me and kissed me all summer long, only to pretend he didn't even know me when school started because I wasn't part of the in crowd. Sure, the Cindys wanted me, but only if I played the game their way and didn't ask questions. Ryan only wanted me if he could pull me out of sight for a quick make-out session. And even then, only if I kept my mouth shut when he felt suffocated by his hero complex.

The phrase I never thought I'd utter—What Would Fake Blondie Do?—passed my lips as I put together a strategy for the night. I might have more self-control (and self-respect) than she did, but she obviously had something I didn't. If she wasn't afraid to go after what she wanted—to come out with guns blazing (even if they were secure in her C cups)—I needed to be ready with weapons of my own.

I started grabbing things off hangers and digging through drawers until I'd put together the most extreme outfit I could dream up. Bold-flirty-sexy. I put on dangly earrings à la Fake Blondie and left my charm bracelet in my jewelry box. I didn't need that today. My image was my own creation, Cindys be damned.

Dad had swept Mom away for one last romantic hurrah before Mom would have to stick close to home for the babies' sake. That meant there was nobody home to tone me down. Just me, a micro mini, a midriff-baring shirt, and enough mascara to choke a canary.

*Come and get me, baby.*

\* \* \*

"Explain to me again why they're here?" I asked after we'd been seated at a local Italian place. "What happened to wanting to get me alone?"

Ryan and I had our heads together as Tina Price and her linebacker boyfriend, Steve Ogden, bickered over whether to split a pepperoni-and-mushroom pizza or a calzone. "They were coming here anyway, so I thought it would be fun," Ryan said as he looked at our shared menu.

If the bickering was wearing on him, Ryan showed no signs of it. But sharing our evening with a chief Wicked and her Villain boyfriend was giving me a monster headache.

"So, Jess," Tina said in her most syrupy voice, "you're looking very *Playboy* tonight. Is that for our benefit or Ryan's?"

Steve eyed me like I was a cream puff and he had a sweet tooth. "Does it matter?"

"I don't mind if she shows it off. As long as she doesn't share." Ryan slid his arm around me and raised his eyebrows in question. "Unless that's a tempting idea?"

I glared at his disgusting remark as Steve and Tina cracked up. Steve made a couple of rude comments about girls who show it off, which Tina punched him for (though I think she secretly liked that particular association with Paris Hilton), and Ryan laughed like Steve was the funniest thing since Adam Sandler.

I gave a silent prayer of thanks when the food finally arrived, because talking took a backseat to eating. Though I didn't say *backseat* out loud or it would've set off a whole slew of new innuendos.

By the time we made it back to the car, I was fuming. Not once had Ryan made a genuine comment to me. Not once had he defended me against Steve's degrading jokes about the female body. And not once had he bothered to tell me why he'd ruined our date by inviting along my enemy's bud and her wretched boyfriend.

"Hey, Jess," Steve called from the backseat as I buckled in up front. "There's plenty of room back here if you and Tina want to make a Steve sandwich."

*Puke, anyone?* "Not if you were the last sandwich on earth."

He couldn't hear me, of course, because Tina was smacking him again. "As if I'd let her within three feet of me."

"You're within three feet now," he snarked.

"Suddenly you're the Math King? What a joke."

"Last I checked, it wasn't my brain you were hot for, so what does it matter?"

The rage welled up inside me, giving me a glimpse into a scary ulcer/denture future of my own, until I couldn't take it anymore. "WILL. YOU. SHUT. UP!"

My yell reverberated off the windows for several seconds.

Tina looked at Ryan. "What's up with the Bitch Queen?"

I spun to face her. "You"—I pointed—"have the nastiest mouth of any female on the planet. It makes me ashamed of my gender. And *you*"—I whirled on Steve—"are the most loathsome creature ever to walk upright. If you mention my clothing or my body again, I'm gonna knee you where you'll never forget it."

I turned on Ryan. "You and me. Outside. *Now*."

I stared him down until he opened the door. My phone was in my hand now, fingers itching to dial Sarah Jane for a ride home.

"This won't take long," he tossed to the backseat gang. "I just need to take care of something."

*You better believe it, pal.*

I waited until we were out of earshot before I lit into him. "If you didn't want to go out with me, why didn't you just say so? You couldn't be man enough to tell me you don't like me anymore, so you decided to go the Lexy route and torture me for the evening?"

"Leave my sister out of this."

"Oh, yes, let's leave your precious baby sister out of this. Heaven forbid we drag her into something sordid and nasty."

Bitter sarcasm ran thick in my blood. "Are you blind? That's where she *lives*, Ryan. And obviously, you're no better."

I wanted my words to hurt him. I wanted him to feel the pain I felt so he'd finally break down the wall and come at me full force. Until he let go, there was no way I'd ever get through to him.

But the guns never locked and loaded. Instead of looking furious, he had the nerve to look relieved. "I guess I'm no saint after all," he said, absurdly pleased with himself.

"Old news. Neither am I."

He skimmed my body with his eyes in a way that should've given me goose bumps but only made me feel cheap. "That much is obvious."

"What's that supposed to mean?"

"What's that outfit supposed to mean?"

"What are you, the fashion police? My—" I looked down at my sex-kitten ensemble, and for the first time all night, I saw how ridiculous I looked.

And I hated it.

I hated that I'd tried to be like girls I didn't even respect. Hated that Ryan could make me feel cheap when he had the capacity to make me feel so special. Hated myself for not being strong enough—or important enough—to break through his defenses.

My anger fizzled out as quickly as it had spiked. "Why? Just answer me that, Ryan. Why are you pushing me away?"

"I'm just showing you the other side of Ryan Steele. Isn't that what you wanted? For me to let you in? Well, congratulations, Jess. You're in. How do you like the scenery?"

"Don't give me that crap. I've twisted myself into a pretzel to fit into your life, but it's never enough. Why is that? What do I have to do to be enough for you?"

"Let me be myself. And while you're at it, try being yourself too. If you even know who that is anymore."

"Don't make this all my problem." Frustration burned holes in my stomach. "You're the one who didn't have the guts to tell me our little fling was over. I don't even know why."

"Because you have me on a pedestal."

"Are we back to that again?"

"You *do*, Jess. You're as bad as everyone else." He clenched his fists. "You wanna know why I was mad about that article? Because I'm not a hero. Heroes don't kill their mothers."

If someone had smacked me with a newspaper, I couldn't have been more stunned. "How can you even say that?"

He looked at me for a long time, then stared at the neon restaurant sign. "Do you know why she was in the car that day? Where she was going?" His voice sounded flat, lifeless. "To pick me up from football practice because I was grounded from the car. I'd been out partying with friends." He flicked his eyes toward the Escape. "*Those* friends. I'd missed curfew again. No car for two weeks, which meant my mom was on chauffeur duty."

"Ryan." I reached for his hand. "You have to know it's not your fault. What happened was—"

"An accident, yeah." He tucked his hands into his pockets, out of reach. "I heard all that from the police. But try telling that to my dad, who hasn't said five words since he checked out after my mom's funeral. The accident wouldn't have happened if I hadn't been such a screwup in the first place."

The walls had finally come down, but I hadn't been prepared for so much collateral damage. Ryan was broken inside. Why couldn't he let me help him put the pieces back together?

"So you painted yourself the villain and played that role. I get that. But it's not really you."

"Oh, yeah? Look at Lexy. She blamed herself for the accident for months. Closed herself off from everyone. When she finally broke down and tried to talk to me about it, I couldn't deal. So I cut her off, told her to quit whining and live with it, even though I knew it was *my* fault, not hers. But I never told her that. I just let her seal all the blame up inside because I was a coward. She was never the same after that."

The Wickeds had seen their opportunity and seized it. Lexy broken and battered was the perfect target to steal from the legacy of the Cindys.

"It was a mistake, Ryan. No one expects you to be perfect. You'd just lost your mom."

"So did Cassie, but she didn't fall apart."

*Because she had the Cindys.* "What happened then, it's in the past. You've done so much to be proud of since then." I caught myself before I mentioned the Fun Zone. "You work so hard, but you don't let yourself enjoy the rewards. You let the bad stuff in but block the good. All it does is give you a warped perception of who you are."

"It was warped already."

I wanted to shake some sense into him. Instead, I struggled to keep my cool and understand. To channel Sarah Jane's infinite patience while my heart was breaking. "I can't imagine how I'd feel if I lived through what you did. But being on the outside, I can tell you it wasn't your fault. It *wasn't.* A thousand things had to fall into place for that accident to happen, Ryan, only one of which had anything to do with you." I resisted the urge to touch him. "You're entitled to feel however you do about it. All I'm saying is that if you can't shake feeling responsible, don't live your life as an apology. Live it as a tribute. Don't you think she'd want that?"

"Being a failure is a pretty pathetic way to pay tribute."

"That's not what you are."

"How do you know? You don't even know who *you* are anymore." He glanced at my outfit again, distaste evident. "That's not the Jess Parker I ran into at the bottom of the stairs that day. And it's definitely not the girl from the lake. It's like you have this picture of how things are supposed to be, but it's all an illusion."

"That's not true." Was it?

"Of course it is. You're pretending to be something you're not because you think that's how you're supposed to be. And you want me to pretend along with you." Ryan took a step back. The beginning of good-bye. "I can't play that game anymore, Jess. Not with you."

My cell phone chimed as another couple passed us, calling out a hi to Ryan. But not to me, of course.

*Always on the outside.*

I glanced down at the phone in my hand, reading through a blur of tears. A text message from Heather lit up the display.

**911...test at school...HELP**

The couple went on their merry way, and I looked back up at Ryan.

He crossed his arms. "Don't let our discussion interfere with your busy social life. We're done here anyway."

I hesitated, torn by desperately wanting to help two people. Paige's words rang in my head: *You can't fight other people's battles for them.* Especially when they didn't want to be saved.

"I'll never be enough for you, will I?" I said. "If I won't support your villain act, you'll never really let me inside your world."

"This is what 'in' looks like. Stay or go, it's up to you."

I went.

* * *

"Are you sure this is where you need to be?"

I had to give Sarah Jane credit. She'd come and picked me up from the restaurant and taken me to school without batting an eyelash. Even though I knew she was still upset about the security breach. She did a double take at my getup but never said a word except to ask if I was okay and did I want to talk about it. Yes, and no.

"There's something I need to do," I said. "I'll find a way home."

"I'll wait." She pulled into the side lot and turned to me. "If this is about Lexy—"

"It's about me. I'm tired of not doing the right thing. I need to prove I'm ready to be the new leader."

"There's nothing to prove. We wouldn't have voted you—"

"Then I need to prove it to myself." I unbuckled my seat belt. "It's *my* mission, Sarah Jane. If you trusted me enough to give it to me, trust me enough to finish it. Letting Heather down isn't an option. This is what a real leader would do."

I thought about Heather calling me a role model. If I wanted to save the Reggies, they needed to know there were people as strong as the Wickeds who were out there fighting the good fight. Even if they could never know how massive that fight really was.

"I don't want to see you hurt in the process. It's too important . . ." Sarah Jane's voice faded away, and I watched her take a slow breath. "There's so much more at stake than you realize, Jess. This is only one piece of a much bigger puzzle."

"But it's the piece that matters now. What good is a plan to defeat the Wickeds a year or two from now if it leaves a trail of destruction in its wake? If I don't stand up to the Wickeds and show the Reggies there's another kind of power—the *good* kind of power—then what are we really fighting for?"

She looked on the verge of tears. "Do you know what you're getting yourself into?"

"Enough to know I can handle it." I softened a little at the fear in her eyes. "If I'm outnumbered, I'll call for reinforcements."

She bit her lower lip, then pulled me into a quick hug. "Go be Crusader Girl."

❋ ❋ ❋

The doors to the school were locked, and I didn't see any cars in the student parking lots. I made a slow trek around the school, making sure to stay close to the building for cover.

I'd made it almost the whole way around when I saw movement near the football field. I ducked behind the wall of the teachers' lounge and watched the snack bar behind the bleachers. Heather was there, sitting on the ground under the boarded-up counter. From the jerky movement of her shoulders, I knew she was crying.

I stepped out of my hiding spot as two figures emerged from the tree line in back of school. Lexy and Morgan had come to make good on their promise.

They crossed the field quickly and yanked Heather around the side of the stand. I moved around the building to keep them in view, just in time to see Morgan knock Heather's purse to the ground and Lexy shove a furious finger in her face.

*Oh, no, you didn't.*

I covered the distance as fast as my stupid sex-kitten heels would take me, wishing I'd worn my butt-kicking boots instead.

Heather's sobs came through loud and clear as I closed in on the scene. "Problem, ladies?" I asked, my voice strong and all business.

"What are *you* doing here? Stay out of this, Thief."

"Just out for an evening stroll." I moved between them to put a shoulder in front of Heather. "Looks like I'm just in time for the rumble."

Morgan snorted. "Puh-lease. We're so scared."

"Back off, Lexy," I said, ignoring her sidekick. "If you have a problem, you go through me."

Lexy cocked her head in surprise. "Still playing the hero?" Her mocking laugh set my teeth on edge. "You're in way over your head."

"Funny how I'm not worried." I leaned in to lock eyes with her. "Step. Off."

I'd made eye contact with the bull, and I knew it was seeing red. She looked at the quaking girl behind me. "So that's how it's gonna be, huh? Have fun explaining the photos, Clark Bar. Not that anyone will believe you."

"Everyone has a moment in their lives that changes everything," I said, using my body as a shield between Heather and the Wickeds. "The thing they wish they could go back and erase from history. You have no right to hold that over their heads."

"It's not my fault if they're careless. Secrets are only

secrets if no one knows. Once they slip up, their secrets are fair game."

"Heather's not the only one with secrets. Can't you see what you're doing to people?" I tried reasoning with her. She had to be human in there somewhere. "How would you feel if someone spilled your darkest secrets?"

Lexy's hand stilled on the cell phone I suspected now held the incriminating photos. "Like I'd care."

But she did. There was no mistaking that momentary blip of fear in her eyes.

I saw her mind putting things together. I was a Cindy, an insider in the world she'd worked so hard to leave behind because the Cindys were the only ones who could expose her.

I hadn't meant it that way. It wasn't until it tripped her up that I realized she thought I was talking about the accident. But it was out there, and I'd gotten her attention. The shift in power was palpable, and I held on with both hands. "Really? You mean there's nothing you've ever done that you wanted to keep secret?"

Morgan looked between us, confused as always. "What's she talking about?"

"Shut up, Morgan," Lexy snapped. She studied me intently for a minute, then barked at Morgan, "Watch the loser." She looked at me. "You and me. Two minutes."

A sharp nod of assent from me, and Lexy headed off around the edge of the bleachers. If they'd brought backup, I hadn't seen them, but I was glad the bleachers were in sight of SJ's car anyway. I still didn't have a death wish.

Lexy stood staring out at the track, turning as I approached. She gave me a once-over. "Little heavy on the primp meter today."

"Is this a fashion consultation?"

"When did you grow a backbone, Parker?"

"When did you start blackmailing people, Steele?"

Her laugh was as dark as her soul. "So quick to point fingers. What do you know about what happened that day?"

"Enough to know there's more to the story than the rumor mill lets on." That's about all I knew, but I could bluff with the best of them. "Enough to know you don't want it getting out."

"So we scut the pictures of Clark Bar and Captain Mop and you keep whatever you think you know off the grape-vine?"

"Heather doesn't deserve this. None of them do."

"No one's as pristine as you think, Thief. Not even my perfect big brother."

I wouldn't let her push that button. *Don't think about Ryan.* "What's your choice?"

Lexy looked from me to Heather and Morgan, then glanced over her shoulder at the red convertible tucked around the side of the school. "You can't win, you know. I can't wait to see this come back to bite you in the ass."

"My butt, my problem. Do we have a deal?"

I held out my hand, and she looked at it with disgust. She grabbed it for one fierce shake before wiping her hand on her too-short, too-tight skirt. An outfit, I realized, that looked appallingly similar to my own getup.

"Morgan!" she yelled, and both girls snapped to attention by the snack bar. "Let's go."

Lexy turned back to me, contempt oozing from her cosmetically tightened pores. "You're delusional if you think you can save them all. You have no idea what you're getting yourself into."

"I'll take each one as it comes."

I watched Lexy and Morgan until they disappeared into the woods, Morgan nipping at Lexy's heels like a puppy. Heather was leaning against the snack bar, shaking. I might not be able to save them all, but I'd saved Heather. At what cost, I didn't know, but at least Heather was safe.

For now, that had to be enough.

# Chapter 19

**DEFEATING THE WICKEDS** when you're outnumbered, even just two to one, is a win of the highest order for the Cindys. Sarah Jane, Paige, and Kyra couldn't sing my praises loud enough. They took me to The Grind to celebrate, all the while complimenting my amazing leaderly prowess.

All night, I'd dreamed about the showdown at the school. Over and over again. Sometimes it ended with Lexy backing down; other times it ended with her winning. But every time, I made the same mistake. And every time, I had to watch it unfold like a helpless bystander. Like it hadn't been my choice in the first place.

We waved to Audrey (who gave me double thumbs-up— seriously, she knows *everything* that goes on in this town), and Paige and Kyra went to grab us celebratory iced lattes.

Sarah Jane, who was blissfully unaware of exactly *how* I'd gotten Lexy to back down, was convinced I walked on water.

"I can't believe you talked Lexy out of posting the photos," she gushed. "I don't agree with what happened in the—well, you know how I feel about that—but you did what none of us have been able to do. You stopped Lexy in her tracks."

*By blackmailing her in return.*

And there it was in reality, just like in my dreams. Only now I couldn't pinch myself and wake up.

I'd crossed into Wicked territory not once, not twice, but three times in the last forty-eight hours. I'd snooped through confidential files, put my toes over the slutty line with my Wicked-esque date-night outfit, and taken a walk on the dark side where my mission was concerned. What kind of role model showed the Reggies that the only way to win was to fight like a Wicked?

Kyra grinned at me as she and Paige slid in next to us with our drinks. "Word travels fast," Kyra said. "Audrey says to tell you you're a hero!"

The word left a bitter taste of how Ryan must feel every day of his life. Except he actually *was* a hero, even if he couldn't see it. I was a Fraud with a capital *F*.

I thought about the charm bracelet and butterfly charm tucked away in my jewelry box along with the high-heel pin that had started it all. Bypassing the charm bracelet yesterday should've been a warning sign: DANGER LINE APPROACHING: DO NOT CROSS. The facts had been staring me in the face the whole time.

My metamorphosis was a failure. I never should've left the cocoon.

Sarah Jane was still showering me with praise, making my butterflies more uneasy with every word, when she stopped mid-rave and stared at something behind me.

I turned as she said, "Wait!" but it was too late. There in all his beautiful glory was Ryan, cozied up at one of the round tables with Fake Blondie. I gazed at his profile just as Gennifer-with-a-*G* saw us. She gave me a sly smile, then angled Ryan's face and locked lips with him in front of an entire table of Wickeds and Villains.

I looked away amidst whoops and hollers from their spectators, feeling acid rise in my throat that a thousand iced lattes couldn't soothe.

The events of the last few weeks crumbled around me. A guy I'd fallen for who would never love me back, a blackmail mistake that put me on Lexy's level, and an image that made my skin crawl.

Ryan was right. I didn't know who I was anymore. I wasn't even sure I wanted to know.

SJ immediately sprung into protective mode. She guided me to the hallway, waited until the coast was clear, and opened the employee door so I could lick my wounds in private.

But the Club with its do-gooder vibes was the last place I wanted to be.

"I can't." I told her, taking a step back. Another. "It won't change anything." I turned and pushed through the doors to the patio.

Sarah Jane was on my heels. "Let's get out of here. You don't deserve this today. We should be celebrating your big win."

"*Stop*, Sarah Jane." I spun to face her. "I failed, okay? *Failed*. And no amount of *CMM* work is going to fix that."

SJ jumped when I said *CMM* and quickly scanned the area to make sure no one had heard. No one was near enough or paying attention to us, but Sarah Jane moved closer and lowered her voice anyway. "How can you think you failed? You *won*."

"I told her I knew about what happened that night. The night of the accident. I traded her secret for Heather's: if she didn't post the pictures, I wouldn't tell what I knew. *That's how I won.*"

"But you don't really know, do you?" she asked, alarm peeking through her calm facade. I could see her hastily reviewing what she'd told me. "How could you know?"

"I bluffed." I scrambled to explain as horror crept across her face. "I didn't mean for it to happen. I was trying to find common ground, something that would make her see Heather as a person, not a target. She misunderstood what I said."

Sarah Jane's shoulders relaxed a little, but I wasn't finished. "I didn't let it go, Sarah Jane. I could have, but I didn't. I saw her fear and jumped on it. It was a way in, and I took it because I couldn't think of any other way to win. All that mattered was saving Heather."

Sarah Jane stared at me like she'd never seen me before. Her normally peaceful aura was cracked and splintered because of me, which only heaped on my guilt. After everything she'd done for me, I'd let her down too.

Oh, sure, I could rationalize that I would never actually *out* Lexy. Never in a million years would I do that to someone, not even my worst enemy. But that's the thing about blackmail. Its purpose isn't to be used. It's just a way to control people through fear.

Protector or not, I'd stooped to a level I couldn't justify even to myself. And I'd indirectly implicated Sarah Jane in the process, the one person who'd been my personal cheerleader in the face of everything.

I dropped onto a nearby bench. Admitting it out loud made it all the more real. I was horrified by how easy it had been for me to step over to the dark side when it suited my purposes. And I'd used something far more heinous than a poor choice of rebound guy as my bait. I'd used the death of someone's mother, a well-respected Cindy, to contain my enemy.

"You made a mistake, Jess. No one's perfect." Sarah Jane tried to soothe me, but it felt off. Something had shifted in the air. Despite her best efforts to stay calm, fear rolled off her in waves. "You'll find a way to fix it. Once you find another way to win—"

"I don't even know if we *can* win, Sarah Jane. I'm fighting a battle even Paige doesn't know how to win, and she's been in the know for two years. How am I supposed to figure it out when I just got here? Where's *my* leader?"

She blinked. I saw a lightbulb go on in her head. "You need a support system."

"I don't need another support system. I need someone to show me what the heck I'm supposed to do."

"I can't help you there," she said, leading me to her car. "But I can get us out of here. We'll figure out the rest after that."

With a promise from me not to move an inch, Sarah Jane darted back inside The Grind. She came back out with her purse and a look of determination on her face. Less than a minute later, we merged into traffic.

She drove toward the middle of town, in the direction of my house, but took a right instead. We were headed for the lake. *Too many memories there,* I thought, and started to say so when she made a left past the railroad tracks and we drove out toward the mountains.

"Where are we going?"

Sarah Jane's eyes never left the pavement. "Road trip."

✳ ✳ ✳

It's ironic how failures in life are often preceded by warning signs that we don't pick up on, either because they're not loud enough or we're not paying attention. Like choosing to leave my charm bracelet behind. When the little warnings fail to do their job, the universe simply bumps up its campaign to get you back on track. Even if it means clocking you over the head with a major disaster to finally shake some sense into you.

No doubt about it, I'd been clocked a good one. I had the blackmailer scars to prove it.

When you hit rock bottom and start to bounce, sometimes you need to get away. No tunes, no talking, just the wind in your hair and the sun on your face. A total escape from past, present, and future. That's what Sarah Jane did for me.

Or that's what I thought she did.

Montgomery University sits snuggled into the foothills of the North Georgia Mountains. Its pristine campus has an Ivy League feel, but with a Southern charm all its own. It's also the top women's college in the country. My mom had gone there. Nan had too. I had no plans to, mostly because there were no guys. Although that did sound tempting right then.

Sarah Jane pulled onto the main street on campus, passing ivy-covered buildings and slowing to give snappily dressed girls with books the right of way. The grassy medians overflowed with flowers in purple, red, and yellow, and the sun didn't seem quite as suffocating here as it had in town.

SJ found a visitor's spot, cut the engine, and looked at me for the first time since we'd passed the THANKS FOR VISITING MT. STERLING sign. "Let's walk."

We wandered through the campus, taking our time and not bothering with small talk. We stopped occasionally at large etched tablets giving the history of some unusual buildings along the way, but mostly we absorbed the peace and positive energy of the campus. The air felt lighter here, and I was pretty sure it had nothing to do with altitude. Sarah Jane had picked the right place if she wanted to calm my nerves.

Which wasn't surprising. Sarah Jane had always been there for me. No matter how many stupid things I'd done (the list was long), no matter what kind of debacle my makeover had become (*debacle* was too kind a word), no matter how much I wanted to forget everything and hide under my bed, Sarah Jane had never let me down.

The Student Union was open, so we wandered inside for some water and a smoothie to quiet my rumbling stomach. We'd intended to grab something at The Grind, but those forgotten plans felt like forever ago.

We found an empty wrought-iron bench under the canopy of a shade tree and just watched people go by. Little by little, a tiny thread of peace wove through my veins. Just enough to confirm that Sarah Jane knew exactly what she was doing when she brought me—

"My parents are getting a divorce."

I almost dropped my smoothie.

She said it like it was a simple fact, like it didn't bother her at all. But one look told me that was far from the truth.

"I'm so sorry, Sarah Jane." I was dumbfounded. "I had no idea."

"No one does, except Mark."

"How long have you known?"

"A couple of weeks. My dad's living in an apartment during the separation. They've been going to counseling, but my mom told me yesterday she's pretty sure they're going to file for divorce."

"Is there anything I can do?" It was a lame attempt at soothing, but what was the right thing to say to someone whose family life was collapsing around her?

A ghost of a smile flitted across her face. "Not that I can think of. I just needed someone else to know."

I thought of all the times I'd been clingy and needy, complaining about Ryan or Lexy or how I couldn't figure out how to defeat the Wickeds. I always expected Sarah Jane to prop me up and tell me things were going to be okay. Not once did I ever stop to think that Sarah Jane might need propping up. That she might need to hear things would be okay for her too.

But I never knew. All those superhuman peace-and-love vibes, all the die-hard optimism. How could *anyone* have known?

We were quiet a few minutes, letting the magnitude of her news sink in. I was honored that she'd confided in me. I'd never done anything to earn that kind of trust from her, which made it all the more humbling. "Why did you tell me now?"

She took a deep breath and let it out slowly in a way I recognized as Sarah Jane's centering technique. She was a master at quieting her emotions to remain calm, cool, and collected. I so needed to learn how to do that.

"I guess I needed to get it off my chest more than I thought. There's only so much you can control about life, you know? Even when you think you've finally got things running great, sometimes they fall apart anyway. And they can't always be fixed. At least not by you." She turned to me, her eyes earnest. "The only thing we can control is how we deal with it."

Sarah Jane is what Nan would call an "old soul." As always, I wished I had half her wisdom and poise. A quarter, even. "I'm sorry if I made things worse for you."

"You haven't. I've been more . . ." She grasped for the right words. "More hands-on than I probably should've been with you. But being your Big Sister was the one thing I thought I could still do well, even with everything going on at home."

And then I'd failed her. She'd never admit that, of course, but I knew it was true. "I should've trusted you more, Sarah Jane. I wish I had."

"No, that's just it. You had to do this on your own terms. If you took a couple of wrong turns, that's all part of your path. All I could think about was not being a failure as your Big Sister."

I couldn't imagine Sarah Jane failing at anything, although I could see how she might feel like that, given my recent crash-and-burn as leader. And as Makeover Girl.

Sarah Jane glanced at her watch and stood up to stretch. "I've got an appointment over in Artemis Hall."

"Do you need me to call someone for a ride?"

"It'll only take a minute. You can come with me, and then we can walk some more if you want."

I did want to. For once, I wanted to be there for Sarah Jane.

"Can I ask you something?" I asked, as we tossed our cups in the trash.

"Sure."

"How do you stay so . . . Zen?"

"I've been meditating like a fiend," she admitted with a laugh. "Plus doing yoga like you wouldn't believe. They both help a ton with stress. But mostly it's remembering to breathe."

I thought of my favorite Drew Barrymore movie, *Ever After*.

*Just breathe.*

I followed her back toward the far corner of the school. The building there was even older than the others but had no tablet proudly proclaiming its distinction. The arch over the door held an ARTEMIS HALL, EST. 1868 carving, and I wondered how buildings that old could still be in use. It seemed like they'd be nothing but rubble by now. Sometimes things are stronger than you give them credit for.

Sarah Jane opened the heavy wooden door, and I was surprised to see that the inside looked more like the lobby of a high-end hotel than the dungeon I'd imagined. She went up to the small tidy desk in the circular entryway and spoke with a middle-aged woman.

"I just need to deliver a package," she explained when she came back. "We can sit on the benches for a minute."

I took my seat next to her, feeling mellow within the sanctuary of the ancient walls. The red tufted pillows lining the bench sank beneath us, and I leaned my head against the wall tapestry, breathing in the cool, still air.

I'd started to relax when I heard footsteps and a familiar sound. Two women approached from the side hall, and I stood in anticipation.

The older of the two women smiled at me fondly. "This is quite a surprise."

"Sarah Jane just had to—" I turned toward my friend, only to find she'd disappeared. The wooden door behind me creaked, and I watched it close softly behind Sarah Jane as she descended the steps outside. "Oh."

I looked at the women and considered my predicament, the truth dawning on me too late to be of much use. "I guess I'm the package?"

"Indeed you are, my dear. It seems a little tour may be in order."

I looked around, trying to figure out what kind of tour Artemis Hall of 1868 held in store for me. The older woman laid a gentle hand on my shoulder, and I saw the delicate locket with the ornate swirled letters hanging from her wrist.

I looked at the locket, then back at her warm, smiling eyes, and knew this was no ordinary road trip.

"We weren't expecting you quite this soon, Jessica. But Sarah Jane did the right thing by bringing you."

"Thanks, Nan."

* * *

If I'd ever imagined what ISIS headquarters looked like—and I had, a little—this wouldn't have been it.

Nan and the other woman, who introduced herself as Meg Garner, keyed in through some plain doors to an area that looked like any boring office you'd ever seen on TV. "This is our home base for ISIS, Inc., our corporate identity," Nan explained, "and The ISIS Foundation, our nonprofit side. We have satellite facilities in other locations, but this is our headquarters."

I followed them as they wove through the office, feeling dazed not only by being inside Cindy Central but by being taken on a tour of it by my own grandmother. The same woman who'd never given me the tiniest clue that she was part of the Sisterhood.

Would it have killed her to have given me a hint?

My gaze left the back of Nan's head, scattering the hundred questions in my mind, and I checked out my surroundings more closely. Women sat in front of computers at small cubicles that ran in rows the entire length of the building. Nondescript offices lined the sides of the room, and classical music filled the air. It wasn't ugly or depressing. It was just ordinary.

Except the view out back. It took my breath away.

In the middle of the lush, manicured lawn was an enormous, perfectly round concrete patio edged with a beautiful pattern of bricks. The circle was surrounded by small geometric ledges holding a series of brightly colored fountains, carved wooden benches, trees, shrubs, and flowers. It nestled up against a vast, grassy hill that plateaued before blending into the mountains, providing a brilliant green backdrop to the landscape that made the circle feel hidden, almost sacred in its privacy. And so restful.

"I thought you'd like that best."

Nan shared my passion for outdoor beauty, and I smiled at her words. "It's amazing." I wondered if she'd had a hand in its creation. There were so many questions I wanted to ask.

"That's only the beginning," she said, guiding me onward.

Nan and Meg (she asked me to call her that) led me into a small elevator. Nan pressed level S3, and we descended beneath Artemis Hall. *I knew it.* The main-floor offices had been too plain, too average, for the Society I'd come to know and love.

The elevator stopped, and I tried to breathe normally. Stress and anticipation were duking it out inside me. I'd just tarnished the Cindy name with my walk on the dark side, and here they were taking me behind the veil of the Cindys' secret world. Why now? What did this have to do with me and Heather and taking down Lexy and the Wickeds?

The elevator doors slid open, and I was rewarded for my patience.

With a well-stocked, neat-as-a-pin storage room.

Boxes labeled with different holidays, bins of office supplies. Reams of paper perfectly stacked on metal shelves.

I'd thought I was getting a sneak peek at the inner workings of the Society. Turns out they just needed an extra set of hands for the Fourth of July decorations.

Disappointment sent the air out of my lungs in a whoosh. *Just another day behind the glass.* I stepped out into the storeroom.

Nan and Meg each grabbed an arm and pulled me back inside.

"Patience, Jessica," Meg said. "Watch."

Nan lifted her wrist and passed her locket over what I'd thought was the emergency call button. A beep sounded, and the doors closed again. A few seconds passed before panels I hadn't noticed on the rear wall slid open to reveal a wide, brightly lit corridor as long as three football fields. Longer, even.

I followed them through it, glancing this way and that as we passed side corridors that seemed to extend out to the rest of the campus. I looked up at the bank of lights above us. If my directions were right, we were walking directly under the outdoor landscaped circle behind Artemis Hall, and well beyond.

We reached the end of the corridor, and Meg touched a finger to an ornate carved butterfly on the wall. The nondescript wall in front of us disappeared into the floor. Another elevator opened, this one much fancier. Mirrors graced both sides, and a set of carved doors decorated the rear. Nan punched a button, and up we went. Up and up . . . straight up into the mountain.

The rear doors opened and, for the second time that day, I found myself speechless.

"Welcome to the real ISIS, Jessica."

# *Chapter 20*

**WHEN YOU SUDDENLY FIND** yourself in a mountainside bunker that looks like it belongs on Fifth Avenue and are instantly surrounded by the most celebrated women in the world, all of whom are happily chatting up your eccentric grandmother and saying how nice it is to "finally" meet you (that would be *me*), it can be a little overwhelming.

Especially when one of those people is a movie star you happen to idolize.

Brooke Tatum is no ordinary movie star. Yes, she's an Academy Award winner. Yes, she ranks number seven on the Hollywood Power 20 list. But she's also spoken before Congress about strengthening animal-cruelty laws and is the founder of Girl Gab, an online group that helps disadvantaged girls find positive mentors.

That last one suddenly made a whole lot of sense.

I stood there stammering and trying not to trip over my own feet as Brooke extended her hand in my direction. "Welcome to ISIS, Jess."

"Um, hi." I hoped my handshake wasn't like a limp fish. Or clammy. Even though it was probably both.

She offered a knowing smile that had been the undoing of

many a leading man on-screen. "It's a little overwhelming the first time. Try to pace yourself."

"She's right, you know."

I did a double take, insanely relieved to hear Audrey's familiar voice. She must've left The Grind right after we did. I wondered if Sarah Jane had tipped her off.

Audrey stepped out of the crowd and gave me a hug. "You wouldn't be here if you weren't destined for this yourself. Welcome to the big-time, honey."

I looked around the room. Governors, first ladies, media tycoons, actresses, Olympic athletes, heads of Fortune 500 companies. If a woman had ever graced the cover of a magazine—from *Entertainment Weekly* to *Time*—she was there. I felt like a guppy swimming in an ocean of mermaids. It was almost—

*Wait a minute.* What was *Audrey* doing here?

No way would they let an outsider, contract or not, into a space so secure it had to be built inside a mountain. Audrey had to be a Cindy too.

I looked at Audrey and Brooke, brain finally catching up with my surroundings. Brooke was a California girl through and through. Audrey was from Australia. If they were both real Cindys . . .

I took a closer look at the crowd, at the famous faces surrounding us. They weren't just faces I recognized. They were faces *the world* recognized. Wimbledon champ Silvana Moretti from Italy chatted with German skier Ingrid Jansen and Korean Olympic swimming phenom Park Soon-Yi. British pop star Cate Hamilton exchanged hugs with the reigning Miss Universe, Brazil's Isabel Ferreira.

This was no Mt. Sterling class reunion.

When Paige had said there were Cindys from Maine to

California, I'd thought she meant TCS was nationwide. Here, Cindys from all over the world looked as comfortable as if they were at home. But home for them wasn't a speck-on-the-map college town in Georgia, U.S.A. And definitely not an underground—under-mountain?—complex that put Beverly Hills to shame.

Meg, obviously sensing my impending overload, wished me well and made her way through the crowd. Thankfully, Nan waited until she was gone to explain that Meg was the president of ISIS. Which basically made Meg queen of the Cindys.

Thank goodness I hadn't known that from the beginning or I'd have been a wide-eyed mess long before I saw Brooke. Or Cate. Or Ingrid.

"The ISIS you saw upstairs is our public face," Nan explained. "The real heart of ISIS is here in our private headquarters. From research and development to international relations, it all happens here. When we're ready to take a mission public, we pass it along to ISIS, Inc. or The ISIS Foundation, and they roll it out for us. It allows our real work to remain behind the scenes."

Nan led me through the gilded reception area (complete with a glass atrium ceiling streaming in sunlight—or faux sunlight, courtesy of full-spectrum sun bulbs), mingling along the way. By the time we went through the double glass doors at the far end, my hand was ready to fall off from all the welcoming handshakes.

The hallway beyond the double doors was much quieter than the entry had been. It was also mind-blowing. Nan strolled along next to me, giving me plenty of time to take it all in. Portraits of some of the women in the lobby graced elegant burgundy silk–covered walls, and a row of glass cases housed everything from gold medals to Academy Awards.

"It's an incredible thrill to be recognized in the Hall of Honor," Nan explained as I stopped in front of Brooke's Oscar. Right next to it was a picture of Brooke with a dozen or so girls in ragtag clothes, everyone smiling like it was the best day of their lives. "Brooke is being honored this month for her accomplishments as an actress and for the foundation she created to empower girls in need."

I didn't get it. "All of this." I gestured around me. "What does it have to do with me? How do those women know my name?"

"They're Sisters, Jessica, not just women. And they know your name because you're on the Watch List. You have been ever since you proved your leadership potential in community service."

"Which was . . . ?"

"About three years ago. You've been on the Legacy Scroll since before then, of course, as all legacies are at birth. But the Watch List is for legacies with extraordinary potential."

I had no response for that—who would?—so I trailed her down another long hallway. If Nan was a Cindy, wouldn't Mom have to be one too? And if Mom was a Cindy, why hadn't her name come up in the database search?

And why had no one ever said anything to me about this stuff before *now*?

I wanted to ask all of that and a million things more, but I didn't know where to start. My brain struggled to stay focused.

We stopped at the end of the next hall, in front of a solid steel door that required another scan of Nan's locket and, I'm not even kidding, a full hand scan. I thought I'd died and gone to *CSI* heaven.

Nan held the door open to a room that was the polar opposite of the elegance and sophistication that led up to it. The octagon-shaped space was sleek and streamlined, with gleaming floors and chrome and glass fixtures. Definitely not what I would've expected deep inside Cindy headquarters.

"This is the Gallery of Discovery." Nan's voice was library quiet and church reverent. "You remember our creed?"

"To celebrate our strength, embrace our future, and be extraordinary."

"Very good. This room is the embodiment of those ideals. Our Society was founded on the principle of empowering women. To reestablish a balance of power around the world that had been missing for centuries."

"Time for women to rule the world, huh?"

Nan's face was grave. "Never joke about that, Jessica. You must be very clear: the Sisterhood works to *restore balance*, not to shift power from one extreme to the other. The Society has long been at war with those who desire power for the sole purpose of dominating others."

I gazed at ancient-looking books and scrolls displayed in stark contrast to their high-tech living quarters. "I still don't understand what this has to do with me."

"How do you think the Sisterhood achieves its mission?"

*No idea.* "Hard work and dedication?" That sounded like the Cindy way.

"Each Sister plays a role in bringing the mission to life by following the creed." She gestured toward a round glass case, where a very old book seemed suspended in midair. "The ISIS Manifesto was created by the founding Sisters to guide us in protecting those who have no voice. Centuries later, it's still as relevant as it was back then. It's why The Cinderella Society exists."

Which reminded me. "Not to be disrespectful, but why would they name a girl-power organization like ours The Cinderella Society? I understand the fairy-godmother thing with the makeovers, but wasn't Cinderella pretty passive? She let people walk all over her and only got what she wanted because someone else made it happen for her." Truth was, I'd always had issues with the Cinderella comparison where we were concerned. "Doesn't that go against the whole empowerment thing?"

"Joining a Society like ours can be overwhelming," she explained. "The Cinderella Society name was adopted to help us quickly and easily transition girls into the Sisterhood using a metaphor they could understand. Cindys, Wickeds . . . these are concepts girls can relate to."

I guess I could see that. I already knew the Cindys were all about symbolism.

"As for it being beneath us, I would disagree. Sometimes it works to our advantage that people underestimate us. It allows us to exist largely off the radar of the people who would wish to undermine our efforts. Only two other organizations in the world know ISIS exists, and one of them is currently mounting an offensive against us, the likes of which we haven't seen for generations. What you saw in the lobby wasn't a social affair. Meg has called for a summit on how to address the surge. You and your Sisters in Mt. Sterling will be on the front lines of that battle."

"Every Cindy will, right?"

"Not everyone, no. ATHENA appears to be testing the surge with a few select chapters for now."

"But you're thinking they're doing this as a trial run before they roll it out worldwide?"

"That's the concern. It would be a significant stretch for

their resources, one they wouldn't be pursuing unless it was part of a much larger plan of attack. The women you saw when we arrived are here to formulate a plan to counteract a full-scale recruitment surge if our suspicions are correct."

Thousands of extra Lexys banding together under one evil purpose couldn't be good. "So your war with them is ramping up?"

"*Our* war, Jessica. You're the leader of a surge location."

Which was something I needed to talk to her about.

"Look, Nan, I understand that you want me to be in the Society. But the reality is, I'm a mess. My Power Plan is a disaster, my just-barely-a-boyfriend dumped me because I don't even know who I am anymore, and I blackmailed a Wicked to complete a mission"—Did she know about the mission?—"after Paige specifically told me to leave it alone. No way do I belong leading a group of supergirls."

Nan folded her arms. "Did you or did you not embrace an outsider who was hurting so you could understand why the Wickeds were tormenting her?"

Okay, she definitely knew about the mission. "Yes, but I still don't know what the deal is with the secret vault under the school."

"That's classified. Did you then protect that girl from being publicly humiliated when she chose not to give in to the blackmail?"

"By blackmailing them in return, yeah. A proud moment for Cindys everywhere."

Nan ignored my sarcasm. "A poor choice, to be sure, but one that can be fixed in time."

Since we were talking about poor choices, I figured I might as well air all the dirty laundry. She had to understand the magnitude of my mess to know why I wasn't the right

Cindy for the job. "I also accessed some of the confidential legacy files in Paige's office."

At Nan's frown, I added, "I was trying to find out something about Lexy that could help me get through to her. I never meant to use it as blackmail, even if I'd found anything. Which I didn't."

"What you *intended* to do with the information is neither here nor there. The fact that you accessed the files is inexcusable. No Cindy is permitted to ignore protocol to further her own agenda."

Nan sighed. For the first time since we'd arrived, she looked at me like the Nan I knew: with love. "Sometimes being a leader means doing the hard thing, Jessica. When everyone else has tunnel vision, you have to be willing to stand up for what you believe in and do what's right, even if it makes you unpopular. I may not agree with your methods, but I'm proud of you for making a difficult choice and following through on it to help someone who truly needed it."

But that was as much love as I was getting. Nan slipped back into business mode. "Do you know why a newly initiated member would be chosen for a mission after only being in the Society for a few weeks?"

Because they were hard up for suckers? "I'm guessing you're gonna enlighten me."

"Indeed I will, Miss Smarty-Pants. It's because we've been waiting for you. Watching you develop and waiting for the right time to bring you into the fold so you could take your proper place. There's a reason you were selected to become the first leader in the history of the Mt. Sterling chapter to be named as an incoming junior. I don't think you understand the significance of that historic event."

So Nan had been watching me develop while we were

traveling the country. What if Mom hadn't gotten pregnant and moved us here? Would there have been a Cindy chapter at my next school? Because if there wasn't, I never would've become a Cindy, much less been on the receiving end of a historic event. "See, here's what I don't get. If Mom—"

"Your mother has nothing to do with this, Jessica. Your legacy is complicated and not something I'm at liberty to discuss right now."

I'd obviously struck a nerve. Given the tension between her and Mom, it wasn't surprising. But I wasn't about to let it go without some kind of explanation.

"As you progress, there will be many things you'll want to know before it's time," Nan said. "The vault and your lineage being only two of those things."

"She's my *mom*, Nan. I deserve to know why you and I are Cindys and she's not. What happened to our legacy?"

"It's not my story to tell," she said, then shook her head. "But your mother won't be much help either." Nan seemed to choose her words carefully. "Every Cindy has a choice to make. You have to want the Sisterhood as much as it wants you."

"Mom *rejected* the Sisterhood?"

"It's not that simple. As I said before, it's a complicated situation and not something I can go into now. When the time is right for you to have the answers, you'll find them. But you won't find them from your mother."

Nan's double-talk was making my head spin. I needed concrete answers. "Any chance you can enlighten me about the vault then?"

"I can confirm that a vault does exist beneath the land where your high school now resides. For years, it protected some of the most sacred possessions of the Sisterhood, placed there in the days when your campus was the center of ISIS activity. When Paige shared your discovery with our leadership, they quickly made arrangements to bring the remaining artifacts here." Nan pursed her lips. "If they've given Lexy a mission that involves the vault, it's not an arbitrary request. There's a specific reason they're after it now, and a reason they've chosen to involve Lexy in particular."

Nan ruffled my hair like Mom always did. "The intelligence you gathered allowed ISIS to protect a critical part of our mission. If the Wickeds had accessed the vault without our knowledge, it would have been a serious compromise to our security."

At least I'd done one thing right. One out of two hundred forty-seven wasn't bad.

"Right now, your fellow Cindys need you to get back on track with your preparations. You have a lot ahead of you in the next few months, and you need to be up to any challenge you may be faced with. They need to know they can count on their leader."

"Their . . ." I'd thought she meant get back on track with my *CMM*. "Oh, no. No way, Nan. Those girls can run circles around me. I'm the last person who should be spearheading a battle against Lexy and the Wickeds during a surge."

"That's not what I meant, Jessica."

*Whew.* "Good, because that's totally not—"

"School leaders are chosen by their peers and board members. Guardians are chosen by destiny and groomed by an elite task force within ISIS. That's why Sarah Jane brought you here. If you're to successfully battle the Wickeds, you need to step into your full legacy."

The butterflies swooned.

"You're not simply your Cindy's leader, dear. You're a leader of your generation."

Sarah Jane must have anticipated my complete disbelief when I saw her again outside Artemis Hall. She immediately ordered two chocolate chip shakes from the Student Union (extra whipped cream for me) and guided me back toward our bench without saying a word. We sat and drank them in silence, the air feeling much heavier now than it had before.

Poor Sarah Jane. No wonder she'd been stressed out by my crash-and-burn. They'd charged her with mentoring a break-with-tradition leader who was selected a year late and—oh, by the way—also happened to be a Guardian-in-Training. It was one thing to screw up my own life. It was fifty times worse to take Sarah Jane down with me. I wanted a do-over.

I didn't know what they'd been thinking back at ISIS, but there had to have been a mistake. Even if Nan had insisted the entire task force was not delusional and no, they didn't need a recount.

The icy condensation from the cup dripped onto my bare legs, the equivalent of pinching me back into reality. "So," I croaked. "What happens now?"

"Now," Sarah Jane said simply, "we work."

# *Chapter 21*

WITH MOM'S PERMISSION—I didn't even have to bribe her this time—I threw some necessities into a bag for an emergency intervention at Sarah Jane's. She'd gotten special permission to remove our *CMMs* from the Club and take them to her house, under strict guidelines that they be returned to safety within twenty-four hours. Those ISIS ladies didn't mess around.

As a tribute to the old me, I managed a ponytail twist for convenience's sake that actually looked pretty cute. Simple but practical. It felt good to get back to real life.

I checked my e-mail to see if there was any news about our next cheer practice and was getting ready to e-mail Nan for my work schedule—it hadn't exactly come up during our visit—when an IM window popped up.

First&Goal: can u talk?

I stared at the screen. So much had happened since our final date. Our breakup seemed like a lifetime ago, and in a way, it was. An old life I could never go back to.

I pondered the deceptively simple question. Could I talk?

Yes. Did I want to? It depended. If he was IMing to apologize for acting like a jerk and to beg my forgiveness, I might be open to that. Not only had he acted like a jerk, but he'd moved on without waiting a respectable seventy-two hours. Plus, it was painfully obvious that Ryan didn't have a problem with PDA in general. He just didn't want to be seen kissing *me* in public.

But the worst? No matter what else had gone wrong between us, the bottom line was that we were too different. Ryan pushed away anything that got too close, and I needed someone I could connect with. That meant getting down to the real deal, scars and all. If he didn't care enough about me to let me in, nothing else mattered anyway.

No, the truth was that I didn't want to talk. We'd crossed a line and couldn't go back, but I wouldn't have wanted to even if we could. I needed to keep my eyes straight ahead, not looking over my shoulder at what could've been if only I'd been enough. I seemed to be enough in the eyes of the Cindys, so maybe they saw something in me that Ryan didn't see. Something I didn't see myself, but wanted to.

Swallowing against the tears, I closed the IM window and shut down my computer.

* * *

I'd never been to Sarah Jane's house before. It wasn't as big as the Steeles', but it was way bigger than mine, and so cozy. Cool blues and greens, soothing yellows, and gorgeous flowering plants abounded. No wonder she could manage to be cheerful and relaxed, even with the chaos of her parents' divorce. If I lived at Holly Hobbie's house, I'd be perky too.

"Tazo Brambleberry or Wild Orange?" she asked, poking her head in the fridge.

"Either. Are you sure we need all this stuff?" I hefted a

large partitioned bowl filled with snack bars, yogurt raisins, organic chips, and a bag's worth of Twizzlers.

SJ grabbed a few bottles of each and closed the door with her hip. "Power food. We'll break for lunch and a yoga breather, but we need sustenance if we're doing *CMM* triage."

I followed her upstairs to her room where Kyra, Gaby, Paige, and Gwen had already set up shop. SJ's bedroom was bigger than our living room, and each Sister had created her own little nest around the room. Kyra had fanned out all the latest fashion magazines and was categorizing outfits by style to create a visual aid for Alphas working on their Signature Style Portfolios. Gwen was doing a dream collage for her *CMM*, Paige was working on her transition materials for me, and Gaby had her laptop out so she could review the guidelines for training a leader with Guardian responsibilities.

Sarah Jane, in all her fairy-godmothery wisdom, had decided that I needed a double helping of support system. Given the whole you're-a-Guardian bombshell, I couldn't agree more. I'd gotten a lump in my throat when we'd pulled up to her house and found them camped out on her front porch waiting for us.

It was a happy little reunion laced with somber undertones. I wanted to be the kind of leader I knew they needed. But we all knew there was a lot of work to do to get me ready to face down the Wickeds and win for real.

To get things kicked off, Gaby handed me a sealed envelope with another version of Sisterhood history to add to my *CMM*. These were pages only given to Guardians, which explained the Guardian mission and how it came to be. The envelope had come sealed from ISIS, and—I'm not going to lie—it gave me a little rush knowing I was the only one in the room who would know this stuff.

Nan had shared some of the details while we were in the Gallery of Discovery, but I took them in with a different mindset this time. It mattered now. Not in an abstract, isn't-this-cool kind of way, but because my future depended on it. This was my legacy, no matter how weird those words felt in my mouth.

When I finished reading and tucked the pages safely away in my *CMM*, Gaby planted herself next to me and handed back each of my *CMM* assignments one by one. My Signature Style Portfolio needed an overhaul now that I knew for sure where my comfort zone was. Fun-feminine-sporty had been right all along.

I'd done some work on a Personal Strength/Weakness Summary that most of the other Alphas had long since finished, but I went back and fleshed it out a bit with some things that were glaringly obvious in light of recent events. Like my willingness to help others (a strength, though also a weakness if pushed too far) and my overpowering need to fit in at any cost (definitely a weakness).

Kyra sat down on the other side of me, twirling a Twizzler in her fingers. "You okay?"

"One step forward, three steps back takes a while to recover from."

She surveyed the stacks of paper surrounding me. "Try to think baby steps. You don't have to conquer it all at once. Just take the next step. As the famous FlyLady says, you can do anything for fifteen minutes."

I didn't know who FlyLady was (Kyra tucked her book into my overnight bag to remedy that situation), but the strategy sounded doable. I'd listened to Mom drone on about the babies' development for hours on end. Fifteen minutes was a cakewalk. Investing fifteen minutes at a time in a Power Plan that actually made me feel powerful? Definitely worth the effort.

With Guardian training on the horizon and a surge to take down, I'd need every ounce of power I could get.

✳ ✳ ✳

"You haven't talked to him at all?" Gwen asked as we munched our healthy dinner on the Petersons' relaxing screened porch.

"Not since I left the restaurant. I saw him at The Grind, though."

Paige looked ill. "That was mostly Gennifer, you know. She's been dying to get her claws back into him since the pool party."

"Takes two to dance the tongue tango."

"You know," Kyra said, looking suspiciously chipper, "my cousin is moving back. He broke up with his girlfriend—"

"Don't even think about it."

"It wouldn't be a *date* date. Just testing the waters. Alec's super nice, plus he's pretty cute and could use the distraction. You're going to be overhauling your look again, right?"

I popped a blueberry in my mouth. "So?"

"And it would be cool to launch Jess 2.0 at the Fourth of July carnival, wouldn't it?"

Technically it would be Jess 3.0, but who was counting? "And?"

"It would be great to have a trial run before then. Alec would totally give you a guy's opinion. Plus it would be good for you to be seen out and about. Not making out with some new guy—just getting yourself back on the market.

292

Unless you'd rather be the girl at home pining away for a lost love."

*Gag.* "Point taken. I'll think about it." I took a swig of juice and changed the subject. "So, have you guys all been to ISIS already?"

Everyone had but Gaby, who would get to go as soon as she went Gamma.

"I was pretty blown away the first time I went there," Gwen admitted. "It never occurred to me there was something beyond us like that. But when I thought about it, it made sense."

"My mom goes to Paris and Amsterdam all the time to work on projects with their local Delta teams," Kyra said. Then she laughed. "My dad thinks it's because they have great spas."

I chuckled along with everyone else, but I was thinking about Nan's comment. The whole underestimating thing did seem to make life easier. Less explaining to do, anyway.

"I did my first international assignment over spring break this year," SJ told me. "My mom thought it would be good experience, so I accepted one in New Zealand. My teammates were from Japan, Poland, and Denmark." Her eyes lit up. "Tamika Yoshida from Japan was a Guardian-in-Training. Maybe you'll run into her sometime."

I couldn't see how I would, but I was learning never to say never when it came to the Cindys.

"What are Gamma assignments like?" I asked.

"It's different every time," SJ explained. "Different places, different projects. Just helping out a little wherever they need you."

"And proving yourself to the ISIS bigwigs at the same time," I said. That much I could figure out on my own.

Gwen bounced a grape on the back of her hand. "We're like the minor leagues. Not everyone goes to the majors, but if you're called up, you'd better be ready to go."

"We're all competing to be in ISIS?" That made no sense to me. The Cindys were about banding together for the greater good. I couldn't see ISIS pitting us against each other to join their ranks.

"Oh my gosh, no." SJ looked shocked. "I mean, I guess we might compete for certain assignments. We can't all go to Hawaii every time. But joining ISIS isn't a competition."

Gwen nodded. "I just meant not everyone chooses to be involved beyond graduation. But if you do want to be part of ISIS, you need to be ready. That's what all the training is for."

A great strategy. Unless the majors called you up before your training had even begun. Speaking of which . . .

"When does the Guardian stuff start?" I asked Gaby.

"I've got the preliminaries for you in a folder," she said, polishing off a carrot stick. "Your mentor will design a training schedule for the rest."

I batted my eyelashes at Sarah Jane. "Looks like you're stuck with me again."

"Only for your *CMM*. You have Paige for your leadership mentoring, and your Guardian mentor"—the doorbell rang as if on cue, and Sarah Jane pushed back from the table—"can tell you about that part herself."

I had a hunch who she meant, and I wasn't sure how I felt about it. I hadn't seen Cassie since the fallout with Ryan or my blackmailing episode with Lexy. If Nan knew about it, Cassie definitely would. Had it changed how she felt about working with me?

I wouldn't blame her if she was angry. I was still angry

with myself. Not so much about Ryan. He'd forced the issue on that one. Or maybe we both had. But where Lexy was concerned, I definitely understood. I had some serious explaining to do on that end if I wanted to make amends.

I followed SJ back into the house toward the front door, preparing a mini-speech to let Cassie know I was fully prepared to atone for my sins.

Sarah Jane checked the peephole and opened the door. "Thanks for coming on such short notice."

"No problem at all. This is a priority for me." She looked at me and smiled, taking off her incognito baseball cap and sunglasses. "How's our new Guardian today, Jess?"

"Fine, Brooke," I mumbled. "Just peachy."

# Chapter 22

**AFTER A QUICK MEET AND GREET** in Sarah Jane's living room to get to know each other, Brooke had given me the rundown of my duties for the next few weeks and made plans to meet me at the Club the next day.

I'd come into the office early so I could work more on my surge plan before our meeting. I wanted to reorganize my notes and see if Brooke had any ideas about what we were missing.

I pulled out my notebook and rewrote what we knew.

*WHAT THE WICKEDS ARE DOING*

1. Doubling their new recruit class (strength in numbers)
2. Targeting people in key positions (either directly or by getting to someone close to them)
3. Getting the Reggies to do their dirty work (building spy network to boost intel)

*WHAT THE WICKEDS WANT*

1. To keep the Reggies isolated

2. To eliminate any strength that poses a threat

3. To exploit any strength that can be used to their advantage

The question was still *why*. What was all of this working toward? How much of it was ego driven, and how much was part of a bigger plan?

I was still pondering when the knock on my door signaled prep time was over.

"I come bearing gifts," Brooke said when I opened the office door. She held up her right hand, then her left. "Chocolate or hazelnut?"

"Chocolate, always," I said, taking the biscotti bag and coffee from her right hand. "Thanks, Brooke."

We settled at the table in the leader office, and Brooke opened a folder with a double-G logo. She handed me a matching one. "Why don't you start by telling me what you know about the Guardians?" she said.

I'd read through the packet of info Gaby had given me, but a lot of it was still swirling around in my head. "It's a branch of ISIS formed about fifty years ago to protect the interests of the Sisterhood. There are Guardians all over the world, just like there are Cindys all over the world, and all Guardians are trained by an elite task force in ISIS."

"That's a good start. Every Guardian is a Delta. Most begin as Guardians-in-Training in high school. You'll train to be a Guardian until you're eligible to become a Delta—usually around the time you graduate from college—and then you can apply for formal admittance into the Guardian Guild."

Which explained the *GG* logo.

"ISIS has branches in forty-seven countries," she

continued, filling in more blanks for me. "The Cinderella Society varies a little by region and by culture—it may not operate exactly the same in Spain or India or Sweden as it does in the U.S.—but our creed and our mission are the same worldwide. The training you get during the high-school phase of the Cindys, or the equivalent in other countries, is a fairly universal experience. When she graduates from that training, every Cindy makes a choice about her future."

"We graduate from it?"

"Not in the same way as graduating from high school. At the end of your three years—two years for you, since you're joining late—every Cindy transitions onto one of three paths. That's where 'embrace your future' comes into play," she explained. "The first path is *Influence*. I think of it as paying it forward. You take the knowledge and skills you've gained as a Cindy and use them to make a difference in the world in whatever way you're compelled to."

I'd always loved the concept of paying it forward. To think Cindys were out there doing that right now to combat the Wickeds' network of targeting was a glimmer of hope for Reggies everywhere.

"The majority of Cindys follow the Influence path. There are alumni groups all over the world—once a Cindy, always a Cindy—but those Cindys' active participation in the Society itself effectively ends after graduation.

"Now, for the Cindys who want a longer-term commitment, there's the *ISIS* path. Once you become a Gamma, you can go out on assignment for ISIS. It's not a full-time status, but it allows Cindys to continue making contributions to the ISIS mission throughout their lives."

Hence Sarah Jane's New Zealand assignment.

"Some Cindys move beyond Gamma level and pursue

Delta status, but it's all part of the *ISIS* path. Being a Delta provides you with the clearance to work for ISIS as a career. Instead of going on voluntary assignments, you have the opportunity to earn your paycheck from ISIS. So, rather than being, say, an environmental engineer for the government, you could work in the ISIS R&D department."

Gaby's dream come true. I'd bet anything that's where she was headed.

"Not every Delta chooses to work for ISIS. Your grandma is a good example of that. But they're all intimately involved with the inner workings of ISIS."

I could figure out the rest on my own. "And we're the third path."

Brooke raised her coffee in a toast. "Long live the Guardians." We tapped our coffee cups together. "Guardians have one mission and one mission only: to protect ISIS from ATHENA, while stopping their attempts at domination. Every assignment you receive as a Guardian is directly connected to the Wickeds.

It was bad enough that the targeted Reggies were tied to the Wickeds for all eternity. Becoming a Guardian meant I would be too.

We went over the Cindy calendar Gaby had given me and compared it to upcoming Guardian events and milestone dates. Brooke wanted to make sure we identified any conflicts in advance so I wasn't pulled in too many directions. My first priority was preparing to take over as leader, so the only major Guardian event I would have this summer was the Guardian Summit in New York City. According to Brooke, the Guardian Summit was like the Cindys' version of the UN.

Schedules in place, we shifted to the topic I'd been waiting for.

"Where are you with the recruitment surge?" Brooke asked, taking a careful sip of coffee that somehow didn't leave a lipstick mark on her cup. Was there no end to her magical powers?

I polished off the last of my biscotti. "I was hoping you could help me there. Nan said the Guardians are on the front lines of the recruitment-surge problem, right?"

"It's one of our major priorities. In fact, you've been assigned to the Guardians' Recruitment Task Force because you're in a surge location. You'll get to meet the other members at the Summit. The task force needs eyes on the ground to understand how the surge is playing out in real time. You'll be their eyes, and they'll pass along new intel as it comes in to help you. It's a partnership."

A partnership I desperately needed. "Can I ask you something?"

"That's what I'm here for."

"Paige explained about ATHENA's network of Wickeds around the country." Or around the world, now that I knew better. "What do they gain by targeting the Reggies later on? I understand wanting the power trip, but is it just an ego thing?"

"What do you think?"

"I think there has to be something tangible they get out of it."

"Put yourself in the Reggies' shoes," Brooke said. "Let's say you're in your mid-thirties, and you've been targeted by the Wickeds since you were in high school. That's twenty years of bowing to Wicked pressure. You've learned it's easier to go along with it than fight back because they always come after you worse if you disobey. And then one day, you get the promotion you've been hoping for or the political position you've been working toward your whole life. It's the pinnacle of success and finally puts you in a position of power. What happens then?"

Things started clicking into place. "They use you as a puppet."

"Exactly. Or, if you got the position over a Wicked, they blackmail you into stepping down so the Wicked can step up. The more diverse their power is, the harder it is to fight."

The alarm on Brooke's cell beeped, and she checked the clock while my mind buzzed with possibilities.

"My private number is in the folder I gave you," she said, getting up to go. "Call me any time you have a question or need a sounding board. Don't be shy, okay?"

"Thanks, Brooke. I won't be." *Much.*

Brooke gave me a quick hug—rendering me momentarily speechless (and once again wishing I'd been a Worthington Estates girl)—and left the office. I immediately opened the door to the War Room, making a beeline for the whiteboard.

The photos were still in the columns we'd left them in. If Brooke's take on ATHENA held true for all the Wickeds, she'd just given me the final piece of the puzzle.

We knew the Wickeds were targeting people who had something they wanted. Power, position, a strength they could exploit. If they wanted it, they went after it. Period.

If they wanted to control the entire high-school landscape, they needed to have puppets in every major area. Or be in the positions themselves. And they needed to eliminate any threats to that control. If they succeeded—and it looked like they were well on their way—we were in trouble. Once they controlled the entire social structure, stopping them would be next to impossible.

The problem with their plan was that with such a diverse

reach at school, there'd be no way they could effectively control all the groups and still keep their network of spies active and in fear. It left them no choice but to spike their numbers.

And we had no choice but to take them down before the surge was complete.

Their reach was already more extensive than we could possibly battle one on one. And therein lay the problem: I'd been banging my head against the desk over a strategy that had never been an option in the first place.

*"There are way more Reggies than there will ever be Cindys or Wickeds. The real power is in their hands, but they have to embrace it for it to do them any good."*

Sarah Jane had given me the secret that day at the ball game, but I hadn't understood what it meant until now. If we wanted to take the Wickeds down for good, there was only one thing that could guarantee success.

It would take nothing short of a full-scale Reggie uprising.

But an uprising needed a leader on the inside; the Reggies needed one of their own to look to for leadership and strength. Heather had finally found her voice with Lexy at the Range. With a little guidance and a support system she could count on, who knew what she was capable of? I might not have had all the details worked out, but I had no doubt she was the right person for the job.

I just needed to convince *her* of that.

※　※　※

If I had any hopes of talking Kyra out of setting me up with Alec, I was out of luck. Everyone thought it was a fabulous idea, so I finally caved and let them take control of my social life. They couldn't do worse with it than I had.

Our doorbell rang, and I gave my fun-feminine-sporty

look a last once-over before heading downstairs. To be honest, I really wanted to be a piner, even if it did look pathetic when the pinee had gotten over me in twelve seconds. But I'd made my decision, so it was off like a herd of turtles for dear Jess.

"Sorry if Kyra roped you into this," Alec said, once we were safely out of the house. Kyra hadn't lied about him being cute—dark hair, charmingly crooked grin. He helped me into the car, so he got bonus points for politeness too. I could do a heck of a lot worse for a non-date date.

"She didn't," I offered with a smile. "I wanted to come."

He paused with his hand on the doorframe and gave me a *don't kid a kidder* look.

"Well, she did say she thought it would be good for both of us."

He laughed. "I'll take that."

We decided to see an easy romantic comedy and had so much fun whispering comments like "Gee, I didn't see *that* one coming" and "No way would she ever say that with her boss sitting right there—is she insane?" that I didn't even mind when the kissing scene came on. Alec and I just looked at each other and laughed. It was like hanging out with my best guy friend, if I'd ever had a best guy friend.

Kyra had let Ben drag her to see the latest action flick—ah, the things we do for love—and we caught up with them in the hall on our way out. We stood around for a few minutes, laughing and joking like we didn't have a care in the world. I almost forgot Alec and I were supposed to be nursing broken hearts.

We followed Ben's car to Arnie's Frozen Custard and got waffle cones to go, then took them to the lake. I made sure we kept to the main areas so I didn't have to face any memories head-on.

Alec had grown up in Mt. Sterling but had moved away after eighth grade. He'd been back a few times, but not since The Grind had started testing new menu items here. Audrey's mouthwatering balsamic chicken wrap was deemed a must-try, and our dinner plans were set. Kyra and Ben walked ahead of us, and Alec took my hand in his, swinging it back and forth between us as we walked. No lacing of fingers, just nice hand-to-hand contact.

"You look great, by the way," Alec said. "Kyra said you might want a guy's opinion on your new fabulousness."

I thought about how I'd felt dressing this time around. Finally living up to a signature style that really felt like me. I'd gotten a little dolled up for our date, but I was still 100 percent Jess Parker. Funny how when you dressed for yourself, a compliment was like icing on the cake. Not that I couldn't appreciate good icing the same as the next girl.

"Thanks. You're not so bad yourself."

"Flattery will get you everywhere."

I laughed. "Can I tell you something?"

"Sure."

"I'm having a lot more fun than I thought I would."

Alec grinned. "Me too. It made me forget about things for a while."

"Same here." I glanced over at him. "Do you want to talk about it?"

"Not much to tell. We dated for about a year, but I broke it off because she was more serious than I was."

I thought about Ryan and me. "That's hard on guys, isn't it?"

"It's hard on anyone, I think. But I've always been kinda into someone else, so it wasn't fair to keep leading her on."

"Oh."

"I didn't act on it, if that's what you're thinking. The other girl doesn't know I exist."

He had to be kidding. "You're totally cute and funny. How can she *not* know you exist?"

"She didn't go to my old school. Even if she had, she's preoccupied with studying and wouldn't have noticed me anyway. I used to date her twin sister. By the time I realized the girl of my dreams was hiding right behind her, I was moving."

I did a double take. No *way*. "You and . . . are you serious?"

He blushed but didn't offer any more details. "Want to tell me about yours?"

Did I? My eyes drifted to the stretch of boardwalk where things had felt so right.

"I don't know," I said, honestly. "Too much too fast, maybe? Not super intense," I added, not wanting Alec to think I was *that* kind of fast. "More like the whole thing happened really fast. All of a sudden it was there and overwhelming, and then it was just . . . over."

"Incompatible?"

"A little. But mostly we couldn't accept each other at face value."

It came out so naturally that you'd think I'd actually realized this before I spoke the words. But you'd be wrong. This was a news flash to me. One that, sadly, was right on the money. And embarrassingly obvious given my last conversation with Ryan. I must be a slow learner when it comes to love.

I thought about Alec's dilemma as we headed to The Grind. What kind of girl wouldn't like a guy like Alec? He was total boyfriend material—cute, funny, sweet. Although I only liked him as a guy friend, so what was up with that?

Was that how guys saw me too? Buddy material but not girlfriend material?

Thankfully, The Grind wasn't too busy when we got there. I was having such a great time that I didn't want it tainted by the Wickeds and their sniper comments. We grabbed our wraps and drinks and piled into a booth.

Just like at the lake, we joked and hung out. Ben and Alec started talking about a sci-fi movie they'd both seen. When they just missed knocking Kyra's drink off the table while reenacting the final action scene (which Alec won), I decided a slice of raspberry cheesecake sounded good. I got up to escape the melee. "Anyone need anything?"

"I'll come with you," Alec said, following me out of the booth. "I have won this battle. Now I must collect my hero's dessert."

"It's just cheesecake."

"With swirls," he corrected. "The cheesecake of champions."

We waited at the counter, and Alec put his chin on my shoulder. "Good thing Kyra's drink had a lid," he said. "I spilled grape juice on her favorite shorts when we were nine, and she's never forgiven me."

"You did have some mad skills back there with the fake karate," I teased. I turned toward him when his chin lifted. But instead of looking at Alec, my eyes locked on a silvery-blue pair as their owner held the door open for his entourage.

"Well, since it was *boxing*, not karate, I'd say my moves need some work. Maybe a left-left-right would've been better. . . ." Alec's voice trailed off as he realized I wasn't moving. Or breathing.

His eyes followed mine. "This must be Face Value Guy," he said quietly. "What do you need me to do?"

I tore my eyes away from Ryan and looked at the sweetheart of a guy who'd managed to give me my first night of angst-free fun in days. I relaxed. "Nothing. It doesn't matter anymore."

He gave me that lopsided grin, and I linked my arm with his. Alec paid for our dessert, and we returned to our date, ignoring Ryan and his gang for the rest of the meal. Ben excused himself briefly to say hi to Ryan, but he didn't make a big deal of it and didn't try to merge the two groups. All in all, I thought we made the best of an awkward situation. And we didn't even resort to making out to get a dig in. Not that it didn't flicker through my mind ever so briefly when Gennifer slipped her arm around Ryan's waist, even though he didn't seem to notice.

"You do realize he hasn't taken his eyes off you since they sat down, right?" Alec said when Kyra called her mom to let her know they'd be heading home shortly.

I flicked a glance toward the table where Ryan had positioned himself directly opposite us and was watching me intently. His face was expressionless. Not mad, not sad, just . . . distant.

Kyra grabbed her purse and went off to the ladies', probably to freshen her breath for a good-night kiss. Since I didn't have one in my plans, I stood by the table with Alec and Ben and pretended to be absorbed in a conversation about the WWE. Which was much harder than it sounds (and pretending to be absorbed by pro wrestling is *never* easy), because Ryan had gotten up from the round table and was heading toward us.

I felt his presence as he approached, just like I always did. He was like a magnet for me. If he was within a hundred-foot radius, my body naturally leaned in that direction.

This time, I leaned a little into Alec for protection.

Ryan stopped next to Ben—who looked distinctly uncomfortable—and extended a hand to Alec. "Good to see you, Alec."

Alec shook his hand. "You too, Ryan." He eyed us warily, clearly not wanting to overstep, even though I'd told him it didn't matter. Or shouldn't have mattered.

Ryan turned to me. His voice was quieter. "You look great, Jess."

"Thanks." No squeakiness this time. The icing on that cake wasn't quite so tempting anymore. With enough time, maybe I'd be able to nix the craving entirely.

Ben and Alec resumed their wrestling discussion to ease the tension. Alec gave us some space but was obviously keeping an eye on me in case I needed support.

"You look happy," Ryan said. His eyes were soft. Sad. "I'm glad. You deserve to be with someone who appreciates how incredible you are."

I could feel my defenses melting. "Ryan, don't."

"It's the truth." His voice was only for me. "Don't ever settle. Not for anyone."

My knees turned to jelly as he gave me the sweetest petal-soft kiss on the cheek, then stood back. The pain was right there, so close to the surface. And for once, he didn't push it back down. He didn't let it out either, but he didn't try to hide it away. I could see the strain as he battled the demons that kept everyone who cared about him at arm's length.

And then he turned and walked away. Away from me, from his friends, from everything. Ryan simply disappeared.

I was so stunned that it took me a minute to register Gennifer's cries of indignation. She rushed out to the parking lot, yelling at the top of her lungs for Ryan to stop, and caught him as he opened his car door. A few heated words on her part and one emotionless response on his, and he was driving away. Alone.

I looked at Alec.

He groaned. "Oh, man. This is *Pretty in Pink* and I'm Ducky." He shook his head. "Always the sidekick, never the hero."

How many guys would know the one '80s flick that happened to be my all-time favorite? Only my very best guy friend, that's who.

"You're *my* hero, Ducky."

But just like in the movie, my heart belonged to someone else.

# Chapter 23

**"WHAT DO YOU MEAN I GET PAID?"**

Nan pulled a roll of raffle tickets out of the backseat and looked around the Fourth of July carnival grounds for bystanders. "Your Guardian development schedule will leave little time for regular employment," she explained quietly. "You'll need to cut back on your hours if you want to take it seriously. The Guild understands that and offers a small stipend to Guardians-in-Training to offset the income lost by reduced hours. Didn't Brooke go over all of this?"

Given the amount of work I'd been juggling, I certainly wasn't complaining about the income. But payment? I'm pretty sure that would've stuck in my mind. Even though I'd been starstruck and dazed for the first part of my little shindig with Brooke at Sarah Jane's house.

"She might have. But what about covering the rest of my hours? You still need help at the store."

"I'll figure something out. One of my regulars might be looking for work, or I can put an ad in the paper if need be." Nan led me across the mostly empty parking lot as we walked toward the tent she'd be manning on the carnival midway. "Regardless, you don't need to fret over that. You'll be quite busy enough without worrying about your shifts this summer."

I knew it wasn't my responsibility, but I still felt guilty as we headed over to Nan's booth. Celestial Gifts was a part of our family, even if Mom wouldn't be caught dead there during events like summer solstice. Or most of the year, for that matter. Leaving Nan in the lurch felt like letting my family down.

I helped Nan and the other members of the Ladies Auxiliary set up their raffle booth for a swanky romantic getaway at Grand Hyatt Atlanta and kept an eye out for Sarah Jane. She and Kyra were helping Mrs. Peterson set up a ring toss to benefit the children's hospital, but I hadn't seen them yet.

I did, however, see Lexy stalking down the midway like she wanted to maim someone. I figured as long as I kept out of her tunnel vision, I'd be in good shape. Until Heather stepped out from behind the brats-and-hots station at the end of the row and Lexy picked up her pace.

*Time to earn my paycheck.*

Heather carried an empty box toward the rusty El Camino pulled up onto the grass. She dumped the empty into the trunk and pulled out another box full of hot-dog bun packages. I kept an eye on her through the slats of the empty cotton-candy booth one stall over.

Lexy smelled blood.

"Look what we have here," Lexy said as she closed the distance to Heather. "How's it hangin', Cheater?"

Heather sounded tired. "What do you want?"

"To give you a warning: your little hero won't always be around to protect you. You screw me over again, and I'll take your boyfriend down with you."

Heather blinked. "My boyfriend?"

"You remember him, don't you? Rocker guy, cute in a white trash kind of way?"

Heather nodded slowly. "So if I don't do what you ask, you'll go after Cam to get to me?"

"What are you, slow? Let me repeat it so you'll understand. *Get us. In. The vault. Or Cameron. Goes down. Too.*"

If I hadn't seen it for myself, I never would've believed it. Heather threw back her head and laughed.

"You really do think I'm dumb, don't you?" Heather said, her laugh harsh and cynical. "You think I don't know you already tried to get to Cameron but he told you to go to hell? That he told you there's nothing you could have on him or on me that he would give a damn about?"

I knew that last statement must have felt like a knife to the heart for Heather. I wanted to hug her.

Lexy's eyes got round as hockey pucks.

"I've already ruined the only thing I care about," Heather told her. "Nothing you can do matters to me anymore. I'm done being your pet."

*Oh, yeah.* I'd definitely found the right girl to lead the uprising.

"Happy Fourth of July!" I called, striding around the corner to stand next to Heather. "Gorgeous day for a carnival, don't you think?"

"Beat it, Thief."

I smiled sweetly. "I don't think so, honey bun. What kind of hero would I be if I took orders from you?"

"You can't save everyone, though, can you?" The look in her eyes gave me chills. "Especially if they're all hurting at the same time."

"I don't have to," I said, standing my ground. "Once they know what you're up to, they'll save themselves because they're stronger than you." I gave Heather a nod. "Way stronger."

Lexy scoffed. "You have no idea how strong I am or what I'm capable of."

"Possibly." I flicked a lazy glance Lexy's way. "And you have no idea how strong *they* are. All they need is the right inspiration. Once they know your game, you and your yes-girls won't get past square one."

"Please. This is just the tip of the iceberg. But I'm glad to see you're on the *Titanic* for the duration. It'll be fun to watch you sink."

"I'll bring the deck chairs. In the meantime, stay away from Heather. As you can see, she has no use for you. If I hear you threaten her again, or anybody else for that matter, you and I are going to have a little powwow of our own." I went nose to nose with her. "You got me?"

"Like I'm afraid of you. You're all talk, Thief. You don't have the balls to follow through. If you interfere with my mission, you'd better come with backup."

"I've got her back," Heather said, standing taller. "I'm sick of being your doormat, Lexy. I'm not the only one either. You go after Jess, and we'll come after you."

I was so proud of Heather I wanted to scream. *Celebrate your strength, baby!* But even better than Heather finally going on offense was what happened to Lexy when she did. For a split second, fear flashed in Lexy's eyes.

That's when I knew we'd finally found their weak spot.

What the Wickeds feared most was a Reggie who could fight back. A Reggie who *would* fight back instead of letting the Wickeds manipulate her.

Because without the Reggies to control, the Wickeds had no power.

If one Reggie fighting back gave Lexy a jolt, imagine what kind of damage a full-scale Reggie revolt could inflict on the Wickeds.

True to form, Lexy's hate face was back up in a heartbeat. "Nice try." She dismissed Heather and looked at me. "You'd better come armed with more than just losers on patrol."

"Just tell us where and when."

Lexy's head whipped around at Sarah Jane's voice to discover SJ, flanked by Kyra and Gwen, joining our happy little group. "You mess with Jess," Sarah Jane said, "and you mess with us."

I'd seen Lexy and SJ interact before, but they'd always played surface nice. I was glad I'd told Sarah Jane about incriminating her in the course of my own ugly blackmail episode. If Lexy was going to target her too, SJ deserved advance notice.

"Well, captain," Lexy purred, "you certainly put me in my place. Can't have you angry with me, what with us spending so much time together this summer." She curled her lip in Heather's and my direction, then dismissed all of us with a flick of her wrist. "Later."

"I hope you're not really spending time with her this summer," I said as the trio stopped in front of us. "Are you being punished for something?"

"We're both going to be spending time with her," SJ said, clearly not liking the idea. "Amanda Hamilton called me this morning because her dad got transferred to Dallas. They're moving at the end of the month."

I hadn't gotten to know Amanda very well, but she was

the back spotter in my stunt group. Losing her would stink, but we'd get by. Except—

"Please tell me she's not."

"Oh, yes, she is," SJ confirmed. "Lexy just got promoted."

✳ ✳ ✳

"Where are we going?" Heather asked me after she'd gotten the okay from her supervisor to take a break.

"Do you usually work for the brats guy?"

"Not usually. My dad was supposed to be working off his community service today, but he's not feeling well."

I read between the lines. Mr. Clark was drunk again, so Heather had taken the shift to keep him from getting in more trouble.

"You work at Burger Palace, right?" I asked as we headed down the midway. "I saw you there when my mom was having an extra pickles craving."

"Yeah. They can only give me twenty hours a week this summer, so I work at The Dollar Hut too."

I knew both jobs paid minimum wage, since I'd checked when I thought I might need extra hours for a car. Instead, Nan had been happy to give me as many hours as I wanted, because she'd been knee-deep in her summer projects for the local seniors' center.

Or so she'd said. I wondered now if that was a cover for her ISIS duties.

"Does that happen a lot with your dad? Covering for him?"

"Pretty much. He used to be a nasty drunk. Not physical, just hurling insults and stuff. Now he mostly doesn't bother with me. With anything, really." She didn't even look embarrassed. "Not that I ever cared that much. Most of it rolled off my back."

As a defense mechanism that might have worked, but as a life situation it bit the big one. Not only had she lost her mom, but she was surrounded by people who wanted to grind her soul to dust. What Heather needed was some good old-fashioned female influence of the positive kind. There were big things in store for Heather Clark, and she was going to need a strong support system to see her through. Time to pay it forward for two of my favorite people. The thought made the butterflies smile.

I ducked into the raffle tent with Heather at my side.

Nan greeted Heather with a hug. "Heather! How delightful to see you, dear. Are you girls heading over to the gazebo? I understand there's a band from the high school playing today."

"No time for small talk, Nan," I said. "We're here on business. You know that opening you have?"

Nan raised her eyebrows.

I guided Heather forward a step. "Meet your first applicant."

\* \* \*

A little while later, an overjoyed Heather headed back to man the brats station, thrilled that Nan had hired her on the spot.

Nan wrapped me in a hug. "I'm proud of you, Jessica."

"She needs to embrace her future." I shrugged. "Who better to help with that than you?"

Sarah Jane had gone off to help her mom again, so Kyra, Gwen, and I hung out near the gazebo to watch the band set up. Dale played guitar, so I knew we'd be getting a front-row seat once the show started.

Dale tuned up, and they did a few bars from John Mayer's "Neon" as warm-up.

"I like the acoustic version better."

I jumped at the voice behind me, but the old shivers of excitement had been replaced by a wistfulness of what could've been. *Should've* been, if either of us had been strong enough.

I didn't turn around. "Acoustic is always good. It gets to the soul of the song."

"Sometimes acoustic is the braver choice."

"Sometimes it's worth it."

Ryan was so close his breath tickled my hair. "Can we take a walk?"

We walked side by side without touching, but I still felt the pull. In time, that would go away too. I hoped.

We stopped by the fence, and Ryan turned. "I owe you an apology."

"I'm listening."

"You were right." He took a deep breath and plowed ahead. "I panicked because you were getting too close. Things weren't easy anymore, and I needed them to be. That's kind of how I roll."

"Easy is good. But it's not always realistic."

"I can't be what you want me to be, Jess. I'm not that guy. But you didn't deserve what happened. I should've come clean with you in the beginning."

"Why didn't you?"

He tucked his hands into his pockets and lifted a shoulder. "You overwhelmed me. I felt this amazing connection with you. And even though I knew I'd never be the kind of guy you deserved, I couldn't bring myself to cut the tie."

"So you set me up to be the scissors."

"I'm not proud of it." He kicked a stone through an opening in the chain-link fence. "I can't change the past. I would, though, if I could. I just thought you should know that."

I ached to reach out to him but couldn't open myself up to more rejection. "No," I said. "You can't change it."

He looked at me then, and the pain was there, raw and uncensored. We both knew we were talking about more than just us.

"I thought about the tribute thing too," he said. "I'm not sure I know how to do that, but it makes more sense than what I've been doing."

*I could help you,* I wanted to say. *Let me try.* But the words never left my mouth. "I'm glad."

"So the thing is, I want another chance." The old fence creaked as he leaned hard against it. "I don't deserve one, and I don't know if I'll ever be good enough for you, but I want another chance anyway. If I'm too late, I'll live with that. Either way, I wanted you to get an apology."

"Why?"

"Why an apology?"

"Why do you want me?"

He looked at me as if I were mental. "Because you're the best thing that's ever happened to me."

I didn't even blink.

"Because when I'm with you, I can almost see the guy I used to be. That's why I didn't want to sit at the round tables on our first date. I didn't want you to see that part of my life. I didn't want it to scare you off. But I screwed up anyway, because I couldn't get past it myself." He looked away. "You make me want to be a better person just so I'm worthy of you. You're beautiful and smart, you care about people, and you stand up for what you believe in. I'm in awe of you most of the time."

"I'm flawed too, Ryan. I made a mess of my life trying

to be what other people wanted me to be. Or what I thought they wanted." I shook my head. "I've done things I'm not proud of, and I've got a long road ahead of me to make it right again."

"We could be flawed together." He paused. "Unless you're with Alec?"

"We're just friends."

Ryan looked hopeful, but I had to see this through. "I need to know one more thing," I told him.

"Anything."

"Why are you so different with me?" I braced myself for his answer. "Like the day at the banner party. I got all the intensity. But the minute you walked away, you had a smile for everyone who came your way. It's like you save the best for everyone but me."

He looked taken aback. "You honestly don't know?"

*Would I be asking if I did?*

"Because you're the only one I can be myself with. I don't have to be *on* when I'm with you. I don't have to pretend things are always okay." He drew an arc in the dirt with the heel of his shoe. "That's why I couldn't take it when you tried to force the hero card. And then you started pretending to be something you weren't because you thought that's what *I* wanted?" He shook his head. "You stopped seeing me and only saw the fantasy you had in your head. It wasn't real anymore."

It hurt to hear him say the words. But I couldn't deny he was right. "I admit I got caught up. But that doesn't change what happened. The people you care about most deserve to be treated the best, Ryan. It's not an optional thing."

He flinched. "I know."

"Everything fell apart because we both let it." Maybe

if I'd trusted and given things more time, it wouldn't have blown up in our faces. Or maybe it still would have. "If we let it, maybe that's how it was meant to—"

"*It wasn't.*" Ryan's denial rang out before I'd even finished my thought. "I don't believe that, and I don't think you do either."

I opened my mouth, then forced it closed. It was too easy to let it betray me.

He was right. I didn't think that. At least, my heart didn't.

"Look, Jess, I know this is a major long shot. But can we go back to the way things were before they fell apart?" He looked at me, the tenderness in his eyes weakening my resolve. "Being with you feels like coming home. I haven't felt that in a long time."

My mouth was already forming the word *yes* before my brain intercepted. The familiar battle of heart trying to override head. But I caught the word in time, despair twisting me up inside. "No." I didn't want to say it—I had to. "We can't."

"No." He nodded, defeated. "I guess not."

"We can't go back, Ryan. Life isn't like that. You can't change the past, no matter how much it hurts. And you can't fix what's wrong by pretending it never happened."

"What if I can't fix it at all?"

This time, I did reach for him. He deserved to have hope. "You can. But you have to forgive yourself first. You'll figure out the rest as you go."

A warm wave of peace washed over me, one I'd begun to recognize. Maybe it was time to follow my own advice. And maybe, just maybe, it was time for another leap. "We can't go back," I said, gently squeezing his hand. "But maybe we could try again."

Hope lit Ryan's face. "Are you sure?"

"On one condition."

"Name it."

"I don't want to pretend anymore. We accept each other at face value, or what's the point?"

He thought about that for a minute. "Acceptance has to go both ways. You have to accept the good *and* the bad," he emphasized.

Fair enough. "And if it doesn't work, we call it off. No harm, no foul." *Please don't let that happen this time.*

It sounded so easy, like we were planning some project for school instead of opening up our lives to the possibility of more heartbreak. But love wasn't always easy. I was pretty sure it was worth it, though.

Ryan lifted my hand in his and pressed his lips to it. "Agreed. But I think we need to seal the deal, just to be sure."

The sinful smile on his face had my toes tingling before he even leaned in. He cupped my face in his hands, caressing my cheek with his thumb. "You have no idea how much I've missed you."

The kiss was incredibly soft and sweet, and I knew things were going to be alright. He deepened the kiss, and like flipping a switch, the magic flowed through us like it had been there all along. We'd been given a second chance. All we had to do now was make it work.

For two workaholics like us, that should be a no-brainer.

We walked slowly back toward the carnival, easing into a fresh start with eyes and hearts wide open. Ryan linked his fingers with mine, and it felt like everything good I'd ever wanted was finally within my grasp.

We neared the now-bustling midway, and Lexy caught my eye. She leaned against the snow-cone stand and watched us, decidedly unthrilled with this latest turn of events. She looked at our hands and at me, her eyes narrowing into slits. And just like that, I arrived at the crossroads of my new life.

Heather might be safe for the moment, but other Reggies were still on Lexy's radar. If I had to be the one to unite the Cindys and Reggies in a revolt to bring down the Wickeds, so be it. Was I up to the challenge? I had to believe I was. Or would be when the time came.

All I knew for sure was that with a movie star as a mentor, the prom queen as my fairy godmother, and a chance for a real-life fairy tale with my very own Prince Charming, no way was I backing down. Heather wasn't the only one ready to embrace her future.

Lexy lifted her snow cone in mocking salute, and I knew that whatever she planned to dish out, I could take. Because that's what Guardians did.

I inclined my head to show I'd accepted her challenge. *Bring it on, Ice Queen.*

*The other shoe drops in . . .*

# The Cinderella Society
## CINDY ON A MISSION

Coming from Egmont USA in Spring 2011.

# *Acknowledgments*

Sometimes in life, people touch our lives without ever realizing it. Or if they realize it, they don't fully understand the magnitude of how much they've helped us along the way.

Sending heartfelt thanks:

To Holly Root—for being Agent Extraordinaire. I'm so blessed to have a fabulous business partner who is also a lovely person (and who can always make me laugh). Thank heavens for you!

To Elizabeth Law—for being an amazing editor, exceptional helpmeet (I still love that word), and all-around brilliant publisher.

To Regina Griffin—for bringing me to Egmont's attention and championing the story from the start. (I owe you one!)

To Mary Albi—for being one of the nicest and savviest marketing professionals I've ever met.

To the Egmont USA team—Doug Pocock, Nico Medina, Greg Ferguson, Rob Guzman, and Alison Weiss—for being enthusiastic cheerleaders for all of your authors. What an amazing team you've put together!

To the TCS design team—Lisa Overton, Alison Lew, and

Becky Terhune—for making this debut author's dream come true with a truly gorgeous book.

To the incredibly talented authors whose work made me fall in love with the genre—Ann Brashares, Meg Cabot, Ally Carter, Julia DeVillers, Shannon Hale, J. K. Rowling, and Kieran Scott.

To my wonderful writing buddies, whose unwavering support, friendship, and humor have made this journey so enjoyable (even when it was nutty)—Tera Lynn Childs, Becca Fitzpatrick, Rachel Hawkins, Celesta Hofmann, Adrienne Hogan, Lindsey Leavitt, Jenn Stark, Leshia Stolt, and Wendy Toliver.

To my lovely friends who also lent their expertise to The Cinderella Society (any errors are mine!)—Kristina McMorris and Linda Yoshida for their assistance with all things Hawaiian and Japanese, Christina Diaz Gonzalez for her Cuban fabulousness, Nisha Sharma for being my go-to girl for Indian culture, Melissa Walker for her fashion savvy, Chelsea Campbell for her mad Latin skills, and Steve G. for answering my career questions at the eleventh hour.

To the fabulous Tenners, E-Nation Team, Success Sisterhood, and Pixie Chicks—I couldn't be more thrilled to be traveling this road with you.

To Team Cindy—for really *getting* what The Cinderella Society is all about and embracing it in ways that make me burst with pride to call you Honorary Cindys.

To my family and friends—for love and cheers and having faith that I could do it.

To my very own real-life Charming, (aka my husband)—for unconditional love and support and so much laughter. I couldn't have done this without you, nor would I have wanted to.

To the wonderful and utterly amazing JW—SHMILY.

To Girl Scouts®, Girls Inc.®, and the Dove® *Campaign for Real Beauty*—for their research on self-esteem and body image and their extraordinary commitment to helping girls embrace their full potential. Your work changes lives.

And finally, a big thank-you to the author of a short newspaper column back in the mid-'80s that eventually gave birth to the Cindys' Rule of Fives. I've looked far and wide for the author's name to give proper credit, but to no avail. Wherever you are, thank you! (And thanks, Mom, for passing along that gem to the drama queen that was teenaged me.)

**KAY CASSIDY** is the author of teen fiction she wishes were based on her real life. She is a former college cheerleader and sorority alum, an MBA, and a member of Mensa. Kay is also the founder of the national Great Scavenger Hunt Contest™ reading program for kids and teens and the host of the inspirational Living Your Five™ Web project. She hopes that *The Cinderella Society*, her first novel, will inspire readers to embrace their inner Cindy.

Visit Kay online at www.kaycassidy.com.